Tales From the Renegade City

Tourniquet

Tales from the Renegade City

Tourniquet

Kim Lakin-Smith

IMMANION
PRESS
Stafford England

This is a work of fiction. All the characters and events portrayed in this book are fictitious, and any resemblance to real people, or events, is purely coincidental.

Tourniquet: Tales from the Renegade City
By Kim Lakin-Smith
© 2007
First edition

Author Contact Information:

http://www.theginfairy.com
http://www.myspace.com/theginfairy

Cover by Lucas Swann
Cover model: Dean Hathaway
Author photo: Ingrid Shiel
Interior Layout by Storm Constantine
Editor: Donna Scott

Set in Footlight MT Light

An Immanion Press Edition
8 Rowley Grove
Stafford ST17 9BJ, UK

http://www.immanion-press.com
info@immanion-press.com

ISBN 978-1-904853-35-0

For Del

my immortal

Contents

It is not so much that we are afraid of change or so in love with the old ways, but it's that place in-between we fear...

Marilyn Ferguson

What's real? You can't find the truth, you just pick the lie you like the best.

Marilyn Manson

Chapter 1

Super Beast

Nottingham, aka Renegade City. The future

Watching from the fire-stained dark of a side-aisle, the Angel was intrigued by the subtle interplay of her movements; eyes that shone out from deep inside the hood, hands that flinched ever so slightly. His tongue snaked. For him, fear's texture was raw and palatable. He delighted in its taste.

The girl had been soaked by snowfall. The slick of a black PVC raincoat fell just short of shin-high platforms, each boot being glossed, multi-buckled and festooned with some type of rubber spike...as if to better intimidate her enemy? He turned his attention to her pursuers, a pack of Skinwalkers slipping, sliding and clattering down into the sludge, and whose militants wore standard apocalyptic bikers' dress: leathers, ratted manes spooling over giant shoulders, and faces shot full of metal. He smiled thinly. It would take more than a pair of nasty boots to out-freak a freak show.

He *was* impressed, however. A petite in torn orange fishnets, red denim cut-offs and a child-sized raincoat, the girl's battledress was more honest than the stained musculature of the Skinwalkers. It also acted as ballast to his initial idea that she belonged to the drifters, loners who fed off the city like a tick or a disease, without tribal code, creed or conduct. Yes—his eyes were moons in a face of grave mist— the strength of her body language, the way that she stood her ground, fists cocked like a bantamweight, was too principled for those dissolute ranks. The girl had a *cause* to fight for. But in the name of which of the four key tribes?

She did not belong to Renegade's capricious faery folk since she lacked an obligatory pair of garish, nanofibre wings. Moreover, no self-respecting Fae would abandon the absinthian ambience of the city's nightclubs or the heat-haze of its bars for the corpse of a building before him.

Just as evidently, she was too earthed to be a Trawler. Those sea dogs rarely put a foot ashore unless it was to refuel or repair one of their black-sailed junks or sampans, graffitied canal barges, tubs, or downsized riverboats. Ever elusive in their technological pirating activities on the reinstated canals, Trawlers were never the type to actually go *out* looking for trouble. Hunters of the world's conspiracies and secrets, they were more inclined to trawl the neuro-waters of the Internet, or don an earpiece in a lightless cabin to listen in.

One of the DarkLed then? When a Skinwalker lashed out and she sidestepped the beast in a flow of arabesques that barely stirred the dust motes, he thought he had her boxed. Except—the fork of a vein grew prominent at his brow— where he would have expected one of Renegade's general gothic populous to run for the safety of a graveyard, or just dissolve into a mess of shrouded bones, the girl was brash and all too tangible, as if imbued with *practical* magick.

But her allegiance to the second largest tribe was also questionable given that when she had first entered the seemingly deserted ruin of the Great Library—so very bold, if on edge—he had been standing behind this self-same column, but a metre or so away. Inhaling gently so as not to irritate his gullet, he had detected her aroma; sweet yet uncomplicated, like freshly-laundered linen. In other words, she was clean of sage, patchouli, myrtle, chamomile, lavender, and all the fusty witch scents.

Not a sister of the Castclan then. But she *was* a natural Believer in the rural wisdoms. That was clear from the pentagram ghosting her third eye chakra, painted by a seer from one of the travelling circuses, he supposed, and engineered to keep her safe. Now, as a great insidious zoo of grizzlies, tigresses, bulls, bull elephants, wild dogs, lions, and all the other despicable breeds of were-beast crawled out from the side aisles to join her in the nave, he wondered, would faith be enough to save her?

Head at an angle, he was just beginning to enjoy the idea of the girl's vague face put to sleep under his fingers when she plunged into action. Thrusting a hand into each side pocket of her raincoat, she wrestled pink silk lining inside-out to produce...

The leathered bulk of a wolfhound blocked his view. Panicking, he drew back a fist, to punch in at the spine then extricate the heart...But the beast had already crumpled, its forehead cradled in ham-like fists.

In abject delight, he let his gaze travel back across the mired flagstone floor to where the girl stood, left arm extended, a catapult sling quivering below her slender wrist. Her eyes darted off to the side aisles then up and down the nave. With a sudden thrust, she was off, sprinting in and out of the burnt bones of bookcases, leapfrogging a threadbare chair, a gilt-laced mess of drapery, and the torn base of a lover's seat. At the door, she clasped and turned, turned again, then shook the handle.

His heart skipped a beat. 'What now, Miss Hood?' he whispered, manipulating the key in the silk lining of his pants' pocket. "Give up or go down fighting?"

Neither, he realised in soft dismay as, defying the boundaries of the physical, the girl became like a spider. Opting against the dark ruins of the nave, she arced off to the nearest section of wall, located between two vast, ornate columns. A pace short of that dead end, she stared up, as if gauging her ascent.

Where the wall was once stacked with row on row of polished oak shelves like an elfin hill fort, now it had deteriorated into a mass of flaking stone, sooty residue, slats of wood, filth-greased and blistered like the flesh of a gnome king, that hung at a slant or barely supported a thin stack of books. Twisting at the waist, she made a quick study of the circling beasts, tore her gaze away, then lunged at the rock face.

Her ascent was swift. Part thrilled, part furious, he felt a serpent flex inside his throat. It had not occurred to him she might actually *know* how to climb, that fingers could knot the makeshift carabiners of bent nails, hooks and brackets, that a leg could twist, crook then stretch at an unexpected angle like an insect's segmented femur, tibia and tarsus, that the toe of an outsized cyber-boot could inch out onto a putrid overhang, then lever up.

She assailed the rotted web with aptitude, a fact not lost on the beasts that tried to bait her at the wall's base or mimic her ascent. The fragile maze turned to dust beneath their weight.

The Angel frowned, a small expression that lay like a thumb-print on the space between his eyes. He was bored of

Skinwalkers, their idle joy in malevolence as well as their brutal wading-in when a light touch might fare better.

A third of the way up, the girl seemed equally distracted by the brutes' efforts. Half-kneeling on a sliver of shelf, she tore the slingshot from her teeth like a chicken-thigh and reloaded the cup. Spine arched, she drew aim and fired.

Tiny, silver pellets flew from the cup, prompting those brutes assembled in the pit below to raise their great, dull snouts in wonder. The shot divided into five glittering arcs then fell as a flesh-slicing rain.

The mob erupted like a cackle of hyenas. Their ugly yelps hurt his ears. He grew weary of the game. "Fetch," he said, and at the order, his lightest henchman skulked out from the wings.

More athletic than its counterparts, with a spine that bowed under the weight of its long, dragging arms, the Skinwalker broke into a half-hunkered run. At the base of the wall, it wove back and forth in a thrice-repeated figure of eight, as if mapping the best route of ascent. Tensing suddenly, it powered down on the hard, swollen meat of its lower limbs, then launched. Black claws grated off the stone, ensnarling a metal bracket. Grunting, the creature pulled itself up by the muscled ropes of its arms, dispensing rust and filth with each grip and thrust.

Uniting his palms, the Angel rested his chin on the apex of a prayer. Up above, the spider of a girl stalled on a narrow perch, edged out and seemed to peer down at her pursuer with intelligible interest. Anger spiked his throat. Didn't she fear the reaper?

Suddenly the girl let out a gasp, and, snatching the hood back so that it fell in soft folds about her neck, half-hissed, half-cried out, "Harry, it's me. Jez!"

From his priest-hole, the Angel felt bile wash over his tongue. What distasteful twist was this to an otherwise pleasing situation? Or was it now an aggravation? It was difficult to choose, more so since, as the girl knelt, steeped in the soft, red aureole of light filtering in at the inverted heart of the rose-window, she proved boyishly pretty. He liked the eyes, dark as sin, reflective as a blade. Meanwhile, her face's delicacy was captured, like a fairy in a jar, by a sharp little chin, cutthroat cheeks and oh so very pale skin! He felt a flush of desire. She looked like a living dead girl.

When the girl reached down to offer a hand to the clambering brute in a clear gesture of aid over assault, he felt air bake inside his lungs. He choked on it, a human sound that echoed off the reverberant ribs of the bone church. Smothering the reflex, he stared at the girl—and, yes, she had noticed, sitting up on her haunches to survey the horrid crowd. Her huge, dark eyes devoured the shade, appeared to focus in. He retreated.

When the beast slashed her wrist with its claws, the girl froze for a few enticing seconds, as if shocked by something far more acute than the pain. Then she reacted, wrenching herself up the mildewed timbers to a higher shelf. Half-stumbling onto one knee, she tore the weapon from her teeth again, drew shivering aim and fired.

The slug hit home. With a guttural roar, the Skinwalker careered down, shattering the rotted tiers on its descent, while the girl, seeming to regret her self-defence in an instant, lunged forward, hand re-extended as if in a bid to conquer time and space. But the hour was bred for war, not magick. The creature smacked down onto the flag-stoned floor with a sickening thud.

For a split second, the girl was a torn thing. Then her face turned to stone. She hauled back about to face the wall, hands splintering into ten stiff, little hooks, and clambered on.

Manifesting in the central aisle, the Angel parted the pack with a breaststroke. The beast was alive, if barely, its rusty dreads fanned out over the floor like a nest of dead sea-snakes. Maori tattoos spiralled each cheek. A four-inch titanium tusk pierced the diagonal of each spiral. Blood wept from a pebble-sized nick at its forehead.

The man swept his robe aside and squatted. Why did Skinwalkers make it impossible to distinguish man from beast? He dabbed at the tiny crystals collected at his upper lip with a sleeve.

"Girlfriend?" He rested the tip of a finger on one of the beast's titanium tusks. His unusual gaze lifted; the girl had dragged herself up and over the ornate balustrade at the base of the rose-window. Arms held out horizontally for balance, she was momentarily transfigured in the bloody moonlight like a girl Christ. Then she edged off to her right, the first few spiralling steps that led to the highest lord's tower being visible from that view point, he supposed.

He manipulated the bodmod in a slow, tearing circle. "Wife?" The circle's circumference increased. "...Whore?" The creature whimpered, and he leant in, a sin eater devouring the confession of a dying man.

"She...is...my...sister."

The Angel's long, pale fingers caressed her distant shape. "Ah, sibling rivalry. A joy to behold. Isn't it picture-perfect that the goliath lies prostrate at her heels, yet still she is outwitted?" Unfolding, he shaded his eyes with the flat of a hand and watched her skittish return to the centre of the ledge. "Barricading the stairwell was a masterful step. You *do* take instruction well. Skip left, hop right, skip left, hop right...You'd think she had nowhere else to go."

He pressed a heel into the chest of the prostrate wolf. "See how our little Miss Hood is so very desperate to abandon you. Any second now she'll disappear in a puff of..."

It was the rustle of flexi small-core coaxial cables, kited tissues and electrodes that made him break off, his white eyes slitting. *That* whir of manmade wings, buoyant, insectile, mixing the air in long, slender strokes...it hurt his ears, and less by way of the noise—souped-up to the dry whiskey rasp of a V8—but because he now knew which tribe the girl indelibly belonged to.

His throat felt scorched. He used a fist to stifle his Adam's apple as she tipped back onto one leg, drew the opposite knee tight into her chest, then unleashed a swift kick to one of the lower petals of the rose-window. The glass exploded into a thousand pink, glistening shards and an oval of night opened up, ice-wild, howling.

"Or there's always *that* option," he said dryly as the girl dipped her head, skidded forward on the plump toes of her boots, crested the edge of the hole, and flew free.

She didn't look back.

Chapter 2

The Dead of Night

From behind a vast wall of tinted, one-way glass that dominated the upper floor of his watchtower, Druid watched the city lose itself beneath a layer of snow. Another evening, he might have marvelled at the spectacle. Tonight, he was nauseated by the black and white of it all. Logic, illogic. He found it hard to split the difference.

"Murder?" The word left its imprint on his tongue.

Sophia ran her fingertips over the glass as if reading the landscape like Braille. "Renegade City. So morbidly exotic; like the dark side of Eden. But what is it really? Nottingham reincarnate. A fairy-tale of flawed ideals?" Her gaze slid sideways. The turquoise eyes seemed to deflect his disbelief. "Call me blasphemous, but I'm sick of pretending. I've endured the highest lord's preposterous state funeral, thanked a world full of strangers for sympathy and sentiments, and all the while, I've despised them for it. Our...." Her scarlet mouth budded. "...*fans* bled him dry in life then made his death a mockery."

Her pearlised, green talons traced the silhouetted ruin to the south, and Druid's gaze panned over the districts of Bridge, Dunkirk and Lenton, Clifton North, and Clifton South. He felt his skin crawl. It was hard to quantify why the south of the city looked so very *cold*. There was no miraculous intensifying of the weather at the border, only a sense of passing from the light. Obscured by distance (or the shadow of authority, he thought acidly), the region was devoted to law and order, civil service, and information garnering. Lynchpin of the Knowledge Quarter was that sliver of city centre containing New Market Square and the business premises of the Management, the colonnaded, domed Council House. Other legislative strongholds were Shire Hall and the Galleries of Justice, the Coroner's Office, and the Victimisation Magistrate's Court. Druid pictured the austere glass foyers and dependable, seventeenth century brickwork disguising a warren of well-appointed chambers once used as museums and film sets, now resurrected as court rooms, a felons' exercise yard and gaols. He didn't need to be able to make out the details to see that the Knowledge Quarter was so much more than the sum of its buildings. It oozed a sense of superiority next to the frivolous nature of the rest of the city, more so since he knew that southernmost, as far removed from the central hub of melodrama and role play as possible, lay Clifton Village. A bastion of quintessential Englishness with its thatched cottages, dovecot, and village green, the area also housed Clifton Hall, a stolid country estate and training academy for the Grallators, Renegade's own police force.

If there was any degree of fluidity to the quarter, it was closer to hand at the waterfront, where sheets of dark, oily glass were arranged as office blocks, reflecting the thick, green waters of the Grand Communion Canal. Branching off the mother artery, the rejuvenated canal network crisscrossed the city in trails of blue-green silver speckled with hundreds of Trawler vessels. And what of below? Underpinning the streets was a labyrinthine of medieval caves. Excavated from the Triassic sandstone by the city's long dead, the cave system was an underworld left to the rats, and the Skinwalkers, although—Druid's gaze stalled where the southern skyline was interrupted by a coagulated mass of spires—if rumours were to be believed, the latter breed of rodent had relocated above ground to an up-market if undesirable address.

The ruin of the south watchtower shape-shifted in the storm, spiking out at all angles like hot wax plunged into icy water then thawing back to something barely there, an etching on glass. Established on the oldest religious foundation in a city grown young again, the exquisite corpse of St. Mary's had been home to the lost saviour, Roses. Once upon a time, a city had risen like a phoenix from the fire of a million candles lit in homage to his effigy. Tonight, those flames were eclipsed by winter's star-fall. Touched by loss, Druid brought his focus back inside the room.

Sophia lifted her chin a notch. "Roses set me on this course to a darker shore. He was a living icon. He was also my husband—a man who loved this city so much it exhausted him, with nothing left over for the rest of us." She paused for the briefest respite then threw back her shoulders. "Don't expect me to mourn, *my* high lord, Druid." His name on her lips was subtly acrid, like a curse word spoken by a child. "I haven't the stomach for it. I'm more interested in establishing *why* my husband died, and *who* should be brought to account for his death."

Druid pressed his forehead to the glass. What Sophia proposed was the very thing that had had him stare into the city's light-haze every night for the past three months, only for the red oils of dawn to find him in the same petrified pose. Anger bled behind his eyes. Three short months! He wasn't ready for this. He needed time, long, stretching hours that bled into days like watercolours. There was the biography to write, or was it more of a bible? Either way, the separation of fact from fiction was mathematically principled; it required the precise arrangement of this detail and that, data maps and chronological charts, the pinning down of what was said when and why and with what intonation…all the small things that he had tried so hard to forget but which now mattered so very much, he determined.

Avoiding Sophia's eyes and those dreadful, painful questions of hers, he stared out at the Mystic Quarter surrounding his home, a world that at once sustained and repelled him. His was an elevated vantage point. A towering shard of steel and dragonfly-wing-green glass, orbited by three oak-decked platforms, the north watchtower had been designed as a window onto the city. Fifteen years ago he had thrived on such epic notions of romanticism, locating his watchtower in the disused arboretum alongside the ruins of a Chinese bell tower and a band stand, a sparsely-populated aviary, and a forest of rogue botanicals. Now he shivered at a sense of being contained by the park. Its many walkways glistened like fairy paths, each one a ruse to lead the vulnerable back to the beginning again. Snow lent the self-sealed garden an enchanted quality; his should have been the sleep of the undead, a spindle's pinprick at his thumb.

The mysterious air suited the adjacent neighbourhood. Taking in the districts of Arboretum, Berridge, Sherwood, Basford, Bestwood, Bulwell and Bulwell Forest, the north was a world of staved wood, glacial glass and troll bridges, where suburbia cohabitated with the crooked and the tumbledown. Timbered guild houses represented the casters and weavers, robe dyers, bookbinders, leatherworkers, symbol embroiderers, ritual jewellers and other artisans. Tea rooms housed little-old-lady waitresses serving sweet and sour pastries, seeded breads, potted meat, stew and soups. Thatched round houses burgeoned like fields of vine-strung pumpkins. Old curiosity shops nestled in the dust of university halls. Spirit guides assembled from scraps of metal, stone and timber guarded the quarter's numerous cemeteries and parks like Angels of the North.

The Castclan pod spread over a five-mile circumference, a giant, white, quilted dome full of craft-knowledge, and secrets.

There was one challenge to the fantastical feel of the quarter; City Hospital. Its four great, reflective wings stretched to every compass point, like a sterile cross nailed to the body of the city. That blot on an otherwise mystical landscape was located to the rear of the watchtower, and as long as Druid kept his gaze fixed forward, he could pretend there was no such thing as sickness or death, only castles in the air.

Pixie-boots, laced with a scar of red ribbon and cut from moss green suede—oh yes, he'd noticed them—tapped a soft minuet across the black marble floor. A faint rustling came from the direction of his desk. He whipped around. His eyes burnt like rusted nails into the backs of her hands.

"It's a marvel any of the Great Library's documents survived the fire when so much of the south watchtower was reduced to ash." Sophia sifted the papers. Her frown echoed their confusion of elements. "Word of your efforts to amalgamate what was salvaged has reached the city," she said quietly. "People say you document the scriptures."

Storming away from the window, Druid snatched the glossy stag-beetle of a leather office chair back on its castors, slid heavily into the seat and fed his legs below the slab of trollish walnut. "It's a biography, nothing more," he spat. "If folk wish to make more of it, it's because I write the truth, not any one tribe's corruption of Roses's wisdom." He re-filed the scraps into neat little dusting piles. His lips pursed to echo the dark twists of wood grain.

Sophia lifted a hand delicately out of the way. Her opal betrothal ring flamed. "This isn't the time to celebrate his life, Druid. In a few months, years even, it may be appropriate to write about the glory days, to commission bards in his name, to shout 'Halleluiah! He died so He could save us'." The turquoise eyes lit up with harsh incredulity. "*Now*, the city needs time to heal itself, to learn how to survive without the one thing that made Belief credible. So write your bible by all means, take it to bed and self-love every syllable." Her mouth was a curl of red sealing wax. "But don't try to share that dirty secret, or it'll be salt poured on an open wound. At best, the tribes will turn on themselves in an unholy war of blame-shifting. At worst, they'll turn on you, and let's make no bones about it, if the mob comes knocking, they'll take down the whole dynasty. You, me, Adeudas…"

His fingers splayed over the glossed surface of the desk, Druid thought about the High Lord Adeudas; violet-eyed, angel hair cut into jags and gelled so he looked like the most incredible cocktail of a man, all Andy Warhol'ed and punk plastic. "Adeudas will always find a way to right himself, no matter how strong the headwind," he muttered.

"And me?"

Glancing at Sophia, Druid saw himself reflected in her eyes, a creature gaunt as Tolkien's Gollum, fingering the Precious of his paperwork. His stomach tumbled. He pushed back from the desk. "Relax, Sophia. My days of caring and *sharing* are over. I've no desire to publish one line," he lied.

Sophia studied him.

He drew in a lungful of air, expelled it through his nose. "That's not to say I agree with you. If you put aside your *fashionable* grief…" His eyes devoured a dress that spoke of bayou mourning: a stiff bodice decorated with jade, a thigh-skimming hemline, trailing, antique green lace at an elbow, the cusp of a slim shoulder, the naked throat. "…for a spell, you'd see the city's dying. Belief's breaking down and taking the old ways with it, and that means its reigning nobility, High Lady of the Drathcor."

He propped the shin of a crooked leg on the opposite thigh, and reclined. "Drathcor. We are the kings and queen of modern vampirism. Circus grotesques of the modern age, in a city that can't live without us, can't live with us. So what are our options?" Jet-black claws cradled the bare foot resting on his knee. His expression was complex. "Sensationalise the circumstances surrounding Roses's death, or—and this strikes me as the more credible option—we help the tribes *we* created regain their trust. Trust in his vision. Trust in his words. They came when he called. They'll take strength from him now."

"Rather than mourn Him," Sophia replied blankly. "That's no solution."

"It appears to work for you."

If he cut her, she gave no indication of the fact, just stared back with a look of condescension. "It's ironic. We Drathcor live inside the honeyed walls of our watchtowers and we think we are untouchable. Yet Death still finds us."

Druid slid his arms about his ribs. Was there a trace of real emotion in the flicker of her lips? It made him want to hold her until their mutual pain erased—or she ripped out his throat.

"I won't accept it, Druid!" she hissed, brilliantly reformed into an ice queen.

"Of course you won't, Sophia," he bit back in confusion. "You won't accept *anything*; responsibility, mistakes, consequence, *loss.*" His top lip recoiled from the gum, exposing twin, white blades. "Yes, you play the wounded widow very well. But let's face it, Sophia, black was always your colour."

Her eyes glazed. The mask had fallen.

"Leave me alone," he muttered, running a hand over his forehead. She had hurt him again and, like a blind fool, he had let her. "I haven't got the patience for your mind-games."

She turned away. Her elfin boots tapped neatly over the marble floor. Pausing before the window, she ran her fingertips back and forth across the glass, her exquisite face angled to the east and unsolvable. Druid moved besides her. Gazing east, he wondered how *she* felt, staring out at the quarter of the city that had evolved in her image. Did she like what she saw there, and did she recognise the irony of all that she had once traded in to be its queen?

The eastern landscape was branded on his mind. Scooped out of one half of the city centre and incorporating the districts of Mapperely, St. Ann's, Sneinton, and Dales, the Trading Quarter was a mixed bag of historical, commercial architecture and northern-England grime. In the Lace Market, exquisite three and four storey Georgian town houses stood shoulder-to-shoulder with blocks of rust-red brick. Some of the mills had been restored to their original purpose, regurgitating textiles for sale in the rest of the quarter, or for export. The remainder were converted warehouses, strung up with neon and operating as apartments, dance studios, radio stations, art galleries, and entertainment agencies. In contrast, the regenerated shopping malls of Broadmarsh and the Victoria Centre were the dream of the futurist, their steel exoskeletons fleshed with blue and storm-grey glass. Further east, the faux-medina of Sneinton Market spiralled round upon itself like an ammonite. Of an evening, the alleys were packed with vendors touting the wares of Camden, the Indies and the Orient, all the gusting scents of spices, hand-moulded soaps, charbroiled poultry, slashed flower stems, fresh and rotten fruits, glazed pastries and animal dung perfuming the city. But not tonight. Not when the sky was delivering on its promise of a storm. Not when the east watchtower's huge, white, gardenia-petal sails were eerily still and phantasmic.

Staring right, Druid swallowed back his sourness. Sneinton Windmill was a far grander structure since its reincarnation as the east watchtower, but it was the west of the city that had seen a fresh injection of razzmatazz. Soaking up the rest of the city centre and stretching west to Radford and Park, Leen Valley, Bilborough, Aspley, Wollaton West, and Wollaton East and Lenton Abbey, the Pleasure Quarter was a rich palette of self-indulgence. This was the precinct that attracted the vast majority of the city's tourists, a La-La land where hostels and rent-by-the-hour rooms were the poor, if sensual, relations of stiff-upper-lipped Victorian guest houses and sumptuous, designer-morbid hotels. Restaurants lined every street, their weird and exotic menus drawing on a variety of themes and cultural-influences: medieval, eastern, vegan, antipodean, Palaeolithic, and much, much more. The wedding-cake exteriors of the theatres seemed in competition for the title of Most Extravagant while the art galleries were steel cubes rigged with spots and mirrors like porn studios turned inside-out and hung up to dry. Sin Street Corner House, with its flambé, roasts, dough-scented eateries, real-ale inns, dirty little vodka bars, and CGI-cinemaplex, was a hedonist's heaven. Devil's casino, a star-shaped colossus on Maid Marion's Way, was a puritan's hell. Along with a glut of revamped venues and bars, the quarter's many destinations catered to a quagmire of appetites. All except for Legacy. The rock club grew out of the swirling night like the engorged heart of the city, extraterrestrial, unapologetic.

Tormented by the ache of good times lost, Druid forced his eyes west to the quarter's outer limits, populated by myriad ethnicities and thrill seekers. Chinese water gardens basked in the steam and spice-scents of Turkish Hammams. Mosaiced courtyards gave centre stage to ornate fountains. The tourist traps of the opium dens glowed alongside the fetish boutiques and strip clubs on Booty Boulevard. Floodlit skate parks tore up the one-time golf course, the enormous, snow-filled depressions glinting like the hubs of alien spacecraft. A stock car circuit cut its giant doughnut out of a couple of acres of parkland. The silhouetted funfair and kited tent of Le Cirque des Magiciens sprawled alongside.

In contrast, Wollaton Village was a bed of preservation, the higgledy-piggledy rooftops of cottages and Victorian gentlemen's residences seemingly superimposed on the winter wonderland. At the westernmost edge, Wollaton Hall had long since been appropriated by the Management as a private members' club. Tonight it was a study in shadow.

Unlike the floodlit castle on a hilltop. Like a paste crown on the head of a natural beauty, the west watchtower was an inelegant, squat mansion at odds with its precipitous setting. Renowned the world over as a site of folk law and national heritage, the stately pile had been reduced to the playground of the sensual sheriff, Adeudas, and his host of salacious deputies. With a wave of nausea, Druid turned sideways, leant a shoulder on the glass, and stared intently into the turquoise eyes of the city's ice queen.

Releasing his gaze, Sophia dipped a hand into the side panel of her dress, produced a tiny, purple lighter and a slender case which she flipped open. She took a thin, white Cartier cigarette between her fingers, lit it. Smoke ghosted at her lips.

"I've one more game to play. It's called 'Let's pretend we're detectives'..."—her voice carried over his attempt at interruption—"...let's pretend we give a damn about a crazy little thing called justice." She kicked at the floor with the silver stalk of her kitten heel. "You want to write the truth about His life, Druid? Don't waste time on such an easy tale. Leave happy endings for children's stories and write the truth about His death." Swapping the cigarette to her opposite hand, she raised a beautifully pale and taloned finger. "There is one way to reunite the tribes and that is to provide an honest explanation of how and why their saviour died. Otherwise everything we ever set out to create—equality, darkness's celebration, the freedom to live whatever life you choose, no matter how fantastical, thanks to pure *Belief* in the fact—it all equates to a big, fat, adulterated lie."

She paused to return her cigarette to her right hand, put it to her lips and take a long, luxuriant drag. At the same time, Druid felt his mind becoming curiously painful, as if awakening from an enchanted sleep. "Go on," he said slowly.

"So, here's what I remember. The guards—their stricken faces, the mess of lips that failed, several times over, to get the *fact* out, which I knew already of course. There *are* windows in the east watchtower. Three months ago I watched hope burn like the rest of the city." She flicked ash into the dome of a thin, waist-height, silver cylinder. "Roses embraced death in the same artistic guise as any healthy citizen in Renegade, and, yes, he was angry. But suicidal?" Her eyes crystallised. "What do *you* remember, Druid?" she asked through a pall of filmy smoke.

Druid crushed his jaw around the soft, wet meat of his mouth. He remembered it all, carried it like a storm in his pocket. "The Trawler who smuggled me back into the city came to fetch me from my bed inside the cabin. I remember he was a tall man, a strong, substantial man, who carried a welt of muscle on tanned, tattooed bones, and whose face was markedly gaunt, as if that part of him alone had endured the fatigue of long term combat..." He swallowed hard, fighting against a reactive impulse to shut down. "Barely a word had passed between us. Then, on the night of our return, the Trawler suddenly plunged into the cabin, his tough features destroyed by some internal agony. And I knew then, pushing past him, slicing my palms up the rusty grip either side of the ladder, slipping out across the wooden boards..."

His brow twisted in an effort to wring out the truth of the event. "What else? The look of flames from the bow of the Trawler's junk, like giant forks of blood. The smell, rich and bitter, like burnt chocolate." He drew his hand over his face. "Having successfully reminded myself why I rejected the outside world in the first place, I came back to Renegade to learn how to live again...only to find myself immediately returned to dust. Why's death always like that, a mix of sweet and sour?"

"Because it is unnatural," Sophia avowed, adding, "And because he was meant to be immortal."

Druid smiled tightly. "Even Roses couldn't deliver on *that* account."

"Couldn't he? Fire was one of the rare means to guarantee His death."

"Oh, come off it, Sophia." Leaping up from his chair, Druid cast his arms towards the city. "We *created* this game of gods and monsters. Drathcor, the four key tribes, the drifters, a brand new religion called Belief, every part of the city's makeup, even its political structure in the power we conceded to the Management. Just don't kid yourself it's anything but fantasy. Yes, Roses was extraordinary, but underneath the make-up, he was still just a man. He was still just ordinary."

"We're all entitled to our Beliefs. You have yours. I have mine. But one thing we *agree* on; Roses died before his time and no one has the guts to find out why. Not our Drathcor brethren, the High Lord Adeudas, not the Management or their squad of stilted iron men..."

"The Grallators in charge submitted a full and accurate report."

"...not even his brother it seems."

Druid swallowed audibly. He glared through the glass at Haunted Hill, an artificial mound separating Forest Field and the sweeping acreage of Rock Cemetery, and he despised that it was his destiny to join his brother in the grand sarcophagus at its apex. "Sophia." Tears pricked his eyes. He blinked them back. "The fire at the south watchtower was an accident caused by human error, the result of some small kindle, the Grallators said. A cigarette left unattended, perhaps?" He gazed purposefully at the silver column of the ashtray.

"A neat conclusion!" Reaching up behind her neck, Sophia twisted her waist-length, anaemic-blonde dreads fiercely up into a knot. "Because who'd dare to openly accuse me, the blackest of widows, of causing my husband's death, however inadvertently? I know the Management. Rather than rock the boat, they prefer to conspire in quiet acceptance and collusion of the fact."

The acrimony in her voice was thick; Druid felt it cling to his skin like clotted blood, like oil. "Give me a motive." His neck muscles tensed.

Smoke bled from Sophia's lips. She thrust a talon at the wintered city. "Do you ever think back to what was Nottingham was like before we moved here? Gun-city, remember that tagline? Dead-end splurge of gun-crime, gang warfare and dope dens. Fifteen years ago, we put a stop to all the tours and studio sessions and music Moguls getting fat on our riffs, our licks, our profit, and returned to this beautiful, terrible wasteland we call home. Who'd have thought a *rock band* would have the power to eclipse so much eye-blinding corruption? Would you? I wouldn't have believed it if I hadn't seen the way Roses went about regenerating what was then a lousy cesspit called Nottingham." Her eyes coruscated to the hue of moneyed green. "And we worked at it, didn't we, Druid? For fifteen long, long years we worked like dogs to spit our profits at every filth-encrusted nook and cranny of this city, and didn't it polish up well, Druid? Didn't our *new* Nottingham, our *Renegade City* scrub up well?" Her voice held a tinge of cynicism, or was it wonder? "Ironic then that the good folk left as the dark masses descended; ironic that we slaved to bribe local government only for the dour-suited do-gooders to swiftly move away. And yes, tourists were still drawn to the city, but now they came to experience what happened when a real live Robin Hood bestowed the riches of fantasy and Belief on the city."

"I know my own history, Sophia."

"I'm sure you do, but do you *feel* the true magnitude of what happened here anymore? Roses showed hundreds of thousands the way and they loved him for it. He was an extraordinary man who, at the age of forty-five, had many years of leadership ahead of him." She smiled gorgeously, as if lit up by the gold dust of memories. The smile ebbed. "But that violates the code of martyrdom. Far better to snatch him in his prime. Then he'll shine forever."

"Self-sacrifice without the collusion of self? That's a twisted notion, even by Renegade's standards. Your evidence?"

"Needs careful assembly before we present it to the Management."

Druid fed his hands either side of his face. He sighed gutturally. "Sophia. Where would I *start?* I'm as out of the loop as you are. We've shut ourselves up in the watchtowers for, what must it be, six, seven years now? A unique brand of retirement, but, for a deified superstar, the options are somewhat limited." His upper lip flickered in a sneer. The cynicism faded though as he felt a pang of guilt. "I still think the city needs Belief. I *have* to, otherwise this whole grand performance has been a spectacular waste of time. But I also accept that Roses's death has had a hugely detrimental effect on the unity of the tribes. Which is why I find it impossible to believe any member would wish their mentor dead."

Sophia's turquoise eyes burnt into his skull, seemed to leave their mark there.

She stubbed out her cigarette. "And precisely why it is time to engage with city life again and establish which of Roses's fans robbed the rest of us of his glory. For you, at least…I haven't the taste for it." Her tongue touched her left fang, appeared to recoil from it. "I've given enough. The fans have made wormsmeat of me."

Druid was unnerved by her bitterness; it was a match for his own. He also thought he recognised the motive. Studying the crazed, silver veins in the black marble underfoot, he grunted, "The guilt is said to pass in time."

"Guilt!" Sophia's heel smashed down, tearing at the root to hang by a thread of glue under the shoe. Her expression was vitriolic. "I know nothing about guilt. I loved and lost through no fault of my own. I know *that* with the same conviction of Belief that made me abandon the outside all those years ago. The only difference is that then I was searching for ways to open doors, now I'm looking for ways to close them." She sighed wearily, bent forward, undid the clasp of her shoe and let it slide to the floor, beautiful yet broken.

The vivisection of his death's most gruesome enigma. Did he owe Roses that much, Druid wondered sorely? And what of Sophia, did he owe her a debt? He knelt at her feet, took the shoe in hand. With care, he retried the heel against the sole. He peered at the damage with the same scrutiny reserved for his paperwork.

"You want me to prove the fire was arson?" he said gently.

"I want you to take that shit apart, piece by sinful piece." Sophia stood stiffly over him. She took a cigarette from the slim, silver case, lit up and inhaled. The paper flamed, blood and gold. "Go back into the dark of the city. Seek out the truth. Finish your bible *the right way*. And Druid…" Pale green claws fed over his shoulder, locked in. "Hunt down Roses's killer. Then show me their throat."

Chapter 3

Save Yourself

Ever glimpsed your kind in the Metal aisle of a music store, on a graffitied sit-up-and-beg bench in a hippy café, or across the sweated flesh of a nightclub? Ever wished you'd got a way to preserve that sense of kinship, in a glass vial, say, that's kept in a bedside cabinet, a rucksack pocket, or a shoe-box alongside love-letters, scraps of art, a poem, the threads of severed friendship bracelets, and a few old, faded photographs? Imagine how tempting it would be to rise up in the dead of night, remove the stopper and inhale that precious scent. Yes, your lungs might balk at the effort, your head begin to spin. But you'd persist, and for one elemental reason; if you just learnt to breathe that dark gas instead of oxygen, you'd stand a fighting chance against the weight of so much nothingness.

Imagine four young rock stars started it all with their love songs for the unchaste, the alone, and the guarded. And that rather than stay on their wild-child ride to rock'n'roll gluttony, they made the most unexpected choice of their career; they jammed the cogs of the great commercial machine, then just stepped off. No more tours, no more albums cut, no more promotional work, no more blur of hurt-drug-girl-boy-drink-lust-raw-emotion. Instead, the most revered band in the history of rock sank roots into the earth where they stood, and watched a city blossom.

Imagine the fans came at His request. Thousands in their ghost-greys and hide-behind black, studs and stilettos, platforms and flares, cloaks and pentacles, leathers and feathers, latex and lace; such a complex armoury to guard against a lifelong assault. And they worshipped Him like any other idol.

Imagine His word gave wings to a new Creation, where a boy in make-up was adored and not despised, and where a girl expressed her sensual liberty without fear of judgement. Imagine a founding ideology that came to alter how we, the darker half, chose to live. No preconceptions, no barriers, no need to run and hide, just the freedom to desire it then live it. In a hyperreality made believable by the will to breathe a different type of air. In Renegade City: Mecca of the damned.

Imagine what you'd give for just one hour inside those walls. Imagine how you'd repay Him who lit the way.

Roses. A gothic Messiah, His prose held all the colours of a sensual dream: reds the shade of blood oranges, greens aflame like emeralds, hazy purples, and purest black and white. His words were palpable, seeming to swell in the mouth like passion, like a kiss. His tongue caressed the soul of all those who would listen, and the strangers listened hard to their newfound saint and martyr. Yes, I do not think martyr too strong a word because, without a doubt, there was an element of self-sacrifice to His lyrics. Every time His fingers touched the strings of His guitar, the pain would arise, a black-eyed pain, born of disenchantment – and how He would suffer it! Notes flowed like rain and somehow He was drowning, but in a way that gave voice to a shared disillusionment so that the simplest songs became anthems for all of those who felt themselves drowning in the world beyond Renegade City. Punch-drunk on the fantasy, His poetry became a mantra for every dark dreamer who had ever longed to swap mortality for the romance of myth or legend.

And while He lived, our new world was brave and glorious. He fashioned Renegade City because He was the very first to choose its new reality. Adopting the name of 'Drathcor', He introduced those nearest and dearest to the blood, namely, His fellow band members; myself, the drummer, Roses's very own ice queen and bassist, Sophia, and, on lead guitar, Adeudas, a fiend of flamboyant superficiality and flagrant depth.

We three adapted to exist as Drathcor. Roses, on the other hand, seemed born to it. Dressed in embroidered jeans and collarless shirt of blackest suede, He was a testament to gothic glamour. His naturally exaggerated canines were all too suggestive of a supernatural birthright. His hair was poker-straight and gleaming. Deprived of daylight, His skin became a slip of china while His quiet way of moving gave Him a predatory, if unnecessary, stealth; the 'victims' for a beautiful bloodsucker being both plentiful and willing.

Rock god, hero, saint, and modern vampire – the followers bestowed so many titles upon Him. Yet I knew Him quite simply as Roses, the most glorious front man since the brilliant, black birth of rock'n'roll. He was a soul mate and a friend. He was also my brother.

Together, we dared to dream. Foremost, we longed to escape a world in which music had become the ultimate commodity. A soulless world where the alternative community were hung, drawn and quartered, jeered at and leered at while being held up as examples of devil worship, sexual depravity and asocial tendencies. Not fit to raise children, not fit to hold down a job, not fit to walk the streets, not fit to dream...

Our answer was to reject the corruption, alongside the jaw-achingly-sweet monopoly of the music industry by plastic-fantastic airheads and false idols, and start again. We concentrated our efforts on Nottingham city, an area of some 28.8 square miles, and left alone the surrounding boroughs of Rushcliffe, Broxtowe, Gedling and Ashfield. A sizable stake of our royalties bribed local government; soon, we regenerated great swathes of once-polluted wasteland, rebuilt the hulking wreck of City Hospital, sponsored schools, repaired an endless sludge of architecture...Ironically, as a plethora of exotic strangers descended, it wasn't enough to convince the 'good folk' to stay.

Something in excess of 10,000 are said to have come, or so it is rumoured (and rumour is a truth not often disputed in this city). The strangers brought with them the sweet scent of longing and, in the pit of their bellies, rebellion's fire. Infiltrating every store, tower block, and leafy street, they came at His beckoning, for in a way He spoke to them, and in a way they answered, His accidental doctrine becoming as vital to their existence as air or earth or fire or water. Free to come and go as they pleased, most chose to stay. Families and solo artists alike took up refuge in Renegade's dazzling nocturne, since ours was indeed a tale of beauty in darkness. A fresh start. A life choice.

Druid laid aside his fountain pen, took a sip from his whiskey tumbler then returned the glass to the damp ring on the table. With one hand tucked between the pages, he closed the notebook and fingered the insignia on the cover. The seal of the Drathcor dated from the dawning days, its tying together of a range of mystic elements being all too representative of a time when all four band members were united by Belief.

The basis of the design was an abstract key. A crusaders' style cross represented the handle, its centre point marked with an all seeing eye. The four arms of the cross were diamond-pointed. The arm that pointed south was three times the length of the others to denote the key shaft. At the handle, a quarter-circle looped the space between each arm to form a roundel, and each roundel contained a symbol. He traced each icon in turn; the three rays of the Awen glyph associated with his own north, the spiked head of a black Mackintosh rose representing the south, the seven-petals of a lotus flower for the east, and a silhouetted Luna moth for the west. He slid both hands over the insignia, pressed down hard as if to protect or erase it, and was aware of a shallow homesickness.

"Alright, youth!" In a tumble of dirt brown limbs, the intruder fed into the pew opposite.

Emotion sank back into Druid's bones. He inched up a sleeve of his leather. The Storm Navigator coiled at his wrist like a strip of exposed internal cybernetics. He scanned the LCD display. 01.49 a.m. Since crawling out of the gates of his north watchtower, navigating the dark web of streets, and securing himself in a crevice of this less than salubrious bar at the northern edge of the Pleasure Quarter, he had gone for precisely one hour and forty nine minutes without attracting undue notice. But now, it seemed, his number was up.

Slowly, as if, given time, whatever was seated opposite might have the sense to thaw and resolve itself into dew, he masked the open notebook with five jet-black claws, thrust his shades further up the bridge of his nose, and lifted his gaze. He was face to face with the epitome of teen angst.

Sucking noisily on the tip of a wizened wizard hat, the kid seemed clumsily self-assured, in a way that suggested he considered himself smarter than his contemporaries and, irritatingly, he was right to do so. The mouth was a twist of stretched Hubba Bubba. The eyes were globules of vibrant, oily green. Freckles smudged his nose and cheeks—or was it mud-specks? He was the sort of boy who made it difficult to tell.

"Rude to stare, surprised you dare," hissed the kid churlishly. He spat the drip of fabric out his mouth and shifted from one buttock to another as if the seat of his pants were aflame. Making a fist, he stretched a thin, brown arm across the table.

"Castclan!" Black claws shot out across the bleached shelf of wood.

"Devil Man!" riposted the boy, yanking his arm clear. The gem-like eyes grew beady. A long, sharp nose twitched at the tip. He glared at Druid, like a sewer-rat lifted out of the filth by the scruff of its neck, and held out his fist again. Tiny, blue grains trickled from his fingers.

Brushing his palms against one another, he explained, "Sand. To help the ink dry." He flashed the older man a bright, white grin. "Did you think I meant to cast a spell? In this hole? Now *that* really would turn toad-ugly. Can you imagine the beasts and monsters we'd attract?" Tossing a thumb over his shoulder, he indicated the bar's residents; a tiger with latex whiskers and a perma-wig of amber fur, five mournful pierrots, two inebriated molls lazing off the suit of a Chinese gangster, and various other shady miscreants...drifters in other words, who survived by their own creed and rules rather than those prescribed by the Drathcor, Druid mused acidly. Yes, he had already taken stock of that rogue contingent. His tongue travelled to the sister blades at his jaw.

"Go away, boy," he muttered. Scraping his glossed claws back across the table, he closed the book. "Save your parlour tricks for the city's newbies. I haven't the patience or the pennies."

The boy raised his eyebrows, which were thin, brown and shiny like a pair of garden slugs. "If you'd any idea of the sort of clientele you're cosying up to in here, you'd be less free with the abuse. See that moll with the killer lips and the shape of a holster at her stocking top? Come midnight, she'll take a stroll along the banks of Ninth Canal and gun down a love rival. The pierrots? Black-market pirates trading tips on future Grallator raids. Each one of those clowns totes a blade hidden in the folds of their silk pyjamas. Think you're safe here? This is an oubliette, my friend, reserved for fiends, freaks and libertarians...or, as you may know them, general scum. On the rare occasion that a tourist sets foot inside this dive, they take one look at these bad asses, turn heel and scoot, and I'm talking even the sleaziest sightseer, of which the Pleasure Quarter attracts more than its fair share." He balled his hands into two tight fists, then flashed his fingers. "Louse House,

*Distillery for the Damned...*slogan says it all." The kid stared
hard across the table. He blinked once, and softened his tone.
"Least with the tribes, you get it laid on a platter. Wanna ride
a broom or brew poteen in a cauldron? Get digs with the
Castclan. If you're the flighty sort, Fae will take you under
their wing. Pale and *dead* interesting? Opt for the DarkLed.
Fancy messing about in boats? Set sail with the
Trawlers...Whatever the Belief, we got a tribe to match. Funny
then that not everyone's peachy with the deal. Some don't
want to fit in. Craaazy as it sounds, some *like* living on the
outside. And they don't care for visitors." His green, flaming
eyes indicated the dark corners of the bar. "Believe me, mate.
You're no tourist. You know this hell ain't no place for
Castclan or any *other* pure breed."

"Precisely why I chose it," Druid said under his breath.
He imprinted his brow with cool, fisted fingers. All this talk of
danger was too flamboyant for his taste, and not because the
kid lied. In truth, his nostrils had been piqued by the stench of
lawlessness the moment he eased his slender frame beneath
the low-slung rustic lintel and stepped inside that human
cesspit. No, what his young compatriot failed to grasp was that
a man could lose the will to care.

"What'd you say, mate?" The kid leant in on his elbows.
Druid snapped back his head and stared up at the ceiling,
the bare light bulb, the brown-gilded cloud of a water stain.
His eyes felt moist. "I said pure breeds use this hole just the
same, which is why it strikes me as odd to hear a Castclan
deny his heritage." His gaze dropped. A long digit slithered
out towards the boy. "And before you deny it again, you *are*
Castclan. That's clear from your attitude."

"My *attitude*! I'm not the one making free with the
pokiness, although I am happy to give you the finger." The
mini-wizard grasped Druid's hand, turned it around then
twisted it up. He cracked a smile. "Besides, I don't see any
other freak befriending your bad-natured ass."

"I didn't ask for company."

"Yes, you did." The kid manoeuvred Druid's hand in a
sweeping arch until it came to rest on the soft black leather of
the book. "Might want to stow *that* away for starters. This
ain't the place to show you're higher-minded."

Druid slid the book into the inner pocket of his leather. "I
didn't come here to make friends," he glowered.

"But you *did* come in, and that signals one of two things. Either you're a willing victim to drifters…" The boy arched one eyebrow. "…Pastime of the stupidest, dirtiest pure breeds, of which I'm not convinced you're one—or, and here's the science bit—you're so busy scribing away in that little black book of yours that you've forgotten to care if you live or if you die." He tapped at his forehead with a finger. "Either way, you're on the fast-track to smack-down unless you exercise this muscle."

The kid's rat-like face lit up with mischief or malevolence; Druid couldn't pinpoint which, but despised the idea that he was being played with. Rage flushed his breastbone, the dark heart of each pupil. He parted his lips to warn the brat to run hell for leather. Then he noticed the tiger man.

Long, pearly claws fed between the tarnished poles connecting floor and roof, while the beast's agile bulk slunk in and out of the shadowed booths and tables. Two red slits shone out from under deep-fleshed hoods; inimical and wholly intent on their prey, which Druid took to be his right breast, or, expressly, the contents of his inside coat pocket. Glancing across the table, he realised the kid's sly expression had nothing to do with him and everything to do with the approaching feline. His own gaze sharpened.

As the thief slid within a metre or so of their table, the boy leapt from his pew and a few steps out into the room. He secured an arm about the drifter's hard-muscled shoulders.

"Anger management! That's what we're talking about, my spiky friend," he said cheerily, and shook his head at the Drathcor. He shrugged at the cat as if to gain its sympathy. "Think you got probs? See our kitty here. Fish-breath, hairballs, not to mention a nimble tongue for those hard-to-reach spots. Ask me, it's gross, not to mention unsanitary, but do you catch our friend complaining? I think not."

Stretching up, the kid stroked the tattooed fur at the creature's head. "Some nights this city can seem a craaazy place. You know the score, kitty. The head starts to spin, the mind to boogie-woogie. Times like that, I fear I'm on the fast track to the funny farm. Then I think of you and I feel strangely sane."

33

A dirty bulb overhead caught the glint of lethal silver. Druid flinched, his fists shot apart and clawed, but instantaneously a brown hand fed over the cat's paw.

Leaning in by its triangular ear, the kid softly breathed, "Four clean sheets to retract that shiny claw." A roll appeared out of thin air. The kid drew off four notes with the dexterity of a card player and wafted them under the twitchy nose.

The cat drew a puckered tongue across its lower lip. Flexing the muscle in its mechanical grafted-to-skin tail, it spoke in a voice that slithered, "IQ. I know you, Castclan." The red slivers of its eyes lingered on Druid. But it returned the blade to a secret sheath in its fur and padded noiselessly away.

"Glad to hear it," the boy hissed after the retreating beast. "Go spread the word. IQ's the brain chief, the wisest warlord, the mental...ist man." He pressed a finger to the spot between his eyes, evolved the gesture into a sharp salute.

Deaf or oblivious, the cat took a seat at the bar, rested forward on crossed muscle and breathed its order over the luckless waitress. With a supple yawn, the beast slicked its tongue inside the offered tumbler. Its tail thrashed then curled about the metal legs of the barstool.

"IQ?" said Druid slowly.

"Irvine Quirk," the kid supplied with a trace of 'not cool' awkwardness. "Nice to meet and greet..."

Druid downed his shot of Jack. Every part of him hurt. "I just want some peace," he said softly and to no one in particular.

"You won't find that here." Resting his head sideways on the table, the kid forced Druid to meet his witch-green gaze. "I reckon it's going to be a good while until you find peace *anywhere*. From the looks of it, you're a man who shoulders a cross of a thousand secrets and doesn't have the first idea how to go about laying it down. For what it's worth, I'd say you need to break all of your problems down into bite sized chunks, start at the, well..."

"Start?" Behind the dark, horizontal teardrops of his shades' lenses, Druid's eyes widened. Rusted cogs began to grind into motion in his mind. To rewind to where the dream of a world made for renegades had originated. It was the only place to start.

"Rock City." He breathed the name as if it were a sacred incantation.

IQ sat upright. "Blimey, mate. Haven't heard it called that for a while." He beat at his mouth with the damp tassel of his wizard hat. "You mean Legacy, right?"

"If you say so."

The kid blew out air from between his lips. "This late? We'll never get in. Legacy is at capacity an hour after opening tops. Unless..." With a superior air, he leant back, interlaced his fingers then dead-locked his arms in a long, casual stretch above his head. "There's this bouncer. His take-no-shit peers call him Einstein on account of his being anything but. Anyway, this Einstein owes me since this time a couple of months back. There was this *incident*... " IQ released his hands and used a couple of fingers to mime a pair of inverted commas. He looked ready to continue with the anecdote, but his sole audience member was already upstanding.

Druid indicated the exit door with a talon. "Let's call in the favour."

Kaleidoscopic light lurched and rotated on an axis, paint-balling the walls with exploding, citrus jewels. Music bled up from the floor, sluiced out of the blue, metal-veined grid-work overhead, and the sound was colossal, a turbine of lashing growler bass, waspish guitar, electro-glitch and feedback. Druid felt off-kilter and, having lost sight of the kid, utterly alone. His black and flame cowboy boots ate into the cigarette butts, glass, spit, grit, and silver foil underfoot. His nostrils flared, spooling in the scent of girl-sweet and man-sour. His hands, tough-fleshed and bloodless, trailed the small of the back of an undulating stranger, steered a plethora of human obstacles aside, and his only option was to flow with it. Flow with the pain. Flow with the insanity.

He felt drawn to stay and dissolve into the maelstrom. If he could twist up the volume, maybe he'd stand a hope in hell of drowning out the inner ghosts. Then he spotted the kid, pogoing at the dance floor's edge, the limp wizard hat performing its own weird ballet over the heads of the crowd. Reality spiralled in. He pressed against the tide of inked chests, nipple-rings and whipping hair and breasts until the glittering mass expelled him in a rush on the far side.

Beyond the mosh pit's crush, the air felt icy. Druid pulled his leather close like a shield. He flinched as the mini-wizard vaulted up alongside, face aglow with sweat and smiles.

"Now *this* is more like it. Check out those torches; silver-plated nickel with real flames! We like those. And I always say you can't go wrong with semi-naked nymphs on a trapeze." IQ's skinny lips pursed in a mock whistle. "Swing-a-ding-ding!"

Druid showed no discernable emotion. His gaze lifted to the striking burlesque. Clad in beaded thongs, ostrich plumes and tasselled nipple pasties, as well as their own pearlescent, ebony and olive skin, the beauties dipped in and out of smoky eruptions of dry ice, their movements guided by a stiff yet gliding repetition. Suddenly he thought of Sophia, her perfection, the stylish technicality of her grief.

He pictured Renegade's queen in the velvet gloom of Rock Cemetery, the dress she had worn (black, knee-length, corseted and crinolined), her hair, spun-sugar blonde pinned up under a pill-box hat and veil, and her face, gorgeous and awful in silk and shadow. He saw the stem of a cardinal rose, how she had distributed petals over the lid of Roses's sarcophagus, like blood-coloured tears, or sighs she had no capacity to utter.

Sophia, an enigma he'd longed to unfold, only to find his flesh etched with paper cuts when he'd tried. If she'd shown herself capable of one trace of raw emotion, it had been spite at the idea of Roses's death—this notion of his murder—and cold hate for the truth of the event, which was that he had died and no one was responsible, Druid mused sullenly. And no one could bring him back.

Long, tapering legs cut through the smog. Druid watched the pretty circus, his mind soured. He was here though, wasn't he, in the sticky, black heart of a world that would rip him to shreds just as soon as it clicked who the hell he was? His gaze dipped to the predatorial underworld, where clubbers moved in packs. Their eyes were flares in the dark, their claws stake-like streaks of red, black, plum and ultraviolet, and their hunger, palpable. He wondered when the burnings would begin.

His complexion took on a harsher, reddish hue. "I'm thirsty," he glowered, applying a single digit to the kid's left shoulder and shunting him in the direction of the relative quiet of the upper level bar.

"Uh?" The green eyes shot wide in nervousness.

Druid recoiled, as if the kid had gone up in flames.

"A shot of the hard stuff! 'Course man," perked up his young companion. Hands burrowing in the pockets of low-slung jeans, the kid started to ascend the nearest of two flights of neon-beaded stairs located either side of the main dance floor, leaving Druid to wonder what, if anything, had just happened.

He followed at a distance, his flesh feeling iced and fiery in equal parts. What had he thought, a Drathcor could just retread the boards of Legacy with a fresh haircut and shades, and not a soul would notice? That he could sit, nose to snout, with that inquisitive little rodent (called IQ, for Goth's sake) and not reveal his origins? Even he wasn't *that* crazy!

Although...he peered left, then right...here he was swimming in a savage sea of rockabillies, punks, skaters, velvet goths, cyber goths, gothic Lolitas, metallers, greebos, glammies—the whole strawberry switchblade assortment—and not one batted a sequin-encrusted eyelid. Were they really too blinded by a life on the dark side to notice a mentor in their midst? No, that was too convenient, he mused, screwing up his fists so the claws bit into his palms.

But if Renegade was just an elaborate dream, and all its citizens just reflections of that fancy, then might he not be too? In other words, in the eyes of the inhabitants of Legacy as well as the city beyond, he was just a wannabe, or to use the technical term for Origin's die-hard devotees, a Drathy.

He hunched, his shaded eyes eating into the shadows. He'd forgotten about the Drathy, or Origin's personal doppelgangers; fans, in other words, who mapped their flesh to match his own, wore exact copies of his old stage ensembles, and mimicked his every quirk and mannerism. His lips twisted. He existed in self-parody then, and was most likely a hell of a lot less convincing in the part than his imitators.

He eased his claws over the blue chrome handrail. At the top of the neon-beaded staircase, his disguised gaze fell upon the bar. Yes, the counter was the same wet-look metal strip as it was all those years ago, a surface you could lick a spilt pint of beer off, and once upon a time he would have. But that was before, and in other ways, the club was not the same. Alongside being given a new name, its dark edges had been buffered, soaped and slicked afresh. The arches of catacomb-like alcoves were set with bundled fibre optics, like night-lit diamonds. In place of wooden benches, he saw semi-circular sofas, upholstered in silver swirls and midnight purple skulls. Where the walls had boasted a haphazard mural of garish street graffiti, now a sensual manga arose in pinks, smoky purple, and flesh tones. And, underfoot, no longer the glue of melted-tar rubber but a rink of pure, black glass. He stepped awkwardly across it, troubled by its lustre.

"Oooh, shiny," the boy enthused, feeding his wiry, little arse onto a barstool. "Shinier," he murmured appreciatively as a PVC cat-suited coven shimmied by.

To the rear of the group, a pretty, buck-toothed witch shook her wand in their direction. Scarlet pollen escaped the tip. Druid sneezed. Giggling, the girl captured a kiss in her palm and cast it out. Looping an arm around the waist of a tiny blonde, she skipped away.

"Minx." The boy grinned lopsidedly, his mouth faintly stupid. "You've gotta agree this place attracts a better breed of feline," he remarked as a waitress in silver hot pants and a red, latex halter lined up their drinks. "Come on now. All this bountiful beauty. Would it hurt to crack a smile?"

Tripping off his stool, the kid disappeared behind Druid, who stiffened as a dirt-flavoured finger slid either side of his mouth and tried to stretch the lips.

They observed each other in the mirror behind the bar optics.

"It'll be a cold day in hell."

"The coldest."

The kid let his hands drop. He returned to his barstool and concentrated sulkily on a half pint of Guinness while Druid dared to edge his shades down a millimetre and linger on the mirror or specifically, his reflection.

Time had loved him like a prodigal child. The lines and signs of aging were subtle. In fact, he'd occupied that same spot in the past and not looked so dissimilar. The mirror had been tarnished then, rather than the pool of blue mercury he gazed on now, but, for the greater part, his image was unaltered, sallow at the jaw, strongly shaded at each cheekbone, hollow Saturn-ring eyes and irises of too pale blue; and it was *only an image*, since he was a very different man inside. A younger face had tilted to meet the heat of fame. Now his chin was tucked in and guarded. The eyes, once arrogant and self-annihilating, were tapered and shifty, ever watchful.

He took his glass in hand, swirled the amber. Once upon a time, he'd drunk the bright blood of strangers aside a bottomless shot of whisky, known every which way to kick and punch and bite at life. Grunting, he threw back the liquor. There was no rage in the beast he had become, only emptiness.

"Hell's bells, but you're a tortured soul," hissed the boy, prompting Druid to flinch again, as if the kid had seen inside him. "Staring at your reflection like *that.*"

"Like what?" He thrust the shades up with a single digit.

"Like you'd sooner rip out your eyes than spend another minute in your skin. All this flogging of the psyche. It's a helluva dull hobby. Ask me, you need to indulge that drained flesh of yours with a little TLC. Look out there!" He threw a thin, brown arm towards the dance floor. "Awash with the pleasure principle. Dare you to jump in!"

"I'd sooner drown, thanks."

The rat face moved close to Druid's. "Believe me, friend, you're already drowning. Sorrow stagnates in the crease between your eyes. Let it go, mate. Life's rush'll leave you gasping…and where better to draw breath than amid those golden sands." A finger poked up at the ravishing acrobats. He grinned. "I'd direct you to the Fae and their pretty Basement Boys, but I've seen you people-watching and your eyes are on the girls. Okay, so you're the sort to take your time and I'm not going to force you. I know you can take a horse to water but if it's a stubborn, bad-tempered git, you can't make it…"

"Drink?"

"Erm, yeah, why not?" The kid's gaze shifted from his barely touched drink to Druid's empty shot glass. His eyebrows swelled slightly. "So do me a favour. Just hang on to this." Deft as a street magician, he unclasped his fingers then drew back his hand. A tiny, red velvet pouch was left behind on the bar.

"A love token?" said Druid dryly.

"Charm," corrected the boy. "I was saving it for a special occasion but, hell, it's been a dry spell recently if you catch my drift. I don't go in for screwing with the Goddess so it's a general blend of herb and invocation. If she wills it, let it be so, that's my preferred arrangement. Otherwise you're into threefold repercussions and the risk of being eternally bound to some psychotic bunny-boiling loon you once swapped spit with." His wild, green gaze fixed hard on Druid. "This city's shady. The perfect place to lurk unseen, but it also makes for a hell of a non-existence. So I urge you, friend, come out of the dark."

The kid spoke with surprising sincerity. Druid squinted at the rat-like face and the rough-cut emeralds worn for eyes. He tried to fathom the weird creature.

"Starting with a good old-fashioned effort to get beered up, hey?" said the kid, twisting round on his stool then leaning back so that both of his elbows rested on the bar. He surveyed their surroundings. "Legacy. You gotta love the sleaze and gothdamn rock'n'roll of it all. Never been another club to rival it..." The kid's voice trailed away, his gaze intent on some fresh distraction. Coming to, he grinned and pressed a manly hand to Druid's shoulder. "If you'll excuse me a while, my hard-hearted amigo, my Miss Twelve O'Clock appears to have got herself waylaid while Miss One and Two O'Clock seem keen to come at once."

Druid traced the kid's line of sight to the pretty, bucktoothed girl who was hovering at the end of the bar, accompanied by the dainty blonde. The girls cooed and pawed at one another idly.

IQ swaggered off the barstool. "So you just stay here and give that little old charm a rub and I'll...be back soon." With a failed attempt to resurrect the cone of his wizard hat, IQ threw back his shoulders and strutted off.

Druid raised a finger to the waitress, took up the fresh shot as soon as it was poured. His gaze shifted to the far end of the bar, where IQ had sidled up to the giggly girls and was planting his mouth inside each offered palm.

At that instant, he envied the youth. To lust without love, to kiss simply because lips knew how to part and press, and to enjoy it for being so...Good Goth, but what he'd have given for such freedom! Because IQ was right in one respect; he *did* evaluate every female who intercepted his view with a strange, glow-eyed intensity. But the boy misinterpreted his hunger. If he took account of their pale flesh, it was in place of another's. If breasts arose on a wave of breath, he saw only *her* girlish ghost. And if he felt any hint of desire for those beautiful strangers, it was for the silky red in their veins; anything else was foolishness.

He rested on his elbows, the pads of his fingertips at his forehead. It was difficult to maintain the flow of breath to his lungs, let alone indulge in the trifles of life's pleasure. Stretching a hand out to the tumbler, he crushed it hard between his fingers. No, he needed to tunnel his mind to the truth, fix in on that ever-decreasing black.

"Penny for them," said a voice, and for the second time in an evening, Druid found he was addressed by a stranger.

Air bled from his lips in a silent sigh. He glared sideways. A thin girl in emerald eye shadow returned the harshness of his stare, magnified it three-fold. The finer part of him stayed anaesthetized. But, despite himself, he lost sight of the tunnel and was utterly intrigued by the Snow White with bite.

Her skin was silvery, not unlike Sophia's. But there the similarity ended. While Sophia's was a grown up sort of elegance, a frigid allure that begged to be melted but always revealed a fresh layer of ice beneath, the girl exuded a simpler, almost childish femininity. She had an otherworldly face, pink, frosted lips, and eyes that were huge, dark and unfathomable.

A spotlight swept across the bar. The girl's spiked updo seemed awash with dark and sparkle. She swept a stray strand from her throat with a dismissive hand flick, allowing Druid to linger on the polished camber of her clavicle and the rope of a scar there.

He forced his eyes away. "Straight to the chase, hey? An honest Fae. Makes a change," he muttered then added derisively, "But while I may be a fool, I'm a particular fool. Most I can offer is a double-shot of Bourbon."

"Ice-cubes into the bargain?"

"If you have to sip it like a girl." He signalled the waitress, pointed to the dregs of his empty glass and held up two fingers.

Swishing out the tail of her raincoat, the girl nudged up onto the stool that IQ had recently vacated. "Interesting how you presume I'm Fae because I have the audacity to make small talk," she said, starting to shell a handful of pistachios from a nearby dish.

"Interesting how you presume, as a man alone, I'd appreciate your audacity."

"Touché." The girl licked her finger, streaked it through the air. She flicked a nutshell at the mirror opposite. "Ice please. I said ice! Thanks," she managed coldly as the waitress deposited a single lump in her glass.

Druid watched her closely; the faint tremble of fingers that reached down into the liquor and scooped out the melting cube.

"Usually I'd defend my integrity with a little boot-to-groin persuasion," she continued. "But I've had a bitch of a night. So how's about we forgo the bullshit and cut straight to the pleasantries." She worked the ice up under the curl of her left coat sleeve. Her small teeth clenched.

"Is that a proposition?"

"Look, mister!" The tone was hostile. But her eyes betrayed a different level of emotion. She looked exhausted. "You supply the alcohol. I'll make conversation," she said quietly, grasping her shot and slugging it down.

Druid ordered two fresh measures. He cradled the refill, put the glass to his lips and inhaled its whiskey sour. As he did so, he detected something more remarkable from the girl than idle chitchat. A smear of blood marked the outside of her glass.

"Like what you see?" she managed, jutting her chin towards a flock of Fae. He followed her gaze, and observed the professional sirens with dispassion while keeping half an eye on the weird sister at his side.

Drawn from the exquisite ranks of models, showgirls, gigolos, and players, Druid recognised the Fae as fallen angels at best. The jet set and more solvent tourists paid richly for their company, which was girlish, distant, playful and impeccable. Mixing emotions like spirits in a glass, each winged delicate would bite the 'hand that feeds' as soon as learn to love it, and for the simple reason that Fae were as disfigured as any other by the loveless world beyond. Only difference was, their scars were on the inside.

Druid studied the flock's tiptoeing movement, the way the shadows of their fibrillating wings interplayed on the wall. While the males kept their torsos naked, the females wore slips of silk, gauze or satin, the fabric bound about their breasts with criss-crossed, streaming ribbons. In the case of both sexes, the key emphasis was on the feminine. Their eyes were variegated chrysanthemums. Their mouths were sensual and glossed. Their hair was long, flowing and garishly synthetic. Embroidered with self-reflecting light, vivid hues and metallics, they struck Druid as human butterflies, or exquisite cyber-geisha; traditional, desirous, yet not quite of this world.

The girl, meanwhile, was a darker sort, and, to his mind, a million times more provocative. Not that *that* made her any easier to bracket. An opaque pentagram ghosted at her brow. He frowned at the icon. She was traditionalist then, yet also theatrically adaptable. That was plain from the jet crucifix which lay at rest against her breastbone.

"They'll steal your heart." The toxic angel pointed loosely to his wrist and jeans' pocket. "...Or, at the least, your watch or wallet."

"A wallet or watch, I can replace," he replied laconically.

She tapped the side of her glass with short, white fingernails, not quite in time with the beat. "And the heart?" she asked, without need of an answer, and he saw a hint of solemnity; a bitterness that washed down over her face, her mouth and shoulders. She hunched like a child.

"You need one to steal in the first place," he murmured anyway.

"Oh sweet damnation, don't tell me you're one of *those*. The broken-hearted," she scathed as his eyes questioned her. She sat back, hands on her hips. "It's so manipulative."

He choked into his whiskey. "Manipulative?"

"Yeah, manipulative. Of the atmosphere around you. Wallowing in self-pity and sorrows past. What's gone is gone. Fizz, bang, pop! A heart can ache but only bones can break. Only bones can break..." she repeated sourly before tossing back another shot. She wiped her lips with a sleeve. "Goth knows we've all suffered the illusion of heartbreak." Rolling her drained glass between her palms, she kicked a leg loosely back and forth so that her boot banged off the toughened glass of the bar. "But one thing you can be sure of, it's just a feeling...just an illusion."

She stood suddenly and pressed a hand to the left side of his ribs. He gasped. Her palm made a hot hollow above his left nipple-ring. But then he met her eyes and felt strangely ashamed. There was nothing salacious in the gesture. Instead she trembled, as if caught out in the rain. A spotlight revolved. Beneath its sweeping blaze, her face seemed full of eyes. Her emotions were hidden but not so long ago she had wept. Streaky, black tears webbed each cheek.

"Still ticking," she said in a vehement whisper.

"Now that's a tale of the unexpected," interrupted a familiar voice.

The girl spun away. "You're late!" she hissed, and plonked back down on the stool.

"And you're a brazen hussy, Jezebel." IQ pointed to Druid and added, "That goes for both of you. Soon as my back's turned, you're off with my Miss Twelve O'Clock, my not-so-chilly-hearted friend." He winked. "'Tis a joy to behold!"

"Don't be a knob, Irvine." The girl flicked a pistachio just short of the kid's left temple. "You owe your friend here a drink or several, seeing as he had to sub me in your absence. Where've you been anyway?"

"Chilling," IQ moved agitatedly on the spot.

"Of course. And with whom?"

"Nurse 1 and Nurse 2," the kid muttered coyly, prompting Druid to suppress an awkward smile. "And where have *you* been?" he shot back.

"Hunting," the girl replied sharply. Her pretty lips soured. "For the one that got away."

If Jezebel had stood in the sandy pit of a gladiatorial arena, slain tigress at her feet, blooded sword in hand, she could not have carried herself with a greater degree of defiance. In contrast, IQ was a picture-postcard of astonishment.

As the pair tried to out-stare one another, Druid threw a fistful of notes onto the counter. He melted down off the stool and excused himself. He had neither the energy nor the inclination to eavesdrop. Furthermore, as he descended the steps, hip suckering the stair rail, eyes averted from the crush of lovely strangers, his strongest emotion was relief. Conversation drained him.

A TV, dolled up to the nines in Jeannie Nitro and six-inch Mary Janes, slid past his shoulder. Druid bristled at the touch of another human being. He moved to the far side of an opaque, black pillar, folding in upon himself. Why did life have to go and evolve and forget to include him? All of this sweat, flesh and contact…it was so infected with reality. What had happened to his minders, the roped-off VIP area and the wall of muscle separating the mosh pit from the stage? All dissolved now.

Druid rolled onto his left shoulder blade, laid his head against the pillar's frost. He stared out at the dance floor. Was it so long ago that happiness rested in waves of strobe-lit devil horns, or a storm of petals assuaged the cloud nine of his drum riser? Yes, it seemed so, he realised glumly. Now he was just a face in the crowd.

His eyes felt heavy. He let them rest. The metallic notes which flew from every speaker faded. He heard the nautical creak of stage hydraulics overhead, felt a stick poised in each welted palm and smelled the candy of face paint, the smoke at Sophia's lips, the zoo stench of leather, stale ale and axle grease...

Ever so slowly, he persuaded his eyelids to part. He stared out at the inferno of the mosh pit, and beyond, to the stage that was railed off behind a drop of watery, black satin. The fabric undulated. His nostrils flared. The last aroma was lingering and tangible, which meant that it was real.

"Watch it, you wormy slime!" came a gruff shriek that he attributed to the TV.

"Get your plastic ass out my face then, or I'll have to beat it down," grunted an unseen menace. A few seconds later, the brute delivered on its promise with a hefty, well-aimed slap.

The TV wailed and scooted past Druid on her size nine dolly shoes.

"Warned her!" A snort ripped up from the belly of the beast, its laughter aped by several coarse attendants.

Druid edged to his left. He recoiled as a cat-o'-nine-tails of dreads whipped an inch short of his face.

"Forget that whore," hissed a second with greased malevolence. "Sniff out the girl. Sure as shit, her stink's in the air."

"All these bitches look the same to me," spat the first. "One whore, two whore, three whore, four..."

"Feel the same too," crowed a third.

The brutes howled in savage chorus.

"Enough."

It was an order. The beasts lapsed into silence. Druid inched to his left again, lured and repelled by the speaker's low tenor. He saw a tangle of midnight oiled dreads, amassed on blood-red, armour plated shoulders. A meaty elbow slammed backwards. Druid reeled back behind the column.

"Look for the witch's stain," the brute told its gang. "It'll mark her like a dirty great third eye."

"I'd like to introduce her to *my* third eye," piped up a fourth.

The steroidal hyenas erupted.

"Stop pissing about and get searching!" barked the top dog.

A decree from that behemoth proved absolute. The noise of the pack receded.

Druid pushed off from the pillar. An occult symbol at the third eye chakra? The pack had to be talking about the same girl he had just shared a drink with, which meant she would be advised to make herself scarce before the brutes caught a whiff of her. Some fresh chaos sparked at the largest of the lower-level bars, no doubt, the first port of call for thirsting hogs. He kept his gaze dead ahead, felt for the blue steel handrail, slid his hand up and paused.

Where was he hurrying to? He owed the girl no loyalty. Her very name implied she deserved her fate. Which was what? To be mauled by sadistic mutts, to pay the price for her crimes without a shot at real justice, to suffer shame, and hurt, and devastation because Renegade was too harsh to give a monkey's?

His gaze lifted to the mist-clad sylphs. He recalled Sophia's cold perfectionism; compared that ideal to Jezebel's darkly scissored wit, the torn pockets of her eyes, her quintessential messiness. He felt drawn to the waif. Thus far, she'd shown herself to be rude, fragile and tenacious. They had a lot in common.

He cleared the glowing steps in a few long strides. "Time to go," he said brusquely, arriving at the girl's side. "Seems you've fostered quite a following."

"Skinwalkers." Jezebel bunched back her hair and secured it with a bracelet. She leapt down off the stool, made a quick scan of the area then gripped IQ's forearm. "See you at Queenie's."

"Stop, Jez!" The kid held fast. He twisted her arm about by the wrist. "You're still bleeding." The green eyes poured out a hundred more reasons.

Druid pressed his fingers to his lips. Just below a little, red tattoo, which was a smaller version of the seal of the Drathcor, and the same city key that emblazed the left wrist of every permanent citizen, the wound still wept. He saw nothing sensual about the five deep claw marks. It was a dirty wound, executed without skill.

"Come with me," he managed thickly. "The wound won't kill you, but what inflicted it might."

"That would at least be *something*," she said tartly.

As if grasping some deeper significance, the kid released her wrist. A frown burrowed up at his brow.

She kissed him swiftly on the cheek. "See you later alligator."

"In a while, crocodile," said IQ, falsely deadpan.

Druid used his arm as a barrier. "I'm serious. The bar's a bottle-neck. But I know every glossed-over inch of this dive, and I know a back way out. The question is, do you want to run from wolves or dance with the devil?"

Her eyes sucked him down. "A Russian roulette," she spat, if with a glint of panic as shapes grew about the walls. A hand touched his hip. "Yeah, why not? Life could do with a little heating up." She ducked free of his arm, grabbed for his hand. "Now get me the hell out of here."

"Wait up, love turds!" The kid tripped over a rogue cable drum, and cursed.

"Shouldn't you wait for your boyfriend?" Druid slipped beneath a lowered lighting rig.

"As much my boyfriend as yours," Jezebel shot back. She put a hand on the rig and dipped her body under. "You might go in for little boys, but I prefer my men with a little more bite."

"Do you?" His voice had a seductive edge. The girl stared past him and he refocused on the objects d'art littering backstage: a discarded ice machine, a broken-necked Strat, lime-green fringing that strewed the path like dragons' innards. Remnants of an ended performance, he mused. His chest sank like a stone.

"So how come you know Legacy's rear end so well?" Jezebel interrupted.

Druid tucked his chin into a shoulder. He stopped walking. "I'm...I was in an Origin tribute band." He was grateful for the darkness.

"Uh-huh." The girl cocked her head. "Here's the thing I don't get about Drathy. You wear the clothes, walk the walk, talk the talk, even re-stitch your skin into a brand new shape.

Except, it isn't new, is it? It's Roses's face, *Druid's,* or whichever high lord you think is the bomb." Her tone was bitter. It surprised him. "What's that about? Are we talking idol worship, or something fruitier, in which case, that's one helluva great and secret show of narcissism?"

"Said I was the devil's own," Druid muttered, unsure how to begin to respond to the rest.

"Thought you *were* the devil." She thrust a blunt-cut nail at a spot beyond his shoulder, and he led the way again. "There's me thinking I've hitched a ride with the dark lord himself, only to find I'm holed up with his gofer. Is that ever a let-down?"

"Sorry to disappoint." Druid found the door, shoulder-slammed it open.

He stepped out onto the sparkling ironwork of a skeleton fire escape. Jezebel came out of the dark to stand beside him. The snow was falling softer now. Glued at the hip, they leant in to the wet rail. Opposite was the red-brick cliff face of Legacy's new state-of-the-art car park. They stared six flights down. The alley that ran between the two buildings was deserted, bar an overflowing dumpster and the scattered pages of a broadsheet. An ice-encrusted staircase fell away to their left.

"So why are Skinwalkers after a shy little thing like you?" Druid teased as the girl forced past to take the lead.

Jezebel glared back. But her mouth curved. "What can I say? I'm a shrinking violet with a violent side."

It was a cute response, if barbed. Druid screwed up his eyes, as if to wring a few drops of understanding from them. He wasn't sure how to take the girl. She struck him as a kid, playing verbal hopscotch or sticking her tongue out at bullies. He also sensed jadedness, a darkness which should have made her a model citizen in Renegade's long Hallowe'en. Except the girl didn't seem to want to embrace it. She didn't even seem to want to belong.

As he wove back, forth and down the silver tower, his boots mapped the small, inelegant prints left by Jezebel's spiked pair. His lips twisted. So fate saw fit to hook him up with a fellow aficionado of the socially inept! No surprises there. Then again – his mouth became gentler—it was precisely the flaws that made him want to save her. Was she the sort to let him?

At the final grid, Jezebel leant hard out over the rail. Druid studied her. He risked, "And the real reason?"

"Family business." Her tone was factual.

"Ah, family," he murmured, as if the notion were explanation enough; then added under his breath, "Talking of which, your boyfriend's taking his time."

"I've told you already, he's not my…"

Druid grabbed Jezebel by the collar of her PVC raincoat and shoved her hard against the inside wall. He glared up between the grids. Bang on cue, a spectacular din erupted. Cardboard boxes tumbled, metal clanked off metal, glass fractured, and fabric gave with a flesh-unsettling rip…He glanced at the girl. Like an anti-heroine lifted off a cell of acetate, her flesh had lost its suppleness to a skim of steel. Suddenly she looked less inclined to spar with him than stone cold rip out his throat. He let her go with the immediacy of something that might burn him, took two strides back.

She thought he had lured her out of the crowded club and into the more *discreet* killing field of the alley, Druid realised and with no time to argue the point. All that mattered was she start running fast, and start running now. Long, black claws fed out to touch her shoulder, to make her run from him and never look back. The racket petered out.

"Hick dick devil stick!" hollered the teen nuisance from aloft the scaffold. "Man, sorry about that, guys. Gothdamn rats. All pointy teeth and pokey eyes…Guys?"

Druid balled up his fingers. He retracted his hand.

Jezebel held his gaze and her expression softened. Then she craned out over the railing. "Down here, Irvine!" she hissed. "And for the love of Origin, stop yawping or you'll attract *real* vermin. Idiot," she added under her breath, and reined her head back in.

"We should hurry up," said Druid darkly. He stared past the girl's shoulder. At the far end of the platform, a ladder was raised up above street level to secure the grimy building, he supposed or, more likely, the stock of audio and other gear inside. Except…that wasn't it. His gaze slid between the frosted grids to the square of dark at the top of the fire escape. In the case of Legacy, the threat was never thieves. It was groupies.

But the city had evolved. Like the long-rusted ladder that sparkled faintly in the moonlight, the fan-base was gilded in hurt and hate, and just as immovable. Even the tourists who had flooded the city to peek and fawn at Roses's sarcophagus in the immediate weeks after his death had, to all appearances, deserted the city, as if, at last, it had dawned on them that the great man was gone forever and the realisation froze them out. Druid put a thumb and forefinger to the space between his eyes. It would take a weight of muscle to un-jar the rods of the ladder, plus time they were swift running out of.

He started to say as much. His voice faded as the girl gripped the rail, took her full weight on one hand and leapt overboard, knees joined and at an angle. She landed heavily, spiked boots and hands sinking deep in the snow.

Druid arched an eyebrow. Sweeping his arms out horizontally from his body, he rocked back on a heel and leapt aboard the rail in a fluid, cat-like motion. With immaculate balance, he unfolded, studied the graffitied brick of the opposite wall then stepped off.

He dropped to the ground noiselessly, and held out a hand.

"For the love of Origin?"

"What? Oh, just some stupid phrase." Ignoring his offer of assistance, Jezebel scrambled up. She brushed herself down with all the care of a farmhand. "Guess if you hang with Castclan, their quirks start rubbing off."

"You're a Believer without the baggage of Belief?"

"Not like I'm the first." She beat her hands to shake off the excess snow. "It's the city that matters, not all the religious mumbo-jumbo. Roses's death taught us *that*. But hey, you're the full whack—talk, eat, breathe, sleep and shit Origin—and I'm probably just full of it, so ignore me." Her eyes chased off into the shadows then out to the pavement.

"So you consider yourself immune to the will of the Drathcor?" His mouth stiffened.

"Look, the music's divine. But what lies beneath is no more complex than four musos playing Midas in monkeyville. Belief's the Way? Yeah, right, if you're a good little goth and stay inside the box." Her eyes slid skyward, or, as Druid understood it, to the walls built up around her.

Fired up to respond, he was sidetracked by the distinctive footfall of one of Renegade's loftiest residents. His gaze flew to the pavement, where a strip of tarmac was lit by a solitary street lamp. An elongated silhouette fell across the path. A few seconds later, a Grallator strode into the spotlight, pumpkin head bobbing, a stripy scarf rippling from the flagpole of his neck.

"You don't think Renegade sets its own limitations?" Druid said as the public servant passed from view.

"Maybe. I *do* think we just imported our prejudice from one world to the next. Trust me..." She paused—he supplied the name 'D' with some awkwardness. "Trust me, D. Bitchiness is key to the scene. Shit, it always was." Her face acquired a wealth of shadows. "I also *believe*..." Her emphasis was calculated, "...that desperate folk are easily led. But I'm talked out on politics." She chased an itch at the small of her back. At the same time, her eyes flew up to the kid, who was pogoing on the lowest rung of the rusted ladder. "Time to love and leave you."

"Can I walk you home?" Druid's tone was emotionless. He indicated to IQ to jump down, and the kid skydived off the platform, landed like a heap of rags. Sitting back on his heels, the mini-wizard scrubbed his frosty mop, grinned impishly, and was, no doubt, about to offer some priceless idiom. He was pipped at the post.

"Away with you!" cried an absurd voice from the street. "Shoo now, or I'll be forced to show you the long arm of the law. You there, with the facial hair! If these are your boys, may I suggest you exert a firmer hand? Now, there's no call for gestures like that, and please unhand my person! Didn't your mother teach you not to play with matches? Put those away. I said, put those...Arghhhh!"

Three pairs of eyes fixated on the sidewalk. An instant later, the Grallator streaked past, peg-legs scissoring, the tips of his stripy scarf aflame.

"Thanks, but I'm not walking," said Jezebel tersely.

"Jez, don't. *They're* barely sky-worthy." IQ thrust a finger at the sky, flipped it. When the girl shot him an evil glare, he drove his hands into the pockets of his low-slung jeans and just looked sad. "See ya," he muttered.

If Jezebel replied, her voice was lost to a purr of metal noise. Leather spikes, a metre tall, shot forth at her upper spine. The plumes divided—two a side—then angled into a St. Andrew's cross. With a swish, the fabric unfolded into four gun-metal-grey triangles, ripped ragged and patched with PVC.

The wings stirred, like the sails of a derelict windmill. Druid fell back a step. *This* was alien to the lie of a life he had built for the girl. She was meant to be Castclan; savage wit, a silvered pentagram at her brow, strength in the face of clear and present danger. At the very least, she was a genetic anomaly, stainless steel for a spinal cortex and a few extra pairs of forelimbs.

The truth continued to cut at him. She was just a Fae in a boned harness! His throat felt sucker-punched. He'd felt an affinity with her, dared to flirt even…Why did she have to go and belong to those otiose self-servers? A Trawler, floating above life's current, a DarkLed, death-kissed and fading, a Skinwalker, even, would've been preferable. But Fae? His pale eyes tapered.

With a roar of engine noise, the sails started to rotate. Snow whipped up at her ankles and the girl pitched slightly at the waist. As she did so, she was thrust forward by the dark blades' momentum. Sparks of ice flew out from her heels and, for a brief moment, she seemed set to crash hard into her audience. With a split second to spare, the wings fastened on an updraft of air so she was jerked clear and up.

Her ascent was terrifically swift. In the blink of a kohled eye, she had cleared the fire escape, pitched left of an illuminated Coca-Cola sign and a billboard poster that still preached 'Believe: So Mote It Be' in a faded, copperplate gothic font, and entered the violet pale above. With her body at a slant, she hovered and gave a childlike wave. Then she folded her arms at her chest, stared skyward and soared.

Druid watched her dissolve. The kid knocked up against him.

"Fickle little minx. Flighty too." He poked a finger at the sky, and grinned. "Not that I'm questioning your choice of bedfellow. Just keep your eye on your watch and wallet."

Druid shook his head. Was it only half an hour ago he'd got the exact same advice, and from the girl? He started to offer his stock reply. "A wallet or watch I can…" Breaking off, he encircled his left wrist with a thumb and forefinger. His upper lip tore back. His watch was gone.

"Oops." The kid backed off. "Fae! What they like, hey, with their whispers of sweet nothingness and fingers that go everywhere? Take this one I met last Beltane. Wings like tiger's-eye and big, brown bazookas. Pure angel one minute, the next, she was going..."

"Down!" Druid thrust the boy aside, caught the great ham of a fist square on his jaw.

He staggered back. A stain of metallic coated his inner cheek. Nausea sluiced his stomach. His mind started to darken down, accompanied by a part-audible, part-physical sensation, as if he stood in the midst of a cloud of flies. He batted at his head with fisted claws. The static faded. His gaze left the sparkling ground.

He felt a sharp tug of dread, and also a subtle fascination. The sky had curdled, like a giant saucepan of soured milk. Where the drifting shapes of cloud repelled one another, a stone-washed moon shone down unhindered, and seemingly birthed of that apocalyptic flow were the bulk-encrusted figures of the Skinwalkers.

As his initial fear bedded down, Druid made slits of his eyes and studied their savage detail: the dirt-handsome jowls, the huge, vining crowns of their mohawks, the aged leather, bodmods, spikes, latex, plates, rubber, UV torcs, and other armaments. And the flexing fist of one brute stood forward of the rest.

Dark-red, malignant eyes rolled in his direction. Working the conjoined metal rings of a knuckle-duster down between its claws, the beast growled, "Helped the whore get away did you, Drathy?"

Blood fed either side of his chin. Druid worked his jawbone back and forth. It yielded with a wooden snap. "Looks that way," he muttered.

The brute's second punch had volume; it thumped against the air like a hunk of ironwood. Druid ducked, packed an open fist, and drove that weapon deep into the beast's gut. His claws churned flesh in a half-revolution.

The toadish warrior grimaced. White air bled from its nose cavity. Re-anchoring a pair of huge engineering boots in the filthy ice and easing back its mammoth shoulders, the brute started swinging.

Druid ricocheted back, tied the movement to the breath and reduced down to a tight web of muscle. His hands flowed into, forward and against. Like a Thai boxer, the pads of his feet shuffled, reversed, and closed the gap. Rolling hands blocked, then double-blocked. Low body shots exploded off soft tissue and bone, hammer-fists, uppercuts, jabs, a club elbow to the ribs...The wolf went down, tried a last unsteady slug, then fell off to the side.

Druid stepped away. His lungs felt raw. Breath was a barbiturate. He put a hand to his ribs and laughed ridiculously. As the shadows built at his shoulders, his arms hooked out from his sides. He let his head loll back. His jaw craned apart, his lips peeled at the gum to expose the glistening, red-raw blades. A glutinous sound, like displaced flesh, reverberated in his throat then charged forth in a roar.

"Drathcor!" The wolf at his feet scrambled backwards. Its eyes glistened like blood pools while, perversely, the rest of the brood cocked their muzzles left then right and inched even closer.

Druid was motionless. The dewclaw of a thumb twitched. Very slowly, each set of talons arched to form a bird of claws; and, as if woken from a trance, the Skinwalkers fell back. A curse of 'Living Devil' echoed off the walls. A whispered cry of 'the girl' circulated as the brutes backed up.

"Escaped my grasp as much as she has yours, gentleman," said Druid in a low voice. "Which explains why I was forced to make do with less palatable spoils." He inclined his chin towards a small collection of rags, located a metre or so to his right and superficially immersed in ice.

The gang peered primitively at the bundle. It took time for them to register that they were in fact staring at the body of a boy. The shining dew of their eyes betrayed a bleak awe.

"He feeds!" howled the concussed wolf, falling badly in the sludge so that two of the thugs were forced to support the huge branches of its arms on their shoulders and drag its carcass off in the wake of their comrades.

The dark circus pooled at the alley's exit. Red, devil black and gold eyes burnt back across the distance. Throats arching, they unleashed a rabid chorus. Then the pack moved apart.

A lone dog soldier stood under the street lamp. Bluely lit by that incandescent bulb, the new arrival was less a man than a leviathan dredged to the surface, a great coat of algoid-coral, dead men's hair, ships' rigging, and the fetid bodies of sea serpents dripping off the great mast of its red-plated shoulders. Druid knit his claws across his chest. Gatekeeper of the city's un-chartered depths. It was a fitting guise for Lorcan, chief of Skinwalkers.

The brute shook out two waist-length, plaited ropes of beard, lowered his wormy mane and retrieved a small pouch from the top pocket of his leather. Drawing off several strands, he fed them between his fingers, and all the while, his gaze stayed on the Drathcor. A quick flick of spit along the paper's edge and he popped it between his lips. Scooping up a flame from a match inside his palm, he released the smoke in a slow, pale stream from his nostrils. The briefest snort called the others close and, with a thrust of a single digit, he led the pack away.

As the last beast shambled out of view, IQ sat up and gave an almighty belch. "Struth stranger, got to knock the wind out of me like that?"

Half-turning from the boy, Druid drew his tongue across his teeth.

"Oh that. Tell me something I don't know," pooh-poohed the kid with a flick of the wrist. He stood stiffly, bent forward to brush the snow off the front then back of his jeans. "Not every day you bump into a Drathcor. But hell, if they're all as green as you, I'd spot them a mile off." He poked at Druid's mouth. "Sure Drathy like to splash out on groovy fangs, but that kind of workmanship? Gotta cost a packet. As for the book you like to scribble in, only Drathcor get to use the royal seal for anything other than the city key tattoo. Any fool would know it."

Druid eyed the boy. "Except I didn't bump into just any fool." He dabbed at his mouth with the back of a hand.

"Here." IQ made pincers of two fingers. Reaching up his opposite sleeve, he produced a black silk handkerchief with a subdued flourish. "Bit of a drawback, don't you reckon, having a mouthful of shiny knives when you get slugged on the jaw? Ask me, it's a right queer scene. Rats have pointy teeth too, you know." He scrunched up his nose. "Nasty."

"Rats feast on garbage. Drathcor drink the bright blood alone. Just this once, I may be willing to make an exception." Druid stepped up to the boy in a single stride. His hand slashed through the air, capturing up the handkerchief.

IQ swallowed audibly. "Okay. I get the whole 'don't confuse vermin with exalted ones'. And, hey, I truly appreciate you saving my ass back there. So I'm kind of damp, what with skidding half-way across the city, but worse has come of a run-in with the Skinwalkers. Riotous man, did you see the brute that slugged you? That was one ugly mongrel." The boy bounced from one sodden trainer to the other. He stopped suddenly, and reached a hand up onto Druid's shoulder. "A word of warning from a wise-guy though. You might want to underplay your being a living god and all; he who feeds at the breasts of vestal virgins."

"Is that what they say?" Druid considered his young companion. A ghost of a smile played at his lips.

"Too true, my friend. Gets his freak on with the filthiest. Sinks shooters with Beelzebub. Breaks bread with Zappa."

"Cool."

"But seriously, I think you should be careful. We're children of the revolution now and the hearts of your kind are beating on the block. I don't know why you're out here. From the way you've been flaunting it, I'm not sure *you* know. But it might be worth finding out. First though, you've gotta keep the blades hidden. Speak softer. Move the lips a little less. Second thing…" The kid glanced up and down the length of the alley, "I've had more fun. What say we get off the streets before that ugly mutt lets reinforcements off the leash?" He blew on his hands, cocked his head towards the sidewalk, and started to trudge away.

At the street lamp, he put his chin over a shoulder. "You comin'?"

Chapter 4

The Ghost Woman and the Hunter

Druid raised his eyes. The sky was a drag strip. Snow clouds, soft, dense, and all shades of grey, moved in its element like the residual fumes of burnout. He felt oddly disorientated. Dawn had broken; he'd barely even noticed.

A sub-zero wind raked through his red-tipped mohawk. He dipped his nose and strode on. His boots, a pair of cowboy-styled, red-flame New Rocks, smashed into the ice. His leather, long and worn like an old man's face, billowed out behind him.

The kid was right. He had no idea what he was doing in that bleak, whitened world, bar his acting like a suicidal Lothario for the iciest of beauties. His shoulders hunched, like the stumps of shorn-off wings. The affection he felt for his brother's queen, the inimitable Sophia, was a scab on an old wound. Soon it would shrivel up entirely then fall away.

Folding his claws in on one another, Druid let the points dig in. He knew the tenable reason for his quest, of course, that Sophia had sent him out into the field to gun down an assassin. A grand and awful task, and one he felt in no way qualified to undertake...or was it just that he still didn't want to think in those terms? After all, if he *did* establish that Roses had been murdered (and with the same ease as any other Caesar), he also had to accept the very real possibility that the mortal wound went to the heart of Renegade itself.

He breathed deeply, if noiselessly, and released his talons from the soft flesh of his palms. Was this why he'd been at such a loss as to how to even begin to solve what was, in effect, a hypothetical mystery? And did this explain why, last night, as he'd crept out from beneath the glass-green Saturn rings that encircled his north watchtower, negotiated the tangled wilds and ghost structures of the Arboretum, and made his way to the gate of weathered steel at the entrance, he'd felt anaesthetized to the task. Little wonder then he should have found solace in his notebook, a shot or ten of Jack, and the illicit clientele of Louse House?

Distillery for the Damned. His lips slanted. In retrospect, it was a fitting haunt for Sophia's champion, since she'd damned him to eternity. Now he had no choice but to go in search of answers to questions he had no desire to ask, such as why was he being led through streets of *his* creation by a wiz kid in league with the drifters?

Up ahead, the boy tugged his tattered wizard hat low about his ears, the floppy part of which repeatedly puffed out from the back of his head then gradually deflated. It was a comic sight, but Druid wasn't fooled. IQ might act the clown, but jettison the awkwardness of youth and the kid was all clued up and then some. The deft use of bribery to skin a cat-burglar, his having the dirt on each freak in that dive, as well as a bona-fide sixth sense when it came to Druid's true origins...all were indicative of a sharp little mind, and a hell of a nose for trouble.

Yet, underneath it all, he was *just* a kid, Druid reminded himself, and so what if he was being piped on a magical mystery tour to despair, betrayal or the charbroiled loins of Hades itself, he was grateful just to take the pain inside and let someone else lead the way. Moreover...he smiled a fragile smile...it was the next best thing he'd got to a diversion tactic, a reason to drag his weak carcass into daylight; even if it meant tuning out the inner voices.

He had just reconciled himself to the fact when a great heart began to beat. Boom! The visible breath at his lips acted as a metronome for a count of one, two, three...then boom! Each deep thump reverberated up through the soles of his feet, into his shins, his thigh bones, the girdle of his hips. At the same time, sprays of snow were dislodged from each ledge, awning and protuberance so the street itself appeared to ripple.

Narrowing his eyes, Druid tried to place the sound. So much more than a beat to step to, it was a call for action, pageantry perhaps...or was it hush and reverence? He froze in his tracks.

"Shit!" Dashing to his side, IQ tried to hurry him along with a quick sweep of an arm. "What with all the dramarama, *it* clear escaped my mind." Witch-green eyes darted up to the nearest street corner. "No biggie. We're taking the next right onto Mappley Road anyway. Just need to get our skates on. Come on, mate. They'll be out the gates any time. Oh, for the love of... Shift your bloody feet!"

Druid, however, was rooted. He stared dully ahead. What kind of a sick fool could arrive at a destination he despised and with no idea of how he'd got there? He'd even managed to pass within a mile or so of his north watchtower and still failed to take a blind bit of notice. And, okay, the restaurants, second-hand boutiques and small business premises lining either side of the street were not so extraordinary. Likewise, the dawn-purpled street lamps could light any avenue, the frosted pavement edge any road. Except that this was Mansfield Road and even the iced tramlines had come to an abrupt halt several metres back. Misty lamplight shone twenty-four-seven; a ghost path inside ornate, cast-iron gates...and there, Druid knew, the lights went out. His chest rose and fell jaggedly. Nowhere else was life's brilliance so perfectly eclipsed as at the gates of Rock Cemetery.

The lurid Garden of Remembrance had been renowned for its architectural excess long before he and the rest of the dark revellers gate-crashed the city. Hearsay even went so far as to suggest it was key in the choice of final destination, as if Roses had deliberately fixed on the city because it kept its dead in such salubrious surroundings. Sinking a fang into the wet flesh of his inner cheek, tasting his own blood like a bitter dose of salts, Druid felt too jaded to care or to remember. All he knew was that the original boundaries of Rock Cemetery had been extended to incorporate an adjoining area of Forest Field, thus allowing the tribes to add to its breathless residents while putting their own artistic twist on the 'attraction'.

His mind's eye swept across the breadth of parkland; a gothic mélange of marble mausoleums, guitar-shaped gravestones, plague pits, neat white crosses, caves sealed with cast-iron portcullises, glass casks containing mummified remains, the pockmarks of fire-pits, stone angels, stone arches, opulent sepulchres, inscribed with circles, doves, clouds, crowns, fleurs-de-lis, garlands, grapes, ivy, and the hourglass, as well as more avant-garde icons: heartagrams, punk stars, Eddies, skull and crossbones, rolling dice, flames...He revisited fairground rides themed on the human skull, a restaurant awarded three Michelin stars for its funeral banquets, even a

Hilton hotel in a network of part-contemporary, part-medieval, sandstone catacombs.

Boots entombed in the snow, Druid despised death's allure; for him, no matter how many fairy lights adorned them, the bones of the dead stayed tangible...at least until they fell into dust.

"Oh, don't stop there, mate. We're never gonna make it!"

IQ's words came to him as from a distance; it was all he could do to hear the flap of his leather as it flew out like a sail from his hips, and the flutter of shiny, black bunting tied to a nearby lamp post. Instead, he was given over to a night when rain signified a change in season, on a manmade hill awash with mourners. He felt the iced water streaming in rivulets off his temples, the contours of his chin; how his black, satin cassock had sculpted itself to his body like a fluid organism; how his bones set as he knelt at the foot of the sarcophagus.

Druid started to draw a palm over his face. He froze the gesture at the shrill note of a horn.

"Shit—too late. Okay, just glue your shades to the ground and play like you're respectful," hissed IQ, tearing his wizard hat off his head and clenching it tight between his hands. Glancing sideways, he stared down insistently.

Unable to offer reverence simply because it was required of him, Druid stared out to the street corner. Breath misted at his just-parted lips. Something was closing in.

He heard four rasps of the unseen drum. Two Grallators emerged through the gates, spidering out on long, pinstriped legs like great gothic insects. Their faces were unnaturally smooth and expressionless, as if carved from cold, white wax. Under grey top-hats, their hair was greased back into long, thin ponytails. Their drooping arms moved in fluid, biomorphic motion.

Druid steeled himself to a verbal assault, austere patter being the Grallators' prerogative. But while one cast him a dark, suspicious look, the pair strode on by.

Then the street exploded. Gymnasts, bathed in supple leather, tumbled head or feet first in and out of the snow. Flip. Flip. One of the acrobats arrived at Druid's side, stuck out his tongue, then cart-wheeled away.

"He likes you," muttered IQ with a sideways glance.

Druid batted the boy aside. Feeling his shoulders visibly relax, he buried his hands in the side pockets of his leather and watched each act unfold.

Next came the clowns; not the pantalooned ghouls of children's nightmares, but elegant types of jester, white-gloved mime artists, as well as stock grotesques, the West African arachnid, Anansi, with his cotton-candy afro, the masked contingent of Italy's Commedia dell' Arte—the sombre-suited Doctor, the flamboyant Harlequin, the brash Scaramouche—and also an English fool of ancient, pagan rites, the bonneted, smocked and manly Maid Marion. Each artiste moved with charismatic swagger, as if they played for the delight of an ever-shifting audience...except these smiles were fashioned of greasepaint, not sincerity, while each wig or pom-pom hat was adorned with a small, black feather.

Distracted by the subtle inference of grief, Druid barely reacted when an adult Bengal slashed five iridescent claws just short of his arm.

"Jeepers creepers, it's a live one!" spat the kid, dancing back a pace.

The beast strained at its gilded chain.

"Heka!" boomed its owner, a leviathan of a man who started to draw the metal links back through giant hands, whereupon the cat unhinged its beautiful, stripy jaw and roared: a terrific reverb that was sustained by the wall of buildings either side.

Fingering a leather pouch fastened at his waist, the man freed a curl of raw meat. He pursed his lips and gave a shrill whistle, at which the creature broke off and curved its huge, trophy-hunted head back against one shoulder blade. Its eyes flamed all the yellows of amber, sun, sand and gold, as the man tossed the meat so that it fell several metres ahead and lay bleeding in the snow. A moment later, beast and master lunged off in that direction.

Far from being shaken, Druid felt superbly alive; his heart double-bassed and his skin flushed. Enraptured, he watched as four bull elephants, draped in tapestry blankets and Indian gold, swaggered past. Six white mares followed close behind, their hooves quick-skipping across the snow as if that blinding surface were aflame. His eye left the ponies for a sea of black umbrellas. Under his gaze, each concentric shade twirled widdershins then very slowly lifted.

"Gorgeous," he whispered instinctively.

The dance troop was a riot of colour and femininity. Eyes drawn in languid loops, lips pencilled into a perfect bow, skin so nut-brown and buttery he could almost taste it. The female Castclan were exotically tempestuous. Witnessed en masse, few could deny their centuries-old allure, especially not a Drathcor who saw his brief existence as a pitiful comparison.

Wearing a heavy, satin gown of purple, green, black or plum, slashed open to the thigh and fantastically embroidered, each gorgeous princess twirled an umbrella aloft. And when they shook the coined belts about their shapely waists, or snaked their pretty arms, Druid imagined himself the Baptist, damned by each exquisite footfall, and he couldn't bring himself to care, such was the lure of their wild tarantella. Once, he would have played the odds with that fierce sisterhood, betrothing every one as his one-night intended, yet, observing their beauty now, his tastes seemed less fluid. In fact, their close proximity was unsettling.

It was with relief then that he saw the dancers give way to a fresh spectacle. Trumpet, fiddle, trombone, tin whistle, saxophone, oboe, fife, clarinet, squeeze-box, bodhrán, kettledrum...all lent voice to the furore as a gaudy band strode forth. Draped in ponchos, or patched waistcoats, or coats of tasselled suede, the men were more physical than their womenfolk, earthy even. Necks and wrists were strung with turquoise or amber, fingers wreathed in gold, eyes rimmed in blackest kohl and foreheads inked with all manner of strange symbols. They reminded Druid of ancient braves, or was it modern Pharaohs? Either way, their flesh was brown and faintly leathered as if here were men who had walked the desert for so long the sand had given way to glacier.

Standing on the sidelines, Druid envied them their timelessness. His eyes drifted to the floor. He wanted so much to move beyond that moment, to be incognito, insubstantial, reduced to the ether of pure spirit. Then something interrupted his vision. He re-focused. The card poked out of the snow at his feet like an origami crocus. Flipping his coat out behind him, he knelt, retrieved it with two fingers and flipped it over. 'Progression Not Perfection' said pink letters in a diminutive hand.

"Your respects are appreciated."

A pair of neat, cream leather boots appeared at the edge of his vision.

"Your loss deserves respect," he heard IQ respond.

Unfolding, Druid inched down his shades and stared into a face bleached by the moon. The lips were bloodless, the skin drawn tight about the bone so he might have mistaken the woman for a DarkLed were it not for her eyes. Shot with red, those teary globes seemed to thirst then spill again.

"Soz I missed the ceremony. Forget my head if it wasn't, you know, attached," offered the boy. As if to dissuade fresh tears from falling, he added, "Nice day for it though…" His voice trailed away.

In the difficult silence, the empty hearse trundled noisily out of the cemetery gates, a vast, black whale with a rattling ribcage and a stomach full of darkness. The woman spread her hands beneath her own ribs, and Druid recognised the need to hold the ache within. It spoke volumes for the recentness of her loss, as did the unsteady fingers that moved up to her neckline and manhandled a small crucifix.

"I thought it appropriate to have the burial at first light, when the day is newborn. It seemed significant, you know, although we had to formally request a Grallator escort. Skinwalkers don't respect the sanctity of the living let alone the dead. But it was a pretty ceremony. Cold though…bitterly cold." Her tone was distant. She pinioned the boy with her ever-flowing eyes. "It's funny. I cherished a tattered list of the Beatitudes as a child. One picture always stood out for me; two expectant innocents at the feet of Jesus. *Blessed are the meek, for they will inherit the earth.* I liked that. After all, heaven's an oxymoron if the dead leave those they love behind. But to inherit the earth, they must return to it. So I'll just wait." She smiled awkwardly, the fingers moulding the crucifix into her palm. "Strange comfort, religion. Hard to know if you sell your soul to gods or devils." Her gaze moved fluidly to Druid, and she stumbled back as if he'd materialised out of the icy air.

"Bryony, babe, you'll exhaust yourself," IQ assured her in hushed tones, and he put a hand to her back to steady her. "Less thinking, hey? The mind can weigh you down."

"Gods or devils, I revered them," she breathed, fixating on Druid. He quickly restored his shades so that they disguised his strange, pale, unmistakeable eyes.

IQ beckoned to the nearest group of dancers, who swiftly gathered about. Resisting their efforts to lead her away, the Castclan witch threw herself forward over a reassuring arm. "I believed," she hissed, her beautiful grief splintering to expose raw venom. "Since the beginning, I believed. And still you let them take her!"

"Jeepers, mate. Gotta fade into the shadows more if you don't want to end up spit-roasted on a stake," shot the kid in a harsh aside as the witch was finally led away.

Druid was barely listening. Instead, he stared intently at the diminishing silhouette of a woman who had driven a nail into his blood-red centre, kept his gaze there as, sporadically, she twisted back about. There had been such desolation in her words, everything she said and all that she kept silent.

"Blessed are they that mourn, for they shall be comforted," he murmured. It seemed a flat sentiment.

"What's that?" The boy dragged his hat back onto his head so that it rested just above his eyes.

"Doesn't matter." Druid slid the card into the inner pocket of his leather, behind his notebook. "A friend of yours?" His chin indicated the receding shape of the woman.

"Bryony? Yeah, friend of the family. Not a *special* friend, if that's what you're thinking."

"Bryony, babe," Druid repeated without inflection.

"Oh, that...hell, just being friendly. Friendly guy, me. Make friends with anyone. Take you for instance. Sitting there, desperate as a blue-arsed baboon for someone to notice you..."

"I was not desperate."

"Was too. Crying out for attention with that mouthful of blades. Who notices? Me. Who gets that big, hairy cat off your back? Me. Who's..."

"...got pointy teeth?"

"Good...point. So you made the Skinwalkers scat with your dazzling smile. Guess we helped each other out then." With a grin, the kid thrust a finger over Druid's shoulder then pointed over his own. "Scratch yours, scratch mine."

"Like a rash, you mean?"

"Not so much, although back, scratch... I see where you're going with that. I was thinking more in terms of us being mates." Wrinkling his long, thin nose, the kid threw back his head and sighed. "Don't think she took offence, do you? Bryony, I mean. Not exactly cool to make a pass at a funeral, especially such a serious one. Not that I'm saying funerals in general aren't serious. They are, death being the big full-stop per se, except for the immortals. You live forever...except for Roses of course. That was another, er, serious...funeral..."

Druid stared blankly until the kid's mouth ran dry. He lifted his hands, capturing the falling crystals as it started to snow again. "This hell's freezing over so I tell you what, *mate*. Let's set a course for a new shore, preferably one with under-floor heating and a bar."

"At this hour?"

Druid checked his empty wrist and frowned. Then his mouth turned up at a corner. "Actually, I believe we'll find everything we need at Queenie's."

"Queenie's?" Catching the tip of his hat up into his mouth, IQ chewed in wild alarm. "What do you know of Queenie's? Nothing to see at Queenie's—nothing at all. Who's Queenie anyway?"

The Drathcor tapped at his wrist. "See you at Queenie's. That's what the Fae told you."

"Fae—paah! Don't believe anything they say." Positively sinking under the weight of Druid's glare, IQ curved his shoulders. "Look mate, it's my Nana's pad and, well, she's not one for visitors. Just give us a day or several and I'll get your watch. With interest," he added as the Drathcor stepped closer.

"Look. This isn't difficult," said Druid slowly. He interlocked his hands in a forceful prayer. "Both of us could use a little warmth, a place to rest, perhaps even eat."

IQ looked aghast.

"I mean food. Even a Drathcor has to eat."

"Really? Yeah, well, that's obvious," the boy muttered belligerently. "But Queenie's?" He worked a hand under one side of his hat to reach a sudden itch.

"I've always understood that grandmothers like taking care of family," said Druid, adding almost cheerfully, "I'm sure your grandmother will welcome us with open arms."

The boy looked dubious. "You haven't met my grandmother."

Chapter 5

Lies

Torchlight danced against the gloom, lending the hall a primeval, monastic quality. The flames jittered, then softly undulated as the Skinwalkers slunk by, their hulking shadows playing over every surface like a ballet of grotesques. As if to light that stage, tiny, white spotlights drifted down from the distant height of the roof-space. The snow fell softly to form a shroud, or to weep, because while the temperature was arctic, a number of glowing braziers gave out a semblance of warmth. Each bright basket attracted a host of beasts, who shouldered their way closer to the coals or squatted just clear of the grey sludge pooled under the grate. The rest of the pack showed no desire to share an inch of heat, preferring the black grease and rainbows of a makeshift pit-stop located along the length of a side aisle. There, the dark mechanics worked up a sweat, prising gasket material off the sealing surfaces of a crankcase or scraping a combustion chamber free of carbon. Apart from the hack of spit or ripped release of a ring pull, every beast stayed silent. Waiting.

At the heart of the nave, an old wolf crushed the stub of a roll-up under a weathered para-boot. "*He* should be here by now." Lorcan exhaled two pale streams of smoke.

"Late with the game plan. Late with the currency," snorted a brute at his elbow, shaking out its black and white, tangled mane.

"But always on time with the games." The soft, grey eyes glassed over. "Time to cut him loose. Skinwalkers won't be the Angel's lapdogs anymore."

"What about the blood money, chief? This dive's better than the sewers, but, thanks to the fire, it's one hell of a fixer-upper."

Lorcan dipped his great head. He drove a fist into an open palm. "One last job. Let the Angel call it. We'll be his muscle, but once the deed's done and victim dusted, he pays in full."

His advisor kicked at the slippery ground, sending up a wash of filth. "And if he won't pay?"

"He will," Lorcan declared. "Even if I have to use a scalpel to free it from his fist."

"Free?" A figure stood at the shaded entrance to the place. "To feel the spike of ice at one's chest, the cruellest bite of winter. How exhilarating." The man slid forward, his face illuminated from an odd angle and faintly ghoulish.

At the far end of the nave, Lorcan stared without emotion. Likewise, distracted from the melting suns of the braziers, the flick of a blade into the crown of a piston or a countershaft from a stripped gear-set, every muzzle turned to the newcomer.

"But to lose that freedom..." The voice trailed off. Gathering up the sides of his white robe, the man picked his way over the wet mosaic, taking care to slide around any Skinwalker he encountered. "No longer free to feel the whip of wind at high speed, or play cowboys and carrion in this dark fortress, but caged instead. That's no life for wild things." He arrived at the head of the nave where moonlight diffused the delicate glass of the rose-window, bathing him in pinkish light. The velvety folds slipped from his fingers and he turned to face the group. "I would even go so far as to say they'd find the grave preferable to incarceration, and it would all be such a needless waste if it resulted from a greedy need for *payment*." His features crumpled like a paper rose. "Beware of haste, Skinwalkers! Your indiscretions have been witnessed."

"By him who directed them," growled Lorcan as he worked a claw into the upper pocket of his leather and pulled out a tobacco pouch. He tooled a cigarette between his thumb and forefinger, popped it in his lips then took a flame to it. The tobacco crackled. "We've all witnessed *your* disinclination to reward those in your employment for their services," he breathed.

There was an instant of icy tension in which only the weave of cigarette smoke seemed to separate the warlords. With a crooked finger, the Angel summoned that great wolf closer.

"I will not betray your cause," he muttered. "Do not betray mine."

In a low, assertive growl, Lorcan replied, "One more job. Then you pay."

"You have my word on it."

Their hands crushed.

"I'll make sure the job befits the end of our happy union," the Angel added as if by way of an afterthought, then turned his attention to the crowd.

"Skinwalkers! This ruin is nothing short of a modern miracle. Not only is it now habitable, but you've also taken pains to protect its more...sensitive areas, and, for that, I'm most grateful." A clip of banknotes was retrieved then tossed to Lorcan, who caught and pocketed it without expression.

The Angel's mouth crept up at an edge. "Just a suggestion, chief. Preparations for your winter solstice are well under way out at Forest Field. Therefore, I say it's time to bask in the glow of your success. It's time for mad dogs to party!" He offered up a toast with an empty fist, and, after a moment's hesitation, the pack followed suit, knocking beer cans off those of their neighbour so the brown juice frothed, or offering up a weird, discordant chorus.

At the slightest motion of Lorcan's hand, the pack fell silent. "Preparations have started," he told the Angel through a smoky veil, "but remain appropriately subdued."

"Subdued? That surprises me." The man spread his hands out to the throng. "Hasn't this loyal breed *earned* a taster of its spoils? When it comes to preserving what's right and natural, Skinwalkers consistently deliver. Take the need to protect this library's more significant quarters for instance. It was incredible that your men were able to barricade the stairwell at such speed, and while I would have preferred a more creative arrangement of brick and rubble..."

"Your staircase is secured." Lorcan stabbed a claw past the man's right shoulder, indicating the rose-window. "If you'd said to make the brickwork fancy, I'd have shat a happy smile on it myself." His right jowl swelled, then quickly deflated. "My boys were too busy with the wounded to bother with such niceties."

The back of a hand to his lips, the Angel coughed. "Yes, the wounded." His eyes glazed. "Were there many?"

"Eleven, twelve. All surface wounds except the artisan, Harish. He took a slug to the forehead and had one hell of a rough night. The head-wound will heal in time, same goes for the break to his thighbone. His balancing days are done though."

"*That* is unfortunate," said the other man impassively. He cast his gaze over the rough crew. "He was very talented. Not many have his ability to climb onto a tower or roof or spiral and still turn a claw to the most exquisite carvings."

"I'm aware of Harish's skills. He's done with monkeying though." Lorcan shook his head so the tiny, silver bells knit into the two waist-length plaits of his beard jingled. "That shit comes of unleashing your best dog to beat up on a bitch."

"Yes, which was my fault entirely. But what a fabulous choice!" The Angel threw his small, pale hands towards the muddied heavens and readdressed the mass. "If we hadn't pitched the artisan against the spider, we'd never have known they were kin, if a tad…catty." He clawed at the air. "So, was my choice of assailant just a coincidence or did Fate intervene? It's a poser."

He dabbed at his mouth with a wisp of white silk. When he took the cloth away, his face had altered. Gone, the unsettling half-smile, the dance of too-cold eyes. Now he was a phantom, lips drawn back from the gums in queer disfigurement, eyes crystallised.

"Where is *my* artisan—Harish?" he demanded softly.

With the suck and drag of the tsunami, just seconds before its glittering arc descends, the ten-thousand-strong crowd drew breath. Druid adjusted his posture on the drum stool. A single bead of sweat rolled off his cheek, landing on the snare with a noise that was infinitesimal but seemed to ricochet off every Beyer microphone and all nine giant speaker stacks across the lawned breadth of Wollaton Park. As if in answer to its signal, the filler track blasting from the numerous PAs died away.

Druid raised his drumsticks high above his head, knocking them together three times to set the tempo. Flexing his arms almost involuntarily, he smashed a roll out across the toms. A series of flash pots detonated and, within seconds, they were thrown into a war zone. The stars dissolved, mushroom clouds ballooning in their place. With a boom, he sounded the cannon of the bass drum, and, almost by way of retaliation, flintlocks and muskets released their reedy fire via the snare. The lights went up.

With a seismic roar, the crowd exploded.

Roses cast a kiss out to his queen, Sophia, then snatched hungrily for the mike. "Drink my sin, feed me in, take and break my art, then swallow," he embarked in an inimitable, smoky tenor that seemed to snag the beat then hold it gently. "Heal me, deceive me, hate and drain my heart, 'til hollow." He swayed, his skin transfused beneath steel-blue gels so that, in the artificial midnight, he looked like a seraph carved over a grave. In his hair, he wore a halo of pale yellow roses tied with black velvet ribbon. An unbuttoned shirt of indigo silk flew out from his otherwise naked shoulders, like wings unfurling. No longer man, but icon.

Druid lurched to strike the gleaming crash cymbal, punched his foot against the bass pedal and tossed back his head, a glistening shower of sweat released from the tangled strands of his long hair. His lip curled. If Roses walked off the lip of the stage and levitated over the heads of their audience, he wouldn't be surprised...He could *see* the magick spilling off the crowd, and it was fantastic. Men looked on, their kohled eyes enraptured, while women copied each crest and fall of his brother's lips, as if sharing in a kiss. Druid felt a sting of envy under the left side of his chest. Didn't *he* exude that same fire? Every time he gulped for breath, he sensed it. No one noticed though. Not even angels.

He played softer, throwing in ghost beats on the snare and broken sixteenths on the high hat. His attention drifted to the anaemic peacock strutting up and down the stage. Adeudas was wearing a catsuit in seven shades of purple, his hair white as Old Man's Beard and all scrubbed up. A heather-grey Parker Fly Deluxe was moulded tight against his pelvis, real tight, like the hips of a lover, and he played it with that same erotic expertise. Then Roses took a diagonal step back from the mike so that his shadow fell across Adeudas.

Roses eclipsed even the most flamboyant. Druid bent his neck and smiled. He struck the bell of the ride cymbal, cooling his ego in the shimmering wash of brass. His own exuberance was also lost behind another's wingspan, but he stayed watchful in those shadows...

Like a motion camera on a crane, he homed rapidly in on Sophia. One kitten heel resting on a monitor, she teased the pickups of a vintage white Hagstrom II B bass. The hem of a jet-black dolly dress rode up her thigh, exposing an inch of red suspender, a thing so sweetly intimate, it stirred yet disquieted him. With her four-string moulded to a jutting hip, she alternated between the slap of a thumb bone and the twang of a crooked middle finger, a touch both punishing yet tender...Suddenly he missed her so very much. Tears trembled at his eyelids. He fought to dissolve them. *Don't lose the rhythm.*

Liquid fell against his cheek. He swiped at it with a forearm then refocused. With the tip of a heel, Sophia was cranking up the distortion on her Boss MT-2 pedal. At the same time, Adeudas was matching her. Sandwiched in-between, Roses leant into the mike to match the increased volume.

Druid listened. No mistake about it, Adeudas and Sophia were ignoring the rhythm he set and forging out on their own. He paused, twiddled his right drumstick. With a stressed blow to the high-hat, he forced a sharp 4/4 and fought to reel in the beat. But he might have struck an invisible shield for all the notice they took. Roses shot a concerned glance over one shoulder and tried to match the renewed tempo. But no matter how much they tried to stop the song from spiralling, the others seemed to relish in the mayhem.

"Don't lose the rhythm," he thundered.

Where rose petals had been tossed up onto the stage just five minutes ago, now the four-piece faced an onslaught of plastic cups, cigarette butts and beer cans.

As the crowd started to boo, a bottle exploded beside Roses, spattering him with chips of glass and dregs like holy water. He stared at the rest of the band in utter confusion, and, touching a finger to his cheek, smeared the trace of blood there. "Druid," he mouthed desperately, like a child.

"Come away!" Druid smashed his drumsticks to the floor. "Leave their bitterness for me." He tried to clear the toms. His foot met with resistance. The lace of his left Converse boot was ensnarled with the bass pedal. Heart in his mouth, he kicked at the kit, shook his foot with grit resolve, dropped, then tore at the lace with trembling fingers.

Somehow the string was knotted a thousand times over; no matter how determinedly he approached the task, the knots only seemed to get tighter. Just as his exasperation reached fever-pitch, he saw an orange flash out of the corner of his eye. In seconds, a blitz of makeshift firebombs littered the stage. Pools of fire sprang up all over the floor, black smoke and stench pouring off that rubber surface so Druid thought himself reborn in the bowels of hell itself.

Roses collapsed to his knees, embracing the stand of his mike, almost as if it could save him. *Help Him!* Druid's lips formed the words, but every syllable was lost to the filthy air. Instead, through a break in the smog, he saw Adeudas put aside his guitar and flex ten elegant fingers. Next, that insidious gent produced a cigarette from a soft pack, popped it into his mouth. Leaning in to a burning curtain, he lit the end of the paper, took two quick puffs then leant casually back against a speaker.

Druid thrashed with his foot so that the ankle joints snapped painfully back and forth. But as the boot lace knotted tighter, he realised Roses was already drowning.

Rising through the flames, that dark angel arched his spine dramatically, the liquid blues of his silk shirt enfolding his naked torso. "I'm lost," he said. Then he stretched out his arms, fell backwards into the black heart of the mob and was instantly absorbed.

Locked behind his kit, Druid was conscious only of the pain. No flesh, no earthly substance, just the pure unfolding spread of loss. His chest racked, his throat stung. He was fading from the inside.

Her touch was unexpected; it burned him. Leaning in from behind, Sophia pressed her palms against his breastbone. "Time to step out of the dark," she breathed.

Druid's eyes snapped open.

He found himself staring at the cold, white-silver drum kit in the corner of the room. Moonlight streamed in at the glass walls of the north watchtower. Neck cricked by the hour or so he had spent slumped over his desk, he gingerly raised his head off the dark, glossed slab of wood. His face was damp with tears. The silence thrummed.

They carried the artisan out from a crude lean-to located at one of the vast pillars; bore him high upon their shoulders while his fevered stillness resembled the inertia of death. If there was any emotion involved in delivering their brother to that sly warlord, the creatures did not show it but laid the wounded man down sloppily and withdrew.

"Artisan!" The bark was Lorcan's, and the weak creature did its best to respond, raising its head a little off the floor only to drop back so that one side of its face lay immersed in slush. Sinking to one knee, Lorcan fed a hand around the back of its head and raised the trembling face clear. "The Angel wants to speak to you." One set of fingers crooked the rag-doll neck while the other hand hoisted the invalid's waist until, together, the pair achieved a sort of sitting position.

"Angel?" the creature breathed tremulously.

"Harish. You do look a mess. What a pity. We had such times. Scrambling up this, scaling that. Well, the actual act of ascension was yours, while I'd say where and when. We made quite the team, which is why I'm so very loath to sentence you."

"Don't take the piss. Where's the room for reprimand?" spat Lorcan. He ordered two of the beasts to take up the artisan's weight and relieve him. Locking his knees, the warrior unfolded to his true height. A mass of woad-like tattoos snaked out at the collar of his leather bomber to spiral his neck and the shaved sides of his skull. His skin acquired a high flush of colour. He might have been a savage, bathed in the blood of his enemies. "This dog soldier took a pellet for his pack," he snarled.

A lesser man might have shown at least *some* vestige of fear. The Angel, however, remained unaltered. "Harish has endangered the tribe, and continues to do so. What is a wounded animal but conscious carrion? Offering nothing, he takes and takes to feed his putrefying flesh and, in so doing, drains the strength of the pack. I have the power to cleanse you of this tic. Unpleasant, yes, but what are we about if not the preservation of purity? Let me heal you. Let me ease the pain."

A tangible discomfort settled over the group, several members recoiling into the shadows as the eye of the Angel passed over them.

"Which is why I invoke victimisation by Skinwalker," said the inquisitor, speaking with the absolute authority afforded to him. "In this time of untruths and dissension, we alone represent an impenetrable force and must continue in that vein, especially when the old ways are so much in danger of crumbling. We must shield the city's secrets, protect them from any cheap governmental act that would expose us all and make our past-selves common knowledge." No longer hushed and sweet, now his voice was a bitter rasp. "How can we be expected to live this lascivious lie if lesser creatures insist on sharing our realities? You!" A hand rose up to supplicate a great hog of a Skinwalker at the nearest brazier. "How would you like it if the mantle of Belief was stripped away and the old life re-applied, revealing you as something less than monstrous, revealing you as a man who is...ordinary?"

The enormous beast swung the tusks of its stiffened dreadlocks violently from side to side.

"You wouldn't like it one bit," concurred the Angel, and he thrust a bony finger at the artisan. "Belief is as essential to a Skinwalker as the open road. Likewise, nothing must be allowed to threaten our way of life, as defined by Origin. Secrets are secret for a reason. As Renegade's most prodigious mercenaries, I know that you agree." The porcelain features cracked. "That is why we cannot entertain a sick dog who draws attention to this sacred place. Where one spider leads, others are bound to come a'crawling."

"Jezebel was only after me." The artisan spoke in a feeble burst, his mouth twisted to one side. "She...knows nothing of...secrets, Angel. She cannot harm us."

"Jezebel?" The Angel threw up his hands with an air of self-satisfaction. "Skinwalkers, we've been infiltrated by the mother of all whores and sorceresses herself. A follower of false idols, so the Burners' black book tells it. And does she follow *her* false idol now, Harish?"

"I didn't hold back," breathed the other, clutching an unsteady hand to his chest as the two Skinwalkers held him secure.

"Nor did she!" The Angel dragged the air between his lips, appeared to choke on it. He sighed wearily. "Harish, you are beloved, but you've attracted the interest of anyone in Renegade with the vaguest interest in the secrets of our saviour. And that surprises me, given your own propensity for keeping secrets."

Stillness descended over each party. The Angel, observing with malice, the artisan's wide, blood-lit eyes fixing on the other with panicked incredulity.

"You've threatened our mystery, Harish. Now it's time to share your own," said the tormentor and drew his white robe close, as if to preserve his own purity.

"Enough of the political shit, Angel," spat Lorcan, lacking patience with the trial. "When it comes to victimisation, you can pretend me and my boys know jack, but the truth is there's no secret to *those* sacred rites. Victimisation requires that a perpetrator be condemned by a majority then branded with the Expelled insignia of their tribe." His eyes were fine slits, each iris a steel marble. "And yeah, we're talking one of Renegade's official tribes here, of which Skinwalker ain't one."

"But you and your boys consider yourselves a tribe. In fact, I remember a time that very issue was..." The Angel's cold, white gaze settled on the great wolf. "...*hauled* up before the Management."

Lorcan's left jowl twitched, as if in an effort to control a snarl. "What's more, we've heard no evidence against Harish. Yes, he was hunted to this spot, but he fought tooth and nail to bring the bitch down. You champion a beast's right to hide its history, Angel." Like a Nambu Type 14 pistol, he released a long finger from his clenched fist and shot it towards the artisan. "But then you hound this brute for his enigma."

"Enigma, no. Perversion, yes. We're all free to dream and live the dark epiphany, but one thing we all agree on is Belief is key. Anything more permanent is a vile distortion of that ideal, is it not, Harish?" He appeared to gesture to the small of his own back. "Which is what makes your *tale* all too disturbing...a scientific enigma that is tucked out of sight most of the time but, once released, one that has proven a subtle aid to exception displays of balance, even at height. Lorcan, I know your men took Harish to City Hospital today, but were any in the room when his wounds were cleaned or his thigh-bone plastered?" He paused, the pale ice of his gaze falling over the quiet mass. "I thought not," he said softly.

Smoke flooded either side of Lorcan's nostrils. His canines gleamed while the soft, grey eyes threatened to spill over the edges of his eyelids like warm mercury. "Strip him," he ordered.

Drooping and punch-drunk on the pain, the artisan was dragged into the bloody moonlight and disrobed. First went his leather, with its blazing insignia, then a series of chains and belts and layered T-shirts and bandaging. Working a pair of damp engineering boots free, tossing them aside to drown in sludge, his two assailants clamped their fists around a leg each, and then unpeeled the leather. While cut away at the broken thighbone, the fabric still snagged on the plaster cast, prompting the artisan to unleash an agonising scream.

"Show us all what you've been hiding, Harish," said the Angel. "Harish!" he demanded after a second's silence.

"He's fainted." Lorcan drew powerfully on the vestiges of his rollup. "What now?"

"Turn him over," said the Angel who urged his toe towards the creature then seemed to think better of it. "Do it," he commanded. The two Skinwalkers pressed their hands beneath the naked man and lifted. As they did so, Harish fell awkwardly onto his front, face re-immersed in filth...and like the voices of the damned, the hall resounded with whispered obscenities until one word won out. 'Victimise.'

A few steps away, the wintry figure adjusted the collar of his white velvet robe at his chin. He coughed once, twice. "This perversion of Belief must be cut out like a cancer. I sentence the artisan to victimisation by Skinwalker," he told Lorcan with an authoritative tilt of his fine chin.

With a tinkling of the many tiny bells worked into the ropes of his beard, Lorcan turned on the nest of beasts. "Bring a hatchet," he snarled, and, ignoring the dark nature of the Angel, added, "We do it before he returns to consciousness." He stared at the creature's lower spine. "And heat a branding-iron."

Chapter 6

Cold Day in the Sun

That a woman of a certain age, whose brown eyes held the gleam of hard-wrought know-how and whose lips were a painted, dry, red streak, could propel a fish-paste sandwich with such accuracy and at such velocity was nothing short of a modern wonder. At least Druid seemed to think so as he stooped to pass below the crooked lintel.

"Nana!" The boy ducked too late; the bread stuck to his nose like a limpet.

"Not difficult is it, my sweet? Not 'ard on the squashy brain. Go to market and fetch groceries for the buggeredy wake, says I. Give you wads of cash, do I. And what's my blessed angel do?" Queenie put her fists amid the many pots and pans, jam kettles, jars of herbs and dusty condiments crowding her kitchen table and leant forward. "Blows the feckin' lot."

"Not exactly blows," IQ mustered. "I was, erm…helping a friend in need." Peeling the soggy triangle off his nose, he edged it delicately onto a corner of the table then patted at the bread, as if to mould it back into some semblance of a sandwich lest the violent maid still wish to serve it.

"Ah! One of *them*, 'ey. Always popping up those needy friends, least where my lovely lad's concerned it seems. And what's today's friend needing?"

"Rescuing."

Druid coughed belligerently—and though IQ shooed him back in the direction of the spare bedroom with a hand flick, Queenie peered inquisitively towards the lanky shadow in the doorway.

"Who's there?" she demanded, screwing up the bright, rat-like features that were inherent to the Quirk family. "Come out. Come out."

The shadow stepped into the room.

Wiping her palms against her floury apron, Queenie stuck out an arm. Their hands embraced over the table. Her brown eyes narrowed and she ate Druid up—the androidal shades, the flaming tips of his damp mohawk, the beaten leather, the plump pale of his lips.

She smiled coyly. "Bet you cost a pretty packet to rescue."

"Nana!"

"Oh, cease your noise." Despatching a radish with a well-aimed flick, Queenie ignored the boy's protestations of "Fair blinded me, Nana!" as he hopped noisily about. "I trust you slept well, stranger. That bed is made with me great granny Agnes's bridal quilt, stuffed with tufts of 'er own 'air. No doubt it was that that 'elped you sleep so soundly. Two in the afternoon, you dirty stop-outs. Not of Castclan," she asserted.

Druid looked past Queenie to the smoke that oozed from lit incense cones, the table strewn with leathery volumes, dishes of this bright powder and bowls of that, a geared mechanism showing the movements of the cosmos, and beyond, the squat window showing the pinks and yellows of the Castclan pod's projected sunshine. The Castclan were *his* tribe, and, as such, had evolved out of his desire to amalgamate free spiritedness with a deep respect for spirituality. Except, that wasn't it, he decided with a tinge of inadequacy. It was *the fans* who dictated the nature of each tribe. His had chosen to unite under the umbrella term of Castclan and practise a chaotic syncretism, drawing from Wicca, Druidism, Shamanism, Neopaganism, Buddhism, Kabbalah, Pantheism and other earth-based religions. If the Castclan could be said to share one unifying bond, it was their unshakeable adherence to Belief, which they saw as Nature's gift to the free thinker; and it was in this that Druid also found a common bond. "No, I am not of Castclan, but I am an admirer," he murmured.

"Hey dude. That's my grandmother!"

"…of the craft," Druid clarified with a sideways snarl. "To draw strength from the tapestry of life, and to revere it, accepting oneself as but one thread—that must be illuminating. Most religions feed our egos. We're important, they tell us. We matter. And if you're the right sort, a god'll save your righteous soul. Death becomes the ultimate test of popularity. In contrast, Castclan are governed by a more natural trajectory. You step off life's wheel and accept that it keeps turning. As a branch of the Belief system, it's humbling, and *that* I find admirable."

"Hog-spit!" IQ's witchy eyes rolled. "What happened to 'You *are* Castclan. That's clear from your attitude.' Weren't so loved up of the whole turny-wheely thing back then. Oh no. Then you were all grrr to the Castclan." He made claws of each hand. "Which is ironic really, given who you..." Suddenly remembering his sharp-witted grandmother, he knocked Druid playfully with his elbow. "Just joshing, my friend. Because that's what you are. Oh yes. What we've got here, Nana, is a comrade to the Castclan cause."

Queenie held up a hand. "'Ush, me precious pet, or I'll shove an apple in your trap and serve you as a smorgasbord. Your friend is welcome, though I trust 'e'll leave us as 'e finds us." She eyed Druid with significance. Then she found the handle of her knife and halved a giant lettuce. "And 'e'll be bringing me the cash afore the waning Aries moon. I'm thinking 'e's the sort who'll afford it."

"I'll repay your money in full," Druid affirmed. He nodded towards the heavily laden table. "And while I was grateful for your grandson's assistance, I regret depriving your guests of a kingly banquet in the process. There's enough death in this cold city. Those who mourn deserve such comfort."

"Oh, no matter," huffed Queenie. "No feast can disguise the taste of pain."

She returned to the salad and the shimmering movement of her knife absorbed Druid. It was a minute or two before he asked, "Was the death sudden?"

"It was the life that was sudden." Queenie snorted, her blade fashioning green coins of cucumber. "A blaze of breath set her yelping." With the side of her hand, she pushed the salad into a wooden bowl. Her face softened. "Did you see 'er, Irvine?"

The boy nodded as Queenie put the chopping board aside. "I can still picture the sweet tiny. Six days in this world, no more was she given."

"It was a child's funeral?" Druid raised his brows.

"A babe, yes. And pretty as a cherry pie."

"That's very sad. Also surprising. Going by the scale of the procession Irvine and I witnessed earlier, I presumed it was the funeral of an elder or dignitary. But a child?" Druid frowned. "I've always understood the Castclan's exuberant funeral rights celebrated life. But how do you celebrate a life not lived?"

"It's the idea of *celebration* you confusin'. More than 'igh spirits, it's our way of remembrance, and, for a life cut short, remembrance is everything. Even as we speak, that wee poppet is being celebrated in rites and rituals out at Forest Field since, in our eyes, death's just the gateway to the spirit domain," said Queenie shrewdly. "The spirit, or the soul if you likes, takes its last bow then walks through the gate to a fresh existence. A second chance, if you likes, 'specially for that pretty pie of a babe. And *that*, our needy friend, is worth singing and dancing for. *That* is worth celebrating."

With a skedaddle of a smile, the old maid gathered up her skirts at either side and charged out from behind the table. Bounding back and forth in black and pink, striped stockings, her impromptu hoedown was punctuated with bursts of 'It's Only Rock n' Roll (But I Like it).' With a swift bounce, she arrived behind Druid and tapped him on the bottom. "Giddy up, my lanky lovely!" she caroused.

"For the love of Origin, Nana!" IQ spat the soggy tip of his hat out the corner of his mouth, appalled.

Whether it was in response to the seemingly instantaneous commotion that arose outside the kitchen window or something unsettling in IQ's reference to the Drathcor, Queenie stopped stock-still, hands on hips, stripy legs astride two flagstones.

"'Ere they come," she stated simply.

Druid followed IQ over to the tiny bow window. Beyond the latticed glass, he saw the same black parade that he had encountered outside Rock Cemetery filing into Queenie's cottage garden through a small, white wooden gate, and, all of a sudden, he felt very exposed. At the same time, he was fascinated by the diverse throng who were busy cramming themselves onto the candied-angelica-green, thirty-foot lawn, and doing their level best not to step back into the vegetable patch or trample down the hollyhocks.

He glanced back over a shoulder. Bustling off to the rear of the kitchen and an area where the stone floor erupted, Queenie stooped to gather a sprig or two of sprouting herb. Returning to the table, she lifted the lid of a china soup terrine and tossed the fragrant handfuls in. "Finished, and just in buggeredy time."

"Come off it, Nana," whined IQ, pressing his sharp nose against the window, "You haven't gone and put the wake on here?"

"Somebody's got to feed the sombre. They've been carrying out the rites of passage for nigh on six 'ours now, while you've lain all tucked up in bed and snorting like a wart'og. What's more, you don't think that poor, pretty Bryony 'as the stomach for it. Nay boy, it's a feckin' shame she's to suffer it, and we're fixed for 'elping. For you, me perky petal," she instructed, propelling a pair of oven-gloves at her grandson. "In the garden, if you please."

With an evaluating glance, she presented Druid with a cheese-and-pineapple-on-sticks hedgehog. She urged the plate towards him. "If you want to step back from the wheel, you gotta be a part of it in the first place. Time to jump on, our needy friend. Time to jump."

The garden was heaving. Druid carried the half-depleted pineapple and cheese monstrosity stiffly in and out of the tea-sipping acrobats and clowns, the milling sisterhood (some of whom glanced up as he passed, seducing him with their sorrowful expressiveness) and the broad backs of the band, and found himself irritated, or bemused, by seemingly dismembered hands that swooped in to steal a 'spine' as he passed. A few steps ahead, the boy leant over a white-clothed trestle table, urging the soup terrine out of his arms. He indicated to Druid to deposit his burden between a plate of fairy cakes and a garish, lime-green jelly in the shape of a rabbit.

"See, mate. Told you there was nothing to, er…see here," said IQ in a half-whisper, doing his best to ignore the throng who had taken over every square inch of the cottage garden. "What say we scoot and find ourselves a little action?" The kid flashed his most enthusiastic smile.

Druid seated himself at the far end of the table, away from the crowd and in the shade of the gnarled trunk of a crab apple. "I've all the action I can handle right here, thanks," he muttered, eyeing a procession of gypsied beauties. "Plus, it seems rude to leave before our little kleptomaniac shows up."

"Jezebel? Hmmm…I don't think we'll be seeing her within a thousand miles of this place. But, cool beans, we can do that," said the kid in a vague attempt at nonchalance that made it clear their sticking around was anything but cool, and he poured himself into the bench opposite. "Here's the thing though, mate." He jerked his head towards the savoury hedgehog. "I don't know if it's Queenie's creative catering or the fact you might actually have to mix with the minions, but good god-squad, you're frosty. Why don't you treat us to a smile?"

The Drathcor curled back his lips to reveal two white sharps.

"Second thoughts, scrap that," hissed the boy, checking swiftly about. "These walls have ears, or in your case, eyes."

"What walls?" said Druid dryly.

His gaze moved down the stripy lawn, to a bower of damask roses serving as an entrance arch above a squat, white wooden gate, and then to the dirt track beyond; and he felt a new, softer sense of admiration. Strident mystics and the second largest of the tribes, the Castclan had gone to great pains to create a fresh, if complex, Eden. Externally, the tribal pod resembled a gigantean sky dome, its quilted skin fashioned out of some chemical inconstant always moving in a milky, fluid mass. However, it was on the inside that the structure's otherworldliness *truly* came to light.

He stared up at the distant ceiling and the projected shades of afternoon. "I always forget how beautiful it is," he said wistfully, a little jealous of his tribe's freedom to take control of their environment.

When IQ appeared mystified, he indicated skyward. "*This,* the Castclan pod—it's the white rabbit in this wonderland of ours, what the rest of us are chasing. It's the perfect amalgam of Nature and technology."

"Gotta have the skills, friend," said the kid with a nod of self-approval. "Put another way, if you'd got a history of being strapped to dunking stools, driven from the homestead or plain flayed alive, you'd be inclined to use a little cerebral..." He tapped the centre of his brow with a finger. "...mix the magick up with science, and guarantee a nice little *controllable* pad like this."

"Quite possibly. But to the outsider, it makes for one hell of a contrary ideology."

"I thought you were all down with the Castclan. Or so you told my granny."

"And I meant it. I *do* think your kin have a real affinity with the natural cycle, and that's what makes your dual love of science and nature such a beautiful irony. The very tribe that champions Mother Earth is her worse adversary, in that you deny the real world,"—Druid cast his hands around—"and create your own."

"And that differs from the other branches of Belief how?" A young woman approached. Her hair was a mane of burnished gold, her skin, cream and coffee. As she moved, she kept a slender hand pressed to her pregnant belly. "Moreover, how interesting that you, a Drathy in the high lord Druid's guise, should find his tribe's motivations confusing. But to go back to your earlier point, that ours is a contrary ideology to the outsider, first you have to establish what counts as an *outsider*. A tourist? A citizen who doesn't follow Belief? Or a believer who isn't Castclan? Which brings us to one of Renegade City's founding principles, namely, the very notion of redefining the outsider."

"Nosey nose!"

Druid scowled at his companion. "Of course. All I meant was that while the other trajectories of Belief, the Fae, the Darkled, and the Trawlers, remodel the self, an initiate of Castclan manipulates his or her own nature alongside that of the seasons," he answered the woman courteously. "This pod is a feat of creative engineering, a snow globe in reverse. Winter rages outside, but here, inside the glass, all is summer." He pointed up with a thrust of a black nail. "All you lack is a clear, blue sky."

"Erm, the blue sky gel is currently being serviced," IQ mumbled with pride.

"I take your point, but don't restrict our tribe to the preferences of Queenie and her cronies," said the woman as she reached out to the hedgehog, plucked then devoured a spine. She patted at her mouth with a damask sleeve. "What we have created here is freedom through variation, a feat, as you put it, not so dissimilar from Nature herself. For example, some sections of society retain a nomadic lifestyle..."

"Lest the mob come pounding," IQ interjected.

The woman shot him a chastising glare. "Piebald ponies can be seen relocating the colourful caravans of all manner of peddlers, musicians and travelling folk. Others prefer a carnival existence. You are familiar with Le Cirque des Magiciens?"

"The grandest touring fair in the city," said Druid, the name conjuring up memories of long, candy-scented nights spent in the company of acrobats, fire-eaters, trapeze artists, frothy can-can dancers lured from the Moulin Rouge, bare-chested muscle men, clowns in pantaloons, sword-swallowers, knife throwers, squirrel monkeys, lions and tigers and bears, oh my...

"And home to those who favour the physical theatrics of the craft. But most choose to adapt an allocated space inside the pod to suit their personal ideal. At the south ravine, for instance, you'll find a number of tiny, white cottages set in imported Irish bog-land, in the east, a desert, littered with small, if inhabited, pyramids. I believe I am right in saying, but I feel sure Irvine will correct me, there is even talk of a witch doctor from Bora Bora..."

"Tahiti." IQ shrugged his shoulders.

"...setting up camp under a coconut palm," the girl continued, and she crinkled up her nose in long-suffering irritation. "But who cares for geography! My point is this—we embrace diversity at all levels, even that of the natural order. Because, despite the superficial paradox of an earth religion excelling via science, we do so purely on the grounds that our endeavours succeed because the Divine wills it so. In other words, who are we to question the mysticism of the natural and scientific world alike, or to offer an explanation for either? What's more, ask yourself—is the world we create at odds with natural magick or its natural progression? But I forget myself. Desdemona Quirk." Pretty olive eyes rolled at IQ. "Sibling to the noise maker. And you, friend, you are not of the Castclan?"

The words were Queenie's, but with a softer edge.

"No, but he's an admirer," sneered the boy. "Aren't you, D?"

"Then D is very wise," said Desdemona, smiling, "Unlike my brother, who's just a wise guy."

"Ah my sister, how I missed her, better kiss her." IQ planted his lips sloppily against the girl's cheek. "But you grown-ups are annoying me with your talk of pseudo-philosophical whatnot. I'm in need of a decent conversation." He urged up one side of his wizard hat to reveal an ear and bent down to Desdemona's bump. "What's that? Tell mummy to lay off the chilli dogs. They make you fart. Hear that mummy?"

"Shove off, Irvine."

"Hey, don't blame the messenger. It's junior here who's complaining of the bottom bubbling. Lay off the hot stuff mama. And as for the sauce…"

"I haven't so much as drunk a capful."

"Depends on whose cap you're talking about," IQ rejoined. "A peapod fairy's, that's fine and dandy. But if you're talking a Grallator's, that's a different mouthful altogether."

"Talking of whom, what's a Grallator doing at a Castclan wake?" interjected Druid, disquieted by the envy souring this debate and keen to change the conversation.

He narrowed his eyes at the peg doll in top hat, tails and six-foot long, pinstripe flares who was making a beeline for their party, and was instantly on guard. Once upon a time, a Grallator would have been more likely to bore him to death than stir up any real cause for alarm. Times had changed though, and as he had observed that morning near the gates to Rock Cemetery, so had the Grallators.

In the early days of the city, it had required a peculiar brand of fool to want to rule their world, or, at the very least, police it. A Management-appointed body called the Grallators had satisfied this calling. Stalk-thin, their eyes glazed from the strain of editing the city's many inventories and accounts, the tall ringmasters had proven tireless in their capacity to advise. Seek a new direction, a Grallator was sure to advise you. Don't seek one, a Grallator was sure to advise you just the same. Civil servants born and blessed, the breed had been tolerated for one reason—they alone found pleasure in the mundane chores of government.

But power is a dangerous thing; it breeds ego and elitism. Towering over the other citizens on their ergonomic stilts, it was patent that the tribe had come to believe the hype of their lofty elevation. In place of a onetime role as gentle giants, they had evolved into authoritarian wraiths, death-pale and fleshless, easing their spindle limbs into every nook and cranny of the city. And whether drained the more of living colour by Roses's death, or the increased savagery of Skinwalkers, one thing was crystal clear to Druid. They were hardening up.

"Shit, no! Where? Don't let him see me!" IQ grasped the plated hedgehog and attempted to hide behind its depilated spines.

"Too late," whispered Desdemona. Brightening her voice, she exclaimed, "Peter Pineapple—what a surprise!"

"My darling boy and girl!" The lanky giant bounded up to them in four great strides—and Druid was relieved to see that this particular individual belonged to the old school of Grallators. Reaching down, he shook each sibling enthusiastically by the hand. His Pinocchio face beamed. "Well, there's a pleasure. I was only just saying to Mrs Riddle how long it's been since I saw my two favourite pixies and here you are. Bright as buttons..."

"Brash as bog-brushes."

As if a puppeteer loosened its strings, the Grallator's face dropped. He eyeballed the approaching maid and nodded curtly. "Queenie Quirk."

"Boring Berk."

"Nana!" It was Desdemona's turn to chastise her elder. "Ignore her, Mr Pineapple."

"Ridiculous name for a ridiculous man," sneered Queenie, and she winked at Druid.

"My grandmother means you well..."

"No I don't."

"And it is so good to see you here, even if the occasion is sorrowful."

"Oh, indeed, indeed," interjected the buffoon, his face a little reddened. "Very tragic. Though I have to say it is only by the good will of Origin that I stand before you now, as a figure of strength, as a light sent to guide you through the fog of loss and suffering..."

"Lords 'elp us," muttered Queenie.

"Only last night an assault was made on my good person," declared the Grallator, and he paused until Desdemona uttered a polite squeak. With a sigh, he patted her gently on the arm. "Oh, I know it is alarming, but we cannot hide from the fact. Grallators have patrolled this dark city since the dawning days." His cheeks shone. "After all, it takes magnanimity to weigh up right and wrong, and it is my curse, nay, my gift, to be suited to the role. But I digress." His features turned, as if on cogs, and he looked serious. "I was perambulating near Legacy, our Lords' own nightclub, when whom should I encounter but filthy Skinwalkers."

"Skinwalkers?" spat Queenie with sudden interest and she slackened the slingshot aimed at the Grallator's temple. Gobbling down her cubed cheese ammo, she demanded, "Why are Skinwalkers makin' their buggerdy menace in Legacy? Were they inside or prowlin' without?"

"They were outside, Madam," asserted the Grallator, and Druid and IQ glanced intently at one another as if each urged the other to stay schtum. "A proper nuisance they were, causing all manner of commotion—and the language! Well, it suits a sinner."

"And Skinwalkers are the devil's own dung?" said Queenie with bite.

"Without a doubt, Madam Quirk. They are a pestilence. Can you believe they set my scarf aflame? Desdemona, see here how they singed one end, and after you fashioned it with your own fair hands. Do you remember last Yule? How my neck would shrink in the bitter altitudes. And it was you, my dear Irvine, who said to knit a scarf. I can still picture the two of you, fingers click-clicking as you wove the pretty yarn. Quite warmed to it, if my memory serves me well, young Irvine. Clickety-click for hours on end."

Druid raised an eyebrow at the boy.

"What? I was bored, alright!" said IQ hotly as Queenie openly guffawed.

"I can assure you, this is no laughing matter, madam." The Grallator crossed his arms over his chest. "Where a few Skinwalkers lurk, a pack is sure to follow and what are your preparations? I implore you, my dears—look to your shelter. It's utterly defenceless."

Desdemona put her hand to her belly, sighing, "Oh, Peter. My husband was nothing if not a master craftsman." She gestured towards the timbered cottage, which was of squat construction and painted a sunny shade of yellow. "A ship's beam runs the length of the frame, giving extraordinary strength. Criss-crossed lead adds extra protection at the casements. Each strip is reinforced with steel. The thatch?" She pointed to the finely meshed reeds then let her hand fall. Her eyes lowered, their soft olive shade now hard and flinty. "No other man in Renegade will match Harish's head for heights, his skill or his artistry."

"Well, strictly speaking, Harish is no longer in this city. Is he?" half-whispered the Grallator, as if sensitive to Desdemona's situation yet keen to get his facts straight.

Desdemona ignored him. "Harish built our home to withstand all the rigours of the natural world; rain, wind, fire..."

"And Skinwalkers? What of Skinwalkers, Desdemona?" asked Peter Pineapple softly. He hitched up his pinstripe flares and lowered himself precariously until he was able to sit on one of the nearby benches. His crane-fly legs arched out in front of him. "Believe me, my dear, I make no criticism of Harish, but we would be fools to rest on our laurels. Our security is outdated. Yes, the tourist parties may have tailed off in recent weeks—and who can blame outsiders for staying away given the chill factor to the current climate. But any passing drifter can still enter this pod on a whim. And while I would give my life's blood to live one more day the old way, life has changed and darkly so."

"It is death that has changed us," said Druid, his eyes intent on a patch of grass.

The Grallator sighed. "The city is no longer a haven, ever since the fire destroyed the one true spirit." He crossed his heart, mumbling 'Good Rest Our Roses' then continued, "Not to mention the Great Library, I've sensed the winds of change. We are in a war-zone. I see it every night on my patrol and the violence is growing. But..." He tucked his hands beneath his chin in pompous prayer, "...let us put our faith in the Management, from whom hope springs eternal."

"Those bumbling fools!" Queenie shot a bullet of saliva into the makeshift spittoon of an ice bucket. "There ain't a single one worth the 'alf of 'im that passed. Yet still they sit on their lard-'ard arses and make stupid rules, only for us Castclan to find the loop-'oles. Bloody bum 'oles, the whole buggerdy lot of them!"

In some capacity, Druid was starting to enjoy this homely debate. It was the equivalent of a door that led to some clandestine secret left ajar. He had always suspected the Castclan of being the intellectual subversives of Renegade City. Simultaneously at war and at peace with Belief, the tribe had always maintained a guarded respect for the Drathcor, much as a vampyre for its sire. And on a par with that supernatural bond, the two tribes shared a tacit understanding that each would fight to the death to preserve its own autonomy. Thankfully, the theory remained untested. Casting his eye over the eclectic brew of ancient peoples, all belonging to what was arguably the most influential of the city's tribes, Druid guessed that was probably for the best.

At that particular moment in time, however, he was fascinated to hear what the average citizen made of the Management, Renegade's presiding judiciary, whose sixty-three (albeit, prior to Roses's death, sixty-four) members were elected by their peers to represent each of the city's four key tribes...Not that a wild card like Queenie Quirk could ever be construed as an average citizen, he mused with a savage smile.

"But, my dear..." the Grallator blustered.

"I ain't your dear, sunshine."

"...Mrs Quirk. There are rules and there are consequences, and it is through the application of precisely *that* degree of order that Renegade will find its resurrection. Take, for instance, the will of our own sacred son, that a Bill of Interdependence be drawn up so information might be freely shared. All records on full and permanent display so none can corrupt."

"And none can hide. An idiotic concept," thundered Druid, all trace of amusement evaporated. He glowered at the Grallator, as if the effort of holding his tongue was excruciating—and it had been, he realised suddenly. On no previous occasion had he shared his true revulsion for the bill that Roses had proposed; one that had sought to lay bare the secrets of all who came to the city to live the lie of Belief and to start afresh. In the shadows, he had laboured under the misapprehension that his brother knew best. Now, he felt his hands hook as if to claw back the voice he had lost, and the guilt start to lift.

"You may think so, erm..."

"My mother's cousin," Queenie interjected.

"Oh." Peter Pineapple looked at Druid. He arched one eyebrow. "Very, erm, pale."

"I've had a cold."

"Yes, of course, of course." The Grallator waved a dismissive hand. "But the truth of the matter is that information will be our salvation."

"And that's the feckin' shame of it," spat Queenie, hands bolstered by the wide girth of her hips. "When it comes to that pig's swill of a bill, we witches were the first to grumble. To our minds, naught outweighs man's natural right of privacy, be 'e crook, thief or damned donkey. And trust this old fart when she says if you give folk free rein to nose in others' dirty drawers, they'll come back up with an 'eart full of 'atred. Leave us free to dream, and to Believe, or Lords alone know the devastation when the city walks in an unknown skin." Her wise brown eyes fixed hard on Druid. "Don't know about you, *my mother's cousin*, but I'm preferrin' imagination to information any day."

"Oh madam," blustered the official, wiggling his long legs in agitation. "Imagination is a loose cannon. Who dares guess at the perversities which have evolved in our great city as a result of its unbridled usage? It makes my flesh creep to think of it. Skinwalkers are bad enough, but now a greater threat is being birthed in Renegade's darkest recesses. Things are emerging that have no place amid such beauty. They are vulgar and…"

"Untouchable?" Bryony stepped through the wall of listeners. Druid's chest swelled with hot, dry air…or with shame. "Scared you'll catch difference like you'd catch a cold, Mr. Pineapple?" She spoke faintly, though her voice had an edge.

Producing a handkerchief, the Grallator dabbed inefficiently at his glistening temples. "Well, naturally difference is to be celebrated. It's difference through defiance we have to monitor." He glanced up. "Oh Bryony, it's you. I didn't mean to imply…"

"Its okay, Peter. You're right of course. Every world has its bad guys, even this one." The girl sank onto the bench, a fragile Thumbelina beside the lanky giant. She looked up blearily, focused in on Druid. With difficultly, she swallowed. "For the love of Origin, I meant no harm, Lord…"

"…Lordy lord, Bryony," Queenie hollered. She stepped instantly between them, slamming her strong, brown hands onto her hips. The wise eyes crackled. "Winter's wane is upon you and I bet you 'aven't tasted a crumb. Oh, my 'ours of slavin'! Not that I blame you, precious poppet. You've been dealt the worst sort of 'and, but its time to force some eatin'. Irvine!" The sturdy maid summoned her kin with a hooked finger. "Well, offer 'er somethin', my mucky monkey. Go on,

Bryony. Give it a fair tastin'. Its Bloaty Bert's finest cheddar, you know."

"Oh indeed, Bloaty does craft the most excellent cheddar. Mind if I…"

"Mitts off!" Queenie despatched the Grallator's hand with a determined thwack. "Lanky loons not allowed the luscious cheese of Castclan."

"Are you quite sure, Madam? I can't say I'm familiar with that ruling. But indeed, there is the Law of Protection, designed to keep a Grallator sound of mind and healthful. I suspect one of its fine sub-clauses to be the basis for such teaching and very wise too, oh yes, very wise."

"My grandmother is teasing you, Peter," said Desdemona and she plucked off a cube of cheese and politely offered it.

The giant held up his hand. "Oh no my dear, you will not tempt me with your dairy delicacies. My body is a shrine to virtuosity, nay, a temple of temperance, and it must remain unadulterated."

"Thank the feckin' Lords for that!" Queenie dismissed the officious gent. Instead she looked to Bryony, who was still fixated on Druid, her bloodless lips mouthing a silent prayer. "But if cheese be not to your likin', we will find that which is." Looping her apron over the crook of an elbow, the bossy maid worked her fingers into a small, embroidered purse at her hip. "Irvine, 'ow'd you and me mother's cousin like to go a-huntin' downtown. I'm thinking parfait for our lovely girl 'ere" – she ignored Bryony's attempts at refusal – "or figs. Now there's a thought. Yep, a pound of freshest figs."

"Figs? Where in the name of Roses will I find fresh figs in winter?" protested the boy, "Take me all day if not the night as well."

Queenie pressed a sovereign into his palm. "Exactly." Her voice held a gentle insistence. "Time you return, the wake may be done and dusted and these mournin' folk dispersed. But that's only if you *dawdle*."

"We'd best be on our way then." Druid met Queenie's gaze. He nodded slowly, paused for a few seconds then turned solemnly to Bryony. "This world is cruel, its most unforgiving aspect being that we are *all* ruled by Nature. Even the gods, it would seem." Sinking to his knees, he met those ever-flowing eyes. "Belief can do many things, but it cannot bend reality."

The girl's lips stopped moving and she shuffled to the edge of her seat. Hesitantly, she leant forward. "Not bend, my Lord. But might we not evolve?"

The drowning eyes sparked. Druid, however, was still registering the shock of her. While her words seemed at once wise and nonsensical, there was something excruciating in her suffering: a sense of suffocation as if she longed to demand justice yet feared its reprisals. He interpreted her grief like a palm-reader, one line for guilt, one for hurt, one for tenacity. So many emotions, he sensed, walled up in her flesh. Or was the pain his own?

It was IQ who came by Druid's ear and whispered, "Come away now, mate."

"You leaving us then, Irvine?" Peter Pineapple frowned. "And you too, my new acquaintance? Well, the Lords speed your recovery and rest assured Mrs Quirk will return the roses to your cheeks in no time."

"I'm sure," muttered IQ, raising an eyebrow.

"And don't you worry, Irvine. We Grallators will despatch the heinous Skinwalkers in no time. Send the pack, erm, packing. And no need to shed tears for my well-being. I have a resolve seldom seen in these bleak times, not to mention integrity. Oh yes, my safety is assured. But for others, it is a different matter. Protect you and yours, Irvine, I urge you. Look to the preservation of your home..."

The Grallator's voice faded as the men kept walking.

"Has he shut up yet?"

"That arse of a Grallator? We can but hope so."

"Poor Peter. He's really not that bad," said the boy with forced sincerity. He kicked a stone down the lawn with the tip of his trainer. "Means well, but good Goth man, he's tedious."

Druid cut his eye at the boy. "Given that you were part-responsible for that buffoon's choice of neckwear, you haven't always 'clickety-click' thought so."

"Hey, we all do our bit for charity." IQ launched a well-placed stab at the stone. "Well, maybe not those of us who've got the whole god-status off to a tee. But us common folk like to make amends, and Peter's my bit of do-gooding. You see, once upon a time, Desdemona and I teased that Grallator mercilessly."

"And why the hell would you stop?"

"We all need allies, my spiky friend. Especially when the world starts to turn on an unknown axis. Sometimes friends in the know are invaluable."

"Useful you mean."

"One and the same."

"Then I'm registering a complaint because you've proved nothing short of useless. I was looking for the Fae, not tea and cakes with the family, let alone the whole damn tribe."

"That's harsh. Wasn't my fault the Fae didn't show, and it's not like you objected to meeting my grandmother. Oh no, quite the lethal Lothario when you want to be. First Jezebel, then Queenie. What's more, you weren't the only one put out by the whole wake thing. Threw me as well you know, given that I had business of my own to attend to."

They reached the squat, white garden gate. Druid put his hand to the latch. "Namely?"

IQ's witch-green eyes sharpened, and, for an instant, he seemed on the brink of some great explanation. Then his gaze shifted to the topsy-turvy cottage and its garden party. "Just family business," he murmured.

Was the kid's tone sincere? Druid found it difficult to know. Stuck in that awkward space between child and adulthood, everything about IQ seemed ironic. Love beads adorned his dirty neck. A silver sleeper hooked his upper left ear. Baggy jeans hung low about his narrow waist, as did a barrage of single and double row spike belts and, dangling at one hip, the chain of a canvas wallet tucked in a back pocket.

Druid thought back to when they had first met. Then IQ had worn an oversized, purple hoodie, but in the clement climate of the pod, he'd taken to carrying it, slung over one arm, revealing the old, grey T-shirt he wore underneath. Its sleeves had been ripped open at the seams, then rolled and secured at each shoulder by a safety pin. The puckered neckline was equally distressed. But it was the design of the t-shirt that drew the Drathcor's eye.

Sketched in Tippex and red felt-tip pen, the symbols were at once crudely drawn and beautifully intricate, mathematical even in their innate symmetry. Druid frowned a little. In the costume ball that was Renegade City, it was difficult to judge a man by his appearance. But the design added a fresh complexity, something inordinately ritualistic, disciplined even, to that wise little rodent of a kid.

"Herald for the Castclan. Star of bright hope and Belief," parroted the boy, apparently noting Druid's gaze. "Hell's bells, I was drawing these in kindergarten. First, the circle, you know, of life everlasting. Inside, the waxing and the waning moon, perched back-to-back, each with a beady eye on the ever-ever, and then, naturally of course, at the centre, there's the pentagram."

"Symbol of protection?"

The young brow crinkled. "Among other things but, yeah, the pentagram has a certain big-fisted usefulness when it comes to guarding the homestead." The kid shook his head. "It's a shame its protection wasn't cast o'er Bryony, hey?"

As IQ's face darkened, Druid found himself trying to decipher that young, expressive mind. After all, what sort of devil in kid's clothing would dare befriend a Drathcor? Or strike deals with drifters as Druid had witnessed him do with the human tiger in the bar? And what other child would hide such sadness behind a depth of smiles?

"Bored Lord," said the kid, intercepting Druid's evaluation of him. "What say we blow this joint?" He grinned broadly, his brown hand moving to open the gate.

Druid kept a firm grip on the latch and stared over his shades. "Who are you, boy?" His gaze burned down on his young companion, whose face turned red with frostbite. "You're a child with too many secrets for my liking. Going by looks alone, nothing would suggest you've the gall to approach a Drathcor or bribe that flea-ridden feline in the bar earlier. Yet something drives you."

"Bit scary that kitty cat," said the kid with enthusiasm and he stepped back from the gate. "Bad fur day if you ask me. Or I have heard talk of a mouse shortage. Either way, that was one grotty puss. He's never struck me as a tetchy sort before, but beat me naked with a phoenix feather, with some it's hard to tell. Take you for instance, my friend, all teeth and lankiness."

"I'm not lanky. I'm lean."

"What's a synonym between friends? You're tall is all and have got one hell of a mouth on you. With a temper to match, that I can attest too. But even you've got a squashy side..."

"We were discussing you."

"I'm not squashy."

"Want to bet?"

The boy's lips twitched. "Ok, so you want the truth, mein Drathcor?" He shot a glance over his shoulder then leant closer in. "I'm eyes and ears for sale."

Druid's hand forgot the gate.

"Discretion's landed me the lion's share of my investigative work. It's all in here you see." IQ tapped his brow. "Brain's ahead of the game while the body's stuck in boy-land. Useful though. No one suspects a kid of snooping." He lifted the gate-latch with a clunk and waved the Drathcor through. "That's how I collect my secrets, courtesy of drifters and lowlifes. Example. Louse House. Remember the moll packing a pistol?"

"Some nonsense about her shooting a love rival at midnight. Let me guess. It was your job to locate the other woman, or should I say, produce the warrant for her death sentence?" A wave of loathing hit the pit of Druid's stomach. He strode away with a snarl.

The kid tried to keep pace with him. "Not at all, mate. I tipped off her rival."

"And how d'you know this other woman didn't take a shot at the moll in return?"

"Hey, I'm no Grallator, and whatever my thang might be, it ain't policing. But I can say I'm not down with death. Life? Now that's far more entertaining," insisted the kid, falling over his own feet so that Druid finally slowed down. "Thanks," he panted, offering up an anxious smile. "Look, it's like this. The moll wanted me to find the other girl. I did just that. What the moll *didn't* know was I told the girl to head for the hills. In exchange for a nice little earner of course."

"So you get paid by both parties. One, to locate the missing person, the other, to pretend you never found them. It's a resourceful twist on extortion, I'll give you that."

"It's a living," grinned the kid. He kicked a fresh stone down the dirt track. "Reminds me. You owe me ten notes."

"What the hell..?"

"Call it a retainer. For services rendered."

Whisking noiselessly around, Druid grabbed the boy by the frazzled neck of his T-shirt. "And what services could you possibly render me?" he breathed into that sharp, brown face.

"Man, I'm kidding. I'm kidding," choked IQ, and Druid pushed him away. "Jeesh. You'll have someone's eye out with those claws."

"Or their tongue."

"Okay, I get it! You're not big on the whole gaffs for laughs. Just trying to liven you up, that's all. But you're deadpan, man. Or is that just dead?" The boy balled up his fist to exert a playful punch, caught the Drathcor's glare and poked him bravely with the tip of a finger. "Seriously though mate, you could say I've got myself a new secret, you being a living god and all. But now you've got the dirt on me I reckon we're even. So how's about I take a busman's holiday and we start investigating whatever it is that's got you to leave the safety of the Batcave?"

Druid looked unconvinced.

"Look, let me break it down like this," IQ persisted. "You're after answers and, when it comes to the city's secrets, I'm its goddamn confidante."

"And you'd help me why? Money? Fame?" Druid watched the kid closely. "Deliverance?"

"Of sorts, maybe yeah." The kid sniffed like a bona-fide urchin, and laid a hand gently on the Drathcor's sleeve. "But deliverance from a different devil. Peter Pineapple was right on one account. Without Harish, I'm the man of the house and I'm telling you, friend, it's responsibility with a capital Rrrrr. Not really my style but them's the breaks. So I need to keep my family safe you see, 'specially with Desdemona's baby on the way."

Druid tucked his claws up into the soft recesses of his palms. "Keep them safe from what?" he demanded.

IQ stopped walking. "Got to break it to you, man. This city's not the stuff of dreams anymore. Something's rotten in the state of Renegade and I've no idea where the hell the stink is coming from. But one thing I *do* know is, it's dangerous. Roses was taken and…"

"Is that what you believe?"

The question seemed to perplex the boy, who concentrated on flicking at the tip of his wizard hat with a thumb and forefinger for an unusual length of time. At last, he responded, "When you have eliminated the impossible, whatever remains, however improbable, must be the truth? Or so said our faery friend, Sir Arthur Conan Doyle, and if a man ever touched base with what lay beyond the probable, it was that dude. So we look to the possible…or, in layman's lingo, mate, the facts. I'm taking it you're on a quest to answer the holy grail of posers, namely, did the highest lord choose death of his own accord? First thing; piece together the victim's background."

"And it *will* be a case of piecing, given the veracity of the fire. Very few documents were salvaged."

"Of course! The Great Library." IQ kicked his stone several metres down the path. "I like your style. Very cunning."

"Except I've already sifted the documents." Druid was remembering the charred fragments spread over his desk: the spell book shaped like a spider, the handwritten scrawl, the sooty business card…"Nada."

"I wonder what you missed," said IQ with a glint in his eye. "Oh, there's always something. A piece of rope, a warped candlestick, a revolver wrapped in velvet and slipped behind a bookcase."

"My brother died of smoke inhalation." Druid put a hand to his throat. "What I need to know is how that could happen."

"Not to mention, why. Ah, so we're getting somewhere. Well, I would suggest you go get the evidence and we'll rendezvous in…hmm." Pulling a pocket watch from the wallet suspended by a chain at his waist, the kid checked the hour and scowled. "Four thirty. It's my guess that night's already drawing in beyond these sunny walls. I'm thinking, if it's okay by you, around lunchtime tomorrow might be best, mate. When daylight's on our side."

"What difference does daylight make?"

IQ employed a swifter pace. "Skinwalkers," he said simply, and the Drathcor drew level with a single stride. "Full moon's up and, well, a little friend told me they've found a new lair."

"The south watchtower."

"Precisemondo."

"And that little friend wouldn't be the Fae by any chance? Goes by the name of Jezebel, you say…"

"Who's that? I don't remember saying a name. Did I?"

Druid ignored IQ's squawks and raised a hand in backward salute. "Tomorrow at noon, my *useful* friend."

Chapter 7

Livin' on the Edge

The dark eroded. Every last red cell drained from Druid's cheeks. He hadn't been inside the south watchtower since the fire, letting others sift the remains. A rope of pain tightened at his throat. Never had he imagined such devastation!

Squinting up, he saw that the dramatic architecture of exposed crossbeams was encrusted with bird droppings, the glossy faeces dripping either side of the blackened beams like clowns' tears. Every so often, a caw from the rafters interrupted the quiet. Otherwise, the only intrusion came in the form of snowflakes, feathering the many gaps in the mildewed ceiling. So softly the snow fell, like rice scattered over the head of a bride.

He drifted forward. The dank hall opened up before him, much altered yet familiar, like an age-old friend fallen on hard times. He re-imagined its former splendour; walls stencilled with gold fleurs-de-lis, fat, embroidered floor cushions; pierced metal lanterns, strung up at every apex and perfume-misted, silks that curtained every archway, and row upon row of heads bowed in literary prayer.

The mirage touched him. He drew his coat closer about, as if to trap the lie. When the heat was sustained, he realised suddenly that he had arrived at the front of the nave and stood directly below the gallery of the rose-window. Where the afternoon sun flowed through the pink stained glass, he was bathed in an almost corporeal glow. He lifted his face to it and sensed another's eyes upon him; the shape of Roses, leaning boyishly out over the rail, the drapes of an unbuttoned, satin shirt flowing either side of his chest like wings. Then the sun went in.

The gallery was deserted. In lieu of once iridescent brass, the handrail was warped and badly tarnished. A petal of glass had been shattered at the base of the rose-window. Soot clung hungrily to stone, like an epiphytic vine invading the tower of a sleeping princess.

Druid felt the sting of warm blood at his cheeks. His mind was playing tricks on him again; or perhaps it had never stopped. He was still haunted by last night's dream, traces of which bled into one another like drug-induced illusions. And certainly, it was an illusion since the events had never really happened. He and his fellow band mates had occupied countless stages the world over, but the crowd had never responded with anything other than light and generosity; the only flames to ever threaten to consume them were precision-timed pyrotechnics, and, most significantly of all, their musical tautness as a band had never been compromised. That was why he had found the dream so disturbing. Try as he might to forget, he was haunted by Sophia's acerbic beauty as her hand cupped his heart, and the enmity of fans, hordes of them, baying for royal blood. His spine stiffened. It was just a dream, he told himself. A stark, painful, ineradicable dream.

Added to which, no amount of faery glimmer could disguise the true state of the ruin, or disguise its stench. While the scent of burning was indomitable, a fouler stink pervaded: musk of Skinwalker.

Anger flickered at his lips. What he'd give to find one of the brutes; curled at the base of the reading desk perhaps. Matching his footfall to the rise and shudder of the beast's sleeping torso, he'd move softly in, raise his boot then bring it down with a resounding...

Crash! A bouncing bomb of timber ricocheted off the tiled mosaic by his feet, exploded into a shower of dust and splinters on its second impact. He leapt back as another board smashed the other side. Every nerve found its razor-edge and his claws unsnapped to form slashing pincers. His shades panned up.

A figure busied itself in the left-hand corner of the gallery so that Druid momentarily thought he had come upon a ghost. But, squinting up, he realised the urgent labours spoke more for a creature born of the physical than the spectral; one intent on gaining access to the stairwell and, in turn, the rooms above.

His jaw ground from side to side. The idea that any parasite could choose to work its way up to Roses's private quarters was utterly repugnant. His claws shot apart. Pressing a boot to the lip of a bookcase, thrusting up to clasp the damp chill of a wrought iron bracket, he eased one or two fingers into the smallest of gaps and relied on their strength to support his body weight.

He ascended silently, his fingertips resisting every effort to puncture the skin from a spike of wire or a shard of glass. Luckily the practised rub of drumsticks had toughened those fleshy pads while the repetitive lift and punch of a drum pedal gave power to his leg muscles. He stretched out a foot, nudged the tip of his boot up onto a higher ledge. It took him a second to gain his balance; then he pushed off and locked his fingers around the mottled rail above. Making hard, white domes of his biceps, he pulled his chin level, rocked his lower body back then threw one leg up and over. With the softest swish of his leather spilling over the railing, he crouched down on the other side.

A few steps away, the creature busied itself at the stairwell. Druid angled his head. The body was a shell of liquid black, the head swathed in cobweb. But, otherwise, he could make out no real characteristics. Instead, he watched, revolted, as it sat back on its haunches, loosed one brick, then two more over one shoulder, before returning to worry at the wound like a carrion bird.

Druid powered forward. Smashing his full weight against the back of the beast, he bound its wrists in one hand, secured its head against his shoulder with the other. His chest rose and fell in rapid bursts. Breath spilled hotly from his lips. He glared down. Beautiful, black eyes turned up to meet his own.

"Jezebel!"

He released the girl and stared in horror as she collapsed forward, grasping at the thin silk scarf about her head and throat. She fought to dredge the air inside her lungs, and, all the while, he stayed motionless; his body packed in ice. His mind was racing though. What the hell was the *Fae* doing in the ruin? Why was she trying to excavate the stairway? His thoughts sidestepped. What explained her expression a split second ago, when she met his gaze with the dark serenity of one who welcomes death. For that instant, he saw such annihilation in those wild, prodigious eyes, and it drew him to her as much as it repelled him.

Recovering, Jezebel drew the back of her hand across her mouth. With a swift glance back, she frowned, the soft creases at her brow betraying her confusion. Then the creases vanished.

"D! You arsehole. Lay a goth-glam hand on me!" She bit the brilliant flesh of her lower lip, and undid her headscarf with fresh ferocity.

For all her hostility, she might as well have been a Skinwalker, Druid mused hollowly. "I thought you were a different breed of burrower," he whispered gruffly; although, when the girl uncovered the rope of a scar at her neck, he drew back, as if to give her the comfort of a greater distance between them. "I came to meet your boy, IQ," he said, adding ruefully, "I didn't expect to find another living soul here, let alone a Fae up to her pretty elbows in brick-dust."

Her red mouth widened, as if amused by an ability to destroy his expectations of her...or in reaction to a different sort of flattery? Either way, the smile melted. "So you thought you'd go for my jugular?"

"I told you. I thought you were out to rob a poor man's grave."

"Not so poor and not so much a man," Jezebel remarked sourly, and once again Druid caught a hint of loathing for the Drathcor. He found her tone disturbing.

Slitting his eyes, he tried to read the truth of her. Where her coat had fallen open, he saw a black mesh décolletage and, below, a boned velvet basque. At each ear dangled a cornucopia of stars, crosses, hearts, and hoops, while the jet crucifix lay in the well of her pale throat. She wore a patched suede micro-mini slung low at her hips like the holster of a gun-slinger. When she stretched, her skirt slipped off one hip, revealing a twice-pierced belly button and the tattoo of a ragged fairy.

Her dress sense was eclectic, he mused, less goth than switchblade street kid, one that attracts rather than collects garments from thrift stores, siblings and the odd benevolent vampire. In isolation, her attire was not so remarkable in Renegade's self-expressive catwalk, except this clotheshorse was a Fae, and *that* fact alone signalled her out as a misfit.

"What are you, Jezebel?" he asked, feeling himself a sliver of dark next to her elfin form. "A Fae who prefers the company of Castclan to her kinfolk?"

The girl swept soot off her raincoat with her palms. She sniffed. "Would that be so unusual?"

"Once upon a time, no. Folk have always been free to befriend, even join a different tribe, whether they're kissing cousins, mother and son, or brother and sister. But winter's bought with it new degrees of frost. Most tribesfolk keep to their kind."

The emerald-winged eyelids swept down. "My kind was happy enough to let me go…" Her voice brightened. "Besides, those boudoir beauties weren't to my taste." She wrinkled her nose.

"So you *drifted* to the Castclan?"

The insult was deliberate. No bona fide Fae would tolerate being compared to the city's more seedy vagrants. But where he had predicted rage, he found only cynicism.

Jezebel laughed darkly. "You're one to talk! Who are *you* anyway, with your air of heart-hard-done-by? It's touching, really, if a little overdone. Buffy Summers's shirtless Angel? Not to mention her peroxide spunkmeister, Spike…after a little soul re-engineering of course. Then there's Louis, Anne Rice's self-flagellating, rat-munching antihero…"

"I thought Lestat was the antihero," Druid said without expression.

Jezebel raised a well-arched eyebrow. "Personally, I'm all for Claudia. Drains the blood of her piano teacher, keeps a corpse as a bedfellow, not to mention her meticulous poisoning of Lestat. Any chick that twisted gets my respect." She sighed and flexed her fingers. "Piano teachers. Pure evil. I digress. Apart from your predilection for the tragi-hero, how the hell did you get *here*?" She threw her arms out by way of illustration, and was transfigured by the Parisian glow that effused the stained glass window.

Druid was thrown off-kilter. Not so long ago, he had seen another silhouette, similarly posed at the gallery to the rose-window…Except that *then* the figure was born of his imagination and easily dissolved. "I haven't the faintest idea," he whispered.

"Don't be soft." Jezebel moved out of the light. "How'd you get in?"

"Same as you, I expect," he mumbled, regaining his senses as the girl resolved into a thing of blood and flesh.

"Over the fence? Who'd have known the pale prince had it in him." Jezebel jerked her head out towards the nave. "Skinwalkers must've been expecting you since they tidied up so nicely."

"What?"

"Sheesh, I take it you haven't set foot in this wreck but even a dirt-bag like you has gotta smell a rat, and a giant-sized rat at that. You think fire tidies up after itself? Someone, or some *thing*, has been playing Mrs Mop down there. Who's swept up the books, D, or the remains of them at least..?" Her chin jutted. "Not so quick with the backchat now."

He indicated loosely to the mess of dislodged rubble. "Judging by that well-packed stairway, even Skinwalkers respect the secrets of the dead." His eyes frosted. "Unlike you."

She swallowed the insult slowly then carefully replied, "I have great respect for the dead. Can't say the same for a percentage of the living."

"Oh, I can *see* that much," Druid glowered, his temper freshly aggravated. A claw thrust at her right wrist. "Storm Navigator; compass, thermometer, LCD display, torch, stainless steel casing, the reverse cut with a letter *D*." His mouth became a twist of iron. "Many things in life are for the taking, Jezebel. The piss out of me isn't one. Nor is my watch."

The Fae's expression was playful. To Druid, infuriated by his failure to protect Roses's crestfallen lair from scavengers, her intention was to mock him. He grabbed for her wrist.

"What the hell...get off me, psycho!"

As the girl tried to wiggle free, Druid tightened his grip. A tiny gasp escaped her lips, and he released her that instant, perplexed, wounded even, by the idea he had inflicted real pain.

"Jezebel. I didn't mean..." He edged closer, tried to read her body language. Head down, her face was hidden by the razored slices of her fringe.

"Bastard."

A swift blow to his windpipe sent him reeling. Like a television thumbed off then on, his world faded to black then fired up seconds later. The ground rushed up to meet him then dropped away again, and with a faint sense of sickness, he realised he had folded forward over the tarnished railing. Aware of a small movement at his side, he strained to breathe. The air tore at his throat.

"Just had to ask me for it," bit the girl beneath her breath. "Thought you wouldn't mind the lend, idiot that I am."

"Jezebel," he whispered hoarsely. Out the corner of his eye, he saw her twist a hand around and up at the bottom of her spine. He felt a breeze off some swift mechanical action.

Something black and leathered blocked his view of her. The air stirred; he dipped his head, forced his hips back from the rail, and, at last, glanced up...straight into the eye of the taut slingshot.

Jezebel hovered a foot or so the other side of the rail.

"Nothing new to say," she jeered. "Nothing sweet? Nothing good?" Tall, tattered wings turned cartwheels at her shoulders, mixing up a dust storm.

Druid noticed how her hands trembled to keep the slingshot tensed. He focused in on her short, white fingernails, how they dipped in and out of shadow as the ragged sails revolved. Then he heard an engine's splutter. Launching himself hard against the rail, he caught the whip of the sling against his ear, embraced her in his arms; felt her body slip against him.

"Hold on," he demanded. "Hold onto me."

His stomach churned as she fought against him, more so when her wings turned sluggish then quickly froze. In the fragile instant between flight and falling, their eyes locked. Her brilliant, black globes overflowed with a sweet, electric honesty. Seconds later, his arms enfolded nothingness.

Mr. Oliver Denizel, consultant, accepted the blood-stained business card as it was offered.

"I got *that* from the inside pocket of his leather."

"He was found on the outskirts of Renegade City, you say?"

The paramedic nodded. "Just shy of Gedling, in Colwick Country Park." Staring down at the mess of fur and flesh that lay huddled like a dead bear-cub in the nook of the hospital bed, and which had already soiled the crisp, white linen with its part-stripped, filthy limbs, the man grimaced. "Lost a good few pints of blood to that grassland. Ask me, he was dropped there. No sign of a struggle at the scene, and some of these wounds don't look so fresh."

Flat, white eyes scanned the card. "You think someone..." The doctor lowered his finely-boned hand and let his gaze rest on the patient. "...abandoned him?"

"Or else they were disturbed. Seems more than just coincidence he was found so close to the city lines."

"Indeed." Hand to his breast, Mr. Denizel reached for the water jug and plastic beaker allocated to the bedside cabinet, poured himself a draft and sipped the fluid slowly. The moisture in his eyes ebbed. "Well, I didn't expect to see *this* specimen again so soon."

"You know him?"

"He was here yesterday, as well as a dozen or so walking wounded. I've no doubt he and his fellow rioters had been embroiled in some test of nerve, or fresh violence against the city. And then they come to us to heal them..." The doctor arched a fine, translucent eyebrow. Like silk spooling over a marble floor, he started to slip away.

"Aren't you going to examine him, Mr. Denizel?" said the paramedic with a look of subtle confusion.

"I'm sure my colleague, Mr. Goldin, will have him restored and ripe to plunder again in next to no time." With a flick of a fleshless hand, the DarkLed was already drifting away again.

"Mr. Goldin's secretary has been messaging your PDA ever since the patient was bought in," the paramedic called out after the doctor as forcefully as he dared. "The wound concerning Mr. Goldin the most is one that requires a more...cosmetic approach. It's, erm..." Here the man struggled, as if replaying some image in his head that he found both astonishing and unpleasant. "The patient has been victimised," he blurted. Mr. Denizel halted in his stride. With a sharp glance at the door of the cubicle, the paramedic added, "The Skinwalkers' brand...it's in a very strange place."

"Victimised?" The doctor turned about in a whisper of soft movement. He drifted back over to the bed, made a quick scan of the prostrate beast and fixated on the dark encrusted bloom at the base of the spine. "Or, to some minds, purified."

Distracted by a sharp burst of laughter from the corridor, the paramedic checked his watch. "What's that, Mr. Denizel?"

"Frederick, I'm keeping you from your break. As for my PDA, I have to admit to ignoring that blasted little silver rat of a machine this last half-hour. But I am here now." Raising the blood-stained card up into the light, narrowing his white, inexpressive eyes, the doctor nodded. "I'll take care of the patient at this juncture."

With patent relief, the paramedic started to head out. "I'm leaving you in good hands, friend," he directed towards the bed. Then he grasped the vertical silver strip of a door handle, swished it open and disappeared into the corridor.

The door closed with a soft breath of air. Mr. Denizel slacked the fabric of his pants at the thighs and knelt down at one side of the bed. As the beast slept, hurried rushes of air jittered at bruised lips. The older man reached in to brush a wisp of tangled hair back from its sweated forehead.

Two wild, black eyes fixed brilliantly upon him.

"Hello Harish," said the doctor.

Jezebel opened one eye, hoping to see stars. Instead she struggled with a blur of half-tangibles. She found a face, felt the sensation of an icy hand closing over hers...and then dived back below the surface. Her mind kaleidoscoped; millions of colours bled one into the next until a deeper darkness held her. And now she was floating, like a child buoyed up by armbands, and in the same way a child senses their mother's arms as a circle of safety, she knew herself concurrently embraced.

"Who are you?" she asked. "Friend? Foe? A brother?"

The voice answered her softly.

"The bastard."

Her eyes snapped wide. Straining an arm, a leg, she bucked against his body, kicking out with anything that might help her push off the ground.

Strong arms held her. "Don't fight me, you idiot. You might be hurt. Shhh. Shhh now."

She wanted to be free of him, free of the nearness of this stranger who had struck at her twice this last hour, free of the scent of worn, smoky masculinity as his leathered sleeves enfolded her. It was all she could do to shake away his hand as it tried to close over hers again.

His lips breezed dangerously against her cheek. "Be still," he whispered.

It was difficult to decide which hurt the more; bruises to her bones or the bittersweet warmth that flooded her flesh as the forceful arms enfolded her.

"You lied," she muttered after several minutes had passed.

"About?" His voice was low and easy.

"Your heart. Same as last night, I can feel it beating good and loud beneath your ribs. Veritable boom-box."

"Aha."

His chest trembled against her back, suggesting he was laughing. Surreptitiously, she moved to escape his arms. At first, she sensed reluctance, then a rush of air between them

She went to stand and fell back. "Lords, my head."

"Quite a fall. You look okay though. I'm afraid I can't say the same for your wings."

"What?" She fingered the mess of wires and ragged fabric at her back. "Shit."

"Hell's bells, Jezebel!"

Glancing up, she saw the wizard kid dash the length of the nave, slide onto his bum and arrive at her side.

"You okay, babe?" IQ's face was lit by two pools of brilliant green. "What happened?"

Relieved, or oddly annoyed by the kid's arrival, she snapped, "Poxy wings! Thought you'd fixed them." She regretted her words the instant they escaped her lips. The boy gulped, then stared down at the floor. "I didn't mean that, Irvine. Lords only know how Fae ever managed to design these crazy mechanics. I've never met one could work a false eyelash let alone engineer a pair of human wings."

"The first Fae came from Australia," said D. "For the first few years, the tribe was more bohemian than boudoir. Their wings were the result of years of detailed study. But you'd know all that, of course."

"Erm, hello?" Jezebel pushed herself around on the cold, damp floor to sit cross-legged. "And how'd you know so much, our international man of mystery?"

"D's a historian," IQ intercepted.

Jezebel caught a flicker of amusement at the Drathy's too pale lips.

"It's true to say I document the truth," he replied.

"That so?" With a childish scowl, Jezebel tried to piece together the man seated opposite. He was interesting; not conventionally handsome, but fascinating because he was unconventional. His body was a slip of bloodless pale while the clothes he wore were grave goods; scarlet jeans cut from plush, ankh-patterned brocade, and a dress shirt of black raw silk that appeared to rest, a little stiffly, off his skin. His eyes, meanwhile, were kept captive behind a pair of sharp, black shades.

She glanced at the leather he not so much wore as kept for company, saw the tail end of an intricate tattoo exposed at a rising coat sleeve. There was something comforting in the suggested scale of that design, a bad-boy-bad-girl affinity, not to mention a fearless decision to look that way for life. Jezebel almost smiled; one thing she couldn't stand was a man who played at things, who wore a single sleeper to D's six silver crosses, or whose back boasted an elusive, inch square Chinese symbol where D bore a tapestry of dream-work. No, D was the real deal, she decided, and dangerously so.

His hands tensed, the fingers drawn neatly and instantly together like an oriental puzzle box. She realised he watched her in return and, inadvertently, touched a finger to her scar. "The truth about what?" she asked, a little unnerved.

"Renegade City of course. Great spinning space this!" prattled the boy, changing the subject as he raised his arms out from his sides and twirled. "You should try this, D. Give you a head-rush." He stopped suddenly, his arms wrapping round over one hip. "But not you, Jez. You've had more than enough excitement for one week."

"Really?" The man knelt up on one knee. He directed his head off into the dark crevices of the room then bought his shadowed gaze back front. "Guess that's why your wrist's bleeding," he added unexpectedly.

"He's right, Jez! Look at your wrist, mate."

"What?" A mess of sticky red oozed either side the wristwatch strap. She sucked air between her teeth and realised how damn lucky she was that only her wings got smashed by the fall. "Here." She unlatched the watch, offered it. "I borrowed it to protect my wrist 'til I got to Queenie's and had her dress the wound."

The kid slapped his forehead with the flat of a palm. She tried to appease him. "I *did* mean to get it seen to. Its just I really wanted some answers first." The combination of pain and frustration became too much to bear. "I just needed to know," she blurted.

"Know what?" D's attention shifted to the shadows around them. Refocusing, he fixed intently on the watch, but didn't reach for it.

He posed a key question, Jezebel realised heavy-heartedly. What exactly was it that drove her to pursue a brother who had displayed such savage disinclination to be rescued. Serendipity? Self-righteous suicide? *Love?* She felt nerves starburst in the pit of her stomach. Harish was her kin, and her foundation. He was also her beacon of hope in Renegade's queer dystopia and the cold world beyond.

She tried to formulate a response. "Erm..." The ache at her wrist made it hard to concentrate. She was also loath to share any aspect of her personal history with a man who had attacked her twice in one day. And yet she understood his motives. Indignation and pride were sentiments she recognised only too well. "I wanted to know what was kept in those areas of the watchtower which were hidden away from the general public," she stated, and thrust a short, white fingernail at the rose-window. "By my reckoning, that staircase leads to the upper battlements and, probably, the private quarters. I was forced to escape in that direction last night," she added offhandedly. "Although I had to fly once I found the stairwell blocked. That's why I wanted to come back here in the daylight."

Her face faltered. It was an effort to maintain the bravado when all she wanted to do was break down and scream: *My brother, the only thing that ever made sense in all the madness, is out there somewhere and I need him to make the pain stop.* She dropped her hand like a stone. "Skinwalkers barricaded the stairway, IQ. Doesn't that suggest there's something worth hiding?"

"Why don't you just *fly* up the outside of the tower and take a look yourself?" said D dryly.

Jezebel suffered his cold, inviting scrutiny. She fought to shake the crushed wings down off her back. "This pair of fancy flight aids have, what you might call, a technical fault. Now and then, the motor goes ker-plunk and, hell, I'm no kill joy but I'm loathe to dice with death on more than a once weekly arrangement."

D's lips flickered, in a bid to suppress his amusement perhaps, or was it derision? "And did you dice with death, Jezebel?" His tone betrayed neither.

"Damn right she did," interjected IQ, pulling at the back of his baggy jeans as if to hoist his indignation higher. "As a *neutral* observer, D, I think you'll agree when I say she's a loon surviving on a diet of loon juice on the isle of Loopy Loon." The boy raised his brows meaningfully. "Crawls into a live den of Skinwalkers on a full moon no less."

"That is...loony," said D quietly. Jezebel felt her cheeks flush. As his gaze chased in and out the shadows again, he murmured, "It does depend on your logic though. In some ways, it was a smart move. Catch the enemy off guard."

"Except they caught her first."

The boy ducked as Jezebel's hand grazed the top of his head.

"I missed your sorry ass when the shit came down," she spat, wanting to cut out the kid's loose tongue and wear it as a dog tag. "Tell D the history of our agreement, did you? *'I'll track him, Jez. I know the right, or, is that, the wrong people to ask. Leave it to me, Jez.'*" She threw up her hands. Yes, the Quirks were the closest thing she had to family in Harish's absence, but her very connection to them was a constant reminder of how she and Harish had once lived as life's gypsies, united by a common distrust of everyone else. In time, Harish had fallen in love with Desdemona, and she had allowed herself to feel a sort of flighty belonging among Queenie and her clan. But nothing made up for the fact that Harish had deserted her to a world full of strangers, or that IQ had vowed to return that lost wolf to the fold and failed to do so. "Sheesh, you wanna know the real truth of things, D?" She struggled to keep her voice from cracking. "My brother would be pushing up the daisies if I left things up to Irvine."

"IQ's helping you track down your brother?" D glared at the boy. His claws arched into two crude weapons.

Touched, or shocked, by his cruel instincts, she reined in her need to shift the blame and added quickly, "Irvine didn't find my brother. I did. You might say Irvine rescinded on his bargain then, but innocently so." Taking up the thin, black scarf that trailed loosely at her neck, she dabbed sullenly at her wrist.

"That's interesting." D's upper lip curled. "Isn't it, IQ? I don't think our previous discussion covered that circumstance. A happy ending. How'd you win out then?"

The kid's luminous green eyes found an edge. "Who said anything about a happy ending? Happy endings don't sink their teeth into your flesh and leave your ass bleeding."

Jezebel was ablaze with white hot anger. Harish could hardly be blamed for reacting on instincts that were integral to his true self, or for his being bewitched by the wild underworld inhabited by the Skinwalkers. Moreover, after he had lashed out at her the first time, Harish had run as hard as he could the other way, abandoning sister, bride and unborn child, albeit unwittingly in the case of the latter. And this was why she *had* to track him down, no matter how many times he acted the role of rabid beast. Whether his leaving translated as an act of noble self-sacrifice, or a giving in to the animalistic side of his persona, Harish still had a right to know he was soon to be a father, and she had a right to bring him home. "Screw you, Irvine!" she hissed. "Gonna share my shit with any fool who'll listen? Not to mention the fact I left *his* ass bleeding."

"Hate to contradict you, Jez, but you're the one started blabbing. Lucky for you, I know that D here's the trustworthy sort."

"Any fool?" said D, turning to face her fully. Jezebel could have sworn there was hurt in his voice. It unsettled her, mixing as it did with her inner grief and fury.

"There's something else," she said reticently. "Before his claws got trigger-happy, Harish half-whispered, half-mouthed up at me something that sounded like 'angels watch'."

"Seems that a rep for pilfering timepieces precedes you," D teased lightly.

"Or there's something in the gossip of drifters after all." IQ met Jezebel's desolate expression, tried to temper it with a soft smile. "Just some new Big Bad in town; nickname's the Angel."

"Meaning what?" snapped D, as if this fresh twist added another weighted layer to his own.

Jezebel shrugged. "Meaning this story's only just beginning."

"Too right!" said the kid, brightening with a playful wink. "So whether we're talking devils, angels, or wee kilted kelpies, perhaps we can get down to the real business of catching ourselves a killer. Yeah, a killer, Jez," he reiterated as her features darkened. "I figure you're the sort to help us fix this puzzle. So strap that scarf tight about your wrist. It'll do for a band-aid until we get you back to Queenie's."

Putting his small, brown hands on his hips, IQ tossed the limp end of his wizard hat back over one shoulder and declared, "Now then, D, what you got for me?"

Chapter 8

All Along the Watchtower

Overhead, white-gold, dusty light pierced the torn mantle of a hall that soared away, grandiose and sadly beautiful. Lofty piers acted as sentinels to the whale's ribs of the vaults. Both side aisles were lined with tall, boarded windows. Druid's gaze returned to the nave and a central aisle strewn with the fixed relics of mouldered shelves, the meat-hooks of brackets embedded in each filthy wall, bookcases lazing off their hinges like drunks off lampposts, and monoliths, floridly inscribed with such majestic labels as *Green Magick*, *Musicology*, *History of The Tribes*, *Folk Law*, and *Drathcor and Other Deities*. The mildewed spoils of many hundreds of thousands of books had been swept to one side to form a soft hill of soot at the base of one of the vast stone columns. Deserting the others, Druid walked past the dust of words to the pulpit: a reading desk carved in a spine of bony segments and from some material that looked like ebony, but might have been redwood or oak below the grime. The lectern held the cast of an open book. He dared a finger to the surface. It melted at his touch.

Druid turned away. Like the disintegrating stock of the once Great Library, he realised all his precious documents amounted to little more than refuse from a defunct golden age; song lyrics scribbled in a notepad, an order for Chinese food pencilled on the reverse of a scrap envelope, handwritten scrawls, bills, flyers, a spider-shaped spell book... Nothing of real substance, he glowered, and, from the large pile marked as rejected, IQ agreed with him.

A handful of papers did hold the boy's interest though; one item in particular. "Soz I haven't been more vigilant, Jez," said the kid in the same quiet voice he'd adopted the previous night, when he had told a man who feared the sun to step out of the dark. He offered a singed scrap to the girl. "I do make it my mission to hunt the inner truth though."

Jezebel crouched, one arm scooped about her knees, the other reaching for what appeared to be a business card, delicately, as if it were the wings of a butterfly.

Druid's gaze shifted to the girl. He put the tip of his tongue to his left incisor. It was difficult not to like her, he mused. Like a lemon, halved and squeezed over the tongue, she cleansed his palate of the grease of anonymous groupies. His eyes navigated a lazy path to her collarbone. He traced the scar, was angered by its interruption of her flesh. Yet, it also intimated vulnerability, and *that* he found intoxicating. Little wonder a different beast had tried to take a taste.

Jezebel turned the card over. She stroked it with the shell of a fingernail.

"Something wrong?" Druid moved up to her shoulder.

"What?" Glancing up, she looked ever so faintly confused. Her eyes returned to the card. "No, nothing's wrong." Her finger traced what was written there: *'Harry Geronimo – Discreet and willing donor of the blood type 'AB'.* "Just thinking about the old life, you know, before Roses went to ground. It's sad." She threw her head back, sighed quietly, then tossed the card back to IQ. "It's also unforgivable."

The change in her tone was puzzling. "You find a Drathcor's death unforgivable?" said Druid softly.

Her response left him reeling.

"Sheesh, no! Best thing that devil ever did was go and die on us."

He liked her less then, would have slashed his claws across her spiteful face had his basic humanity not prevented him from doing so. "You knew Roses personally, of course." The childish retort was the best he could manage.

"Never laid eyes on the great 'I am', or any of his brood. They took to the skies way before my time. But it doesn't stop me living in their shadow. I hate to get into the politics of it, specially with a Drathy, but tell me this much, D. If our deities are so goth-damn benevolent, how come they created a city that fosters apartheid? How come, having done exactly that, they sit back and observe us from the sanitised distance of their watchtowers, like we're freakin' mice in a lab? Ask me, I'm surprised they got away with it so long. Would've thought some freak would have taken a pot-shot way before now. Stop interrupting, IQ!" she hissed, shushing him with a hand. "Oh, don't look so prissy. We've agreed on it a thousand times. No, what I find *unforgivable* is how Origin created a society where the misfit is the norm, but—and this really is the killer—the notion of an all-knowing, all-seeing government stayed unchanged."

She stretched out her arms to bathe in the rosy glow of mid afternoon, then fixed her eyes hard on Druid. "How do *you* define an outcast, D? Isn't the common definition someone who exists outside the norm, thanks to choice, fate or fortune? Example: Skinwalkers. To the everyday citizen, they are the untouchables, and, yeah, they may not be the most moral mongrels. But dig below the filth and fur, and they're still men...."

"Wrong!" Druid steepled his jet-black claws. "They are hired thugs for sale. What do they care for acceptance or any form of practical society? Skinwalkers have one motivation: anarchy."

"And yet they're organised enough to bring a broom and barricade a stairwell."

"Skinwalkers cleaning up after themselves?" IQ pulled at his chin as if an imaginary beard grew there. "Perverse, man."

Druid ignored the boy. Instead, he was wholly enraged by Jezebel. "So you think Skinwalkers joined the intelligentsia overnight?"

"Not overnight..." Jezebel threw up her hands. "I don't know where you've been hiding these last few months, D, but any fool can see Skinwalkers are evolving."

"Fool again, hey?" Druid stared out at her from under hooded lids. "Careful, *Jez,* I'll get a complex."

The girl seemed to catch her breath for a second. "Look. Skinwalkers are running riot these nights, whether the moon's full or not," she answered hurriedly. "No one can dispute they're getting organised. Something's changed, and I don't mean their opting to sanitise this hellhole. Something's giving them direction. Something's leading them."

"Or someone?" Remembering their earlier talk of a new, furtive foe called the Angel, Druid softened the hard angles of his jaw. It wasn't such a far out notion. "I'll admit to being taken aback that they went to the bother of tracking you to Legacy last night. It seemed a lot of hassle to go to for one curious little girl."

Jezebel's chin jutted. "I did mow down a good dozen of the brutes," she said defensively.

"All the same." Druid wore a half-twist of a smile. "You're hardly the Chinese Mafia. Would've made far more sense for them to lay low, stretch out the feelers, then strike in a far less *public...*" He broke off suddenly. There it was again; a fluctuation in the air's movement, a solidity to shadow, a sense of being watched. His features took on a darker, aquiline form. "Time to go," he whispered.

"Go?" The girl ground her hands onto the angles of her hips. "No chance. I've got a date with Messrs Brick and Dust at a certain stairwell."

He threw a claw towards IQ. "You got a cell?"

The question seemed to throw the boy, and it was Jezebel who dug her fingers into a side pocket of his low-slung jeans, retrieved the slim, black Nokia and tossed it over.

Druid punched in a string of digits. His gaze flicked up. "You call me if those scraps turn anything up." He threw the cellphone to IQ, who caught it awkwardly. "I'll be waiting."

"Whooah, mate." IQ gazed at the piece of plastic in his palm as if it had been alchemised into gold. "You've never gone and given me *your* personal cell number?"

"What's so great about that?" Jezebel stared at the boy in blind incredulity.

"Nothing...nothing at all," IQ backtracked, and, almost as if he had latched on to the same extrasensory intuition as the Drathcor, his green eyes made a circuit of the nave. "But what would be *great* would be getting the hell out of here. Daylight's fading. Before you can say 'String me up by my innards and feed me to Beelzebub', those outsized furballs will be yapping at that door." His brilliant eyes indicated off to the exit at the opposite end of the nave. "What say we scat?"

The girl seemed torn. She threw a glance up at the rose-window, then out to the square of dark at the far wall.

Druid straightened his spine. "The private quarters aren't going anywhere, or the stairs leading up to them." His shaded eyes pinioned her. "Ask me, the answer you seek isn't kept in a burnt-out ruin anyway. It's made of fur and flesh and it's out there in the ice. We'll find him, Jezebel," he added with a level of sincerity he himself found unexpected. "But not this hour...and not *here*."

As if sensing the wisdom in his words—in particular, that it made little sense to stay and wage war in a shadow maze—

Jezebel stooped, gathered her wings off the damp, oily floor and tucked their remains underneath an arm.

IQ held out his hands, palms uppermost. "Give them here, Jez. Can't promise nothing. Ask me, it would be simpler to get yourself to Sneinton, peruse the wares of the wing vendors, pick yourself out a nice, new, *reliable* set."

"Got to find ways to keep a kid like you busy and off the streets though, don't I?" Jezebel offloaded the broken wings on the boy. Following in his swift footsteps, she moved to the exit and disappeared through the doorway, only to stick her head back out a few seconds later. "Shall we?"

"You guys go on," Druid said softly. His back to her, he stared at the iced strait of flagstones between the two towering landmasses of stone columns, let his gaze lift to the fiery votive of the rose-window. "I just want a minute to pay my respects to our saviour."

"Whatever." With a sniff of irritation, Jezebel dissolved from the room.

Alone at last, Druid walked slowly to the centre of the room, slid his hands into his leather's pockets, then crooked his head to peer into the void of a side aisle.

"Come out, come out, whoever you are," he growled.

The figure stepped into the light with a theatrical flourish.

"Adeudas." Druid dragged his tongue off the roof of his mouth with a dry tut-tut. "Thought I sensed some monster lurking in the dark."

"Rather than reduce myself to a pile of dust in the light, hmmm?" Sallying forward, his fellow Drathcor laid one arm across his chest and the opposite hand to his throat, an effete gesture in wild contrast to his height and taut, muscular frame. "Isn't your sacrifice enough?"

Adeudas's lips crept apart into a smile. Easing a black patched suede cape off his shoulders, he directed a neon-pink claw about the ruin. "Well now, hasn't *this* place improved? And so what if it's still a little on the shabby side. We're all capable of avoiding housework, especially if one's mind is on other things—a secondment perhaps, or maybe a vacation, hmmm?"

In one long, easy step, he closed the gap between them. Druid forced himself not to flinch as a garish claw skimmed his left cheek.

The man's smile broadened. "It's not unusual to find oneself thrown a tad off balance." He waved a hand limply back and forth. "A fish flip-flapping out of water."

The sweet perfume of an Ice Garden cocktail floated over the inch of atmosphere separating them, alongside the burnt-paper aroma of a hand-rolled cigarette, scents so integral to his once wild life that they stirred in Druid the most intoxicating memories: laughter, high, fine, and melting on the tongue, kisses, open-mouthed and revelatory, from a sea of pretty lips, his mouth, trickling Jack into the hollow of a navel, or pressed to one supplicant wrist while his blood-brother took up then bit the other...

Their eyes locked. Druid felt the shell he'd developed over the last few hours erode away. Other than Sophia, no one else alive knew him like Adeudas. Long, lean and draped in yellow velvet, those legs had straddled the bull of a Marshal amp for many a performance. He'd felt those pale hands drape his shoulder for numerous encores, consumed after-show beer after beer while vivid claws braided his hair. And, yes, he'd dipped a jug to wash away an ocean of peroxide, crushed straightening irons to that scalp to spike the natural curls there, seen the true blue behind the sparkling, lilac contact lenses. But, for all of Adeudas's secrets, nothing compared to the ones *he* kept hidden.

He made black rosebuds of his claws. "What are you doing here?"

Adeudas absent-mindedly stroked the plush velvet at his chest. "Ah, Druid, how kind you are to take an interest. Since you ask so nicely, I was reacquainting myself with those loved and lost at Rock Cemetery when I felt drawn to this dark spot. I had meant to pay my respects at the site where Roses breathed His last, but then found I wasn't in fact alone. The only honourable thing to do was stay incognito, except..." He placed a hand on a jutting hip. The halo of each iris flamed blue and violet, "Instead of paying homage to our highest lord, I find you and your merry band of misfits talking a whole lot of bull."

A cat in black and yellow skin, Adeudas looked like he might pounce. He swiftly turned away. "But let us not talk falsely now. The hour's getting late. These walls may be disintegrating but they still have eyes...and claws and tongues and teeth. This is a dangerous haunt, especially when the sun is setting, and yes, the Skinwalkers are busying themselves with flooding Forest Field, but their patrols are ever vigilant."

"Flooding Forest Field?" Druid narrowed his eyes. The statement piqued his interest.

"They require a fair acreage of ice to set up on. But the canals are of limited girth. They are also heavily populated by a splurge of Trawler vessels trapped in the ice. So, as I hear it, the hirsute rascals, shall we say, *commandeered* a pair of fire engines, hooked up the big guns and let rip with several thousand gallons of the city's mains water supply. The Grallators weren't best pleased, but the Skinwalkers only assisted in the creation of a semi-natural ice plane, and the perfect sparring ground for their event," Adeudas clarified with an air of nonchalance.

"Event? What event?"

Easing the gypsied cloak back about his shoulders, the vamp started to shepherd Druid towards the doorway. "We can talk more in the car," he said lightly.

Druid rotated his face on a stiff axis.

"It's getting dark." Adeudas placed a fatherly hand on his shoulder. "This is hardly the most salubrious neighbourhood. My driver's waiting on the street." His amethyst eyes twinkled. "Take a ride with me, my pale wanderer...for old times' sake?"

Druid rested a hand against the door's grimed surface. He stared into the tunnel, black as pitch and festering with the stench of the beast, and felt a leaden sense of compliance. No matter how apart he felt from the bloodless brother at his side, or how much he despised being spied upon, Adeudas was right in one respect. It was dusk. Skinwalkers were coming.

He stepped into the dark.

The black Chrysler 300c slipped through the derelict streets, super-sized grille bared, every iron muscle flexed. Eased into the rear seat of the sedan's satin cockpit, Druid was just conscious of its solid motion. The bulk of his attention, however, was on the hellish realm beyond the window.

"Repugnant, isn't it?"

Ignoring the sly creature opposite, Druid found his mind on a different journey. Three months ago, he'd selected one of the dozen or so unmarked cars in the regal fleet and negotiated the streets surrounding the ruin. Why? He couldn't answer that. Perhaps it served as a sort of a purification rite; or was it more of a face-off? Either way, nothing had prepared him for the sight of the south watchtower, weeping soot as the steam rose in filthy plumes off its groaning shoulders. And yet, in spite of that, the neighbourhood seemed to battle on.

Druid massaged his brow with the flat of a palm. It felt like only yesterday that crisp, black awnings had sheltered the storefronts, folk had repaired their smoke-damaged premises in quiet reverence, and the Grallators had worked to erect a steel mesh fence around the ruin's perimeter, an order of respect that had struck him as blatantly unnecessary; no self-respecting citizen came within a hundred yards of the place. Even the tourists had stayed safely entombed in their cars and coaches, as if to enter the immediate vicinity of the rotting watchtower would be to infect themselves with its decay.

But something had left its mark since his last visit. Now the locality resembled less a salvage float than a necropolis. Everywhere he looked, the street was peeling away from itself. Supporting walls, broken slates, bits of rain-soaked wallpaper, snapped curtain rods, sodden drapes and drains; all came tumbling out towards him like heartache, like a city weeping. Druid shivered involuntarily. He tucked his chin in to his chest.

"Admiring the view?" interrupted Adeudas from across the neo-thirties cabin. "Personally, I'll take beauty any day over this more ascetic affair," he whispered as if disclosing a dirty secret.

"What's the use of beauty if the flesh that lies beneath is rotten?" Druid tore his gaze from the glass.

"None, except it does soothe the mind and rest the spirit," replied the other gent, catching the eye of his driver in the rear mirror. He winked at the pretty dead girl. "But how superfluous it must seem when one is inclined towards more intellectual excess." A pale hand wafted towards the spot above the inner breast-pocket of Druid's leather. "*Tales from Renegade City?*" Leaning forward in his seat, he toyed with the translucent flesh at the back of the DarkLed's neck, and playfully confided, "His brother was the same. Always keen to legalise our secrets."

Adeudas flashed his more reticent colleague a glossy smile. When Druid gave no discernible reaction, he sniffed, produced a polka-dot handkerchief, and dabbed affectedly at

119

his nose. "Although, recent events would seem to suggest that bookish pursuits are passé." His gaze slanted. "Private investigation, it seems, is the new philosophy."

Druid grunted. Adeudas's barbed wit was mildly amusing to him. But when he rested the side of his face against the cooling sheet of glass, his head still pulsed. It was hard to engage in word games when his mind crawled with riddles: last night's dream, the adroit wizard kid, the haunting Fae, the cryptogram of Roses's death, and an odd, if intractable idea that the trail began with Skinwalkers.

He forced a reply. "I like to keep abreast of current events."

"So I've been led to understand," said Adeudas, and seemingly with the same dry indifference he'd displayed in Druid's dream. But then he fixed Druid with his synthetic, lilac gaze.

"And how is Sophia?" he asked sunnily. "I'm afraid it's nearly a month since I last beheld our darling girl. She was haunting the zenith of the east watchtower—I'm sure she cut an enchanting silhouette. Eyes large as saucers; heart stemmed by frozen tears." The vamp made a great show of peeping over his shoulder, then leant in by Druid's ear. "Word has it, guilt stops her from thawing."

"Guilt?" Druid felt his amusement fade. Yes, he'd harboured that same mistrust of Sophia just a day or two ago, still did perhaps. But he was also intrigued by her claim of innocence, enough to flee the north watchtower like a rat piped to the tune of her enigma. That said, he was determined to keep his darker instincts under wraps and his eyes wide open when it came to Renegade's ice queen, for the simple reason that, even if he did out a further villain of the piece, it didn't mean he found her innocent by proxy.

He was consistent, nonetheless, in his hatred of gossip-mongering. "I take it you're referring to the Chinese whispers of the Management." With a fresh reflux of revulsion, he pictured the guts of Council House reduced to an acerbic melting pot of self-interest by ranks of snow-white robed dignitaries; political heavyweights, gleaned from each of the city's four key tribes and elected less for their interest in the city's general welfare than for their shameless intertribal bias. "Since when did you pay any heed to *their* findings?" he shot, a little moodily.

Adeudas twisted the peroxide spikes at his crown. "Oh, Druid, how you make me smile!" He jerked back his lips to reveal two unnaturally sharp incisors. "Those perfect pussies? I couldn't give a flying fig. But rumours, they're a different circumstance. Every whiff of make-believe has its *origins* in fact. Which is why it concerns me to see you adding fuel to their fire."

Eyes darkening to violet, his chin jutted towards the glass. "Hardly the safest place for a flawed immortal."

"Apparently I'm not the only night owl likes to venture beyond the nest."

"Too true," conceded the other man with a pout. "It seems we all need to get out and stretch our legs now and then, dust off the old cobwebs." The smile transmogrified into a snarl. "But we don't all resort to playing Tomb Raider with the first waif and stray we come across. Such tales, my pale wanderer! Lost brothers, a quest to infiltrate the upper quarters of the south watchtower, not to mention the Great Escape from Skinwalkers, unscathed..."

"Hardly unscathed," snapped Druid with an edge of irritation. "The flesh at her wrist was shredded."

"But by whom, my darling boy?" Adeudas let his head fall back onto the beige and grey bolster. "My gorgeous tribe, the Fae, are inexhaustibly beguiling, but if they've homed in on any of *my* less honourable traits, it's an ability to woo without mind of consequence. It's in their nature; quick to lie, quick to seduce. Add in the frailty of women and, well..." The perfect plasticity of his face softened. His head lolled towards Druid. "We are, neither of us, immune to their impropriety."

Ice-cold fingers slipped around the back of his neck and Druid interwove them with his own. With his free hand, he slipped off his shades, folded them then fed them into his leather's upper left pocket. "Maybe you're right, Das." His strange, pale eyes stared into the face that over recent months had come to represent not so much a stranger as an apathetic fiend. Why was that, he wondered, something as fickle as his own jealousy? Certainly, as he slunk in from abroad to find his world aflame, it was Adeudas who took the heat, who wooed the Management, who spoke a mystic mass for the mourners, who came to him with scraps of paper salvaged from the wreck of the south watchtower and told him to write His life story *so the tribes might find religion.* Wise words from a man who stayed picture-perfect as Belief began to fester; and all the while he, Druid, drained away until there was nothing left but a slip of skin.

"I only seek to protect you, my blood-brother," said the vamp into his hair.

"And I only seek the truth."

Adeudas shoved him away. "Whose truth? Yours or Sophia's? Heaven in hell, Druid, isn't it time you revised the level of her influence?" Tearing at his cloak's fringing, he pressed back into the far corner of the seat, pouting, "What dastardly deeds does she claim to have unearthed this time?"

"She speaks of murder."

"Murder!" Adeudas raised his eyebrows. "What do you make of that, Dorothy? A blue-blood put to the knife, or should I say, the matchstick? How sensationally macabre."

"Do you have to share every word with your tramp?" Druid hissed, his claws breaking apart.

"Now don't throw sticks and stones unless you welcome broken bones. Dorothy's my driver," Adeudas chastised with a wagging finger. But his serious tone soon gave way to playfulness. "She's also a tasty little minx: B-negative—your favourite flavour as I recall."

Druid glared at the profile of the beautiful ghoul in the driving seat. "I'm fussier with my food these days," he snarled.

"Ah, now, my high lord, you know better than to dis our esteemed donors, whose numbers are, I'm sorry to say, sorrowfully depleted. Why is that, Dorothy?" the vamp demanded suddenly, and with a violence that far outstripped Druid's.

The driver coughed delicately against the back of a manicured hand. Inclining her skull to one side, she spoke in a voice that was high and almost nasal. "Most of your willing victims fear reprisals from those who say the Drathcor are no longer free to feast as they please," she told them haughtily. "They say the queen drowns in denial. They say the city is disintegrating. They say…" Hesitant, the girl refocused on the icy track of road.

Sidling forward, Adeudas ran a claw along her prominent collarbone. "Continue."

"The old ways will be rewritten and the old ones written out," the DarkLed answered crisply.

"Hand." It was a command, not a request.

The girl responded instantly, prising one set of fingers off the wheel and crooking her wrist to the side of her headrest at an awkward angle.

"Fools' tales, even if they are becoming too commonplace for my taste." The high lord bent to press a kiss to the base of the other's thumb.

"Ouch," whinged the girl affectedly. She drew back her hand, replaced it on the wheel.

Adeudas collected a bead of scarlet from his lips with the hook of a finger. He snaked his tongue over the blood. "Oh, Druid, why don't we put aside our childish follies and take comfort in more salacious matters?" he purred.

"I am most content for *you* to do so." Druid stabbed a finger at the front seat, a sliver of anger shining in each pupil. "Just leave the nasty to the bedroom. I haven't the stomach for it."

Unusually, Adeudas seemed to be listening. He nodded slowly. "Stop the car, Dorothy."

"High lord?"

"I don't care to repeat myself."

The sedan curved over to the pavement. Dorothy cut the engine.

With his gaze locked on Druid, Adeudas waved the girl away. "Wait outside, or run back to your mistress, I don't care either way."

"Mistress?" Effulgent, grey eyes betrayed a fresh nervousness.

"Oh, let's not play games, Dorothy. I'm talking about Sophia. I'm sure your pretty lips are quite a-quiver to spill our every secret."

"Not I, my high lord…"

"Go!"

With sulky obedience, the driver adjusted her slim pencil skirt, thumbed the catch and slid out noiselessly.

The door sealed with a well-engineered, soft thump. Adeudas's lips twisted. "Little girls, eh? What are they made of? Sugar and spice and all things nice? I wish that were true, but deception and decadence and all things deviant, that's nearer the recipe, especially these nights. So let me share a piece of advice. Don't trust a soul peddling the sap in their veins as sacrament."

"You don't pay for it!" Druid rolled his eyes.

"A donor who *doesn't* expect some form of riches in exchange for their pain is a rare diamond; more so since our hour is almost over."

"What are you talking about? The true fans stay loyal," said Druid with conviction. But even as he spoke, the phantoms of his dream started circling; a sea of faces, blurred into one vengeful mass as they crawled towards the stage...Refocusing, he realised Adeudas was staring at him intently. "We have to trust our Belief in others," he insisted weakly.

"Trust our Belief, certainly. But in others? That is not so wise." Adeudas indicated the still-warm driver's seat. "Did you think I was teasing when I ran that young emissary back to her queen? Not remotely. Just as Dorothy was quick to bring news of a fresh tryst between Sophia and yourself, so she will decant our words, like poison, into the pink shell of another's ear."

"Sophia will think I have betrayed her." Druid stared beyond the glass.

"Or that the player has been played." Aged yet beguiling, Adeudas brought his handsome face closer. "Just now, I thought it prudent to dismiss that little driver girl, despite my attachment. I advise you to do the same."

"In what respect?" Warily, Druid let his companion take up his hand and press it flat against the car window.

"Sometimes we have to block out the sun to stay in the dark."

Squinting, Druid lifted his thumb and forefinger. His hand obscured the ivory sails of the windmill that shimmered in the east. "Sophia," he breathed.

"I'm not naïve to your suffering, or to the queen's more embittered fancies. But I implore you, Druid. Beware you don't lose yourself to her fire. It will consume you *anew.*"

"Thanks for the pep talk, but I'm no man's fool." Jet-black claws scraped down the glass.

"*Man's,* no." Adeudas raised his hands and fanned his thin, pale fingers. "But girls, girls, girls. I can already see it hand-carved into the lintel of your crypt." His claws melted down. "Oh come now, my toxic twin, don't be modest. While shying away from the darkest portion of the limelight, you drained the cup of excess, none the less. In fact, as I recall, your hedonism far outstripped my own. And what do we find at the euphoric heart of it all? Groupies. Dreadlocked groupies with pierced tongues and navels, skinny groupies with long, creamy legs, stripy groupies with tattooed arms and candied weaves, black-eyed groupies with lovely, leather wings..." Adeudas placed his own hand over the white fortress. "Another man's groupie."

"With smoke in her hair and blood on her hands, so you'd have me believe." Druid attempted to break free of the other's arm, and for a split second, Adeudas seemed to back off, a sour look on his fantastic face. Then he lunged.

Druid saw pale fingers trickle out, like the blueish polyps of a Portuguese man-of-war. A dark shape—a knee—crushed his breastbone. Simultaneously, the vamp's pristine features broke apart; lips widened as if on strings, jaw dropped at a grotesque angle, each pupil a speck in hot, lilac lava.

Ringing the vamp's wrists with his claws, Druid clamped his elbows tight to his hipbones. His arms dead-bolted. Tentacular claws strained an inch short of his throat. He bucked in an effort to shift the flow of weight between them, but Adeudas's lower body was being applied to his ribcage with such force that the air gushed from his lungs as from a set of depressed bellows, and it was all he could do to keep vertical. His grip became slippery with sweat. His arms trembled then bowed out. Slick fingers crept about his neck and contracted.

"Always the instigator, my darling boy. Always the dark horse, ready to leap from the wings." Adeudas bore down like a biting imp on the chest of his delirious victim. "Are you really ready to sacrifice yourself for that she-devil's cause? To stand against the Management and accuse them of lying or colluding or *mismanaging* the evidence? Roses's death was an accident. If there was ever anything more sordid to the *affair*, it was that no one was prepared to point the finger at the sole fire-starter in the frame. Sophia had access. Sophia had motive. Sophia had *the means*." His livid face close to Druid's, the vamp pursed his lips and pretended to exhale a stream of smoke. "But since we'd just lost our king, it hardly seemed appropriate to victimise our queen. It might be a sacred rite in terms of chastising the average tribe member, after all, the citizens may be free to express themselves, but they remain contained in this escapist fantasy, to be expelled from which would be soul-crushing. Sophia is a different creature altogether, being in part responsible for *creating* the fantasy. Who in hell would be willing to carry out the sentence? Citizens? The Management? You or I? We're all guilty of a never ending game of pass the buck." He smiled a shade too sharply. "I can't help but wonder, blood-brother, are you as confident of the same reprieve?"

"I'll nail *myself* to the cross if it means I get to the bottom of this...*shit,*" Druid spat, and he slammed a knee up into the other man's groin.

Adeudas bucked. But he recovered instantly and squeezed the throat beneath his fingers. "It stops now. Mosey on back to your cold, green crypt, become the tragi-Christ no fucker understands again, and leave the hairy-scary stuff to the big boys. Else someone might end up supplying the wood and nails for *that* crucifix sooner than you think."

A low, electronic tone interrupted the stiff atmosphere between them.

Adeudas glanced down and slackened his grip. Bending his elbows, he gave Druid's face a long, luxurious lick. "You're wanted," he snarled, then broke away.

While the vamp had his back to him and was busy easing over to the far side of the car seat, Druid bodysurfed sideways, slammed a boot into his opponent's cervical vertebrae and restrained that sly face against the glass. With Adeudas pinned, he slid a hand into a side pocket of his leather, brought the cellphone to his ear, and thumbed the green.

"D?"

The air felt on fire as it streamed into his lungs. "Who's this?" he rasped.

"D, it's IQ, mate. You okay? You sound kinda puffed!"

Druid cut his eye at the writhing fish at the end of his line. "I'm fine. Just playing footie with a friend."

"Oh...ugh, dude. Gotta spell it out for me like that? Now I've got a mental picture and everything. Look, I've got the skinny on that info you gave me and I think I've got a lead. Might be something, might be nothing, but thought it best to care and share."

"I'll be there within the hour."

"Where, mate?"

Even with Adeudas in his current predicament, Druid still didn't trust that freak not to listen in. He kept things simple and encrypted.

"Same old."

"Same old? Erm...not sure I'm with you, ma...wait, you don't mean Louse..."

"In the hour." Druid hung up.

He slid the cell into a pocket, eyeing the tall shadow sewn onto the bottom of his heel. "Going to behave now?" When Adeudas jerked his head as far as he was able, Druid released him in a swift spring of movement, righting himself at the far end of the seat. He kept his claws pincered.

"My, my, you are becoming quite the animal," said the artful creature opposite, a faint flush to his pale, plastic skin. "Oh do relax, silly boy." Relocating his polka-dot handkerchief, Adeudas flapped at Druid's warlike hands. "Just a bit of rough and tumble to ease out the knots, keep the old blood flowing, hmmm?" Softer now and hypnotic, his eyes met Druid's. He sighed quietly. "Beware the rat-faced boy. By nature, he dwells in the sewers. The Fae is a fraud—I smelt it in her blood. As for our dear Sophia..." He stared past Druid, in the direction of the east. "Perhaps I'd best instruct the stonemasons to start work on that cherished epitaph in case it's required sooner rather than later." He breathed sharply through his ringed nose, stretched then gave Druid a soft pat on the shoulder. "But, hell on earth, it's your funeral, friend."

"Be sure to pen me a glowing obituary." Easing the door open, Druid twisted diagonally and prepared to step out into the night. As his boot touched down, he felt a grip on his shoulder.

"Wait."

"What?" He whipped his head around with a snarl.

"You and I, we've been through that." Adeudas threw a claw towards the dark world beyond. "This is not our fate."

"What do I care for fate?" spat Druid as he exited the car, the tail of his leather gliding off the seat like spooling, black ribbon. "All I know is the way forward."

Chapter 9

Bullets

A skinny shadow sidled into the pew opposite. Druid shut the notebook and put down his pen. "Hello, IQ."

"Sah!" The kid knocked a hand off his brow in mock salute.

Witch-green eyes swept about the busy bar. "Glad to see you took my advice about lying low. Not!" Drawing a sign with his fingers, the boy quipped, "*Street Smart: The Art the Fiend Forgot.*" He laid his hands flat on the table. "Jeez, D, word gets out there's a bona-fide biter in this fleapit, folk'll soon start scratching. Yet here's you, all prince-pale in shiny boots of leather, waxing lyrical like you're Bram friggin' Stoker. What're you so busy scribbling in that little magick book anyway? Arrest warrants for Grallators' crimes against insanity, or a post in the classifieds for lush lovelies to lunch on? A new clause in your will perhaps?" Snatching up the Drathcor's black and silver fountain pen, he pretended to write in the air, "*I, Mr. Morbid, bequeath the sum of my otherworldly goods to one Irvine Quirk, loyal confidant and friend.*"

"Friend, hey?" Shiny claws disarmed the boy in one clean sweep. "How'd I get so deserving?"

"Your sparkling wit and your big gnashers reel me in like a goth to a graveyard," IQ winked. He spat the well-chewed tassel of his wizard hat out of the side of his mouth and used it to point to the small, black leather book on the table. "Seriously, though. What you got in there?"

"Children's stories," said Druid, spidering his claws over the notebook.

"I bet." Pressing one side of his face to the table, the kid squeezed up an eye and tried to peer under. "Go on. Give us a peep?"

"No."

"You know you widdly want to." Fingers crept towards the gilt-edged pages.

"Touch it and die!" Druid exposed a slim scythe of sparkling white either side of his upper jaw.

"Sheesh, someone got out the wrong side of the coffin!" IQ whipped his hand back as if the flesh had caught alight. "Just being friendly, was all. Like I give a flying fig about what's in your stupid book, anyway," he said sulkily and, swallowing his hat's tassel again, slumped back in his seat.

Resting his elbows on the table, Druid put his head into his hands. He hadn't fully recovered from his shock encounter with Adeudas, added to which, he was plagued by stills from his dream; that dandy's stylised ambivalence, Sophia, all tattered tulle and heart of dark, touching him, breathing him in, as he did her; and, all the while, Roses going down in flames...He scrubbed his fists into his eyes. It didn't take a prophet to interpret *that* nightmare. Trust no one; not even himself.

"I...didn't sleep well," he managed, and forced his eyelids open.

IQ's face had softened. "Quick fix for insomnia, mate. Hoist up the old mattress, shove a handful of flax seeds and eucalyptus leaves underneath."

"Sleep isn't my problem. It's the dreams that accompany it."

"Add a pinch of coarse sea salt into the mix then. Shrivel those night terrors right up." The kid leaned in and, with the earnestness that had caught Druid off guard once or twice now, said, "We all fight monsters east of Eden, friend. You just need to learn to close the door on that dark world when morning breaks in this one." He studied Druid with a wisdom way beyond his years. "Broken sleep, abandoning the safety of your watchtower, moving in circles cast from ash and blood. Why'd you put yourself though it, D?"

Druid laid a finger on his lips and felt them tremble. What was he fighting for? Or—he pressed harder on his mouth— was the real issue, *who* was he fighting for? Adeudas had spelt out how much he despised any effort to bring the city's secrets to light with threat and muscle. But was *that* even relevant? The marks from their encounter still fresh at his neck, Druid seriously doubted whether Adeudas was ever the beast to trust. On the other hand, Sophia had come as close as she ever would to asking him for help, to needing him. But if *she* was the reason he was risking his life out in the wilds, wouldn't he think of her more often, long to enfold her in his arms, shield her like a lie? Instead, her every aspect pained him.

Not that he was going to share his darkest dilemmas with a prying child. Instead, he muttered, "Guess I like the smell of trouble." Pulling moodily at the red spines of his mohawk, he glanced past the kid. "Take this place. It's one of the few holes in the city that hasn't been whitewashed by do-gooders. Reminds me where we came from."

"Funny that. Reminds *me* where we're headed." IQ tossed a thumb towards the bar's shady clientele. "This lot? Discharge of the revolution. Blow your brains clean out if they thought it cool or profitable." He lifted his snout and sniffed. "When you get this much of the brown stuff pooper-scooped into one place, it's gonna stink."

"Strange how I found your little legs dabbling in the midst of it," Druid jibed, if with an edge as he remembered Adeudas's warning: *Beware the rat-faced boy. By nature, he dwells in the sewers.* Taking in the trade of that liquored hovel—a band of scar-faced Amigos, Darth Maul on steroids, a pair of molls hanging off the arm of a PVC-suited gangster, a haggish sea witch, and several squabbling, well-oiled Munchkins (the cat man had, apparently, scatted)—he knew Adeudas had a point.

"Likewise," the kid retaliated. His mouth tied itself up in a mischievous bow. "Don't get me wrong. I've got a soft spot for the worthless, particularly since drifters got the cheap seats when this freak show hit the town." His gaze fell on the tome in Druid's grip. "You see, in *my* book, when it comes to who's in and who's out, we're as judgemental as the Burners."

"Their messiah had no style."

"Jesus had cool hair."

"Given." A tinge of amusement registered at Druid's lips. The smile faded. "Intolerance was never part of our vision though. Origin's music was about reshaping difference into something more substantial. Our sole aim was to unite the outcast."

"All aboard the good ship Anarchy, eh?"

"Not exactly." Druid worked the fleshy part of a palm into his left temple. "But we did have a game plan, of which a body like the Management played no part." Without raising his eyes, he sensed inquisitiveness spark in that lively brain opposite. For a high lord to criticise the one group of people maintaining any semblance of order in their wounded world was beyond foolish, he realised; it was indicative of mutiny. He chose a different slant. "Our dream was to create a city where *difference is cherished and weirdness most wondrous.* Roses's words," he added by way of superfluous explanation. His fingers caressed the notebook's leather cover; it felt like sloughed snakeskin. "Socialism: great in theory, a huge dollop of implausible idealism in practice. Know why?"

"Because we're buggers for consumerism?"

The older man pursed his lips in half-agreement. "Because mankind has *desires,* yes. True egalitarianism could only come about if we stopped caring, about anything or anyone, and that would make zombies of us all." He traced the insignia of the royal seal with a claw. "Looking back, it was inevitable really. Even before Renegade, when we'd nowhere to go except the nightclubs, the rock bars, the online chat rooms, we still divided into cliques. Even then we expelled the uninitiated."

"Hoofing one set of rules aside only to bag ourselves another?"

The Drathcor snorted. "That's one way of putting it. It's why the tribes evolved. They provide structure. Without their guidance, all that's left is a sea of *drifting* souls." Forgetting the book, he stared out at the criss-cross of worn wooden benches with their slouching, hawk-eyed occupants. "It's easy to label society the antithesis of everything that's free and creative. But, for the most part, even we strange citizens want to stay a part of a world that works, else we regress to our baser instincts by design."

Resting a grubby trainer up on the bench, IQ hugged one knee into his chest. He grinned. "If I catch your, er, *drift,* you're saying that by choosing their own path rather than one dictated by a tribe, drifters opt out of a system that has, by its own anarchic right, *already* opted out, thus threatening the very core of this," he flung out his arms. "Our structured insurrection." Hand to chest, he made a show of drawing breath, stopped and arched an eyebrow. "Plop, plop. Smells a lot like dragon shit. Know why?" Waving a hand theatrically aloft, he orated, "There are more things in heaven and earth—and Renegade—Doratio, than are dreamt of in your philosophy." He let his hand fall; leant in. His eyes burned like gobs of marsh-fire. "Ever ask yourself why drifters hate

Drathcor, why it is you should hide that fancy-shmancy book of yours when these under-underlings abound? Simple. The wonder boys and girl of Origin built a brave new reality with one flaw: the exclusion of those who didn't quite fit in." He popped the tassel of his hat into his mouth like a pill and his eyes grew wider. "No one likes to be stuck peering in on something wonderful. Everyone wants to step through and stay inside the looking glass."

"And you think being a Drathcor makes the fantasy any more accessible?" said Druid with a snarl. "To be apart from all that moves around you while standing downwind of the smallest, sweetest waft of freedom? Drifters aren't the only creatures to dwell incognito in Renegade. Believe me, boy, I understand that plight all too well."

"Added to which, you're a bugger for the big bad, least that's the stuff of legends," the mini wizard beamed, visibly delighted by his companion's less salubrious tendencies.

As if on cue, their debate was interrupted by the sound of splintering glass. Its unexpectedness sent a discernible shockwave through the establishment, prompting every patron to sit up and take notice. Druid and the boy remained resolutely still. A gruff demand to, "Fetch me a new pitcher, you stupid broad, or I'll pistol-whip yuh," sounded from one of the shaded booths and, a few seconds later, a neat pair of pins slid out from the dark.

"Aw, whatever you say, Harry," purred the owner of the legs in a thick, New York accent. A sassy moll emerged and, in doing so, offered a flash of gunmetal at the side split of her lime-green pencil skirt. Stepping away from the table, she stopped a moment and retrieved a compact from her handbag. She pinched each cheek to bring a flush of blood to the surface, narrowed her eyes, then snapped the compact shut.

Druid kept his eyes on that particular bird of paradise as she teetered off to the bar. His gaze slid back to the kid. He found the urchin smirking.

"No surprise a player like you gets pally with lowlifes. Dolls like that are a helluva lot of fun to while away the hours with. Especially since, sooner or later, a life of mindless luxury has gotta bore the pants off you; and not in a good way."

"More than you can possibly imagine," Druid mumbled, darkly amused. The kid could have corrupted a kindergarten teacher with his suggestive smile.

"Then welcome to the thunderdome!" IQ raised a clenched fist by way of a toast. "I never drink on duty," he explained with false sincerity when Druid stared at him, bemused.

"Cheers." Druid drained the first of two shots of JD he had arranged by an elbow. The liquor burnt his throat in the best sort of way, a sensation not dissimilar to quaffing the red waters of a vein, especially that of someone he had longed for. The reminder of his heritage cheered him, and he ran his tongue over the blades in his mouth. IQ might be sewer-bound by nature, but it was precisely the kid's connections with the city's underworld that made him so appealing.

"And are you?" he asked the boy slyly.

"What?"

"On duty."

"Of course. Goddamn bureau of friggin' information, me. Told you I had something for you and, boy, have I ever." Wiggling in his seat, IQ met Druid's gaze with a queer little swallow. "How would you describe Skinwalkers?" he posed with conscious flippancy.

"Renegade's filth-encrusted genitalia."

"Not keen then?"

Druid stared across the table.

"That's, erm, good," said IQ, his face bursting with expression. "Actually it's a feckin' relief since I'd sooner drink my own pee than play in the park with those bad puppies. Sure I'm down and dirty with drifters, but Skinwalkers?" He pursed his lips and gave a low whistle. "No sirree. So now we got that sorted, here's what I...excuse me a sec, mate." Squinting at a spot past Druid's shoulder, the kid raised his voice. "Gonna wing your way over and say hi or keep on playing games?" He thumbed his rat-like nose. "Sniffed you out, Trawler."

With an audible sigh, Druid shifted round in his seat. Wedged between a pair of rickety bar stools, one serving as a shelf for a pint of some brown sludge, the other as a gaming table for three carefully-rolled, multi-faceted bronze dice, was a man in black. All dirtied up like a piratic cowboy, he was wearing scuffed, black jeans, a black t-shirt, a black, embroidered waistcoat, a black bandana looped about the neck, and a black tri-corner hat, pulled low over the eyes. The Trawler picked up his dice, disengaged from the bar stools and meandered over. Taking a seat alongside IQ, he flicked his hat brim with a forefinger to reveal a face that was astonishingly leathered. He looked like an executed highwayman, wearing his own pared, vinegared skin. New-romantic stripes of ultraviolet grazed both cheeks. Owl-like eyes swivelled in deep sockets.

Druid tucked his nose into a shot glass. "I thought Trawlers didn't care to step outside of their safety net. Rather like their patron, the august Sophia."

"Venture onto dry land more often than you'd think." IQ raised his fat little eyebrows. "Like to lurk in the secret places where no one thinks to look. Can I borrow those, mate?" Turning an over-generous smile on the man, he held out his hand.

The Trawler stared at the kid, his binocular eyes refracting as if capable of recording the event from different angles. He allowed his fist to hover over the table for several long seconds then let go of the dice.

IQ scooped them up, proceeded to rotate each die then hold it up to the light.

"Rare dodecahedron metal dice, dating from the reign of Emperor Kangxi of China's Qing dynasty. Used for Astro-divination." The Trawler shifted heavily in his seat. His accent was crisp Irish. "First die represents the planets, Sun, Moon, North Node, and South Node, second, the twelve zodiac signs, and third, the twelve houses of the astrological chart."

"A Trawler with an interest in the esoteric? Seems to go against the grain of a tribe employed in techno-mining information." Druid twisted the shot glass round in his cupped palm. He hadn't had many dealings with Trawlers. Then again, not many folk had, given the tribe's preference for a life spent in lightless cabins—made fetid by a Tropicana of wireless CPUs, laptops, LCD monitors, deskjets that spewed forth an incessant ream, chewing gum wrappers, part-crushed, paper coffee cups, and Redbull cans with a rim of swilling ash—alongside a single-minded inclination to ferret out a worldwide web of secrets. What he *did* know was that, as hawkers of everything fast-typing, ferreting booms, and code-destabilising minds could dredge up, Trawlers were valued commodities both inside and *outside* the city. In fact, Sophia's enigmatic tribe were a good part responsible for Renegade's autonomy. Like worker bees, they sustained mutually-beneficial links with the world outside the hive and thus ensured its survival. All they had to do was keep on producing the honey.

"The cleanest data is often found in that we find mysterious. The abacus. Stonehenge. Punch cards. The ZX Spectrum. Pragmatic objects made weird by time's passage. Much as your good self, high lord." The Trawler's romantic lilt was soured by cynicism.

On hearing his official title in the unforgiving environment of Louse House, Druid flinched. He glanced at IQ, who was presenting a die to his open mouth and waggling his tongue.

"Thought they'd like a different view." The kid kept his gaze on Druid. "I'd say matey here is less interested in mystic enigmas as sweet little micro-tech suckers. Say a pinhole camera." He swivelled the die 180 degrees. "Wave to your adoring fans, D?"

"Kid's watched a few too many re-runs of Dark Angel on the Sci-fi channel. Trawlers are skilled in the use of web technologies, not espionage identikits." The man drained a good portion of his pint. He stared at Druid intently. "Got a message for you."

"You saying this *isn't* a camera?" IQ directed the die at one of his nostrils.

Druid felt a wave of nerves break over his chest and stomach. He drained his glass, rolled it aside. "What does Sophia want with me now?" he snapped.

"*That* is definitely a lens!" The kid held up the die again, revolving it like a faceted jewel. "Light refracts off glass in the central swirl of the sun symbol. It's a feckin' camera."

"To share information," said the Trawler, ignoring the teen complainant at his elbow. He hunched a little, as if positioning himself as a barrier against prying eyes or attentive ears. "The High Lady Sophia was recently informed of a development in our investigation into the death of Renegade's highest lord, Roses."

"I could have guessed that Trawlers would have their sticky little fingers in that particular pie." Druid smiled dryly. "Why Sophia got *me* to do her dirty work when her own tribe specialise in rooting out that which is hidden strikes me as baffling."

"Perhaps because we're as much in the dark about events surrounding His death as any other gang of citizens."

There was an edge of disquiet to the Trawler's voice; the man was genuinely sorry for the fact, Druid realised with a flush of shame. It was juvenile to pit himself against a clan of expert information gathers, all because he envied their affinity with Sophia; she who, until that moment, had failed to provide any visible evidence that she cared a jot if he was the living dead or grave dust. "Surely *you've* got to have had access to some sort of backup system?" he insisted, referring to the effects of the fire on the south watchtower's database stacks and the technological meltdown that had thrown the city into several hours of mutinous chaos as a result.

"We collate information for a handful of external global corporates. We *do not* peddle intelligence on Renegade City itself. That would make us not only pariahs, but vultures picking over the carcass of a once-glorious Xanadu." There was steeliness to the lilt now. The eyes smoked with indignation. "But, at the high lady's request, we *have* delved into a number of legacy files belonging to a few key players."

"Of which I'm no doubt one." Druid shuddered internally. To know that his personal files, emails, uploads and internet usage could be exhumed and monitored by strangers was not only unsettling, it smacked of violation. He was oddly reminded of Roses's proposed Bill of Interdependence. If the bill had ever been passed, it would have exposed the secret histories of all citizens. For those not born and bred in the city, it would have been an end to make believe. An end to Belief. A shard of pain tore between Druid's eyes. Increasingly, he despised Roses's attempt to let loose his personal anger on the flesh and blood of Renegade.

"I am sent to divulge specific information and that information only," said the Trawler. His tone betrayed a fresh trace of apology.

Druid's gaze shifted to IQ, still engaged in probing the die with a fingertip, but whom he guessed was in fact listening in with avid curiosity. "The kid's okay," he murmured.

At the reassurance, the Trawler scooped off his hat, swept back a scrub of white-blonde and honeyed hair, and, cradling the hat to his chest, retrieved a tiny paper scroll from the lining. He passed it over.

Druid unravelled the scroll and scanned the contents. "'Deed done. The old ways are going up in flames.'" He glanced up at IQ, who was still playing the role of dimwit. "What the hell is this?"

"A transcript of a transmission that was traced back to the IP address of one of the terminals in the Great Library. Although it was sent through a proxy and anonymiser, we were able to trace it back because the Great Library adds a hidden packet to every transmission within the UDP layer." The Trawler reigned in his enthusiasm. "Email was sent fifteen minutes before the first sighting of the fire was officially logged by a Grallator monitoring station."

"Shit." Finally, IQ allowed himself to show a modicum of interest.

"Who sent it?" Druid's throat went dry. He croaked on the words.

"Chip's registered to one Jaden Phillipe, a five year old DarkLed."

"A cloned chip, in other words." The kid bit down on the damp squib of his hat tassel. His puckish face was alive with morbid fascination. "Goth almighty, D, you know what this means? The fire was started deliberately. *That* says so." He dipped his head to indicate the scroll in Druid's hands.

"Maybe." Druid felt emotions assuage his flesh like a rainstorm. The thrill of knowledge slapped against the ache of loss. Hurt rattled ribs. Vengeance sliced at his heart. He signalled to a passing waitress for a refill. "End of the day, these are just words on paper, albeit originally a screen."

"But for whose eyes?" The kid concentrated his wild, green gaze on the messenger.

It was a key question, Druid realised, taking a nip from his refuelled shot glass. "Who was the email sent to?" he demanded with a resurgence of faith.

Just as the conversation was starting to get interesting, the Trawler stepped out from the bench, pulled the triangular mask of the bandana over his nose, and adjusted his hat so that it sat low at his brow again. Resting a boot on the bench, he leant forward on an elbow and said in a dry, lilting whisper, "Lorcan."

Chief of the Skinwalkers. With the voicing of that one word, the hunch that Druid had harboured ever since his most recent, terrible visit to the ruin of the south watchtower solidified into cold, hard fact. The rabid outcasts *were* involved in his brother's murder, or at the very least, responsible for an act of arson that resulted in his death. Lorcan had received an email detailing as much. How was he meant to feel about that, Druid wondered weakly? Nauseated? Vindicated? The knowledge seeped into his pores, formed a tannin-like coating of unformed questions on his tongue. He lowered his eyes, reread the contents of the scroll then slung it back across the table.

The Trawler gave nothing away, only collected the scroll, applied an edge to a squat, bubonic candle and placed the flaming paper in a nearby ashtray. "Irvine will fill you in on the rest." He held out a hand for his dice.

"Hey, how'd you know my name?" The kid begrudgingly tipped the three dice into the Trawler's palm.

"Shall we say it precedes you?" Inclining his head in a parting gesture, the man closed his fist about the dice and turned to leave.

"One question," said Druid tightly. He waited until the Trawler had turned full around again. "How'd you know I would be here?"

"Cellphone signal."

"You said Trawlers weren't clued up on with the whole spy game." IQ's rat-like features hardened.

The man plucked a die from his hand and directed it at the kid. For the only time in their encounter, he smiled. "Watch your back, wizard."

Druid watched the Trawler leave, Louse House's suspect residents paying him no notice as if he were invisible.

Producing a slip of paper from one of the front pockets of his hoodie, IQ took care to flatten out its charred edges then offered it over. "This flyer, you salvaged it from the Great Library. Don't know if you ever looked at it closely but..."

"'Announcing Fright Night. Gangbang with the ghouls. Come get some if you dare. Just twenty bucks a shot,'" Druid parroted. Staring at the kid, he added without inflection, "I've had a fair bit of spare time to study it."

"So it would appear," sneered the boy. "And what d'you make of it?"

"Not much, just another event designed to keep Legacy ahead of rival nightclubs."

"You reckon?" IQ chewed on his hat tassel like a fat cigar. Out of a corner of his mouth, he said, "What if I said the gangbang slogan was literal, paying chicks twenty bucks a time to do the nasty?"

"As in a fetish night?"

"Well, it does take a certain breed of perv to participate." He waved the flyer delicately before his nose like rotten fish. "What we've got here is one of several hundred handbills circulated in the Pleasure Quarter last December. A shout out to every loose-knickered lass to sign up to the cause, if you like—that being the exotic entertainment of things that go bump in the night."

"And it's relevant, how?"

"Jeez, D. Are you blind as the bats in your bat-cave? Check out the watermark."

Druid slid his hand around the lumpy candle at one end of the table and drew it closer. Holding the flyer over the flame, he succeeded in backlighting the insignia. He felt a pang of disgust and grunted. There was no mistaking the dreadful image: a three-headed hound with the tail of a serpent.

"Fright Night. It translates as those freaks letting their manky hair down for the mother of all parties," hissed the boy quickly, as if the words themselves might turn back about and bite him. "Once a year, all the chapters of the Skinwalkers come together to celebrate their winter solstice in the only way they know how, with shed-loads of booze, bustin' bikes and babe action." He paused, misty-eyed, then shook off the daydream and retrieved another item from his pocket: a second, newer flyer. He tossed it down onto the table. "Recognise anything?"

Druid held the page up before the flame. The same awful emblem shone clear. Rather than agitate the dull throb at his brow, it acted as distraction. His unusual eyes flicked to and fro about the flyer. "This Blizzard Bash…?"

"It's this year's event, yes," IQ said authoritatively. "A bit of legwork and keeping the old ear to the ground and here's what I know. Last year's Fright Night was truly riotous—and I mean truly. You saw Legacy's facelift for yourself. Once the Skinwalkers had finished with it last year, the place was almost condemned, and not in the 'Beware All Ye Who Enter Here' kind of a way, but more your traditional bricks tumbling-down-and-crushing-you-half-to-death deal. Hence the Management ordering its overhaul. Anyhow, the pack's shifted up a gear. This year the solstice celebrations are being held in the great outdoors. The mutts pilfered a pair of fire engines, tapped in to the city's mains water supply and flooded…"

"Forest Field. I heard." Druid pictured Adeudas in the creeping dark of a ruined watchtower. Thinking back, hadn't that sly prince played an all too evasive game when he had confided as much then avoided further questioning? Moreover, in light of the information disclosed by the Trawler, he was loathed to trust anyone with inside knowledge of Skinwalker activities. "'Get ready to grind at the Blizzard Bash,'" he read non-committally. "'Nineteen bucks a ride.'"

"No surprise *that* tariff works outside inflation."

Druid kept his eyes on the flyer. "'This year's Gauntlet. The Seven Wonders of the Wheel. Revels kick off at midnight on the twelfth of the twelfth. Bring a throttle.'" He discarded the glossy page and sat back, chin in hand. "That's tonight."

"Which is precisely why we should settle ourselves in *here*," his companion replied with careful exaggeration.

"What's the Gauntlet? Might help us access their chief and get some answers."

"You craaazy man. Make silly talk. We stay and party like its summer in Jamaica." IQ paused, eyes growing wide and incredulous. "What do you think the 'Gauntlet' means?" he spluttered.

"I've no idea."

"Well…me neither. But it can't be good if Skinwalkers designed it."

"Guess there's only one way to find out." Druid picked up his notebook and slid it, along with the fountain pen, into the inner pocket of his leather.

"Don't be a muppet all your life." The boy masticated his hat's tassel with frantic abandon. "Those brutes'll eat you alive. I can picture the vendors' blackboards already. 'Cotton Candy, Nougat, Flayed Drathcor, ten cents a slice!' Wait it out. I'll fix you up with Lorcan right enough."

"You know him?" Druid raised an eyebrow.

"Know *of* him. Reputation has him on a level with another big biter seated not so far away."

The Drathcor shook his head. He'd thought as much. While drifters welcomed a streetwise kid with an outsized brain and balls to match, Lorcan would as soon roast IQ's weaselly bones, pick them clean of meat, and toss the entrails to his henchmen, as give the kid his ear.

Whereas, if *he* could just get close to the devil, maybe he'd see a kink in that blood-red armour, a window on the man behind the beast. "Well, since we're in the neighbourhood, it'd be rude not to drop in and say hi."

"You're kidding me, right? Firstly, we ain't nowhere near *that* neighbourhood. You're talking all the way across Rock Cemetery and the other side of Haunted Hill. Secondly, we ain't going near *that* neighbourhood, not tonight anyway. Talk to Lorcan!" The kid rolled his eyes. "In which Captain James T. Kirk un-charted universe is that gonna happen? Look, just give me a couple of weeks. I've got this contact, a cute little go-go dancer with one hell of a wiggle..."

"Question, IQ." Druid rolled a fresh shot of whiskey to his lips, sank it. Behind the shades, the faint holograms of his eyes fastened hard on the kid. "Why'd you show me this flyer if you didn't expect me to follow up on it?"

Blowing out his cheeks like a puffer fish, IQ stared up at the mottled ceiling. "Presumed you'd pass it straight to your personal militia, I guess. Alert the odd trillion Grallator guards at your disposal. Send those right-arms into battle, rectitude blazing..."

"Guess I like to be more hands-on," Druid interrupted at the same time as he caught a flash of striped orange at one of the age-crackled pillars. He slid out a leg to sit astride the bench. Tapering his eyes, he devoured each booth's gauzy dark, the sinister gangs at each table, the barflies. On the jukebox, a seven-inch vinyl disc crackled—once, twice—then erupted into the raw riff of "Ace of Spades". The dive overflowing with Lemmy's thrash cacophony, he stood, swept his leather aside and fed a boot up onto the table.

"Get up and make your way to the door," he told the boy with hushed authority.

"Not even listening to me, are you, D?" Cleaning out an ear with a fingernail, the kid shuffled off his seat and, in a move that was spookily intuitive, slid the bench aside. "Goes to show, hey? All the money in the world can't buy you manners. Two weeks, I said. Can't get you access any sooner."

"Shift!" hissed the Drathcor as he slammed his heel hard into the wood grain and sent the table skimming across the filthy floor. Newly materialised out of a back room and headed for them at a rate of knots, the tiger man leapt abroad the crude missile, used it as a springboard to launch sideways, and fastened its powerful limbs around a tarnished pole connecting floor to ceiling.

The creature leant towards Druid, cheek pouches sewn up at each edge to expose tiny, toothpick fangs. *"Drathcor,* I see you."* Smiling like a Cheshire cat in a branchless tree, the giant feline used two claws to point at its slitted, red eyes then at Druid.

Next second, the man in a long, leather trench coat and shades felt every Tom, Dick and Dirty Harry in the room give him their full and undivided attention. There was a grace period of confusion, or interest, or anticipation. Then the voices stared to rise.

"Stone the crows, man. That dude for real?" jeered the overweight Darth Maul, double-ended lightsaber club-fisted, devilled eyes bearing down.

"¡Guárdese de los amigos! Este monstruo es un Drathcor," cut in one of the rotund Spaniards. Removing his wide-brimmed sombrero, he rolled it into his body with a thumb and forefinger; as if threatening to launch it like a cut-throat frisbee.

Meanwhile, the sea hag undulated down off her barstool, one gnarled hand clutching a staff of twisted ironwood. "Been at t' catnip, Stripe?" she teased the tiger man. "Word from the deep be Drathcor got bumped off in their coffins months ago."

"Nah, Bettie Flotsam. That's a bag of drizzle," piped up a blue-suited weeble—and Druid vaguely recognised a re-incarnation of the mini-coroner responsible for certifying the Wicked Witch of the East most sincerely dead after a certain house-dropping incident. He was less inclined to agree, however, with the public servant's next prognosis.

"Everyone knows Drathcor ain't flesh and blood anymore. Their bodies turned to salt years ago...or pewter," said the little man importantly, and with the unequivocal support of his Munchkin comrades, all of whom entered into a rousing falsetto chorus of, "Ding dong, the Drathcor's dead!"

They broke off abruptly when the wee coroner turned on Druid, his squat little gourd of a face even more puckered than usual. "Now begone, Drathy, before we drop a house on you too."

"A Drathy? 'Ere?" The sea witch lifted a great sheaf of tattered, waist-length, grey hair. One of her eyes was missing. The hollow socket tunnelled like a borehole into the skull. "Bilge rat, you got a freakin' nerve. Gonna rub that bloodless scum in our faces? Ain't we good enough t' lick your pretty boots? Ain't we good enough t' splice you?"

The room gave off several glints of silver as blades were pulled.

Unfolding to his full height, Druid shot the jet-black needles of his claws apart and bowed. "At your service, gentlemen...and ladies," he said with a half-smile as, securing a fresh pitcher, the moll in the lime-green pencil skirt teetered back over from the bar. He out-stared that doll until a curl spread across her appliquéd, scarlet lips.

"You see that, Harry?" she hollered ear-splittingly. A measure of the frothy liquor sluiced the grimy floorboards. "Got m'self a Drathy sweetheart. What d'you make of that Harry? Somethin' or nuthin'?"

"If I was you, I'd get to stepping, you crazy broad," growled the mack daddy from the booth. "Your sweetheart's about to get iced."

"Yeah, shift your porky ass, toots." A random Munchkin scurried forward to put the boot in to the girl's tightly skirted behind.

Her efforts lavished on keeping the jug vertical, the vixen did a little kick-back with one of her killer, nine-inch heels and caught the tiny man square in the groin, prompting him to double over and cry out in an even sharper falsetto, "Ooh, me willy winkie!"

"Now, there's no need for us boys to engage the old testosterone," piped up IQ, starting to swagger forward until Druid applied a Vulcan grip to the back of his scrawny, little neck.

"You're the only *boy* in here, IQ," the cat salivated, swinging down from its perch. "I got my money to earn, so unless you're gonna cross my paw with another wad of moolah, you'd best hope this..." The beast eased its stripy, tattooed head over each shoulder in turn then returned its sly face to the front. It smiled knowingly. "...*Drathy's* used to defending his facesake."

While he was aware of the red eyes burning his flesh, Druid paid the cat no heed. He was concentrating on the girl in the lime-green pencil skirt and killer heels.

"Gonna defend my honour, Harry? Guess that Drathy did make me feel...exposed." A couple of paces short of the booth, the moll flashed Druid a sassy, little, gold-toothed smile; and he caught the flex of a trigger finger at her thigh. "Except you ain't the brawling type, are you, Harry? Might get some dawg's blood on that sponge-clean suit..."

As the moll kept up her yabber-yabber, Druid maintained his grip on the back of IQ's neck. "Get ready to move," he breathed by the kid's ear, plotting the locale of each potential assailant en route to the exit. But, far from being grateful for his taking control, the kid busted free of the neck-hold and rounded on him.

"Move, mate? We're just getting started." His green eyes flared. Turning back to his audience, the mini-wizard tossed up his hands. "Stripe, my man. You and I go way back. I was in the same class at school as Oscar, your youngest alley cat."

"Not enough, IQ," hissed the tiger, revolving two sets of pearlised claws. "Time to meet your maker."

Lurching forward, the feline slashed the blade within a whisker's breadth of Druid's jaw, then spun away in a circle on all four paws. Instantaneously, the Drathcor went to ground, one leg extended, one leg crooked underneath for support as he leant forward, a giant, spindle-limbed arachnid dreamt up by an opium pipe. Before the cat had completed its 360 degrees, he tipped forward, sprang off his taut arms, spine bowed in a perfect reversed C of a backwards bend, and cleared the creature's head. He saw the slit eyes elongate in shock as he landed in a perfect mirror-image of his previous pose, opposite leg extended, opposite leg crooked. With an air of meditative calm, he pressed his hands into a prayer. A split second later, he tensed one hand into a fist, body-slammed the base of his other palm forward, and connected with the ringed cartilage of a fur-tattooed windpipe.

"...Because you're a lover not a fighter, ain't you, Harry, you dirty rat!" screeched the moll at that same instant, tipping the pitcher's full contents over the unfortunate Casanova, or so Druid presumed, hearing an instantaneous roar of "You crazy bitch!" and the subsequent commotion of rearranging bodies in the booth. "Seen you two in my mirrawr, haven't I?"

roared the girl at volume. "Kissy-kissin' like you're two frickin' love birds. You and that cheap tramp, Melinda..."

"Who you callin' cheap?" shrieked a second female.

The cat gasped for air as if it was in the process of expelling a giant furball. Druid catherine-wheeled to one side, kicked the brute's legs out from under it, and was back on his feet a second later. Exercising a little strong encouragement, he had frog-marched the boy halfway towards the door before the sea hag lunged; and IQ took her out with an uppercut to her large, hooked nose and a side kick that lumbered her ironwood cane. Then the motor mouth reacted.

"Hey, I'm touched! My own anaemic Hercules. But really, you can let go now, you know. Aw, come on. What's this doing for the street-cred? Folk'll think I'm being pimped. Really not cool, mate. I can talk us out of this. Let me go, you friggin' freakster!" The kid swung hard about, his expression boyish, mortified, and most of all, afraid.

Before he could add to his tirade, the moll let off her first gunshot.

"Think you need the other ball either, Harry?" she squawked as the Chinese gangster tumbled out of the booth and screamed blue murder. She swung the gun around, causing the majority of the bar's not-so-brave spectators to duck while a few meaner individuals stood their ground.

"What about you, jackass?" The doll pointed the barrel at the rotund Amigo who rolled his one good eye at her, then spat. Her arm swung over to Darth Maul, "Or you, giant ladybug? Wanna piece of me too?"

Having apparently forgotten his earlier mission to slay a Drathy, the tattooed Zabrak showed no discernable emotion, just focused on the moll and powered forward, slogging aside several pissed dwarfs in its wake.

"Look where you're going, dickwad!" piped up a whorl-faced munchkin sucking a giant lollipop.

"Screw you," hissed the Dark Side assassin, whereupon the Munchkin whammed the stick of candy into his shinbone.

In the seconds between peace and all-out anarchy, Druid gripped IQ's neck again, slammed a fist of claws into the soft belly of an Amigo who leered at them with a Bowie knife in his hand, and propelled the kid towards the exit. With a determined shove, he forced the boy through the doorway.

Behind them, a fresh volley of gunshots sounded, rapidly usurped by the smash and grind of splintered furnishings and the thwack of connecting flesh.

"Well, bugger me with a banana, guess those Spidey Senses of yours are bang on cue. Cheers, guv'nor. Could've lost my noodle thanks to those naughty ninnies."

"Naughty ninnies?" spat Druid incredulously. "Those are *real* weapons they're smashing against each other's skulls, not the bounce-back-up-when-I-hit-you cartoon kind."

"Oh, I know, I know. Drifters—they're mad and mean when they want to be. Thought they were gonna have your godly guts for garters in there. Guess that's part of the risk you take if you kick it with Renegade's dirtiest. But, being a super sleuth, I have to keep a toe in that not so congenial gene pool." Hat threatening to slip down over his eyes, IQ jerked his head in the direction of the bar. "If you wanna know about the bad things in life, you have to put yourself among them."

Druid lifted his shades. He narrowed his strange, pale eyes at the night sky. "My sentiments exactly," he murmured.

Chapter 10

The Hand That Feeds

On Haunted Hill, the air was soft and faintly spring-like. It was only when the wind whipped up a fresh whirl of snow that Druid felt winter's burn, anaesthetising his lips, the end of his nose, his fingertips. Climbing to the lone apple tree at the zenith—a wise, old thing that wore its fraying branches like a bonnet, and had been relocated from some bucolic spot to that manmade site some ten years previously—he put his head on one side and stepped beneath its lowest tendrils.

He put his back against the trunk. Sensing the bark's texture through his leather, he was oddly reassured by something so rigid in that shifting, snow-white world. A few feet away, IQ busied himself with a cellphone, offering the odd snort or titter as his witch eyes scanned a text. Druid's darker gaze slipped back down the slope to where the line up of ever-diminishing devotees waited to pay their respects, despite the inclement weather.

He found himself contemplating the shivering souls who took sips from a hip-flask or blew hot breath between their palms. They seemed to be from all walks of life: DarkLed, whose trembling fluidity was akin to living ice sculptures, po-faced Grallators, a solitary Fae dressed in shimmering green like a creation of absinthe, and a host of mismatched drifters. There was also a handful of tourists; it was always easy to pick them out, cameras strung about the neck like holy amulets, free and easy cash frittered away on parkas, baseball hats, bags, and similar items of attire bearing the tag 'Renegade City' as machine embroidered logos, as if that gave them any sort of access to the Renegade experience. The city specialised in two types of tourists; those who chose to indulge in its sleaze element, and those who came 'to buy the t-shirt.' This contingent belonged to the later, sneaking the odd, furtive peak at him because a Drathy was still a sight to see, while the prerequisite guide, a grey-bearded wizard in a food-splattered robe, proved a twitchy sort, hands hovering near the group in a scooping gesture, as if any minute now, the city might implode and take his charges with it.

Druid pressed further back into the shade of the tree. As far as he could make out, the unusual troupe of city dwellers and sightseers shared one common bond, the desire to express their reverence. Otherwise, there was nothing to connect them.

There had been once, though, he mused, taking his turn to view the sarcophagus that knew no subtlety but sat above the hardened earth, harsh and cruelly tangible. Unlike the gnarled, old apple tree, its permanence struck him as unnatural. Like an object out of sync with its surroundings, he thought, remembering those first white nights after the funeral, when his eyes had stayed glaringly open, as if to halt the senseless tick and tock of time. But (a stone swelled in his throat) time's tide had continued to ebb and swell, no matter how much he wished it wouldn't. He looked away.

Staring up into the tree, he focused on a snowflake drifting between the naked branches. The speck of ice twirled in lazy descent until it met the frozen ground. There it evaporated, soaked back in as if it had never existed.

Was that meant to be the natural way of things, he questioned testily? The weathered hulk of Roses's tomb would remain in existence long after its resident had sunk back into the soil, *as if our being human makes us the more disposable*, he glowered.

And yet he hadn't objected to that arrangement just a few short hours ago. To step off life's wheel and accept that it keeps turning...*his* sentiments on meeting the belligerent matriarch, Queenie. At the time, they had felt genuine. But now? He concentrated on the icy ground. Such pretty paganisms were all well and good, except Roses didn't *feel* like a microscopic drop in a cosmic ocean. He had lived and he had mattered.

As if intent on driving home the fact, Druid faced up to the extravagant coffin, nervous eyes scouring its intricately carved, yellow quartzite with equal measures of repugnance and wonder. From that distance, he couldn't make out the detail, but he knew each sculpted panel bitterly by heart; the six naked figures dominating the start of the puzzle, men and women represented by spheres in the attendant panel, who re-emerged, human but much altered, in the next. The first, as a

Castclan, haloed by pentagrams, the evil eye, flowers, moons, and stars; the second, as a pin-thin Grallator with a head in algebraic clouds; the third, as a DarkLed, whose milky outline was a subtle polish to the stone; the fourth, as a gypsied Trawler captaining a stylised sea vessel; the fifth, as a Fae with delicate features and intricate wings; and, finally, as the four Drathcor, distended jack-o'-lanterns with wasp-waists and loose, spindly limbs.

Druid almost smiled as he pictured the lid of the casket; a florid wreath of barbed wire, crosses, ankhs, skull and crossbones, bats, black ravens, flowers, hearts and jewels, as well as an open scroll proclaiming, 'Renegade City Welcomes You!' There it was for all to see and subjugate themselves to; Renegade's inimitable metamorphosis of the ordinary into the extraordinary. Save one cruel factor, he mused darkly. Their one true god forgot to stay alive. Plus, while it served as a neat synopsis of their eclectic evolution, the storyboard blanked the most extreme band of renegades in the whole damn, dark city—Skinwalkers. No matter how much he despised that lawless crew, he couldn't help puzzling their innate right to be acknowledged. His eyes followed the lumbering advance of a blue-skinned dragon, a pair of vast, fibreglass wings tilling the snow in its wake. If Skinwalkers deserved a place in their bold history, didn't *drifters* deserve one as well?

But even as the dragon man let out two great snorts of white and bent with difficulty to make a floral offering, Druid found the beast ridiculous. To hoist those monstrous wings across the miles of Rock Cemetery then scale the treacherous hillside, and, all the time, contort a human spine against their weighty angle—it seemed a perverse life choice. Sneering inside, the Drathcor curled his tongue under the synthetic sharps of his fangs. Renegade had always functioned on one clear premise, some fantasies were worth indulging, others worth ignoring.

The snow started to fall faster, like frosting from a shaker, and his gaze left the drifter to concentrate on the fat, shiny flakes. Where were the *true* Believers, he wondered, digging his stiff claws beneath his armpits? Evaporated back into the bleak, hard ground, he concluded dourly, casting his eye beyond the grave and its sparse attendees.

A few miles west, the Pleasure Quarter was in darkness. The Las Vegas-styled strip of Booty Boulevard looked like a ghost town, its neon signage extinguished. The resonant basins of the skate parks were no longer floodlit, nor the opaque skids of the stock car circuit. Even the grand château of the west watchtower was in silhouette. Druid hugged himself harder. If Renegade City was crafted from a web of dreams, its fragile threads were beginning to snap.

Even before the boy thrust a grubby finger in its direction, he saw the flame launch up from the valley and lick the blue-black sky.

"Thar she blows!" shrieked the kid, hopping wildly about like a deranged Easter bunny.

Within seconds, another flare shot up a few hundred metres to the right, then a third to the left. Druid watched, at last enraptured, as seven flames exploded up, as if out of the ice itself. Instantly, or so it seemed, the unimaginative dark was replaced with a vast, floodlit arena, its last beacon detonating but a metre or so from the foot of Haunted Hill.

"Now that's showbiz!" IQ thrust his hands into the pockets of his too-loose jeans and jogged from one foot to the other. "You seen it, D?"

Stepping out from the arbour of the apple tree, Druid snorted in assent, if incredulously, given that it would take a dead or a blind man to overlook *that* spectacle. Of course, he'd been party to rock stadiums all over the globe, each meticulously rigged with coloured filters, props, lasers, lighting grids, robotics, aerotechnics, pyrotechnics, and every kind of theatrical excess. And, yes, those hi-tech extravaganzas had seemed anarchic at the time. But nothing in his experience compared to the monstrous, flaming dystopia of the Blizzard Bash.

His eyes bedded down to slivers. In amongst the trappings of that dark fair—striped marquees, barbecuing fire pits, food vendor vans, generators arranged in rows like battle-poised Daleks, an ejector seat pulled taut on bungee cord in-between two tall, neon posts, and a skeletal Ferris wheel revolving a cargo of steel mesh cages—was a vast, spidering edifice, part rustic coliseum, part gigantic ship's wheel.

"The Gauntlet," he breathed, recalling the flyer IQ had passed him in the bar and its not so subtle sales patter.

"You're not kidding," spat the kid, tossing the wet fibres at the end of his wizard hat back over a shoulder. "Still think we should pop in and say howdy?"

"Absolutely." Druid's tone was steely. His heart, though, was racing, like a man about to be lynched.

His gaze shifted from the iron jigsaw of an amphitheatre to a main stage, erected at the opposite end of the ice field and in-between two brilliant torches. Edged by a spray-painted frame of red and gold flames, the stage itself stood empty. Instead, giant video screens showed car or beer advertisements to the accompaniment of a booming commentary from the numerous PA stacks arranged on stage and here and there about the arena. The scene was, otherwise, remarkably quiet and, bar the odd food vendor sloshing waste into a dumpster or roasting his arse before one of the giant fire pits, uninhabited. In fact, right at that moment, the Skinwalkers were notable less for their squalid occupation of the Blizzard Bash than for their total absence from it.

"Reckon I got the wrong night, eh?" Pushing his hat higher, IQ scrubbed his forehead. "What say we tippy-toe away and have ourselves a few jars at Legacy?" He rubbed a forefinger and thumb greedily together. "As I remember it, you owe me a wedge of the green stuff from the time I stopped that moggy from molesting you."

"I owe your grandmother," said Druid curtly. "And, trust me, the cat posed no danger."

He glared at the boy, who wrinkled up his snout and remonstrated, "What?" when the older man made no attempt to look away.

"Listen."

The atmosphere had changed, and the boy apparently sensed it too since he made no attempt to argue, but crouched down, stubby fingers pressed into the snow. "They're coming," he told the Drathcor softly.

Indeed they were, thought Druid, focusing on the lustrous machines feeding in from the dark and rapidly so, like stealth bombers in forked formation. The escalating thunder of the alloyed devils had more in common with sensation than sound since he felt it infiltrate, then squeeze his soul with iron fingers. Glancing briefly around, he saw that every other creature on the hillside felt it too. Like statues in the snow, the straggling group of mourners stared at the frozen strait of Forest Field and the scourge of Skinwalkers hammering forth. Only the guide showed any immediate reaction, appearing to feel about the pockets of his robe as if in search of anything he could use as a weapon.

If the view terrified the majority, it held a certain lawless majesty for a Drathcor who lived by the taste of blood and thought it freedom. Druid kept his breath tight, focusing on the intricacies of those awesome vehicles; American-styled, angled windshields with smoked glass and shimmering silver mounts, metallic fairings in glittering green, vivid purple, brilliant red and black, customised headlight and radiator cowls, and the chrome feelers of Chubby drag bars on rumbling Harley Fat Boys. The revolutions of polished spokes captured something of the moonlight and flamed iridescently, while each bike's moulded skin was dark, lustrous and insectile, like the anterior wings of a scarab beetle. The whole scene reminded him of structured chaos; ear splitting, anarchic, and cool on every level.

Taking a sharp breath, Druid realised his claws were bruising the flesh of each palm. He started to unpeel them but paused, detecting the first waft of the brutes in the snowy air. It was a crude aroma, of cracked leather coats packed tight in thrift stores, thick, slicked testosterone, oil-smeared tarmac and greasy pit stops. There was dirt also, rich and peat-like as if dredged out of the earth's bowels, and something mouldered, which prompted his soft palette to reflex involuntarily. He coughed to shield any sign of weakness. But the sound was lost to the furore of bikes entering the arena.

"Jeez. It's like Barnum on friggin' ice down there." IQ threw his hands towards the mass of machines. "What d'you reckon, D? Ever seen anything like that before? Beats those wild nights back at the ranch, hey? Oh, that's me." Despite the tremendous roar of the bikes, the kid's hearing was patently attuned to the high-pitched, polyphonic sequence of his cellphone. He held it up, thumbed a couple of keys, and snorted.

"Interesting text?" Druid watched the brutes shift their great carcasses back in the saddle, kick out side stands and dismount.

"Just Jez. I fixed her wings, well, best I could considering the tat I had to work with. I texted her to check she'd given them a test run. Now she's asking if she can come 'n play with the big boys?"

"Really?" Druid refocused on the slope of Haunted Hill and a sugar daddy who was gesturing to his girls to hurry up with a silver walking cane. "Ask if she'd like to play with some big *bad* boys."

"As in with us...down there? Yowza, dude! That's not even right. I know you're pissed at her after the watch-stealing shenanigans, but no bird deserves *that* sort of plucking."

"Trust me. The Fae wants to find her brother. If he's shacked up with monsters, there's no better place to look this cold and stormy night." He thrust a claw at the frozen strait, where the first of the night's brawls had already broken out. "If he's not to be found there, he's not to be found anywhere."

"What'd you want me to text?" said IQ doubtfully, chomping down on his hat-tassel.

"Haunted Hill ASAP. Dress sexy."

"Erm, ok. Although I'm not sure Jez knows what a push-up bra is, let alone how to work her milkshake."

"And in disguise. Don't want those dogs getting a sniff of her. Or she'll need more than my watchstrap to stem the bleeding."

"Wear...disguise," parroted IQ, punching letters in. "Nau...ghty...nurse, dir...ty...geisha..."

"Just tell her to get here," Druid hissed, keeping his gaze on the macabre cabaret below. His flesh crawled with millions of spiders. He'd rather tear out his own eyes than set foot on that hellish plain, but another's words played in his mind with cloying obstinacy. *Hunt his killer. Then show me their throat.* Irises of cool turquoise, a wisp of smoke at just-parted lips...Sophia's intricacies haunted him. He swallowed painfully.

"Excuse me, old fellow."

Druid snapped his head to the side and glared into the great black eyes of the dragon man.

"Hate to interrupt, especially at the unfolding of such an, erm, spirited spectacle. Not my scene of course, especially now I'm prone to the odd touch of sciatica. It's the cold you see, seeps into my joints."

As opposed to the colossal monstrosities of the drifter's wings, Druid sneered internally.

"But I just had to come and congratulate you on a most fantastic get-up. Quite amazing. Yes, quite." Placing a hand of sparkling blue skin on the Drathcor's shoulder, the drifter leant in and rasped, "I was fortunate enough to meet the high lord back in the day, and..." In a swift motion, he scooped Druid's shades down a fraction. "Lo! What a resemblance. The fierce highlight to each eye, the lips, plumped by saline no doubt as was my crest." Silvery claws indicated the triangular bridge of bone grafted above the creature's brow line and the feathers of fleshly skin. "Stings something rotten, dontcha think?"

"The lips were mine in the first place." Druid thrust the shades high on the bridge of his nose with a single digit. Out of the corner of his eye, he saw the guide usher his group away—and none of the tourists seemed in any mood to argue with him.

"Of course, of course, you're the genuine artisan! I spotted that a mile off; the ankh and dagger earrings, even got the kink at the hairline, while I must say it takes guts to substitute the high lord's traditional mane for a more modern hairstyle. Very inventive, and who knows..." He leant in, almost conspiratorially, "...maybe the high lord has adopted that very style himself." Tapping the side of his aquiline nose, the beast rolled back and chortled, "Yes, your use of detail is exceptional, and while there are key advantages to choosing humanoid over the fabled reptilian..." He pointed to his gleaming belly of synthetic scales, "...I admire your bold enthusiasm for the role."

"Well, I, erm..."

"What my *enthusiastic* friend is trying to say is 'Thank you'," intervened IQ, and he and the drifter stared at Druid expectedly.

"Thanks," muttered the Drathcor through gritted fangs.

"He's a little shy," IQ added aside.

"But of course he is! A keen eye for detail, didn't I say, and nothing says Druid like the tortured timidity of the rock drummer. So sensitive, so singular..."

"So simple...Aw, come on now." With a lopsided grin, the kid knocked a finger against his brow and indicated the savage throes of the Blizzard Bash. "Those brutes may err on the side of Neanderthal when it comes to the cerebrum, but drummers? They're positively pre-pupa." Straightening his damp hat-tassel as if to avoid the Drathcor's eye, he embarked, "How many drummers does it take to change a light bulb?

Anybody? Twenty. One to hold the light bulb, the other nineteen to drink until the room spins!"

"Well, yes, very comical." The dragon man smiled, if a little awkwardly.

"Wait, wait. This is a good one. Johnny says to his mum, 'Mum, I want to be a drummer when I grow up'. Mum says, 'But Johnny, you can't do both.'" The boy let out a high titter. "Or, no, this is better. What did the drummer use for contraception?"

"His personality," glowered Druid, and with such malcontent that the dragon man looked aghast and patted him on the arm.

"Oh, I know this world is difficult, old boy. It's hard to find a reason to smile. But the little fellow here means well, don't you laddie?" Squishing IQ's disgruntled face between a set of claws, the drifter smiled benevolently at Druid and pointed to the tomb with his crest. "Hard times, hard times." He peered at the boy, his big, black eyes sharpened. "So take it from me, respect your elders, clean out your ears at bedtime and speak kindly to others." He let go of the boy—who worked his jaw from side to side and stepped away a good pace or two. "Ah, the little angel. Yours?"

"Haven't been that hungry yet."

"Oh, ho ho. Yes, I get you. Drathcor, the whole...may I?" Leaning forward, the drifter dared a spiky finger to Druid's mouth, stuck it between the plump lips and felt around. "Well I never," he chuckled, retracting his claw while the other man stood stock-still. "The things they can do today! And on that note, I'd best be going or the missis and the fledglings will think I've forgotten where the nest is. Good to meet you both," he offered back over one shoulder.

With a quick, unpredicted leap off the ground, the drifter flapped his muscular arms, an action which snapped those tremendous, iridescent wings out on both sides. With a brief salute, he charged full-throttle at the precipice of the hillside then jumped clear. Seconds later, he was soaring; and those wings which had appeared so cumbersome when earth-bound acquired an unexpected grace. The stuff of legends reborn, the drifter circled the Blizzard Bash once, twice, then rose away.

"By George, he's an arse," muttered the kid, still working a hand over his jaw.

"Oh, I don't know." Druid cupped one hand around the tiny winged silhouette. He imagined squashing the creature much like a moth. But he opened his fingers wide instead and waved. "He was starting to grow on me."

"Yeah, well, anyways. Wanna skip the Skinwalkers Shindigs and go party like it's 1199? Get you a sword, a kinky suit of armour, go vanquish us the odd *patronising* serpent, distress ourselves a damsel."

"No, we stick to the plan. Make our way down *there* and make the thugs on the door let us in."

"And without a pair of the old cahooters..." IQ jiggled his own imaginary assets. "How exactly do you suggest we do that?"

Druid put his claws on his hips and glanced restlessly about. "Where is Jezebel?"

Chapter 11

m●BSCENE

"Now you look like a bear who appreciates his meat! Fancy chowing down on this juicy piece?" Druid gave Jezebel an assertive shove in the small of her back, to which the girl responded by twisting her upper body around to give a brief one-finger salute before working her neat hips like a pendulum and sidling up to the sentinel.

She indicated the gleaming plastic dome of the Skinwalker's codpiece. Her small, pink tongue touched the edge of her mouth. "Like me to give that a polish?"

She stiffened as the Skinwalker knocked her hand aside and slid his grotty paws over her shoulders, the small swell of her stomach.

"Ain't nothin' but bones," rasped the hideous creature, unleashing a good spray of saliva just inches from her face. His claws headed south. "I bet even the cu..."

"Cuts me up to see you boys miss out on such a tasty treat," Druid intervened, catching up Jezebel's hands as she reached for the pocket of her PVC raincoat and her slingshot. He pulled her tight against him, but not quick enough to prevent a well-practised strike from a Transformer boot to the beast's cupped groin. "Keep your head for all our sakes," he snarled under his breath, holding her hands secure. Out loud, he insisted, "It's the bones that give you something to gnaw on."

Slightly hunched, the Skinwalker threw back his great shoulders and let out a rip-roaring howl. "Struth, your whore's got spunk!" The wet eyes slithered over the girl's pert form as she struggled free. "Always cool when you gotta beat 'em down first." He pressed the flat of a thumb to Jezebel's brow, over the spot of her third eye chakra. Druid noticed she'd got rid of the silver pentagram design that would have given away her identity in an instant. "We'll take it."

Snatching the girl up by the arm, Druid marched her past, yanking her quickly aside when she threw one more kick at the thug, who just let his snake pit of a head loll back and unleashed a great, fat belly laugh.

"Good call, dude!" saluted IQ, turning his back on the furred Goliath, if all too soon as five gnarly claws slid around his neck and scooped him back.

"Where you scurrying, rat boy?"

"I'm, erm…"

"What Mack Daddy wouldn't cater for all appetites, hey boss?" Druid shouted back, sending Jezebel flying out across the ice with a determined push. Retracing his steps, he gripped the back of IQ's hoodie and pulled, forcing the boy to balance on the tips of his raggedy, soaked-through-to-the-skin trainers.

Glaring at the kid with the kind of revulsion usually reserved for something scrapped off a boot heel, the brute twisted his jowl then hollered, "Look 'ere, Kisscurl. This whoremonger's brought a pretty boy for you."

Thirty or so feet away and patrolling the opposite end of the arena's entrance, an Italian stallion of a Skinwalker tossed his glossy, black locks over a shoulder, cupped his hands to his lips and thundered, "Aw, and I was saving my ass for you, Varick." Resting a meat hook of a hand on one hip, the brute eyeballed IQ. "Not the prettiest skank I've seen, but send the slut on in anyway," he roared, twisting back to level a pimp who was attempting to slink by with a single punch.

"Piss off then," snarled the other guard, eyeing Druid with suspicion. "And keep the girl clean. I get off at three."

"Shit a brick, man. That was close!" IQ scurried alongside, hobbling a little as if Kisscurl had already had his wicked way with him. "You see the way that other greasy brute looked at me? Makes me feel all dirty."

"Like you've room to talk!" snapped Jezebel, dropping back in line with them at last rather than stomping off ahead. "Least you didn't get some leprous arsehole trying to feel you up."

"Don't you mean *lecherous* arsehole?" offered Druid.

"Trust me. I was face to face with the scabby brute, and I was right the goth damn first time. Speaking of lecherous, you have to put *your* sticky claws on me quite so often?"

Her brusqueness set him on edge. "No, but you were acting the shrew back there." He glanced at the girl's wig of neon-blue bunches; the skin-tight latex of her black cat suit. "Quite the athlete with those high flailing kicks of yours."

"The slob was pawing me, and while I'll flirt like a bona-fide pro if it gets us rights of passage, I'll stop short of the grebs copping an actual feel, if that's alright with you of course."

"I didn't like him touching you either," snapped Druid, with an honesty he didn't expect of himself. He thrust his hands into the silky pockets of his leather and tried to ignore IQ's irritating smirk.

Jezebel, meanwhile, faltered in her tirade. She adjusted the collar of her raincoat so that it lay close to her throat. "I just don't like monsters getting too close." Her face brightened, if more by way of a mask than genuine emotion. "How's you anyway?" she asked sunnily. "Assaulted any young women recently?"

"Not recently." His hooded gaze shifted from one band of Skinwalkers to another as their group wove in and out.

"Although he did bag himself a boyfriend," IQ piped up, while twittering, "Oops there, sorry mate, sorry pal," as he ploughed through the middle of one barbaric brood, apparently stepping on three or four freshly shined para boots in the process. "A drippy dragon of a drifter took quite a shine to Grumpy-Drawers here," he continued, emerging—somewhat regrettably, thought Druid—alive on the other side.

"In a similar vein to your attracting that baby butch a minute ago," Jezebel retorted. "Looked your sort anyway. Bulges, pretty lips and a hairy mane you could really hold on to." She made fists of her hands and thrust her hips forward in a vague erotic motion.

"Screw you, Jez."

"Only if you're quick. From the looks of things, I'm gonna be quite the busy girl tonight," she said with stunned uncertainty as they entered the thunderous flame-lit arena of the Blizzard Bash.

Feeding himself between one gang of barbarous brutes and then another, Druid came to one conclusion—if Castclan were the brains behind dissension, Skinwalkers were the brawn. He couldn't explain their height, the large, heavy bones packed with rippling flesh or the whorled skin that lay thickly over each knuckle and elbow, at least not outside the realms of witchcraft, or steroids of course, and yet he knew they were just men. Or had been once. He eyed their chomping jaws, tearing at a hamburger or the cap of a pungent cigar, listened to a strained cacophony of snorts, grunts, yelps, whoops, barks, and howling. It was hard to trace modern man, and yet he had to admit that witnessed en masse, the Skinwalkers had a remarkable, if terrifying, presence.

Part transhuman, part cyber-punk, there was something of honour to each creature's gruesome battle dress: the gold torc worn at the throat and just below the Adam's apple, the woad-like blue tattoos coiling up and out of the collar and sleeves of a beaten-old leather, the waist-length mane of dark and neon dreadlocks, shaved high on either side to expose fresh ink or the crossways spike of a Scaffold ear piercing. Each warrior favoured a kinetic mode of body armour; bolted plates attached to a tube T-shirt, fitted with flashing LEDs, holograms or UV graphics, black, convex plates for shoulder pads, and an arsenal of silver cuffs, steel elbow joints, and bolted shin sections. Some wore spiked codpieces, emblematic of more violent appetites, others, plate lens goggles or flasher wristbands that sent off shots of halogen like sweeping beams. Pouring in and out of the chaotic mass, fists moulded to his chest, Druid couldn't quite decide if they reminded him more of things birthed of the dark ages or of some apocalyptic future. Either way, like a bad acid trip, the image of Cerberus loomed at every angle, etched in flaming oils over the backs of age-crusted leathers, printed on plastic cups, tattooed behind an ear…

"Something of overkill," he muttered to no one in particular.

"What's that?" said Jezebel stiffly as the beasts pressed close about.

"The, erm, tribal wings. Something of overkill." His hand broke through the sea of bodies.

"If you think *that's* overstated…" Witch-green eyes scintillating, IQ directed a hand towards the amphitheatre and its triumphal arch of an entryway, which was a rusting, tattered edifice with a shield at the crest.

Or, as Druid interpreted it, a caveat against free entry, the weirdest materials—21" alloys, slivers of steel, anterior rib sections, telescopic plated armour, and nine inch claw-like nails—having been sculpted into the triple-headed Cerberus in 3-D. It was mounted, like the worst sort of gargoyle, at the Gauntlet's entrance.

"What's with the puppy?" hissed Jezebel as an old walrus of a Skinwalker bowled her aside.

Druid caught her up at the waist, slung her back onto her feet then let go. "Cerberus guarded the gates to the Greek underworld. In that respect, he was the original hell-hound, if you like. What you'd call a potent tribal emblem."

The girl nodded at the arch and the flaming world beyond. "So *in* there must equate to Hell." She stared back at him. Her face acquired a thousand edges. "Shall we?"

Installed on the rustic shelf of a wooden palette, five feet or so off the ground, IQ gave a sharp whistle. "Up here."

Scooping Jezebel back by the crook of an arm, Druid encouraged her to climb the wet rungs of a half-sunken stepladder, slip below a whale's ribcage of twisted steel then inch alongside the kid. He secured the tip of a cowboy boot on a mesh overhang, stretched for the vine of a thick, greased chain, pulled up a couple of feet and poured himself into the throne of a mouldered leather bucket seat. Little by little, as if once he'd laid eyes on its grand, anarchic blueprint, he'd never erase it from his mind, Druid took in the flame-rinsed maelstrom of the Gauntlet.

Initially, he was struck by the oval arrangement of seven towering flats, set almost at the vertical and serving as a cavea of spectator stands. Each flat appeared welded together out of anything to hand, so that the weird and wonderful wildlife were seated amidst girders, self-regurgitating sprung mattresses, cogs, winches, ropes, severed car seats, fuselages, and scrap metal carrion, or hanging off icy handholds, distended pipes, and ledges like a tribe of rabid rhesus monkeys.

Eyes full of stars behind their tinted lenses, Druid stared out at the arena. A bill-posted barrier advertising key brands, Harley Davidson, Budweiser, Back Street Heroes magazine, and their ilk enclosed the vast expanse of a central ice rink. Seven metre-wide ramps, or 'spokes', emanated off the outside of the rink, each built of wooden slats, like a sort of solid rope bridge, and underpinned with rustic trellis. Rising at an adverse camber, each spoke terminated in the radial of a turning circle...or so Druid guessed as a flame-haired brute circled the armoured roach of a Moto Guzzi on the radial of the spoke immediately below, while, at the far end of the opposite causeway, another titan braced the lustrous girder of a chopped Harley Panhead.

"Race fourteen. Lobryn the Lewd versus Mark Meatmangler," hollered an amplified voice—and, hooking his claws into the thick, greased chain, Druid leant out to spy a cave of threaded rags and metal at the crest of the neighbouring lookout. A Skinwalker with a snood of black and white dreads had his megaphone trained on the crowd like an outsized Ted Nugent popping bison with a BB gun.

"Lobryn is thrice-winner of previous chicken runs," the super skunk boomed. "Meatmangler is a newbie on the circuit, so let's give him a big Skinwalker welcome. Got any wolves out there?"

A thousand beasts looked to the moon and howled.

"Sheesh, don't go much on the harmonies," hissed IQ. But his voice was quickly lost to the blistering roar of engines as the Celt nearest to them fought to control the Moto Guzzi's screaming burnout. In the distance, the monstrous Harley turned over with the unmistakeable 'pop-pop' of its dragon throat.

Suspended above the ice rink, traffic lights switched to amber then to green in a heartbeat.

The Guzzi launched off its mark with the sound of a million hornets swarming; insects made of lightning, fire and metal, whose steel wings clashed at awesome volume. Likewise, the Harley powered down the strait with a Jurassic uneven roar, a super-swift tiger moth with stretched abdomen and gleaming feelers. As the road hogs whipped closer, dreadlocks streaming out into the wind like heraldic banners, claws white-knuckling the drag-bars, Druid felt his chest punch back and forth, back and forth, yet with far less adrenalin than the beasts facing one other down, he was certain.

Raking the throttle, the Guzzi jumped a good few feet out onto the ice circle and slid, almost elegantly, across the frozen marble. Seconds later, it reached the other side then floored it up the second straight already occupied by the Harley. Suddenly the riders were hammering down on each other in fat swells of smoke and the stench of burning oil.

"Shit," breathed Druid, claws tensing at the split seams of the bucket seat.

In a blur of motion, the two riders appeared literally nose-to-nose, but it was the Harley that inclined and started to slide at an extreme angle. Its wheels revolved angrily, splintering up the crude highway before shooting off the side. Likewise, the warrior left the saddle and threw himself at the opposite angle. The creature fell with a sickening crunch, plummeting several metres out across the ice in a man-sized streak of grit and blood.

Back on the platform, the Guzzi lashed on its breaks and screeched to a halt in the far turning circle. Triumphant, the flame-haired brute pressed his groin forward then back, and worked the bike around to face the crowd. He raised one arm, a great ham of a fist crushing the air.

The resulting cheer was deafening.

"Lobryn wins!" roared the commentator. "Meatmangler takes a dive and forfeits the race. Lobryn goes through with no collateral damage to bike or person. Fourteen chicken runs complete. Fifteen minutes 'til the Gauntlet!"

A molten mass of bodies poured down off the spectator stand.

Jezebel twisted around suddenly. "That scare you?"

Druid found his face unexpectedly close to hers. "Not as much as some things."

They held one another's gaze until IQ butted in.

"Bitchin'!" The kid's expression was electric. "Seen it, D? That Guzzi had wings on it. And when the hog put an ear in the sand? That's *pain*, man, with added ouch. Talking of the big, hairy loser, what they do with him now?"

"Nothing." Druid pressed his spine into the bowl of the bucket seat, a retreat that apparently went unnoticed. "He'll face no punishment. After all, he put his head on the line and lost graciously. But neither will any of these mutts rush to help him. That suggests weakness and is seen less as an act of benevolence than an insult. Win or lose, do it with dignity. Don't shame yourself or the chapter. You could say it's their mantra. Once you understand that, you start to see why that beast's left to get himself together and…"

"Scrape his ass up off the ice? Nice mentality." Jezebel's elfin features hardened.

All three watched in silence as the defeated beast limped up to his bike, the blooded stub of what could only be bone protruding through an elbow of his leather. It took several attempts for him to adjust the twisted axis of his vehicle but he managed to heave it upright at last and half-steer, half-carry it with his one good arm. In time, he exited the circuit.

"Depends how you look at it," said Druid at last. He poured his long limbs down then reached to assist the girl, only to find she was already safely installed on the ground. "If he was seriously injured, I expect they'd help him out."

"And what counts as *seriously* injured?" said Jezebel, obviously revolted.

"Well, that would be...dead mainly."

"And how come you know so much about Skinwalkers?"

"I considered riding with them once."

"No way, dude!" The kid's eyes grew wide as saucers.

"It's okay. I decided against it in the end. Too regimented for my taste, not to mention pretty unpleasant in the odour department."

"What in the name of all that is wrong and unholy is *he* doing here? Hide me, quick, hide me!" IQ tried to scuttle back into the throng, but all too late as the hand of God stretched down and patted him magnanimously on the head.

"Why, Irvine! How delightful to see you. How the devil are you?" Peter Pineapple hooked a thumb into the pocket of his grey, satin waistcoat. As if at the twist of a key, his clockwork face illuminated. "And your sister, Desdemona? Oh, the pretty dear. She must be nigh on close to birthing, and in this inclement weather...such a bother. Although a child born to winter is less prone to hay fever. A fact not often shared, but one that strikes me as invaluable, hmmm? But, Irvine, this Blizzard Bash is no place for a sweet boy."

"And how d'you know he's sweet, Pervy Pineapple?" The question came from a throat stripped dry by cigar smoke and doused with bootleg whiskey, as did the smell. That pungent aroma oozed almost visibly off the worn and dirty leathers slung about the red-haired titan who lumbered past, accompanied by a motley crew of riders and peroxide pretties.

"That's *Mister* Per...*Mister* Pineapple to you," asserted the official, making a point of producing a notepad and pencil from the inner pocket of his knee-length dress coat. "Any more of your monkey business and I'll be forced to report you to Lorcan. You don't want me doing that now, do you?"

"*You* know Lorcan?" Druid's mind sharpened.

Shooing at the gang, who prowled close about like a pack of starved coyotes, the Grallator bent at the waist and loomed down to Druid's level. He squinted, bringing his round-lensed spectacles to the tip of his nose. His features suddenly revolved. "Ah, but of course. The cousin! I trust you're feeling better. Flu, wasn't it? Oh, it can quite knock the stuffing out of one."

"I'd like to knock *his* stuffing out," interjected a squashed-nosed brute, jabbing a comrade with an elbow.

Seemingly oblivious, the Grallator straightened up to his full, lofty height. "Yes, I do know Lorcan," he said officiously, adding with volume, "He and I have what you might call a mutual respect. He, the fighter, I, the thinker. Oh yes, Lorcan understands the natural order of things. There must be method to one's madness." Catching the marled eye of the dog with flaming dreads, and whom Druid now recognised as the triumphant rider from the chicken run, Peter Pineapple tap-tapped his notepad with the blunt end of the pencil. "Even that of Skinwalkers. Which is precisely why Lorcan requested my presence at this…" He scanned the scene from on high and blanched at what he saw. "…erm, this, shall we say jamboree?"

"Why isn't there a larger Grallator presence at a potentially *explosive* event like this?" Druid wondered out loud. Yes, Grallators were increasingly disquieting, swooping down on any rebel who saw things differently to the Management, but the notion that they were in league with the rabid brutes fencing him in on all four sides was nonsensical.

"This is not an illegal event," Peter Pineapple assured him, the slight acidity to his tone suggesting it would be were *he* in charge. "It is also seen as something of a mutual truce, Skinwalker activity being self-contained for the night, and Grallators steering clear as a result. I alone have been awarded jurisdiction over this impromptu patch." The Grallator pressed a hand to his chest and bowed his head. His eyes rolled sideways to fix on the scathing expressions of the Skinwalkers. He lengthened his neck. "I am to report on…" Licking a fingertip, he leafed through the notepad, halting at a certain page. "…standards of hygiene, outdoor catering, first aid facilities, liquor licensing, and *crowd control.*" The over-magnetised, too-blue eyes stared deliberately at the goading Skinwalkers. "Quite a task, I assure you. Quite a task."

"Introduce me to him," Druid instructed without expression.

"Hear that! The dickin' pimp wants to be *introduced* to Lorcan. Lah-di friggin' da. Introduce him to my fist more like!"

Again, the wild dog laughter so that Druid's claws fused into razored buds.

"It's imperative I speak with Lorcan," he hissed, torn between assaulting the sanctimonious officer or the carousing savages. "I can pay you."

"Sheesh, who'd pay for *that?*" spat the leery Celt, tossing the great matt of his hennaed mane back over a shoulder. His bite crushed around a stubby cigar. "Tell you who." He popped off three or four fat smoke rings then brought his pockmarked, multi-pierced face close to Druid's. "A Drathy pimp with no taste and shit for brains."

"Whereas you bunch of butt-breathed jackasses can't even give it away." Jezebel's black eyes flashed, dangerous or incongruously playful, while Druid simply stared at her; half-amused, half-incensed. Hands on the sharp angles of her hips, fingers worrying at a coat pocket, taking confidence, he supposed, from the close proximity of her slingshot, she hardened her mouth and shrugged, as if to say, "Now what?"

The dirt-encrusted Celt gave Druid a determined shove and arrived beside the girl in a great clatter of his black armour. "What you say, whore?" he roared, jowls frothing.

"Erm Jez. Like, what you doing, mate?" said IQ in a hoarse whisper that only succeeded in attracting the notice of the squat-nosed beast and his compatriot. "All right gents," he beamed, if with an over-exaggeration of his mouth muscles as the brutes pressed closer.

Peter Pineapple also attempted to embrace the role of peacekeeper. Stepping between the two aggressors, he twittered, "Now, settle down, boys and girls. No need for any silliness." His moon face bobbing about on its stick of a neck, he wagged a finger at both parties. "Be nice, my good fellow, and I'll help the little lady run along now." A white glove hovered near Jezebel's blue-neon bunches.

"Try it and I'll break your hand," said the girl with measured emphasis, and the Grallator swiftly withdrew his arm, as if her words had torn a chunk out.

Eyes pinned to the monstrous canine, Jezebel appeared unflinching. Then she bent her neck—and, for a brief time, Druid couldn't tell if she laughed or if she cried. It bothered him. He wanted to ignore the swift flush to his brow, his neck, his armpits, as well as the bitter need and lust and wanting. He wanted the beast to smash down that great club of a fist and end his suffering. At the same time, he wanted to deliver her.

He still hadn't made up his mind when Jezebel loosed a globule of spit onto one of the beast's para boots. "That's my throat cleared," she said matter-of-factly, wiping the back of her hand across her lips. "Now we might stand a chance of communicating. I said…"

"Heard you the first time, rancid bitch." The brute called his mob close with the crook of a horn-tipped claw.

"Me, rancid? That's rich coming from a rabid mutt with halitosis that'd kill Satan's shit-swilled swine at fifty paces. But we're not gonna hold that against you. Not when we have your face."

"Young miss!" Peter Pineapple turned a whiter shade of pale. "We are guests at this splendid hoedown, and, as such, need to mind our manners. Now what do you say to this…nice gentleman?"

"Kiss my hairless…"

If Jezebel had sought to provoke the vitriolic brood by design, she could not have planned it better. In seconds, IQ was facedown on the ice, a shiny, black kneecap pinioning his upper vertebra—and while the girl had obviously planned to back up her verbal assault with a well-aimed slug of shot from her catapult, that strategy relied on her actually having the time and dexterity to take aim and fire. Druid watched in horror as the weapon snagged on the inside-out silk of her pocket, then winced as the beast slapped her hard across the face and mangled her into its arms.

Meanwhile, Peter Pineapple's attempts to restore calm ranged from "You there! Release that child," to "This is most unacceptable. I'll report you!" and finally, "Stop that, stop this instant, I insist. If you push, I will fa…aaargh!" Crisscrossing his peg-legs, the Grallator came crashing down, then slid silently out across that gleaming surface like a spread-eagled fawn.

Last man standing, Druid pulled his fisted claws tight against his breastbone, knuckle to arched, white knuckle. As two fiends powered down, the jet-tipped buds blew apart. He struck out at the first brute, delivering a well-aimed strike to the underside of its chin. Pale eyes crackling behind his steely shades, he struck a blow to the second fiend's shoulder, disrupting a punch and stunning the muscle and tendon there. But, securing the wounded arm with the other paw, the brute still managed to spin a sharp kick at his head. Druid ducked in the nick of time, feeling the sudden rush of air through his mohawk. Stamping out a low strike to the Skinwalker's knee joint, he levelled the brute and delivered a swift strike to its windpipe.

As that assailant wheezed and crumpled over onto its side, the first brute recovered enough to aim one, two, three kicks at the Drathcor's head then his torso. The second strike connected with the top ribs. Druid felt its piercing sting and, all of a sudden, his claws were less weapons than the counterbalance to each streaming movement. He blocked the third kick with his forearm, leant in, powered the heel of his palm against the other's breastbone and sent the brute smashing across the ice.

He stooped, dredging the freezing air into his lungs. When one of the lanky females ran at him hard and prepared to launch a new volley, he scooped his shades down the bridge of his nose, burnt her with his cold, white eyes and drew back his upper lip. The roar that escaped his throat was low in volume—even as he fought to catch his breath, Druid understood that alerting several thousand Skinwalkers to his true identity would be nothing short of suicidal—but it stopped that wild Amazon in her tracks, and with unprecedented immediacy.

"Drathcor," mouthed the she-wolf, her androidal face made the more feminine for her fear. Yanking at the droopy cross of an earring, she dropped back, all the while pointing faintly at him as if he were Death himself. Likewise, any other Skinwalkers that had been witness to the sound backed off suddenly, heavy jaws slacked, yellow eyes flicking rapidly back and forth. Sweat poured and he smelt their disbelief.

Less aware were the two miscreants restraining IQ or the slathering brute whose paws clung with sloth-like tenacity to Jezebel and forced her chin back at an ugly angle.

Druid thumbed his shades into place. His gaze, however, was unwavering.

"What now, whore?" demanded the Celt, unleashing a fine line of drool down Jezebel's cheek.

"Now you let her go," Druid answered quietly.

"But I like her smell." A rasping tongue licked the girl's ear. "Smells like something bleeding, or at least, soon to be."

Not allowing the Skinwalker time to act on that sentiment, Druid shot down to grass level; one leg bent, the other extended to scoop the beast's colossal limbs out from under him. Like a lumbered redwood, the brute came plummeting down, but was on his feet again almost instantly, unlike Jezebel, who fell awkwardly, one arm trapped beneath her so that her head thumped against the ice. Her dark eyes flickered, once, twice. Then she slipped out of consciousness.

With a tremendous clatter of the tectonic plates at his shoulders, pectorals, legs and elbows, the Celt struck a hefty kick at his opponent's midsection. Druid caught the bruising wham against his ribs again. He fed its energy through flesh, bone, and tendons, deflecting a series of twisting punches to his throat and upper body, then flowed in to the monster's chest. With his spine pressed to the rigid body-armour, he reached up behind, seized the dog's stiff leather lapel and hoisted him over one shoulder. Supporting the brute, who crashed down nonetheless in a great splintering of ice, he knelt and raised an elbow.

It was the ragged edge of one of the Skinwalker's claws that grazed his throat, forcing him to spring back into a crab at the same time that the missed strike sent his opponent sideways. Following through the roll, the beast proved surprisingly limber and leapt up onto all fours, stabbing a backwards kick at Druid's face, then twisting up onto one supporting leg to launch the strike again. Arching his spine at an inhuman angle, the Drathcor limboed beneath the second volley then flipped up into a crouched squat. A double turn, and each man mirrored the triangular form of a pivoting leg and arms tight to the body. While Druid focused on a series of tight, elegant strikes, he resisted the sheer brute force of the Skinwalker's multiple blows, which were less precise in aim but robust. Shooting down, he hooked his leg about the soft flesh where an elasticated tube kept the front kneepad in position and whammed it once against the back of the knee joint, once against the upper heel of a filthy para boot.

The noise that issued from the beast was nothing short of godless. Like an executed man, the Skinwalker collapsed onto his knees then fell softly, limply, onto his front, head twisted sideways. After a few seconds, the pierced cheeks turned ashen.

"Breathe," hissed the Drathcor, smacking the base of an upright fist between the brute's armoured shoulders. "Be glad I chose to snap your Achilles tendon and not your spine, Skinwalker."

The blow forced his challenger to wheeze horribly. From under hooded lids, the brute considered Druid with a mix of fear and hatred. His large, brown lips twisted. "Least I killed your whore."

A fistful of knives ripped down, opening a glistening half-moon of wet, raw flesh from brow to ear. "You're right. I do smell something bleeding." Druid brought the blooded tips of his claws just short of his tongue. "You." His gaze left the war torn Celt and fell on Jezebel, whose eyes stirred behind painted lids. "And my whore's still breathing," he muttered, flying to her side.

He crouched and, for the second time in as many days, drew her back against his chest and slipped his arms about her. "It's okay," he breathed hoarsely by her ear. "This was a bad idea. I'm going to get you home."

"Unlikely," said a strong, velvety voice, near at hand and with a resonance that brought an eerie silence to the scene. "It was your choice to share in our revels, your choice to challenge my men and put Lobryn out of action. Now it's *my* choice."

More than anything, Druid wanted to ignore the stranger's voice and sink deep below that moment, keep sinking ever downwards. Even as Jezebel stirred, he tightened his arms about her, his every emotion locked in a painful osmosis. But then she woke, pulled away and he lost her. At last he raised his eyes.

Lorcan, chief of the Skinwalkers, towered over them. Adjusting the great weight of chains, bunches of keys, spent cartridge belts and racoon tails at his vast waist and upper thighs, the creature squatted down and brought his shrewd, age-worn muzzle down to Druid's level. "Gotta have a man take his place in the Gauntlet. What you say, devil man?"

Chapter 12

Fuel

Perched in a black nest of rags and twisted steel aloft one of the spectator stands—IQ on a rusted iron bucket to her left, the folded-down Grallator on a metal lavatory to her right, and in the care of several titanic Skinwalkers, including a super skunk in possession of a megaphone—Jezebel shifted on her own seat of a stitched-to-steel beanbag and glued her eyes to the Gauntlet.

From on high, she saw a cute 'crew' in killer heels and skin-sucking vinyl escort D up the trellis that underpinned the nearest of the seven spokes and out onto the slated plateau of the turning circle. Bathed in moonshine, he kept his back to her so that he was less a man than an elongated shadow, pouring an ever-lengthening limb over the hub of the waiting Moto Guzzi. Her gaze touched him like a butterfly. The fluid angles of his torso, strapped inside some other beast's body armour; the ragged edges of his mohawk, the very tips of which were filtered by the moonlight. She imagined his face. It showed no emotion.

Inexplicably, she longed to climb up behind him, encircle his waist, and hold on tight for both of their dear lives. Instead, she bit at her thumbnail, glaring at a biker babe who leant unnecessarily far over the front of the bike to pass D his headgear. Twisting sideways, his silhouette tossed the open-faced helmet round in his hands then eased it over his head, and expertly so. She watched in fascination as he manoeuvred the bike off its stand, pulled on the clutch and jumped the kick-start. Massaging the throttle, he added the Guzzi's dry-bone rasp to the noise of the six dinosaurs on the other turning circles.

As those sinister machines let out billows of black smoke, put-putted or boomed, she saw the skunk lean his great arms over the uppermost bars of the nest and inform the throng below, "Seven riders start, six riders fall. One brute's victorious!"

A great roar resounded about the arena.

"Welcome back to Dirk Dirt on a Ducati Desmo 900. That Duc shifts like shit off a shovel!"

Jezebel glared at the first rider, a beast in sports leathers, who unhooked a paw from the shiny antennae of a giant wasp and saluted.

"Macarab, back in the saddle again on a Triumph Bonneville. That's one helluva pretty ride."

Several degrees right, it was the turn of a gothic Amish priest, whose waist-length beard was a matt of glossed, tight, black curls. After he had united his palms in brief, if sinister, prayer, the priest mounted a neat little bug with cardinal red wing cases and a polished chrome skeleton.

The girl jumped as a hand touched her. "You okay, Jez?"

"Fine and dandy." Her eye wandered back to D, who maintained the same elongated pose like a strip of greased, black leather.

The boy squeezed her shoulder; released it. His voice brightened. "So who's your money on?"

"Master Quirk! You mustn't waste your precious pennies on gambling!" exclaimed Peter Pineapple, quite aghast. "And I'm quite recovered, thank you. My collapse, but a stumble…"

"Sh!" The girl's eyes went up like a match put to gasoline. She'd missed the patter for the third competitor; a statuesque tomboy in fringed, white chaps and matching vest. The glamorous limbs clung to a great old hunk of American iron. The face was a boyish snarl.

"…Guns blazing on a Kawasaki Ninja," hollered the skunk. He thrust a devil horn salute in the direction of the fourth rider—and, straining to catch up, Jezebel stared out at the farthest platform and a beast whose entire body appeared injection-moulded in gleaming, black thermoplastic. Even the visor of a full-face helmet was blacked out. Enchanted, or afraid, she saw the Ninja itself had bulk, offset by a score of sharply bladed angles. Yet there was something less showy to its rider, who stayed motionless and beautifully backlit by a shaft of moonlight.

"Poet Johnson on his Harley V-Rod. Time to disembark, ladies, or you'll get those tight butts flamed," hollered the skunk, scooping one great paw aside as if to bowl a strike—and, still haunted by the dark maverick on the Ninja, Jezebel shifted her gaze to the next entrant.

Bronzed and ever so slightly fey in spite of his gladiatorial bulk and stature, the fifth rider kept a veritable stable of preening peroxides on his podium. Glitzy, blonde dreadlocks lay across his shoulders, while, even from a distance, she discerned a too-white, wolfish smile.

But while that disco king opted for the power of a smoky gold muscle bike, his neighbour rode a horse of a very different colour.

"Bad Seed!" The skunk trained a spotlight on a "...converted Harley FXSTS with 72 spoke chrome Dayton wire wheels. Check out those bubbas!"

Bioengineered with the lump heart of a triceratops, the trike powered up to its mark. Dark-encrusted and pulsating, it epitomised all that was bestial in the godless machines—as did the reclining road warrior. His muzzle was swathed in a silk, skull-printed mask. Ultra-violet dreads vined at his shoulders. Thick, black-lensed goggles served for eyes.

"Shit a brick, that lot look dangerous," muttered IQ, giving voice to Jezebel's growing unease. "Ask me, it's a seven horse race. Any one of the fug-uglies could take home the bacon, or whatever it is they're in this friggin' race for."

"Glory," said the Grallator knowledgeably. He tapped his notebook with a pencil. "And there's the small matter of Immunity."

"Immunity?" Jezebel heard her own intensity.

"Whoever wins the Gauntlet can move among the Skinwalkers for a year without reprise. Put more succinctly, no beast can lay a claw on you, no matter how obscenely you provoke them. At least until the next Gauntlet comes around, and then, my word, you're in for it!" The Grallator concluded his sentence at volume as the entire stadium erupted.

Jezebel's stomach felt like something separate from the rest of her. "Is that it? Did I miss them announcing D?"

"Well, he's a renegade, forced to partake to fulfil his debt to the clan. There's no respect in that, so his name will not be called. At least that's how I understand it, my dear." The Grallator tried an awkward, compassionate smile out on her.

"And *what* the hell is he partaking in?"

"The Seven Wonders of the Wheel," announced the official, and with such grand pomposity that she noticed even IQ's fingers twitch. "Seven riders, now, how did they put it again?" He leafed through his notepad, ran a finger down a page. "Ah, yes. Seven riders *face off*. Each is given a flare gun, to be stored at the, er, rider's discretion. At the signal, all must *bomb it* down the straight to the central ice rink, where battle will commence until seven become two. The last two riders must then race to their opponent's starting point, the triumphant beast being the first to release their flare."

"It's a test of courage," said IQ simply, twisting the sodden mass of his hat's tassel around his finger as if, by not chewing it, he gave no outward sign of nervousness. "Least D can ride."

"How d'you know?"

"I don't." The kid poked a finger down at D. "But he looks the part."

"And he knows how to start the engine," cut in Peter Pineapple (again, that helpful smile). "Oh yes, never fear, sweet maid." He flourished a silk handkerchief like a banner. "Your knight will prove his valour."

"He's not *my* knight," Jezebel tried to shout over a thrash soundtrack as the crowd applied every sort of implement to every type of metal. But the Grallator just pointed to his spectacles then out to the Gauntlet. She stared ahead in time to see the suspended cage of traffic lights turn thrice amber then a screaming green. Skidding off their marks, all seven riders plunged down the straight in a rush of heat and smoking rubber.

Jezebel shivered. By turn, fire then ice cascaded over her flesh. Breath misted at her lips. Her heart fibrillated inside its cage of bones. Ignoring a sea of visceral mouths that stretched wide and gave off dark, unnatural sounds like things brought back from the dead, she found a space to focus in, on a man, forsaken and alone.

With his spindle limbs arched each side of the metal scarab of the Guzzi, D tunnelled away in a blaze of white adrenaline. Likewise, each brute fused with his or her machine so it was hard to tell flesh apart from moulded body parts. What *was* distinctive, however, was the war cry of each cycle; the tumbling, monstrous-loud traction of the trike against the Bonneville's beautiful, dark, retro roar, the low-mid grunt of the waspish Ducati against the drag-pipe-aided rasp of the V-rod. There was no time to get a grip on the last three. All seven sleds fed out onto the central rink and braked in a wash of shredded ice.

"Now what?" Jezebel said tensely.

Peter Pineapple's large pumpkin face loomed. "Anything goes."

Skating around the far barrier, Druid had also guessed as much. He brought the Guzzi to a dry burn, lowered his heels to the ice and inclined his helmet. At the far side of the rink, the six dark riders were similarly paused; each warrior fixed on the tall, thin shadow of a man astride a shimmering, black dragonfly.

Druid swallowed. His shins, wrists and shoulders ached. His mind was a whirlpool.

"Who's up first?" he muttered through gritted fangs.

The answer wasn't slow in coming forward. Sprawled in the low-slung seat of the trike, the thug with the all too appropriate moniker of Bad Seed slid the dual batons of a martial arts nunchaku down from a shoulder and moved out into the field. Druid's gaze darkened. He had paid heed to the skunk's patter for each rider with the express intent of sizing up his competition, and this beast had sounded one of the ugliest. Easing off to a slow, meaty rumble, the brute yanked the two hardwood sticks apart to reveal a short interconnecting chain. Manipulating a stick, he started to revolve its twin above his head in quickening momentum.

Druid squeezed a warning shot from the Guzzi's steel throat. But even as the nunchaku slit the air like silk, he noted a second rider start his own barbaric preparations.

Flattened in-between the gleaming feelers of the Duc, the brute named Dirk Dirt steered that garish wasp around in a trickling circle. He slowed right down, put a fist inside his black and yellow sports blouson and pulled out a full-size mace. Revolving a dead-weighted arm at a shoulder socket, he sent that medieval weapon powering down then around in skull-crushing revolutions.

Druid manoeuvred the Guzzi up to what he rough-guessed was the 50 yard line. He watched as the two riders swept out either side of him then back in like two sides of a dark heart, passing one another without reaction; and he smiled bleakly. So they weren't even going to pretend to attack one another, not when they had *his* flesh to flail for fun before the real games could begin.

He spun the throttle. With a crackling roar, the Guzzi streaked across the greenish glass while the trike and the Duc powered in, each rider slicing the air with his pick of lethal weapon. As the three bikes threatened to collide, Bad Seed slammed the pivoting nunchaku out from his elbow just as Dirk Dirt lunged up from the wasp's saddle and brought the bone-splitting orb of the mace smashing down. His visor dappled with dirty ice and the whip of wind at his ears, Druid arched dangerously far over to slide the Guzzi just under the crushing weight of spike and baton, and on the thinnest sliver of wheel tread. He swept into a tight, ice-shearing doughnut and righted the bike—unlike his opponents.

With a hoggish snort, Bad Seed flipped the nunchaku back and caught his fellow beast square on the chin, just as the brute on the Duc delivered the buckling weight of the mace to the trike's front wheel. As Dirk Dirt *hit* the dirt, the trike rolled, narrowly missing the Tomboy and her chopper before bouncing up, then ricocheting off the ice rink's barrier.

Druid hunched in the saddle. The sky rained bolts, glass and metal.

"Wipe-out for Dirk Dirt and Bad Seed!" thundered the skunk with bloodcurdling gusto. "One minute twenty in the saddle. Make your way off the Gauntlet, gentlemen."

As the last bits of shrapnel scattered, Druid peeled off to the barrier. His chest convulsed like a fish out of water, and he tried to take a softer, deeper breath; an action cut short by his noticing a subtle signal from the black knight astride the Ninja to the Poet and the Tomboy. The two singled-out warriors coasted forward, the misfiring snorts of their cousin cycles harmonising.

Druid edged through the scattered remains of the trike. He leant forward, trailed a set of claws near the ice and, with consummate dexterity, snapped up the nunchaku. Revolving one stick, he swept the chain over a shoulder to hook the other stick up and underneath his under arm.

With a rush of grit and gasoline, all three gladiators charged. While the Poet pivoted off-axis, the Tomboy eased her war-machine alongside the Guzzi and proceeded to flank that glittering moth for a circuit. Feeling much like a beast separated from the safe swell of the herd, Druid prepared to pitch left and shake her off; except, at the very last moment, he glanced to the side, and was utterly mesmerised by the creature's freakish athleticism. Scooping her knees up, she rocked back onto her coccyx, then leapt aboard the saddle, arms outstretched as counterweights. With the natural poise of an acrobat, she balanced on one leg, tilted then loosed a swift, high kick.

A hefty para boot ricocheted off Druid's helmet. He skidded. Reining the Guzzi in, he twisted at the waist to size up his new, limber opponent, only to take another fluid punch to the head. His neck snapped back, all breath lost from his lungs so that, for a few slow, black seconds, he dipped below consciousness, and the Guzzi was left to snake aimlessly across the gleaming surface.

With a gargantuan effort, he staved off the concussion, just in time to flick his side mirror with a claw. At his back, the wiry Tomboy leapt down, pumped the gas and slid in close again. On instinct, he played dead; head lolling, bike set to a liquored wasp course, eyes narrowed, secretly focused.

Looming up from the saddle like a Roswell alien, the Tomboy balanced, drew in a knee and struck out with a fresh high kick. At that instant, Druid tore the nunchaku off his shoulder, whipped the chain around her supporting leg, and yanked. In a balletic flow of motion, the female spun into a horizontal 360 degrees, scissored her legs either side of the snorting metal hog and slammed back into the saddle. Sending up a great water-shoot of ice, she slid into a tight semi-doughnut and brought her cycle to a standstill; a move that was perfectly replicated by Druid on the Guzzi.

The female's narrow, handsome eyes bored through the tinted visor opposite then shifted sideways to tag the Poet, much as a wrestler might his partner in a ring. While that pretty man-beast had fought shy of the last bout of combat, now he struck a pose, eliciting a whoop of girlish noise from the sidelines, and plunged.

Opening its gunmetal gills, the shark of a Harley sounded much like a weapon in itself. Druid tensed his grip on one stick of the nunchaku, was about to send its twin ripping out when the V-rod pitched off-axis again. Shaking out his golden, waist-length dreads, the Poet massaged the brake, loaded the V-rod's front end and lifted its rear clean off the ice.

The bike slid effortlessly along on a sparkling front wheel.

Decelerating, Druid pressed his heels to the floor and kicked up the ice a little. His brow crinkled softly. Was he meant to be in fear or in awe of the Poet's grand acrobatics? It was difficult to decide. Then again, as his gaze swept past the arena to a rabid congregation, flapping and cawing in their rag-and-bone nests aloft warped metal pylons, he *did* know he felt out of his depth, and not because he faced some great adversary, but because theatrics were no longer his forte.

The diving Poseidon of the V-rod thundered past. He considered steering over to the barrier, ordering a beer off any of the Poet's busty devotees and relaxing there as the main act unfolded. Instead, he was taken off guard when the Poet pivoted the tilting V-rod in a tight squeal and its great shadow loomed above.

"Hell, no!" spat the Drathcor. His heart's blood rusted. For a few goth-awful seconds, he tore at the throttle only to spin the Guzzi's rear wheel in scintillating, if useless, revolutions. Then the tyre gained grip. Dipping low on some stupid self-survival impulse, he sprinted clear—just as the Poet's vehicle crashed down onto the reverberating suspension of both wheels.

A powerful back-draft propelled him far out across the ice. He tried to steer, but his hands were trembling so badly it was all he could do to reach the barrier and ease off the gas. Determined that he wouldn't fall prey to the Poet's cheap party tricks again, he rotated a wrist, whipped up the nunchaku into a vertical shooting star and glared back over a shoulder…only to realise that any threat had only ever been incidental. Far too intent on amusing his fans to engage in any true sense of battle, the Poet balanced up on the Harley's foot pegs, tossed his golden dreads aside, and circled the V-rod in smoky tyre blows.

"Enough already," Druid seethed.

Across the smoke-stained arena, it seemed another figure agreed with him. The black knight astride the architectural Ninja signalled to the last beast by his elbow; the dark father, Macarab, on his elegant antique of a cycle.

Recuperating his steel, Druid snapped his weapon up over a shoulder, downshifted and trickled the Guzzi to the central point of the showground. He stared out from under aquiline lids. Forty metres or so away, the Bonneville gave off its inimitable, deep, soulful revs and idled thickly in-between. With half an eye on the rest of the arena, he spied the Tomboy powering off to the far end of the rink then drawing fast about, on the prowl again. Meanwhile, ignorant to all but his adoring public, the Poet set out across the straight, lifting the V-rod's front wheel off the ground in a sparking fender scrape.

Druid decided the Bonneville was the nemesis to watch as, hugging the ice rink's outer circuit, limbs moulded either side of the Bonneville's lustrous chrome exoskeleton, Macarab passed within a few feet of the Guzzi. His great, dreadlocked head steered in Druid's direction, the dark, oily pools of his goggled eyes expressionless.

In that super, surreal way in which the Perspex window of a visor can make a rider feel at once a part of and apart from the world beyond, Druid watched, eyebrows arched like two birds on the wing as the priest showed him his back, manhandled the throttle and charged on a course set for the V-rod.

While the Poet grazed the Harley's tail-feathers on the iridescent surface, the Bonneville pulled in tight behind. Lightning quick, Macarab put his para boots up onto the red saddle, eased his enormous frame between the raked handlebars and perched on the front of the tank. In an uncanny motion, only executable by a soul already sold to the devil, Druid reasoned, the brute steadied himself on the front wheel's slim mudguard, leant out and snatched what appeared to be a flare-gun from the Poet's back-slung holster. Returning to the saddle in a leap of faith, Macarab slid sideways and braked.

Plummeting forward, the Poet released the V-rod's handlebars and gave a haughty wave to the crowd. At the same time, the priest-on-steroids inclined the Bonneville and secured one boot on the ground. Smoothing the glossed curls of his beard, he held up the flare, took aim and fired.

The cruise missile sluiced through the winter's mist to punch—wham!—just below the V-rod's saddle, sending up a great gush of gasoline. Fuel ignited in a streak of baby blue, destroying the bike from the heart out, and blasting the Poet sky-high to meet his maker.

Hurtling back to earth, the brute hit literal rock bottom then careered across the flaming surface. Bits of glass, ragged tyre fillets, severed metal, soot, and other shrapnel showered down, the odd squawk from a crowd member suggesting a slight case of overbombing beyond the barrier.

"Another wipe-out!" bawled the skunk. "Poet Johnson, taken out at two minutes forty seven. Goth bless that Harley's soul."

The coliseum exploded in ear-splitting rapture.

Even Druid suppressed a vicious smile. He watched as a gaggle of groupies spilled out onto the field.

"Get those bitches off the pitch!" thundered the skunk, a protest that was soon overshadowed by the furore of wolf-whistles echoing about the stadium.

Navigating the patina of the ice, the high-heeled devotees found their hero bruised and unmoving, his once-glittering dreads severed at the crown and blood-greased. In an awkward, slipping motion, the Florence-Nightingales-with-sauce wrestled their patient off to the barrier then used everything that heaved to hoist the brute up and over.

Druid adjusted his eyes to the unnatural dusk feeding off the oil field. If Mars himself had waged battle, it wouldn't have looked dissimilar. Everywhere, hunks of twisted, warped steel, shreds of snaking rubber, nuts, bolts, wheel trims, pulleys, rotors, callipers, and freshly scabbed plastic. All the grisly scene lacked was the dead, he mused darkly.

Although given the ferocity with which the Tomboy was hurtling towards him, *that* vacancy was soon to be filled. By the same token, he saw Macarab zigzag in and out of the carnage, the brute's impassive goggled eyes fixed on the Guzzi. As the Tomboy's gigantic iron hog closed in, the Bonneville reared off its mark, wire-spoke wheels revolving invisibly like spinning silk. Seconds later, shots of liquid flame streamed out either side of the wheel arches.

"What the..." Druid's words evaporated. His flesh tingled hotly, as if already blistered off the bone.

With two or three metres separating them, the Tomboy instigated her acrobatics. Edging the chopper off-centre, she leapt up onto the saddle then actually stepped *between* the bull-bars to steer with a foot. As the bikes aligned, Druid unleashed a sharp sideways lick from the nunchaku, missed by miles as the female arched slightly, flipped into a neat back handspring and righted herself on the bull-bars before abandoning her own bike to step between the handlebars of the Guzzi.

Balanced on one leg on top of the front tank, the nimble beast launched a boot once, twice, at Druid's visor. She thrust forward to drive ten slashing talons into and up the soft flesh of his neck, just managing to dislodge his helmet and send it crashing down before he revolved the nunchaku and jarred it under her chin. Gripping the ends of the weapon in both hands, he blocked a swift karate chop before bringing the sticks smashing up between the Tomboy's legs.

The beast followed through the movement, somersaulting over him to land, cat-soft, on top of the Guzzi's grab bars. Looping the weapon out and around above his head, Druid snapped both sticks into one hand, and twisted drastically to the left. The nunchaku struck a cold silver note off the chrome tubes to his rear, the Tomboy having already leapt back abroad the lagging gas-guzzler. A flick of the left wrist and the iron lady drew level again, just as the Bonneville sidled in from the left.

Sandwiched between the bleak machines, Druid had no choice but to let himself be guided in and out of the debris, his aggressors sending up an unintelligible chorus of shrieks and howls that drew fresh applause. They travelled dead centre between two enormous hunks of molten cartilage, and the Bonneville started to ease alongside, as if to move in for the kill.

At that instant, Druid glanced up. The moon was soft and fat, superbly silver with chunks of bitter dark. By its light, he saw no hope beyond the next few seconds that separated his being alive from a flesh-seared death, except—his heart splintered into a thousand blood-red shards—one image endured; one so unexpected, yet potentially elemental to his being, that it seemed to tear apart the very fabric of life, death and all that lay between. Jezebel's huge, black eyes, reflecting his, reflecting hers.

Get the hell out of there, he imagined her lips shape.

It was a pauper's prayer, offered at the sight of a tiny flicker beneath the Bonneville's wheel arches. It was enough, though. Shock waves of hot, white electricity re-animated his arms, his fingers; he crushed the brake. The Guzzi wailed like a banshee, anchors paring a shimmering froth off the ice. In a fluid motion, he plunged forward and lifted his rear wheel clear of the ground. Then he gave a violent twist to the handlebars, spinning the whole axis left. As the rear of the bike came crashing down again onto a half-pipe of ruptured iron, he rocked back, aviated into a screeching wheelie and flew free.

Chin to his shoulder, he repressed a natural gag reflex as, with nothing standing between her and the Bonneville's more deadly customisations, the Tomboy took a faceful of spurting flames. Like a pig with its throat cut, the creature squealed, executed a flawed back-flip, lost her footing and fell.

Having put twenty metres between himself and the two self-destructing devils, Druid cranked the brake, the heel of a gothic cowboy boot raking up the ice. He studied the Dantesque landscape as, deprived of its rider, the chopper careered onto its side, regurgitated a semi-Catherine wheel of red sparks and ploughed into the Bonneville. Theirs was an inelegant arabesque. Joined at the hip in one great, belching mass of smoky black, the two machines slid, almost silently, across the arena. Seconds later, they detonated off the barrier, the resulting storm of debris making it impossible to guess where one bike had begun and the other ended.

Damp hair clinging to his skull like a sea anemone and the finest globules of salt water at his brow, Druid flexed his claws above the Guzzi's cold steel handlebars then coiled them back about. He watched with a horrid fascination as the mulish warrior arose from the wreckage like the Terminator and trawled the slush and filth. Stumbling across the Tomboy, the brute knelt to punch out the flames, as much as to inflict more damage as to save the creature. And maybe the act was something akin to battered pride and kinship, but Druid's gaze had switched to the black knight astride the Ninja.

"Last two standing," he whispered.

"Double wipe-out for Bobcat and Macarab! Time, three minutes thirty," thundered a voice from the stars.

Without a helmet, Druid swiped the sweat from his eyes with a forearm. He leant determinedly over the Guzzi's handlebars. His eyes drilled into the Space Invader armaments of the Ninja being ridden around in an unhurried loop by the sole rider opposite. Half the distance of the flaming ice rink separated him from the dark knight, who was a thing birthed of the dankest underworld, with posts of coal for limbs, a torso poured from pitch, and long, glinting fingers of jet. One lone differentiator stood out against the black; a skull-white Cerberus, daubed across the creature's helmet.

The awesome Skinwalker inclined its head slightly, as if by way of a bow. Druid returned the nod. As if in reaction to some strange, telepathic undercurrent, both riders raised a boot off the glinting, filthy ice, secured it on a foot peg, and accelerated.

Passing within a hair's breadth of one another, neither tried to joust or otherwise distract their opponent. Instead, each just concentrated on the rustic spoke by which the other had entered the Gauntlet, honing their gaze to it like a fighter pilot to a floodlit landing strip.

Druid's was a clean transition as he flew between the rim of the ice and the wooden slats of the ramp. The crowd's din streamed past his ears, as if he swam in tranquil depths beneath a violent ocean. From somewhere beyond, he was faintly conscious of the robotic pitch and shift of the Ninja. The sound's significance was lost, however, to a world of melting, twisting faces; masks that slipped into one another or poured out their insides. Even the moon's iridescence seemed to burn his skin.

I'll say a prayer. Jezebel's words as they ushered him away from her. *Are you praying now*, he asked as the wheels threw up into a fine, translucent spray that threatened to blind him. *Steady*, he urged, mostly of his bike, but the same sentiment went out to Jezebel: the girl with a slash of a smile and those extraordinary, huge, black, fathomless eyes. He shook a bead of sweat free of an eyelash and gritted his teeth. Re-securing his balance, he bruised the throttle, dipped his head and chased the wind.

It was a filthy hurricane of a tyre blow that brought the Guzzi streaking round, every bit of control applied to scraping boot and brake. Secure inside his rival's turning circle, Druid snatched the flare gun out from the strap across his back, forced that weapon skyward, and fired.

Silence. His pale eyes traced the line of the flare as it cut across the heavens, matched by an identical track that arced to cross right over. Then the whole stadium went up.

"An unprecedented draw!" roared the skunk above the ungodly racket. "Lorcan locks horns with the Drathy pimp at four minutes fifty-nine."

At the far end of the Gauntlet, the colossal beast moved to stand apart from his steaming vehicle, removed his helmet and released a nest of black and indigo dreadlocks.

Druid cut the Guzzi's engine. He eased the bike back onto its stand, felt for the top pocket of his leather, recovered his shades; slid them back into place. Slipping one leg up and over the bike, he raised the flat of a hand to his eyes. The cute crew spilled out onto his platform again to coo sexily by his ear or prop a pert tush up on the Guzzi's still-warm saddle, but he ignored their spidering hands to concentrate on the chief. *Lorcan*, he breathed. The name was a taste of dark.

For now, the chief was locked in conversation with a fellow giant, the skunk, separated from his perch and standing in a semi-relaxed, officer's pose, the meat plates of his hands slung onto his hips, his black and white dreads silvered with frost. By way of conclusion, Lorcan squatted, put all of his weight onto one paw and leapt down off the turning circle. Meanwhile, the skunk part-surfed on his heels, part-jogged the length of the slatted ramp then strode out into the ice rink. Centre stage amidst the smoke and flames and mushrooming carnage, he raised his megaphone.

"A tie it is! Immunity is split. Lorcan gets three hundred and sixty four nights and days, the Drathy pimp, this evening. Which means no brute lays a single claw on the pimp 'til dawn or you'll go the way of Bobcat!"

The reference to the injured Tomboy elicited belly-laughter and applause from the crowd, and, increasingly, Druid felt like a stranger in a strange land. From somewhere amid the strains of black humour and the pack's latent savagery, he tried to quantify exactly *what* it was that he had won. It sounded as if he was at liberty to move as he pleased through the monstrous ranks, to question whoever he chose and on whatever subject without fear of reprise; at least for the duration of the Blizzard Bash. His lips shaped a dry, innocuous smile; the haphazard division of the prize, by which he enjoyed Immunity for one night and Lorcan, the remainder of a year, was hardly atypical of Skinwalkers. What else was there to expect of their rabid chapters—even-handedness? Chivalry?

"Whiskey?"

The chief's voice had a soft resonance, like claret rinsing the crystal bowl of a wine glass, also an earthy masculinity that unsettled men and women alike, if for very different reasons, so that Druid steadied his eyes before raising them. Lustrous, black armour-plated forearms rested on the rim of the turning circle, the blood-red swells of shoulder pads clinking gently as Lorcan eased his huge, old mast of flesh, chains and rigging up onto the platform. He unfolded, the flotsam of two plaited ropes of beard and other armaments washing against his dense bones. Sliding five gnarled claws into a pocket of his leather, he produced a small silver hip flask and unscrewed the lid.

Druid took a good slug from the offered flask, relishing the fire of the spirit as it washed against his soft palate.

"Quite a race, pimp."

"My name is D."

Lorcan's soft, grey eyes met his with significance. Taking the flask back, the Skinwalker held it just short of his lips. "*D*...it is then." He took a long swig, then threw a powerful arm towards the rowdy throng. "You've earned a seat at my table, for tonight at least. So you'll stay as our guest and savour the delights of the Blizzard Bash; beer, swill, and real, live babes."

Druid felt the liquor's gentle flush, could almost envision it mix with his red blood cells like fairy dust. He was exhausted, he realised suddenly. All he wanted was to lay his body down to rest, taste a little more of that sweet whiskey, and, if he could put his mind to business, quiz Lorcan about the south watchtower. "My pleasure," he responded gruffly.

"Oh, indeed it will be," avowed the chief with a roguish smile. The expression hardened for an instant. "And *Drathcor*, the real, live babes? Best they stay that way."

Before Druid could even think of responding, the warlord slapped him on the back, resumed his wolfish grin, and thundered, "Time to get this party started!"

Chapter 13

Deify

Druid crossed his legs and shifted slightly around on the heavily worked Chinese rug. "I have a question," he said with an assertive tilt of the chin.

Cocooned in tasselled floor cushions, the many vibrant satins exaggerating his leathered bulk, the chief drew on a perfumed Cuban and grinned. "Cognac?" Smoke drizzled out from in-between his canines.

When Druid responded with a sharp nod, the Skinwalker glanced over a shoulder, the tiny bells interwoven in the twin plaits of his beard emitting a faery-like tinkle. "Tabitha! Blaze! You girls gonna keep teasing at my spine or give my boy, D, a drop of the sweet stuff?"

By way of answer, two beautiful women rose up either side of the chief's broad back; the first, with her ebony hair swept into a tortured beehive and wearing red lipstick, a chain-mail bikini, stilettos, and a mink; the second, in thigh-length denim fetish boots, black belted mac and a mane of bright red ringlets. They came crawling out and over the cushions, the raven-haired siren brandishing an outsized brandy glass, the redhead, a brass-banded Viking horn. Sidling in, Tabitha presented Druid with the glass then gave his face a long, luxurious lick. In the meantime, Blaze fed five wet-look talons around the horn and popped its cork. Chemical-bright cognac poured into the crystal.

Druid raised his glass, as much to shirk off the sirens as to toast Lorcan's health. He took a mouthful, bathed his tongue in the smoky sweetness then asserted, "I want to ask you..."

"Shut your flapping jaw!" hissed a second Skinwalker. The monstrous skunk had deserted his commentary box for the comfort of a bed of sheepskins, furs, and carnal females. "We don't need a bastard pimp going all journo."

"No, we don't. And yet I like his grit." Lorcan lifted the bubble of his brandy glass, saluting Druid with the oily amber. "You've got a shadiness, D. Always have had, I suspect." The old wolf's eyes sharpened. "Like your revs, life's made for the punishing; live hard, lie hard, never die."

"Once upon a time, maybe," said Druid warily. He recalled Louse House, that hellhole of a tavern, and a Trawler dispatched like some gothic Archangel to bring tidings of their saviour's demise. He remembered the transmission sent to Lorcan; *Deed done. The old ways are going up in flames.* His brow darkened. "All doors lead to winter eventually."

"So this life's left you jaded?" Lorcan slid his caber of an arm around Tabitha's naked waist. "Know what you need? To get out and taste the sins and pleasures of *your* world. What d'you reckon, Tabby? Gonna give that boy some cream?"

The feline's slitted green gaze lazed over Druid. "Only if he's very, very naughty."

"Hmmm, you are a minx." As the spicy creature poured herself into his lap, Lorcan produced his disconcerting smile. He pulled on the Cuban and was enveloped in a tangy, grey cloud. "Alright, D. How's this? I ask you a question. You ask me a question. Sound fair?"

Did it? Druid tensed. He had set himself loose amid the wolves. But had he really intended to fool Lorcan with his masquerading as some deadbeat Drathy who just happened to share a penchant for muscle bikes, martial arts and occult weaponry with his facesake; not to mention one hell of a death wish? Having learnt categorically that Lorcan had been the direct recipient of information regarding his brother's death, he had given himself over to the single task of tracking the chief down. And with no mind to his personal safety? Druid's mouth stiffened. The idea that he could put one over on Lorcan was preposterous, because the chief and he had met before.

Yes, it was all of two nights previously that Lorcan had stood to the rear of Legacy and, suffused in the purple twilight of a streetlamp, tucked a hand-tooled cigarette between his lips, lit it, and all the while kept his soft, grey eyes on the living god opposite. But it was a very different encounter that haunted Druid now, one that had taken place in Council House and under the force nine gaze of the Management.

It was hard to picture the great old wolf suited and booted, his rancid dreads de-tangled and tied back, but it was *that* ghost of a fiercer, wilder man who'd planted two shined pumps on the speaker's dais—an outsized city key, depicted in glossy rosewood and sited at the hall's heart—at what now felt like the beginning of time, but was probably just a couple of years into Renegade's existence. Rooted to that spot, Lorcan had delivered an eloquent address as to why Skinwalkers should be accredited as a new, fifth tribe due to sheer numbers alone, he had argued, and then how his band of rebels was a brotherhood, with its own strict creed of spirit, pride, gall, and, above all, faith.

Druid, meanwhile, had stared at a spot beyond the drifter's head, mapping out a drum lick with his claws on the softly moulded, corpulent arms of his throne, since it was all but set in stone that the Management would fail to elevate such an inassimilable element as the Skinwalkers to the status of a tribe, even if their chief was to prostrate himself at Roses's feet and beg for holy sanction. Just as his mind was starting to fog, he had sensed the wolf's eyes on his, and in returning the stare seen such hurt and humiliation in those self-oiling globes that he was forced to look away.

Now, subject to that unyielding gaze again, Druid realised he had always known the dangers of facing up to Lorcan, and much as death, he had welcomed it. And yet at his back sat Jezebel, whose blackberry sweetness was all too tangible; he wanted to squeeze and taste that firm resistance, her tang complementing his own bitter tannins. He could not ask Lorcan a direct question about the transcript sent from the south watchtower. To do so would be to run the risk of Jezebel asking how he had acquired the information, and revealing his whole Drathy persona as a lie.

His stomach tumbled. The Gauntlet run and the prize of immunity hard-won, he had found her; lower lip caught up between two rows of sharp little teeth. She had reached for his throat tentatively, patterning her fingertips to the ten red furrows gorged by the Tomboy's talons. "Bitch," she'd breathed with harsh anxiety. In that instant, he had seen her exposed as a beast of hate, and of desire.

And suddenly he wanted her; this girl, this Fae, who was not only ignorant of life on his side of the looking glass, but genuinely despised his existence. From what she had said to date her distaste was raw, like something torn and festering, and yet he understood it well enough. So long as she had a foe in the shape of the Drathcor, she was free to ignore the true wolf at her door, in whatever form that might take.

But—Druid met Lorcan's gaze with a subtle shiver, focusing in on the roguish dab of light in each bright pupil—chances were he'd never find out. Once the chief found the right instant to betray him, Jezebel would turn, hackles raised in fresh antipathy, then take to her heels and run.

Shoulders hunched about his ears, he seethed, "Why would an über-beast like Lorcan want to ask me anything?"

The chief bounced the playful feline up onto one knee. "Because you strike me as a man with secrets to tell," he teased, his strong mouth crinkling.

Was this some cat and mouse game, far more ingenious than any played out between the chief and his companion? Druid swallowed. Steadying himself against inevitable betrayal, he muttered, "Okay, Lorcan. Carve away."

The extraordinary beast again broke into a handsome smile. As the redhead nestled down astride his other knee, he hooked a mass of bloody curls back over her ear. "So, Blaze. What'd you reckon we're dying to ask our champion?"

The minx brushed her lower lip with a ruby talon. "How'd he learn to ride and fight as well as Lorcan?" she cooed.

The chief caught up the teasing finger, pressed a kiss to it. "Exactly."

With every beast in that esteemed circle turning its muzzle on him, Druid felt his brow pucker. Surely there had to be a darker intent to Lorcan's questioning? But when that potent Skinwalker said nothing more but merely smacked his lips expectantly, he forced an awkward explanation.

"My brother and I rode dirt-track as kids. Ros...Roland exchanged two wheels for four—a Boss 351 Fastback Mustang. I stuck to sleds—a Moto Guzzi 850 T5. Same model I got out on the track. Seems I got myself a guardian angel," he said with an ironic sort of smile, studied Lorcan for a reaction, saw none, and added, "As to how'd I learn to fight? Guess I picked up stuff off the street." The lie broke down as he sensed the ebb and flow of Jezebel's breath at the nape of his neck. He put five cold fingertips to his temple, muttering, "You learn to keep up fast if you want to survive on the outside."

"That *you* do," said Lorcan darkly; Druid forced himself to maintain eye contact.

The brute shifted his weight to recline against the glut of cushions. "It's a cold world out here. Without immunity, any one of these beasts..." he indicated his coarse entourage,

"...would tear out your throat before you even had time to bite back. My advice, D, if you want to keep surviving? Learn faster."

He unwound the females, pushing them aside as if to better concentrate and, giving the stub of his cigar a brief tap, said, "Now *your* question."

Druid stared intently at the age-wise face. Now was the moment to tear into the beast, to demand an explanation for every rancid word that the Trawler had brought to his attention. Or he could tread softly like a muted assassin. "What do you know of the death of Roses, our one true Lord and Saviour?" he said with restraint.

Apart from Lorcan, whose features softened in slow acknowledgement, the nest erupted into a great, sullied roar. Beer cans dashed to the ground; cigarettes choked against a boot sole.

"Bastard pimp! What have we got to do with Roses?" thundered one ogre, a claw hand reaching to the top of his para boot, as if threatening to unsheathe a weapon.

"Friggin' preacher," bawled his neighbour with a loose slop of saliva. "We ain't at the south watchtower now."

"Preacher? Hack more like. Gonna make a front page spread of us?" growled the skunk, rising from the waves of rich fabric like an aged plesiosaur. "*Skinwalkers killed Roses.* Quite a headline. Quite a scoop." He shook out his skein of black and white dreads, brought his skull within inches of Druid's. "What say I break your claws now and save you the bother?"

"The pimp has immunity, Diezeg," Lorcan reminded that all-too-willing henchman.

The skunk grabbed at his crotch. "Screw immunity."

"Back off, Diezeg!" boomed Lorcan. He waited for the bruiser to skulk back to his patch, then pursed his lips and expelled a single smoke ring. "D and I struck a bargain," he told the sullen brood, and he threw out those enormous arms of his. "You were all witness! So save the brawls for the beer tent, especially since the pimp's question is an empty one. What do I *know* of Roses' death?" The chief bent forward over the crossed hulks of his thighs and scribbled in the air with his cigar butt.

The dissipating streaks were illegible, but Druid got their basic sentiment. "Nothing," he murmured and tensed in irritation. His mouth spiked to demand a more substantial answer, but Lorcan pointed the snowy cigar tip at him and winked.

"What do I *think* of Roses's death? That's a sharper question. So let me give you this much." Smoke escaped the slackened lower lip. "Renegade's going down, I think even *you're* aware of that, hey D, and Skinwalkers'll be the first to cheer." His eyes narrowed. "Roses? For all his rousing anthems, it came down to just one chorus. Are you in or are you out? Are you in or are you out? Are you in or are you out?" He used a claw to conduct the sentiment then let his arm fall like a dead thing. "Kind of catchy, but not so cool for those kept on the outside. So, someone might've topped the great messiah. The frigid bitch, Sophia? There's a neat little bundle of rumour mongering for you, and to my mind, too convenient. Where's the friggin' motive?"

Druid remained wordless and left Lorcan's chocolate voice to draw its own conclusions.

"Or what about Adeudas? Its not like that dandy ain't worked the wrong side of the law before," said the chief, clearly revelling in the freedom to hypothesise, alongside the fantastic secret knowledge that a Drathcor attended his every word. "Or your facesake?" he posed jovially.

"Druid did it," hissed the skunk, crumpling a tin of Stella in his claws. Wrestling himself up to standing, the brute stepped over the many cushions and bodies to squat before a hole cut into the ice. There he reined in a metal chain until a net bobbed into view. Driving a paw into the slackened neck, he retrieved a frosted tin then slung the net back under. "That bastard always had the evil eye. No offence, pimp," he tossed back over a shoulder.

"Taken," Druid glowered softly.

Perhaps Lorcan overheard. Certainly he scrutinised Druid with his wolf-grey eyes. "Or it could've been any other brute in this rat's nest of a city," he said softly, guiding suspicion deliberately away. "Believe me, D, any...*messiah*..." he spat the word out like phlegm, "...who makes outcasts of his followers is gonna breed himself a fair hive of enemies. Wanna know the greatest irony, D? Like us or loathe us, Skinwalkers are the only tribe still united." A heavily bejewelled claw thrust towards the dark skyline. "Castclan? Every bugger knows those sorcerers thrive on brewing mayhem. Fae, DarkLed, Trawlers – them friggin' fairies haven't a hope in hell of standing tall. Especially Fae. They'd soon as slit their neighbour's throat for a piece of something pretty. Grallators? The law keeps them bonded, but look closer. You'll see the rot. It'll bring them crashing back to earth soon enough."

The chief leant through a great wall of cigar smoke, a gorilla in the mist, "As for Drathcor? What are they? A myth kept alive by the old men and women of the Management." He threw up his paws. "Screw Roses's dying. Where's the guarantee any of those bloodsuckers are alive?" Studying Druid with an air of poignancy, he slid the cigar from his lips. "It's not like they're gonna have the guts to come out and walk among us. Oh no, they forgot all about this city's freakin' Belief system years ago. And so it seems we forgot about them."

Druid felt the weight of so many vacant eyes on him. Bar the chief, not a soul registered him as anything more than a living epitaph to a ghost. He twisted slightly at the waist, let his gaze devour the pale silk of Jezebel's skin, her spider gaze. She offered him a lost, awkward smile but nothing of recognition. He turned back to Lorcan.

"Roses created this sweet pandemonium, then tried to fill it with his idea of good citizens; namely those who just happened to agree with him. Whereas Skinwalkers? He didn't like our style. Least that's how it appeared to us all the years we were forced to exist in the nest of caves under the city. Then the flames came, and at last we had a use for Roses, or his palace at least, and yes, most folks might think the south watchtower's fit for bulldozing, but to Skinwalkers, it's a cesspit we've come to know as home."

The troop erupted in assent, battering a beer can against a neighbour's or whooping at the moon. "I suspect that's why you asked the question," said Lorcan quietly. His expression hardened. "So, to put it another way. What do I *think* of Roses's death?" He worked the butt of his cigar through the air, blew the trails apart and mouthed, "Nothing."

There was a subtle shift in the beast's countenance, the mouth and eyes acquiring a crueller edge that reminded Druid he was being toyed with. Not so much intimidated as irate, he spat, "Skinwalkers became outcasts of their own accord. You can't join a world then pull it apart for fun and expect to be welcomed still. Yes, your sort may be loyal to the pack, but when the chips are down, you're just hired hoodlums under piss-poor direction."

While Druid provoked the rough crowd, Lorcan settled them with a snap of his great muzzle. "Yes, we take what we need and we enjoy it. We've no reason not to. But I tell you this much, pimp. Skinwalkers answer to no man."

"Man? In this weird kingdom, maybe not. But you *do* answer to a high power." Druid rippled the sunny liquor in his glass then drained the last taste of it. "Who's sent you love letters from a palace in flames? Who's keeping the Grallators off this patch on a violent night? Who's the Angel, Lorcan?"

The chief stiffened, as did his foot soldiers, their heavy jaws slung open, black eyes shifting edgily in Druid's direction as if he was the devil himself. A moment later, Lorcan threw back his skull and loosed an ear-splitting howl. He cocked his head at Druid, lips in a mad-dog smile.

"Enough questions, pimp. What you wasting good drinking time for anyway? Get out there, man, grab yourself some fat-bottomed girls and have yourself a good time at our expense. That's not a request, by the way," he added pointedly, directing the ring of sentinels to part and provide an exit.

Fiercely frustrated, it took every ounce of inner strength for Druid to bite his tongue then motion sharply to Jezebel to rise up off the ground and follow. Picking their way to the edges of the circle, he glanced back to see Lorcan's shrewd, grey eyes fixed on Jezebel with a hint of suspicion. Feeding an arm quickly around the girl's waist, he hurried her in-between those parted guards and out, just as Tabitha and Blaze wound nimbly back around the chief and caught his mouth up to theirs each in turn.

The next second, the sentries closed ranks and blocked the decadent court from view.

Pop, fizz. Pop, fizz. The vendor cracked two cans of Stella, took one in each hand, and passed them out to the pale prince and his anime goth girl.

"Thanks." Druid sucked at the soapy froth that washed around the top of the can then took a deep swig. Bringing the lip away from his mouth, he noticed Jezebel's hands tremble slightly as she drank. "You okay?" he said quietly.

"What the *hell* just happened?" Her expression was strangely innocent, as if she were freshly surprised, or terrified.

Druid faltered in his stride. Somehow he hadn't imagined Jezebel capable of any emotion but bloody-mindedness. But here she was utterly transformed; the delicate, elfin features, the huge, dark, questioning eyes, the violet bud of a mouth, all reaching out invisible hooks that sank into his skin.

He frowned, at once intrigued and saddened. Yes, she had proven herself all too keen to engage the brutes in combat, but how deep did her self-assurance really run when their human jaws had already had a taste of her; and more than once now? He glanced at the exposed scar that crept over her left shoulder and up her throat, then at her wrist, disguised by a PVC coat sleeve. For the first time, he saw that while she was honour-bound by circumstance, it didn't mean she was okay with being amongst the very beasts that had gone for her throat just two nights ago, nor did it make her any less afraid of exposure than he was. Little wonder she was beginning to wane.

Tentatively, he reached out to her. "Jez..."

"Don't touch me!" she spat, black eyes refracting. "I trusted you. You said leave it up to you to do the talking, promised to ask Lorcan about Harish. What the hell were you thinking, wasting time with dumb-ass questions about Roses? Screw Roses! Where the hell was He when I lost my brother? And screw you, D! Screw you..." Her voice failed painfully. "And screw me for believing in you."

Wracked with confusion, he watched as she moved to stand a few feet away. Set against the great jets of flamingo pink and orange fire that danced filmily in the distance, the many bonfires littering the sloping bank like beautiful, soft phoenix eggs, and a landscape hand-inked by Giger, she resembled a child, lost amid the junk and flames of Judgement Day.

He moved alongside her and, though aware of his own discomfort, stayed rooted. "*I've* never been the man to put your Belief in. That accolade belonged to a finer soul. But nor was it my intention to betray you, because..." His tongue seemed to swell as every instinct told him to shut up and shut down. "I meant to ask the questions we both needed answers to," was all that he could manage.

195

"Except yours took priority," said Jezebel acidly. Her eyes shifted skyward to reflect the breadth of gloom above. "You drank the beast's best Cognac, swapped spit with his sluts, asked your stupid, useless questions, and all the while, I said nothing. Because you'd asked me not to and I trusted you."

"Then who's the idiot?" Druid stormed, finding his own space of anger. "I demanded you keep quiet because it was the only way to stop you raising hell in there. For some weird reason, I didn't want to risk a second stab at Fae slash Skinwalker diplomacy." He thrust a claw at his gashed cheek. "I'm still a little raw from your first effort."

"More fool me for trying to help you then! Because that's the goth honest truth of it. I didn't like the way those grunts were talking, so I socked it to them straight. But I guess you didn't like that, what with you being all big and grrrr." She bared her teeth in a false, gummy smile. "And me, just a girl, all pretty and petite. So I'm some kind of freak for having bigger balls, but hey, you're the one with issues. Me? I was just standing by a friend."

"What the hell is it with you people and trying to be my friend?" Druid bit back, though with no real idea of why. Even as he saw the hurt sink over her shoulders, he couldn't stop himself from falling. "First I get IQ stepping up to the plate like I was some sort of tourist on a day pass to the city. Then you give these dogs a tongue-lashing that sees me riding hell for leather in their demonic Gauntlet. Don't you freaks have lives?"

"Not since Harish got me into this mentalist's Zion," she slung back, her arms crossed and tucked up beneath her armpits by way of a barricade. "Okay, so I was clueless in the outside world, but this so-called freedom is just as much a lie. Take you for instance—one second you're *the* man, blazing a trail no less explosive than Brando's friggin' Johnny in 'The Wild One', the next, you're puckering up like a pro to Lorcan's not-so-hairless ass. At least until that Ug bares his wolf teeth. Then you turn on your heels and bolt." Her face was river-run with emotion. "And *you* call *me* the freak?"

His head hung low, Druid circled a finger around the inner lip of his beer can. He hadn't meant to wound the girl, particularly since they were surrounded by a sea of beasts that would readily do that for him. "I didn't run from Lorcan, in the same way I didn't mess with any of his eye candy. If you want to know the real reason I left so quickly, I saw Lorcan take a good hard look at a girl—a slip of a thing with the strength to elude his best warriors but with a brazenness that outstripped his filthiest whores—and before things clicked in his nasty brain, I got us the hell out of there."

Parting her lips to speak, Jezebel faltered, seemingly torn between flattery and an unsure sense of insult. Instead, she said nothing, only frowned and listened harder.

"I didn't mean to betray you," he insisted, sliding a palm down over his eyes. "My idea was to ask about Roses by way of intro, then move onto the subject of Harish once the brute warmed to me." It was only a half-lie, he told himself. Pain snagged at his brow. He had intended to ask Lorcan many things, in particular about the transcript provided by the Trawler, but the subject of Harish? *That* he had barely given a second thought.

Now, watching Jezebel's harsh expression soften and remould, he wondered what sort of fiend he had become. Under the whetted porcelain veneers, black and flame New Rocks, distended limbs and snowy flesh was a far crueller monster; one that would make an empty promise then feast on the consequences.

"Peas in a pod," he said aloud, if subconsciously.

"What's that?" Jezebel spoke without an edge.

"You and I," he managed, determined to offer some small glimpse of truth. "We're very much alike. You lashed out at these brutes to protect…a friend." Glassy humiliation slipped back over her eyes, and determined to wear it away, he told her, "I've distanced myself from many things: grief, shame, dependability. For the longest time, I've lived beyond the needs of any other, taking, tasting, touching anything or anyone I'd even the slightest desire for."

He avoided her eyes, took a draft of the cold beer instead and scanned his surroundings. Beyond their conversation, the Blizzard Bash had settled into itself, the majority of hell-raisers drawn to the distant stage, now occupied by a thrash-metal four-piece. He watched the jagged motions of each marionette, remembered the thrill then chill of a crowd's adoration.

"This skin," he breathed. "It weighs heavy on me now. Seems I'm drenched from head to toe in cynicism. Lorcan may be right; life has left me jaded until all I know is how to wound, then feed. Okay, it sounds a shade morbid, but at least I'm a realist. Annihilation of the self; it's a vein best served cold and it's sustained me this far. Ask me, it's a taste we share. Yes, your actions may have been in defence of me but also something more besides. You don't engage so readily in combat unless you're predisposed to a death wish. Believe me, it's a home truth I'm all too familiar with."

"His eyes, they seemed darker, you know." Jezebel spoke with haunting, child-like acumen. "But he knew me. Below the fur and grime, Harish knew I was his sister. Then the lights went out." She polished a wet cheek with an angry fist. "Months I gave him. Eight long, ugly months devoted to his trail, and all because I thought him worth more than a bag of butcher's bones and a scratch-post. Every time I asked after him, it was the same old abuse. Why the hell you wanna go searching for scum like that? You're tracking a Skinwalker? Best hope he's dead if you find him, or we'll have one less crazy bitch in Renegade." Pausing, she swallowed a good measure of her can, gave her face a swift rub with a coat sleeve, and, in so doing, exposed her wrist and the sweat band of a black bandage. "No one wanted to know, not a goddamn soul except for Irvine."

Before he could respond, a gang of slavering warriors bullied their way in-between them so that he reached for the girl's hand and pulled her to him. "Talking of whom, let's find the kid and get going," he said, shifting his eyes about the crawling arena.

"Not a chance," hissed Jezebel, and she tried to pull away. "I still need to find Harish. You go if the atmosphere's too wild for you."

"I got you in, I'll get you out."

Her gaze narrowed. "I think you'll find *I* got *you* in. Either way…" Her eyes danced over each approaching beast in the hunt for something more familiar. "I'm going nowhere. Irvine's gone walkabout and, while I trust the kid to do his best by me, I reckon I'll still rely on my own investigations."

Probably just as well, Druid mused darkly, since, by his own admission, IQ was another specialist in happy lies. Whatever that urchin was up to, it probably had little to do with detective work, especially if girls were dangled before him like a far more naked truth.

He breathed deeply, savouring the indelible sweetness peculiar to fairgrounds and the clean, crisp, winter's air. Releasing Jezebel's hand, he indicated ahead. "You'll be leading the way then."

For two long hours, Jezebel felt the sting of a thousand red, gold, and pupilless eyes, the surrounding hoards of Skinwalkers seeming to feed on her as effectively as if they had shot her full of plastic tubes and wires, and drained off her elixir—and she let them drink her in, concentrating instead on each new Slipknot child or bride to loom, crawl or gambol past.

Their horrors tumbled out to meet her: boyish beauty marred by scars that clung, vine-like, to a throat or snaked from jaw to brow line; the yellowed marl of canines; tattoos on the tongue, the shaved sides of each skull, the chin, the neck, the eyelids, and thick, fibrous dreadlocks stretching to the waist. So many creatures came swarming across the mudded ice, but she saw nothing of Harish.

Her disappointment felt strangely physical, and she was sinking suddenly, buried waist-high in the pointless pursuit of it all. "I'm gonna get a beer," she muttered. "You want one?"

D reached inside his coat and retrieved two cans. He cracked one and passed it over. Cracking his own, he teased, "Thought we might need some sustenance for our journey."

"Glad I keep you amused," she glowered, and sank a heavy draught.

He appeared to consider her then said, "Your quest does. For any sane person to pursue the very beast that attacked them—in your case, twice now—with such grit and tenacity...yeah, strikes me as funny."

His words cut like throwing stars. Instinctively, she put her hand to her throat to protect it.

"I understand it, though," he continued, and his brow crinkled beautifully. "This need to track down the beast, even if you risk your life in pursuit of it. Your dedication, your resolve." He indicated the hideous throng. "The nightmares that see you torn limb from bloody limb by these dogs, only to wake, sweat-drenched and tearful." His shades reflected the supernatural glow of a nearby bonfire. "That isn't so humorous to me."

His intensity confused her. Without really thinking, she said, "Drathcor's groupie. That's what the creeps on the street say, poking stupid fingers at my neck like it's something wrong and twisted."

"But it's an honour to be selected," said D with a slight tilt of his chin.

She rolled the cool aluminium of the beer can over her frown lines. "Jeez, have you been lost in space for the past few months or what? Good Goth, I'm no expert but I know this much. Once upon a time, all was vile and well with the hoity-toity bloodsuckers, while their willing victims enjoyed a cosy enough life of casual pain and reverence. Then the Drathcor gave up feeding. Okay, so there's talk of wannabes sneaking in via the underground sewers in a materialistic bid to tempt them. But most folk agree nothing's passed their razor lips for well over a year now." Her gaze shifted sideways. Of all of the strange, twisted breeds in Renegade, a Drathy would be acutely aware of these facts. "Hardly surprising folk got twitchy," she added thoughtfully.

"...Or blamed the blood whores, freshly expelled from seventh heaven, for matters they had no knowledge of?"

"I told you," she sighed, catching sight of her reflection in the beer can and despising it. "Harish left my neck, and now my wrist, with this false legacy. It's up to me to hide it."

"But any fool can see the mark's too crass," said D vehemently. He gave a short, bleak laugh. "To a Drathcor, preparation for the blood rite is paramount, as is the slow yielding of the skin to each injector. But to hurriedly sink the jaw, tear into flesh, rip it open—*that* demonstrates nothing of sacred execution. Psychologically, it's cruel. Visually, it's nothing short of mutilation."

"Hey! I'm right here." Blood pooling at her cheeks, Jezebel adjusted her coat collar and turned away. Why the hell was she still standing there? A stone wedged in her larynx and she felt frail, wordless and alone; a child in the company of wolves.

But D surprised her anew. "It's our scars that make us dazzling." Long, cool fingers encircled her good wrist, conveying it just short of his lips. Warm breath soothed her fragile skin. "Here the scar would be discreet; a pinprick from a small antique lancet. The procedure lends itself to a slower suckling rather than any actual biting down, and as such is less intrusive for either party, and less intimate. Whereas the throat is reserved for lovers."

His gaze faltered. He tipped the tin to his mouth and swallowed a draught. As he did so, Jezebel glimpsed the slim, exaggerated canines; they aroused a lingering discomfort, alongside less puritanical sensations that rouged her flesh.

Withdrawing her wrist, she fiddled with the nylon bangs of her wig. "Well, you might've lost track of the real world, but you seem to know your stuff about our darkling demi-gods."

D showed no obvious emotion, just retrieved her hand and gripped it, vice-like, in his. "Let's take a break," he commanded—and though she meant to break away, it was easier to follow than to fight. He led her away from the maelstrom to a soft incline and she clambered a little awkwardly, unused to being led. Shortly, they came to a plateau where the snow had been packed more densely by countless para boots, but abandoned now except for the semi-precious embers of a fading bonfire.

Releasing her hand, D shook his leather off his shoulders and spread it on the ground.

"You'll freeze to death," she offered, unsurely fascinated.

The man hid a half-smile. "Little late for that," he teased, adding more sincerely, "Besides, I like the cold."

"Oh yeah, I forgot. You're an honorary affiliate of the Broken Hearted. What became of them, hey?" Her smile was less reticent, if harder to sustain. She took a seat, her spiked Transformer boots sticking up out of the snow like bits of scattered aircraft. Settling back, she tapped her beer can lightly against D's. "So here's to heartache."

"I'd rather drink to Harish." His shaded gaze appraised her. "Tell me about him," he urged.

Jezebel squinted, trying to read this solitary man who had seemed to betray her trust just two short hours ago, but was now asking to hear her most private memories while retaining secrets aplenty, and all without the slightest hint of irony. A changeling of the most elusive kind, he had seemed to welcome death like a long lost soul-mate, plummeting heart first into the jaws of the Gauntlet. Yet, afterwards, he questioned Lorcan with a careful hand, withdrawing at the first sign of trouble.

Resting on her elbows amid the ruby satin coat lining, she said matter-of-factly, "He was the man I'd choose to be if nature would allow it. You've heard plenty on his skills as an artisan? Well, that was just the tip of it. Example—growing up, we'd climb trees, as kids are prone to. But while I'd scuffle up, all hands and scrapping boots, Harish would pause, take a leap at a branch and balance, then take another leap and balance." She moved her hand across the cobwebbed sky, tracing a lost boy's progress. "Monkey, that's what the kids at school called him, chasing him with words, with sticks, with knives. Little wonder he grew into the part. Acrobat, fire fighter, steeplejack, lighting technician, scaffolder—he tried his hand at so many trades. But still the fingers pointed." She poured a good quantity of beer onto her tongue, took comfort in its slow blending of forgetfulness with pain. "Then one day we're together for the first time in three, maybe four, years and this song comes on the radio, and it just hits us. Roses, screeching the truth like goth-damn Jesus in confession. A day later, we kissed the old ways goodbye and headed for the homeland. And, god, let me tell you, the first glimpse of Renegade's blue-neon landscape, the watchtowers, the exotic markets in the east, the infamous nightclub, Legacy—saviour of the broken, the beaten and the damned—the vast, quilted sky dome of the Castclan pod, the Mystic Quarter in the north..." Her eyes grew large as dusk-veiled chrysanthemums. "As for the people? I fell in love with every shade of goth, glam, punk, and psychedelia in this big, black bubble."

"So what burst it?"

"They say riches can't bring you happiness. Isn't that the cliché? Ask me, it's the same for those of the heart and the soul. We spend our lives searching for a new breed of freedom, somewhere we can show our true colours no matter how gaudy, only to run screaming at the first real glimpse of it. You think we've changed because we dress odd, because we cage a bat not a canary, because we've built the greatest shrine to hedonism since Sodom and Gomorrah? Have we hell! Look at the city's grinding heart and you'll see we're the warped mirror image of any jock or cheerleader. We're still throwing weapons, still pointing fingers."

"And who's to blame for that?"

"Blame? It's quite a burden. Always best to share it. On the one hand, I'd burn the Drathcor in whitest heaven for their mismanagement of what was, undoubtedly, the best idea in friggin' history. Where they should have cherished difference, they chose to box people in instead. If they'd only let folk breathe and live a little, perhaps Harish would've found a place inside the mixing pool rather than resorting to the one tribe who treasured him. Skinwalkers."

"How do you know?"

She predicted the question even as it formed at his lips. "Because, more than anything, Harish wanted to belong."

Thirty feet below, the wasteland was spilling out and over itself in an ever-fluid motion. In her mind's eye, Jezebel pictured the same beasts pouring out from every orifice of the south watchtower, multiplying like a virus until she could no longer differentiate him from so much flesh, tooth and bone. Except for the dark circles of his eyes. Those bruised her heart.

Quick to dismiss the childish sentiment, she said, "Harish was always wild. It makes sense for him to make his nest among them; especially since *this...*" She thrust a cropped white fingernail at the rope of a scar at her neck. "His parting present to me. Oh, don't look so alarmed! I find it hard to stomach on a face made for wounding. One dawn Harish took off, his whole life sewn up in a backpack. Just got up and left, without the first idea of how I'd survive or even feel about it."

"I'm sorry." D's tone was unanticipated. It held a weight of sincerity.

"Not your fault, was it?" she snapped wearily, focusing on the soft interplay of snow clouds overhead. "We all have skeletons in our proverbial closets, even you I'd suspect."

"I *do* know what its like to lose someone you care about," he said quietly.

Puzzled, she sensed real sadness, tenderness even, and anger. *That* was writ sky-high in the blaze of his mohawk; the pencilled loop of each eyelid. "Did you find them again?" she asked more gently.

"They're dead to me." He fell silent, picking at the many bracelets circling a forearm.

Jezebel waited awkwardly, then lay back against the bloody satin. She regretted asking. But hadn't D been the first to open those particular floodgates? He had chosen to confide in her, be it ever so slightly, and yet, given his sullen reaction, she wasn't sure she really cared to hear any more.

"Is that why your research is all consuming, even to the detriment of others' needs?" Her question had an edge. "So you can forget those who are gone?" It was pop psychology, but his dark state left her floundering.

"Not forget. Remember." Sliding round onto his belly, he put the can up to his lips and drank deeply. "I need to document the truth before these walls of gold come crashing down and murder every one of us."

"Sounds hunky-dory, if kind of brain-numbing. Somehow, I just don't see you as the bookish type. I know you said you thought about riding with these grunts once. From what I've seen tonight, you've got the necessary: shit-hot manoeuvres on the road, plus a keen mind for violence." She lifted an arm and whipped an imaginary nunchaku. "Aside from preserving that pretty face, what the hell stopped you?"

His expression became fearfully intense, the dark brows knitted, the lips locked tight. "You think I belong with these brutes? Do you, Jezebel? Because Roses only knows, I've fought, tooth and bloody nail, to drag myself out of *that* particular gutter. Yes, there was a time I'd have wallowed in their mire. No ties to anything that's decent or clean or of value. From the outside, it looks cool. A nice little motorbike chapter, all about brotherhood and *belonging*—is that what you think? Shit, Jezebel, IQ was right. You were a loon to risk their lair, helpless and unaided."

"There's nothing helpless about me!" she spat through gritted teeth.

"Oh yeah? Your slingshot might have saved you first time around, but it was proved pretty useless this evening."

Her temples pulsed. "It snagged inside my pocket! A stupid fluke that won't happen again."

"And you can guarantee that, can you, when you find yourself abandoned to the godless heart of *that*?" He thrust a thumb back over a shoulder, at the crawling mass below. "You're lucky they didn't pin you down and pour their sticky claws over every precious part of you, go at it again and again and again until they forced out the last drop of Belief and left you buried."

"You told IQ it was a smart move, my going it alone. Catch the enemy off-guard, you said."

He stared down at her, his pupils swirling with life like two black universes. "That was before I gave a damn!"

Her lips parted, rejoined. Any trace of anger dissipated.

"I may have suffered a crisis of faith for a while," he said gruffly. "But any idea of banding with Skinwalkers was short-lived. Instead, I found a different path, one that steered clear of vigilantism, even if the price was my soul."

"Let me guess. You were at this crossroads at midnight...?"

He suffered a smile. "Like Harish, I packed up my life and set off one dawn, abandoning all that felt right and familiar, abandoning Renegade. On the outside, I put aside these clothes and wore a false palate to disguise my more obvious discrepancies." He pointed to his jaw. "I even found a new name. Mark Anthony. So, yeah, my soul, in exchange for a shot at good old-fashioned normality. Okay, so I hung up my goody two shoes soon enough and stepped back aboard the joyride. But I did get to wipe away the greasepaint and see what made the man beneath. And what did I find? A superstar? A people's hero? Nothing more than skin and bones, made slippery with sin. Even when I returned to Renegade, there was nothing of value or substance, just an endless melting down."

"So what changed?"

"This."

Arching forward, his mouth softly crushed to hers, and perhaps she should have worked her hands tight beneath his shoulders and pressed away the weight of him, or kept her lips closed, like a locked door before a secret. But his kiss was velvety and urgent, and the taste like fire and ice on the tongue. She slid her arms around his neck and brought him closer, surprised by his mohawk as it prickled her fingertips. Bleakly disorientated, every part of her fibrillating and unquenchable, she grasped for his back, squeezed, then slid her hands up to his shoulder blades. Moulding him with palms that cupped and pressed, she caressed the good, soft silk of his black shirt higher, and again a little higher, until she found his skin. Her wintry touch caused him to gasp then flow hard against, and she moved her wrists in slow, glittering circles to just inside his waistband. Barely tangible, his breath fed beneath her lips, like hope, like cherry wine, and she drank without pause, and still thirsted.

205

"Ah, slip it in there, mate!" hissed some vitriolic creature.

She broke instantly away, tumbling aside to sit back on her haunches. D, meanwhile, lay prostrate for a moment and let out a guttural sigh. Bringing his knees into his chest, he rocked back then rolled up to sitting.

"Can I help you, gentlemen?" he said wearily.

"Not you, pimp," said an enormous bear that Jezebel recognised all too readily as the guard she had been promised to at the gate. "Me and my boys ain't that way inclined. But seems a shame to warm the bitch up then leave her out to dry. What say we all get to grips with the pretty piece?"

D sat back on his heels and gradually unfurled to his full height. "Not right now. She's has had her legs spread for the best part of the night now."

"Smells fresh enough to me."

"Just right for the plucking," snarled a coarse companion.

D reached down and tugged her up. "That's as maybe. But my good girl's staying put. I suggest you try the Gangbang tent instead. That's got whores aplenty." Indicating down the slope, he murmured, "Let's go, Jez."

She moved softly, afraid to crush a single grain of snow; and there was nothing familiar in her reaction, just a cloying impotence, as though his kiss had drained her. Retrieving D's coat, folding it meticulously over one arm, she noticed a hard shape in the fabric and slid a hand inside the pocket. D urged her to back away, his gaze fixed on the brutes, and she stepped clumsily back down the incline; all the time, her hand cupping a secret history, *his* history perhaps. The finer part of her said, 'Leave it well alone. This book is not for you.' But her darker curiosity urged, 'Take it. You need a way in.'

D's noiseless descent meant that he arrived unexpectedly at her shoulder. She flinched, and slid the book into her pocket.

"I want that one," the guard bawled after them. "I told you to keep her clean for me. You're lucky I'm still willing to ride it."

"*It's* coming home with me," hissed D in audible annoyance.

"Not on my watch, mate," snarled the bear, his furred limbs ploughing forward. At the signal, his fellow Skinwalkers offered up a grotesque chorus and swaggered out across the snow.

"What now?" Jezebel stared up at the ghost soldier by her side. But D gave no response, just held her arm as they hurried out onto the teeming arena again. At their back, the hideous patrol moved ever closer.

"You can run, but you can't hide, pimp!" quipped the salivating brute—and Jezebel glanced back over her shoulder to see the creature draw a blade, narrow his dead eyes, and take aim.

The blade tumbled out of the whorled claws, flipped over and over in violent somersault. At the same instant, she felt power rip into her limbs, and, as if imbued with a true sense of self, snatched back her arm, threw out the folds of the coat, and sent the knife off kilter.

"Hey, arsehole!" she thundered, slamming the bundled coat against D's chest. Her voice was a bag of broken glass. "I know you're a big man, all gut and tiny balls. But, thing is, you see, I'd rather sink a pint of cow-shit than have you even breathe near me. So how about you and your boys go find a…" she glanced at the brute's codpiece, raised her right hand and gestured meaningfully with her little finger. "…*little* love elsewhere."

D secured her shoulder. "Don't make things worse, Jez."

She shrugged him off and stood as a barricade between him and the monsters.

The guard flexed five thick claws then shaped a fist. "Gonna fix that yapping mouth."

"Yeah, give the bitch summat to chew on."

"Sommit to muzzle her more like."

"Will you really?" she spat, fronting up to the beast like some gothic Tinkerbell to a grizzled Captain Hook. "Gonna beat my boy up good as well, I take it?"

"Too right, whore." The Skinwalker lowered his great jaw to her level, and unsettled her bangs deliberately with his breath. "Gonna peel the skin, inch by sticky inch, back from his bones, then scoop his innards out. How'd you like that?"

"Well, to tell you the truth, not very much. Would we, D?" She looked round and, ignoring the sting of D's obvious disapproval, added, "Then again, given your principled creed of Immunity, as bestowed on my friend here—an honour-bound law by which no beast can lay a friggin' paw on him—I'm guessing Lorcan wouldn't like it either." Her gaze shifted sideways. "Would you, chief?"

Briefly alarmed, the guard's expression hardened. "You're done for," he whispered, his ugly mouth twisted in an upside-down smile.

The brute slunk back to his cronies at the periphery of the thickening crowd. In the meantime, flanked by the skunk Diezeg and a battalion of henchmen, the chief stood in silence a few feet away.

Jezebel focused on the lifeless glass eyes of a wolf's head, a creature whose remaining skin had indeed been flayed back from the bone so that it was worn much as a cloak, with the hood of the skull leering over Lorcan's own studied features. Her heart quickened, unsure if the presence of that top dog assured their deliverance or damnation.

"So, what *is* the score?" she challenged with a jut of her chin.

The kingpin stepped forward, his well-worn para boots compacting the snow. Arms crossed, he appeared to think for a moment, a great stream of white exuding from each nostril. When his eyes met hers, they were unnervingly gentle, and Jezebel almost smiled in spite of herself. Then the brute's gaze slid past her to D.

"You tell me," he commanded without inflection.

Suddenly every organism on that hell plain found her fascinating. So many snake eyes slithered across her skin; and she might have crouched at the base of the rose-window again, torn at the wrist, torn in the heart, and without the faintest idea if she would even see the night out. Here she was, surrounded by the self-same beasts, and subjected anew to their pawing scrutiny.

D, meanwhile, was nothing short of useless. Worse than that, he seemed to melt back into the monstrous ranks and likewise feed on her impending isolation.

She cleared her throat, finding the role of snitch a bitter one. "These grunts are intent on bedding me like rabid St. Bernards while mangling my mate with every fist or weapon to hand. Now I know I'm just a brainless bitch who wouldn't know her arse from her elbow, but seems to me your so-called *honorary* Immunity's worth shit. Am I wrong?"

Lorcan caught her chin firmly between two claws. "Wrong," he breathed, directing her face towards a breaking haze at the horizon. "…and out of time."

"That's bullshit!" she spat, wrenching away. "You deal out Immunity to lull us into a false sense of security. Stay, you say, don't waste good drinking time. Enjoy every sick sin the Blizzard Bash affords. But at first light, we'll torch you. Where's the honour in that?"

The chief's gaze softened and he looked beyond her to D. "I never get why civilians insist on making us more human than we are." His eyes returned to Jezebel. "Skinwalkers'll screw up your world then rape your granny. We're raw and wrong: humanity unhindered. Honour? What's that, *Miss Spider*—a devil that keeps his cock under wraps, or a girl who stays home alone and doesn't come a knocking?" He grasped her hurt wrist, squeezed it so that she flinched ever so slightly, fighting to control the excruciating pain with every bit of self-honour. "Sometimes you gotta take what's coming to you."

"That's as may be, Lorcan. But the girl's faultless. Feed your fury on me." D stepped up, slid his hand around Lorcan's and urged the claws back from about the black bandage.

Jezebel paled, feeling the rough abrasiveness of the fabric as the chief showed no resistance, but let his enormous paw drag a little then fall away.

"The fury isn't mine," said the brute simply. He met her violent stare, tossed a thumb towards the guard, and grinned, "Skinwalkers, we're pretty basic creatures; we ride, we rage, and we always share the booty." His arms grew out from his sides like branches and he turned anticlockwise, towards the brightening sky. "Gonna be a beautiful winter's day," he declared wistfully.

Jezebel stared in utter disbelief as the chief and his coarse entourage strode back towards the crowd. With the beasts starting to close in, she called out hoarsely, "Don't be an arsehole all your life!" She reached automatically for the slingshot, but D closed his hand about hers.

"If you show that weapon here, they'll know who shot their brothers down at the south watchtower. They'll eat you alive, Jez."

Her mouth curved in a bleak, determined smile. "Bring it on, then."

With a swift snap of thumb and finger at her coccyx, she felt the fluid assent of the tall, folded rotators then the weight of their descent. As each branch unfurled, the complex horror on the faces of those circling beasts was almost good enough to bottle, and she breathed it in for one delicious instant. *Please work*, she urged the tattered mess of web and wires while yanking on the starter rope. Pfft. Pfft. The sore mechanics turned over chunkily.

"It's the fug-ugly Fae!" hissed one of the monsters at last, swiftly followed by a great noise of clamorous, rabid howling. Eyes turned dark and glassy, claws felt for a secret arsenal at a boot lip, a turned-up trouser cuff, a hidden pocket in the lining of their leather, and the call went up: "Keep the bitch grounded!"

Her wings started to revolve sluggishly, and she felt herself rise up an inch or two like an enormous metal dragonfly.

"Abandoning me again, Fae?"

D's tone punched a hole in her heart. He turned his back on her and she plummeted forward, scooping under his arms to secure her hands about his chest. Then she rose up, taking the weight of him across her aching shoulders. The beasts crowded in, swiping their great fists into the air so that D raised his legs, causing her body to dip. Like a black wasp, punch-drunk on mouldered apples, she meandered above in generous zigzags, felt D slipping and worked to secure him.

"Let go," he cried over a shoulder. "For Roses's sake, Jez. We'll never make it. Just get yourself away."

"What's the matter?" she snorted between breaths. "That masculine pride wounded again? Jeesh, D, you really need to get over...What the...?"

The rock slammed hard against her arm so that she pitched awkwardly off to the left. A fresh volley of missiles caught her direct on the neck, the cheek, D's chest, the base of her spine, and with wild alarm, she heard the engine falter.

"Going down?" she snarled through gritted teeth.

Seconds later, they plunged back to earth like ghosts of Icarus.

It was difficult to tell whether the score of mangling fists helped cushion her descent or made it hurt the harder. Regardless, before she had recovered as much as one breath, their hands were on her, ripping D aside to force her throat back at an ugly angle.

"Now you pay," slathered the guard, swaddling her in his cruel embrace.

Opposite, D took a slug to the face, his lip bursting open like a split pomegranate.

"What now, D?" she spat against the matt of fur and sweated armour.

Two streaks of scarlet wept either side D's mouth. "Pray for deliverance," he mumbled as a fresh hook jarred beneath his chin.

If angels had raised the purest brass bugles to their lips and piped out a concordant call to arms, the Burners' god could not have answered sooner. The sky rained flames; brilliant orange cannon balls that slammed into the rows of Skinwalkers, knocking them down like skittles. Brows swelled with fat, black bruises, ankles twisted, teeth dislodged, as, again and again, the great stars flashed out across the ice. Jezebel tried to spin around, desperate to see the heaven-sent destroyer since she could only hear its terrible advance, like waves of iron on a chain-link ocean. The Skinwalker held her fast, but it seemed even that leviathan knew himself no match for the ceaseless pitch and grind; of what? Looped metal traction, the unexpected high-pitch then snort of an engine, the crank of a gun shaft; so many sounds of war, tumbling out in a tin-man heartbeat, and at last, the guard tucked her up under one arm then swung around, skating her boots over the snow in a semi-circle.

They met one dark eye face on. If this was the death-giver, Jezebel mused in a hollow daze, it was the most twisted of kaleidoscopes; a 360 degree night, awash with diamond stars, each of which bled one into the next. There was nothing before, nothing ahead, just a tunnelling.

The gun creaked then dipped low. She blinked.

"Queenie?"

Sitting high aloft what appeared to be some desert-style military vehicle, made up of graffiti-daubed sheet metal stapled together one haphazard square at a time and dominated by the long-nosed cannon, the grande dame gave a brief salute.

"Alright, Jez. 'Ave we gone and got ourselves a bloody buggerdy situation?"

Chapter 14

The Reckoning

Arms twisted high behind his back at an excruciating angle, split lip staining his chin with blood, Druid smiled despite the pain. Of all of the unlikely saviours, IQ's tyrannical grandmother was, without doubt, the most surreal and the most welcome.

"Well then," hollered the aged Tank Girl astride her apocalyptic land creeper. "Seems old Pervy Pineapple was right. Second 'e gets off shift at this lively bash, 'e's 'ollerin' down the old blower at me. Tales of little monkeys running riot in this 'ell's own jungle. And what do I find when I gets 'er? That devil's got me girl, Jez, in a saucy clinch and this dog's got me lanky lover in a vice. So tell me boys. What's the friggin' deal?"

Druid tried to ease his stiff wrist joints but the brute at his back held him good and fast, snorting, "Not your business, witch. Fire up your tank and fly away before I'm forced to beat you down."

"You and whose army?" spat the cantankerous maid. "This gaggle of goolies?" She gave her rat-nose a firm rub, lifted up one bosom with the flat of a hand and jiggled it. "I'd ave to play nursie to each and every one afore you'd grow balls to try it."

"Come down here and say that, witch!"

"Ah, feck off!" Launching herself off the vehicle's kick-out step, Queenie hit the ice with a determined crunch. Druid just had time to wince as the feisty old girl sliced the air with a hitherto unseen crowbar. He flinched as she whipped it an inch short of his ear. He heard an audible thwack as it hit something, just as his arms and shoulders felt suddenly liberated. He glanced behind to see the creature doubled up, bleeding head in paws.

"That's *Mrs* Witch to you," Queenie thundered, swinging the crowbar up onto one shoulder where she rested it, like a seasoned Ghurkha returning a kukri knife to its holster.

Druid flinched as a strong, brown hand touched his shoulder. Unexpectedly tender, Queenie directed his face to the right then left and, with a playful tap to his cheek, said, "You'll do, friend. You'll do."

Her lips fashioned an odd, shrewd smile. Then she twisted at the waist suddenly and tossed the crowbar into the tank's foot-well. "You alright there, Jez?" she called, returning to her vehicle to rest a flowered Doc Martin up on its fold-down step. Druid moved beside her, his back pressed to the tank's graffitied armament.

Holding a hand up to her brow, the stern maid surveyed the guard. Her expression brightened. "Ah, you're in safe 'ands there, Jez, even if they're moth-munched and filthy. Wash your momma's dishes with those 'ands, Bernard? 'Tis Bernard, ain't it? Bernard Bobbins Junior. I'd recognise a Bobbins anywhere, not many 'as got the breadth of you, nor the furriness. 'Ow's your ma, Bernard?"

"She's, erm, fine ma'am. Bit of a bad knee this winter," the dimwit garbled before recovering and looking shiftily about. A pair of oil-stained, outsized paws eased in a notch at Jezebel's throat so that Druid longed to bare the slim, white fangs at his jaw and tear out the brute's trachea. For now though, he fought to recover his own balance, as did the guard.

"I'm telling you, witch, it's time to hit the road before my buddies inflict some serious pissing damage," snarled the brute indignantly.

Queenie wrinkled up her nose and quipped, "Kiss your momma...?" She was up in the guard's face in seconds. Then, bam! Her fist slugged the brute square in the jaw, rupturing his lip in two places.

"You be sure to send her my regards," snorted the squat Amazon, giving her hand a quick rap to shake out the knuckles. Back at the tank, she re-installed a boot on the step, then let out a long, sharp whistle. "Well, my beastly buggers, what now? Fight on, or kiss and make up? I knows what I prefer, so come on boys." Eyes clamped shut, she puckered up.

Slowly, she opened an eyelid. "What? No takers?"

"I'll take you," said a voice of steel and velvet.

Druid arched his claws, each jet-black tip readied like a blade. But Queenie surprised him anew. She settled a firm but careful grip around each of his wrists. "Not needed, friend," she said, and, patting his shoulder, eased out from the tank.

Hands square on her hips, the witch fixated on the goliath emerging from the crowd. "Lorcan. Still alive. And still think you can take me? Not feckin' likely, soldier. I always *did* 'ave the upper 'and."

A low hum of malcontent was brought to order when the chief raised a giant paw. "Easy, boys," he said softly, and then gathered the swathes of wolf fur about his arms and bent at the waist. Capturing up Queenie's hand, he licked it lightly and, in return, she nodded.

Unfolding, the chief threw his great meated arms wide and, twisting his head so that the dark-navy ropes of his dreads whipped over one shoulder then the other, told his nervous attendants, "No need for aggro. This is Queenie Quirk, mistress of the wide glide chopper. Back in the day, this hell-babe had the abs and legs to match that monster. Quite a sight, Queen."

"Yeah, well, I'm old and crabby now. So get over it already."

"Bet you could still crank it out on the freeway."

"Your buggerdy winkle I could, but now's not time enough for the testin'. So what's all this palaver? 'Ere's these sweet things all messed up and mangled by your squad while me precious boy, Irvine..." Her eyes roamed. "...why Origin only knows where that tot's holed up."

"Diezeg!"

The skunk stepped forward of the mob, monochrome dreads worming in every direction.

"Chief?"

"Find the kin. If he's a chip off the old block..." Lorcan's eyes flashed in Queenie's direction. "...I suggest you try the poker den."

"What am I? A friggin' nursemaid?" grunted the warrior. He thrust a claw at the crowd, let a gangway open up, and then stomped away in a rumpus of chains, aged leather and squeaking PVC.

Queenie's face shed its deepest creases. "I appreciates the 'elp, Lorcan," she said with careful measure. Then she threw her head back over a shoulder and hollered, "Just as I appreciate you boys cutting us squids a little slack. Soz I 'ad to roast your asses, but sometimes momma's gotta curb those 'orny ways."

Where Druid expected to see the raised hackles of beasts prepared for war, instead the pack nudged one another and leered almost jovially. A tough crowd, they warmed slowly to Queenie's comedic qualities, pressing in as if to get a better look.

Lorcan held Queenie's gaze for a moment. Breaking away, he crossed to where Jezebel stood, her black eyes flitting hatefully from one monster to the next.

Towering over the small bird of a girl, the chief presented a paw. "Time you abandoned us, Miss Spider," he said with barbed gentility—and suddenly Druid wanted to smash that fur-draped arm aside, anything to keep the Fae and that old, grey, *dangerous* wolf a million miles apart. Queenie gripped his shoulder. He sank reluctantly back against the vehicle.

As for Jezebel, her fragile mouth acquired a new rigidity. Glaring up at Lorcan and into a face that Druid knew epitomised her greatest fears, she ignored the gesture and calmly said, "Not without my answer."

Lorcan cast out a paw, rippling the synthetic bangs of the blue wig while Jezebel remained stock-still. "By rights, I should sling you to these dogs and think no more about it. A Fae who buries herself in the walls of my nest but two days past, you aware of that, Queen?"

"I gather so."

"What were you thieving, Miss Spider? *There's* a question needs answering."

"Like I'd steal anything off your skanky ass! Some cheap smokes, a bottle of Bud coated in rat's piss. What exactly do *you* have worth stealing? Nada."

Lorcan tossed the black waterfall of his weaves back off both shoulders and hollered with laughter. Twisting at the waist suddenly, his steely eyes pinioned Queenie's. "These young 'uns have a lot to learn about respect, Queen. Surprises me. I'd have had you down as the first to show a solid hand."

"Too right, mister chief man. Her aim's keener than a shot-putter's," gabbled a youthful voice suddenly.

The crowd parted to reveal IQ's skinny butt aboard Diezeg's shoulders. Dispatching the boy out into the centre of the circle with the same motion as a Canadian curler sliding a stone towards the bull's-eye, the brute dusted off his paws, snatched a beer off a neighbour and sank a noisy draught.

"Alright, Nana," IQ drawled, arriving at Queenie's feet in a final, slow rotation.

Unimpressed, the matriarch reached down, lifted up her grandson's left arm, dropped it and tried the right, checked behind his ears then inside his mouth. She sniffed his breath, pinched one of his cheeks, and slapped him twice about the head.

"Ow, Nana!" protested the kid. His brown fingers scrabbled ineffectually to lessen the blows.

"Too right the pissed precious gets an 'efty dose of Bertie Backhand." Queenie pinned the boy's head underarm in a deadlock and gave his skull a knuckle-rub. "Ask me, it's summat lackin' in these perishers. Gate-crashin' Skinwalkers shindigs? Bleedin' bonkers, not to mention impolite. No invite means *no* admittance," she shouted down at the head in the nook of her great arm. She let go and approached Lorcan, leaving IQ to spin around on his bum and smile daftly. "No respect. You're right there, Lorc. Although…" She fixed quizzically on the old, grey wolf. Her wise eyes sharpened. "We all made our own bed when it comes to *that*. Is the 'ighest lord's tower a comfortable one?"

Druid's interest was piqued, and judging by the inscrutable smile that crept over her lips, so was Jezebel's. By way of contrast, Lorcan's brown mouth stayed resolutely still. Similarly, the rest of the pack may have sought to re-affiliate their long lost queen a few short moments ago, but now they stared her down, cold-eyed and menacing.

"Bar the odd splinter and a faint stench of burning, it's a class above the caves. You remember how cold they got, don't you, Queen? Only place that was warm was nose to tail in bed." The top dog put a fresh cigar between his jaws and tore off the end. He spat the excess wad off to one side, unlatched a Zippo too late as Queenie held up her cupped hands. She threw the match aside as he inhaled. "I'm surprised you've the gall to criticise. Once upon a time you weren't so high and magick. Once upon a time you were happy to fester with the rest of us. What happened to that good time gal?"

"Remembered the *real* reason she'd believed in the friggin' first place," answered the witch. She matched Lorcan's gaze with clear assertiveness. "Beer, age-old whiskey, biker bars paved with spit, blood and sawdust, metal mommas 'ammerin' down the strait—its *physical* magick. But it weren't enough,

216

Lorc. You knows *that* better than any beast in Renegade." Five brown fingers tapped at her brow. "Gotta use me noggin. Gotta sleep at night without slaving to me conscience. We all make our choices, Lorc."

Druid noticed a mutual sadness writ deep in well-creased skin. He imagined each veteran replaying a thousand wild memories, precious as gold dust, in the resultant silence. His eyes were drawn to the small shape of Jezebel. Her face was a storm of hurt and loathing.

Perhaps Queenie noticed also. Swaggering back to the tank, she returned her Doc to the step and rested forward on an elbow. "So, the south watchtower, eh? Seems you boys are going up in the world! Lets 'ope the same's true for your method of *employment*." Her eyes lit up like miniature suns. The fire ebbed. "So let's shake on no more bovver; no more shenanigans. What d'you reckon, Jez?"

The girl's thin brows arched. "I reckon that's bullshit."

"Ah, come now, Jez. Give these lads a breather. I know they're testy but you just ain't askin' them right. See, Lorc, my girl Jez, 'asn't the motive to infiltrate your pack and go a-stealing. Nah, her style's more along the personal. You've got summat that belongs to 'er. Now she wants it back."

"I know what she's lost." Lorcan ran five claws down the dual strands of his beard. His gaze stayed hooded. "But it's not hers for the taking."

"Likely as not, you're right." Queenie hunched and threw up her hands. "'Cept I'm 'ere now." She motioned to the silent cannon then patted the side of her vehicle. "Never would have come to you, Lorc, you know that. Not the way I like to work. But these feckin' squids have got me implicated. So, 'ere's me offer. I'm looking for me boy, 'arish. 'Ails of Castclan, small lad, strong build, bit of a monkey."

"*Your* boy?" Lorcan's voice had an edge.

Queenie leant her broad back against the graffitied metal. She sighed. "Always the games, eh Lorc? What if it *were* your son that was missin'?"

She held the chief's gaze, which was an assault of dark elements: sleet, hail, forked lightning, and, at the heart of each iris, a twister. In that protracted instant, the beasts stopped circling. They huddled in as if thrust from the wings onto the set of some Aristotelian tragedy.

"Okay, so 'e's not," supplied the clever crone, giving faint relief to the atmosphere. "But 'e *could* 'ave been."

A wealth of sentiment passed between witch and wolf, though neither said a word.

"So what's it to be?" snarled Queenie, breaking off to step back abroad her land-ship. "Indulge a wrinkly, old broad and fess up?" Grasping the cannon's handles, she swung the weapon around in a whirr of greased cogs. The barrel halted, aimed dead at Lorcan. "Or do things 'ave to get nasty?"

Claws spread above the tank's rusty sheet metal, Druid felt a stab of anguish; misinterpreted it as a need to hear the fate of Harish on some personal level. But at last the truth flooded his mind like light through a window. His main dread was that Jezebel might just get her answers.

Lorcan sighed. "Let us say the Management calls you to action, Queen, and you don't like it. I suspect you voice your objection loud and clear. But orders are still orders, no matter how you dress them up. Same with Skinwalkers. The Angel sentenced him. We were *law*-bound to obey."

"What the hell do you mean, sentenced him?" Jezebel stepped between Lorcan and the gun.

"To victimisation by Skinwalker."

In that instant, Druid felt Jezebel torn from him like a thorn from flesh. A red fog swirled before his eyes and he saw her, pale as a lily, emotions unfolding like petals gone over. His rage was all-consuming.

"Victimisation is a sacred rite, sanctioned only by the divine law of the Management. The accused always has the option to leave the city rather than face whatever punishment their tribe decides to inflict and be physically branded as an outcast from that tribe. There is a proper process to be followed, designed to guard against exactly this sort of malpractice," he thundered, re-animating his claws. "How dare Skinwalkers instigate such punishment?"

Lorcan swung around savagely, the swathes of waist-worn chains and keys jangling. "I told you, *we* didn't instigate a damn thing...pimp." The title stuck to the dog's rough tongue, as if protecting Druid's identity took every ounce of self-restraint.

"The Angel? Who controls the belly of these beasts?" Druid snarled, crucifying his arms on an invisible cross. "Tell me, Lorcan. Who *is* your lord and master?"

The chief turned away and strode to the edge of the circle. He stopped, twisted his face back around. Eyes lightened to the colour of dove's wings, he said simply, "He is the death-bringer."

"Wait! That won't do!" hissed Jezebel and she lurched forward, fists flailing. Powering over the space that separated them, Druid caught her up by the waist and swung her hard around. "That won't fucking do!" she choked, tearing at his claws so that her nails drove out chunks of his flesh.

"Hush now." Lorcan's voice was cream and black.

Druid held the girl as she stilled a little, limbs jerking back against him spasmodically. He watched darkly as the chief turned full-about.

Flanked on either side by his feral legions, the old wolf told them, "I may have Immunity from this hoard, but I still risk my life in sparing any information." He stared into the barrel. "For the sake of my one-time queen...Turn your rage to City Hospital, Miss Spider. You'll find your answers there."

An instant later, the gun creaked out of commission and Queenie dismounted. The fine streaks of first light created an auburn warrior of her. She strode up to Lorcan, hands clenched, chin aloft. Stepping in, she touched her tongue to his cheek. "We'll expect you," she said defiantly.

The great wolf dipped his head, the skull of the animal borne above beholding that scene with its deadpan eyes. "Watch your back, Queen," he muttered.

Queenie nodded and turned swiftly on her heel. Traipsing back over to her chariot, she said in a whispered aside, "Come away now, Jez. You'll get nuffin' more."

Jezebel shrugged Druid's hands aside.

He kept his eyes on the graffitied hulk of a tank as the search party of a wise old crone, a kid with a cockeyed grin and a tattered wizard hat, and a black-eyed, wondrously savage, strange little girl climbed aboard; and a shard of ice lodged in the underside of his lowest left rib. As Jezebel clung to the metal shell of the cockpit, his gaze caressed her every dip and curve. Sorrow had infected every inch. For now at least, she was beyond him.

Busying herself with a couple of levers, Queenie spared a moment to glance up. "You comin', me lush lovely?"

Sensing that, here, their paths divided, Druid shook his head. *That* road was not his to take.

The witch's sharp, brown eyes settled on Lorcan. "You'll do right by me boy, D, 'ere." It was a statement, not a question. Then, reaching down, Queenie cranked the iron monster into shuddering motion. Two colossal chain-webbed caterpillar tracks began to grind in reverse, trawling a fresh path of grit and glossed ridges back through the ice. When there was space enough to manoeuvre again, the witch tugged on a huge ship's wheel so that the whole vessel sledged 180 degrees.

Queenie signalled adieu with a deep toot of a bullhorn while IQ offered a brief salute, his usual sanguinity replaced with a graveness that strangely aged him, as if a weight of shadows had been hung about his face and shoulders. Only Jezebel was static; a pillar of salt dusting in the wind.

The great rattling monster pulled away, a coruscated mist rising in its wake. Druid felt his soul threaten to unravel. For a few short days and nights, Jezebel had acted as his tourniquet: a valve on the river of hurt, hopelessness and living lost. And perhaps, in return, he had stemmed that dark flow in the Fae—certainly he had thought as much from her slow, exquisite, bud-like unfolding. The treasure of *her* had soon turned the rest of the world to ocean-tumbled glass; Sophia's jaded reserve, the subtle menace of Adeudas, the loss of Roses...

The hoards of great lumbering beasts at his back started to slip away. Druid's brow furrowed. Was it possible he had allowed himself to drip away into such a dilute measure of his true existence that all he saw was a chance to lust, even love again? If so, it was a cruel, tenacious lie. Meanwhile, the real issues had got clouded along the way; he still needed to hunt a killer and he still needed to sink his jaws into the city's skin, get at its cankered heart and drain the rot before the whole damned fantasia turned to spit in the rain. And he was a very different creature to the one who had crept out of the weathered gates of the north watchtower. He was alert to the surreal prejudices tainting his and Roses's most glorious dream, to the extreme elegance of a dragon man in flight and the savage swells of Skinwalkers, brutes that would victimise their own kind but remain the one group of Believers to demonstrate strength in unity, to the shadow of an Angel over Renegade's glam charade, if ignorant to a creeping soul-salved inertia that came from his need for Jezebel.

He pierced his inner cheek with a slim fang, savoured the dark flavour of pain intermingled with his blood. It wasn't enough. He wanted to rip the soft silk of his black shirt open, sink his claws in and root around under flesh and rib until he located that shard of ice, which was his heartbreak, and his weakness.

"Be seeing you, *D.*" The voice was Lorcan's.

Druid hooked off his shades, slipped them into the upper left pocket of his leather, and felt the shape of some object he didn't recognise. Closing his hand around it, he drew a small, red velvet pouch out into the light. It was IQ's love charm, the one the kid had bestowed on him in the bar at Legacy. Druid tugged on the thin, gold string at the neck, held out the pouch and emptied its dust of crushed herbs into the wind. Then he slid back his shoulders and slowly turned around.

He stared into the wolf's dark-grey, enigmatic globes and saw his own strange, pale eyes reflected. His gaze moved to the smouldering wasteland; the ravaged carcasses of spiralled iron ore, the hot spots of bonfires reduced to ash and embers, the vacant stage, the corporeal glow of a fresh, new dawn.

"Yes you will," he said quietly. Tugging the collar of his leather high about his throat, he walked away.

Chapter 15

Famous Last Words

The man in the bed should have been in his mid twenties, but numerous bruises at his jaw and cheekbones meant that his flesh had an aged, sallow quality. Hair radiated out over the pillow; wet, black, and bur-tangled. Scabbing blood escaped one ear. Sweat smeared his exposed skin while, at a nostril, the back of a hand, and disappearing under a thin cellular blanket, myriad tubes were siphoning off and feeding in.

Anguish tore at Jezebel's throat. Harish looked so quiet, almost foetal, lying there on a hospital bed that shone with technology like a cultured pearl. It was difficult to believe that this was the same animal that had pursued her in the south watchtower just a few short nights ago, leaping from one mouldered shelf to the next like a human-monkey hybrid. She tried to swallow. The pain was too acute. What grisly events had taken place in the hours in-between to reduce him to this...this *ghost?* Like a mother tending a sick child, she longed to rest her palm over his brow and absorb a portion of his fever. Except, Harish looked *wrong* in his torn, muddied leathers. Wrong and at odds with the pristine nature of the room.

While Jezebel longed to escape the dark city, the *light* inside the hospital was even less appealing. The room scintillated. Walls were moulded from what looked like extruded polypropylene plastic, and lunar-white. A spaceship deck of tiled iron mesh sustained the lustre of the walls. Miscellaneous apparatus erupted from the floor, drip bags fruiting off the many steel arms. At the far wall, a large, oval window was just visible behind a semi-transparent strip blind the colour of unbleached calico. The internal door was a satin-silver oblong with a slim handle that cut into the palm when depressed; Jezebel remembered how it had sealed noiselessly in her wake, and suddenly she felt not so much protected as *contained.*

Her eyes darted up to the lacunar ceiling; it seemed to press down on her with an oppressive weight. She fingered the rope of a scar at her neck. The one time that *she* had required medical attention in recent years, Queenie had served as nurse and apothecary. The witch's salves of fetid plant stuff, and an agonising if neat row of butterfly stitches, alongside a quarrelsome bedside manner, were polar opposites to this stark cell. They were rustic and earth-brewed, much like Harish—which went some way to explaining why he'd been left in such a state.

Bruised and filthy skin soaped with a washcloth, a cotton bud dipped in iodine and applied to the crusted blood at an ear—was it so extraordinary to expect Harish's care to extend to such? Ordinarily, she would have been up in arms at his neglect. Today though, she recognised something aberrant about her brother. Harish didn't fit the blueprint. He wasn't exotic, dangerous, beautiful or sinister. He was a filth-stained pariah in a clean, white heaven. And yet—Jezebel felt her flesh burn up as if she stood in the direct path of a flash-fire— if Harish was untouchable, then *she* was a carrier of the same leprous gene.

Her eyes greased with tears. She circled her bandaged wrist with a thumb and forefinger, wincing when the pressure aggravated the claw marks. A nurse had set up a drip feed and applied electro pads to his chest (should the area not have been shaved first?), but she had steered clear of actual tender, loving care. Harish had lashed out at the one hand offered in aid, as if to evade her touch. Up until that moment, Jezebel had refused to dwell on the fact. Now, finding Harish in a bleached environment from which he was powerless to escape, she realised just how much he had hurt her. The wound was more complex than a bite mark at the throat or gauged flesh at the wrist. What cut to the quick was how Harish had rejected *her* for being something other, just as the city, and before it, the rest of the world, had rejected him.

Pinioning her lower lip between her teeth, she wanted to scrape at her skin, rip and peel it off the bone to expose the glistening girl inside, anything to remind Harish that he had loved her once, and the love they shared was unconditional. She fought back waves of nausea. Her stomach twisted up in knots. Blame wasn't so easily allotted now that she was, in turn, responsible for *his* wounds. *She* had gone looking for

Harish. *She* had tracked him to the unforgiving lair of the Skinwalkers. *She* had extended her hand, and in so doing, exposed him as an average Joe with emotional ties outside of the chapter. Only, Harish was far from average and *that* was the crushing irony. Were it not for her intrusion, the brotherhood might never have noticed a fantastic creature in their ranks, and chastised him for the fact.

She crouched down, fingered the hem of the stiff bottom bed sheet where it had come untucked, but didn't attempt any physical contact. "Harish," she murmured.

The flaking lips broke apart and a slit of dark appeared at each eyelid. "We're all full of...lies."

Jezebel lost all restraint. She prised five long, keratinous claws off the blanket and clutched them. "*We're* not full of lies. *Renegade City* is. We should leave this place." Applying a gentle pressure, she added, "Get Desdemona to join us."

Harish tried to work his head higher up the pillow, his face distorted in agony. "Can't...Not safe," he spat, a fine salve of foam at his lips.

"Bullshit." Jezebel backed off but didn't release his hand. "It's obvious why you ran away. When you christened me with this," she indicated the scar wreathing her neck and left shoulder. "It made sense to discard your humanity and embrace the beast within. In your mind, anyway. Isn't that why you abandoned Desdemona and why you deserted your unborn child? Afraid you'd hurt them too?"

"Life screwed me over, so I screwed over life." Harish thrashed at the rumpled sheet and blanket. "Don't try to make me moral, Jez. I...didn't...fight to live free of judgment only to be re-caged by my own sister. I'm not the man you want me to be." His expression was vitreous and pain-melded. But a few seconds later, the eyes began to glaze.

Jezebel gripped his hand with mercurial savagery. "Stay with me, Harry." Her cruelty brought him round. Deep-set, black eyes revolved in their sockets, settling on her face like drops of poison. "I just want my brother back," she said, outraged by a creeping paranoia that he would shake her off, had he strength to do so. "Shame your so-called brothers-in-arms can't claim the same. What was your *crime*, Harry? Why did they do this to you? *What* did they do to you?"

Her questions seemed to settle over Harish like embalming fluid. The face that had revealed so much soul-break and inner anguish became calm, serene even. "My crime? I was the outsider, Jez. Always the outsider." His breath was vapid, his voice phantasmal. "I was a reminder; this body, this flesh, is never really ours. We...inhabit it, but can't mould it if biology says otherwise, can't...*contain* it if biology says otherwise."

Jezebel scrunched a fist into the dip below her ribs. She felt as if her heart was being wrung out. The injustices of Harish's birth defect, or was it a genetic throwback, even a natural evolution, burnt her insides like acid. "So rather than accept you, Skinwalkers chose to punish your diversity. Or should I say, slice it off?" She put a hand to her mouth. The aversion was instinctual. "And you say *I* want to re-cage you." Her tone was bitter, yet also tinged with sadness as she scanned the sterile lock-down of a room.

"The Skins were honour-bound. They did me in with kindness. Lorcan saw to that. He tried to get me out before..." Harish's eyes flickered. His tranquil expression froze into a death mask. Jezebel sat motionless for a few seconds. She was on the verge of extending her hand and resting it on the damp brow as she had longed to do earlier when Harish's jaw craned apart, his lips laced with spittle.

"The boys tried to get me out of the city," he gasped, his flesh drained of all residual colour. "The chief said they were to save me from..."

Jezebel gripped the hem of the bed sheet, massaging the stiff fibres like prayer beads.

"...my own guardian angel," Harish forced. And then he slept, eyes tracking demons behind thread-veined lids.

Jezebel yanked the blind aside and stood in front of the window, arms straitjacketed over her chest. Below, the city was blanketed in white, the rust of a rising sun at the horizon. She pressed her nose to the pane, clouded it with her breath, scrubbed at the spot with the hem of her coat sleeve. Suddenly it was vital to see clearly. The oval window served as a magic mirror; it restricted her view to only the central districts so that, for a time, she was able to pretend nothing existed outside of the city and she was just an onlooker, staring in from behind a wall of glass.

Like any other sun fostering life, the wyrd world of Renegade originated in the east. She gazed left to where the

Trading Quarter sparkled in the red and white-gold light, the diaphanous sleeves of the east watchtower revolving at a gentle pace while, gathered at its fluted skirts, the spiralling streets of the medina were brilliantly if uncharacteristically frosted, like an Arabian tale displaced to C.S Lewis's Narnia. In stark if appropriate contrast given the mercantile nature of the quarter, the bastille-like warehouses in the Lace Market also twinkled. Neon spluttered into life at the rows of outsized, 'watch me' windows, cranking up the pulse in sleepy studios, unhooking answer phones in agency offices, hot-wiring eyelids with strong coffee. Jezebel felt a thrill of affection, a reaction that confused as much as comforted her. What was it that drew her to the quarter? She suspected it was *ordinariness*, a word that she had never expected to apply to any aspect of Renegade. More than any other sector, the Trading Quarter struck her as a polestar of cooperation, where Castclan, Trawlers, DarkLed, Fae, Grallators, Skinwalkers and drifters alike were united by a common language of barter and exchange. It was this *practical* application of the dream that would drive the market traders to spoon out their wares across the medina's hand-scrubbed, rustic benches despite the subzero temperatures, the malls with their armoured hides of blue and storm-grey glass to claw in the punters whatever the weather, and the scissoring, iron-clad teeth of the mills to keep masticating yarn into linen, cloth and lace.

Her brow shadowed. She had enough of a grasp on local history to know that, over the centuries, Nottingham's economy had relied heavily on a lauded textile industry and a ripe flow of tourist traffic. Staring out at the waking world to the east, she saw that nothing had changed. Autonomy was a lie, the separation from the rest of the world touted as Renegade's USP a sham. Cream away the greasepaint and the flats of gothic scenery, and the great cogs driving the city were still powered by age-old trade links with the outside world.

Like Eve cast out of a maudlin Garden of Paradise, Jezebel felt a sense of loss. Biting at the littlest finger of one hand, she wondered if it might be possible for her to forget and believe again?

The roses and cream quality of the light was just filtering west to the Pleasure Quarter, residents having a few minutes remaining of undercover-of-dark decadence before the sun threatened to turn them back into statues, or to dust. Unnerved by the ease with which she gnawed on her own finger, Jezebel returned her hand to the glass. There were still sections of the city that gorged on the dream. If the reason for the lie was to be found anywhere, it was amidst the patronage and glitz to the west.

Unfazed by the light, Booty Boulevard was a strip of sequins on the showgirl behind of old suburbia. Listening intently, Jezebel could almost *hear* the cicada-buzz of hundreds of neon signs, the crackle of foils re-examined many times over for residual traces of blow or hash, and the pump of hearts conjoined by damp, hot flesh. If she stared long enough at the writhing mass of buildings, she might see *through* the dark to the pirouetting sheets of newspaper outside the foyer of a theatre, the alley cats scooping and bickering amongst the dumpsters in the backyard of a restaurant, a crow circling the sparkling, white bowls of the skater parks, and the last few stranglers camped on the great sweep of steps outside Legacy.

But there was nothing supernatural about her vision, the view stayed clouded, and instead, she concentrated on the hill of cave-riddled sandstone and its diadem, the west watchtower. Torchlight lent the building eyes; it stared back at her across the semi-dark, triumphant and defiant, a bearer of secrets.

Jezebel pulled back her mind. She was aware of conversation in the room. The doctor's tone was precise and measured, while, fetched from her bed rest by Queenie, Desdemona cut in now and then, her voice strained yet intelligent, and the elder witch restricted herself to the odd grunt and gripe.

Refocusing on the glass, Jezebel saw Harish reflected there, a man enchained by his own bruised and twisted flesh. What terrified her more, that Renegade was a masquerade grafted onto Nottingham's old, tired bones, or that what stood for fantasy and what reality was increasingly blurred? One thing was certain. She didn't want to deal with the harsh events inside that hospital room. For as long as she could, she wanted to remain standing there, eyes intent on what lay beyond the window.

Rooted in law and cold, hard fact, the collection of districts to the south *should* have appealed. But despite its sunlit aspect, the Knowledge Quarter had always struck her as the darkest sector of the city. Harbouring a host of key municipal buildings—each one, a hunk of bloodless stone with a grand foyer and a door bell that sounded, far off and hollow, like a toll to wake the dead—it came *too* close to the outside world. Squinting, she tried to make out the nuances of the neighbourhood, but it was an ever-repeating seam of grey. Even the neo-classical Council House had the taint of an asylum.

If there *was* a theatrical presence, it was the ruined church in the south-east, and yet even that spired pile looked more sober than formidable by daylight, a fact that prompted Jezebel to draw her hands back over her head, lock them at the base of her neck and sigh. She had always viewed the south watchtower in terms of her own personal perdition; it was a gorgon in cloaking black, festooned with statues like the corpses of armies it had conquered, and she had passed through its unholy doors, banner held aloft like one of the Knights Templar. In the cold light of day, however, that act didn't feel so worthy. She and Harish had scarred one another inside and out. Nothing else seemed real. Not the threat of Skinwalkers; men who clothed themselves in the flesh of beasts and were tainted by the scent of blood ever after. Not the hell of a sunlit, dusting ruin.

She felt weightless, emptied of purpose. If she had placed any stock in Belief once upon a time, her faith had worn away to a wafer-thin sheen…hadn't it? Wide and liquidly black like those of a young animal, her eyes flew to the iridescent lance soaring over the enchanted grove of the Arboretum, a mile or so away. The north watchtower basked in the glow of a weak sun. At its apex, an ornate copula flamed with green-gold light like an underwater supernova. Three oak and steel platforms orbited the upper third of the tower, aglow in earth light.

Jezebel placed a hand to her throat, a tourniquet to her breath. If she was a true believer, she would have said the gods had conjured a column of pure, organic energy by cover of night, as if to say 'Remember us. Our eyes are always watching.' But if that was the case, what did the Drathcor make of their domain now the dark had gone?

She scanned the white faeryland of the Mystic Quarter. The Castclan pod was shrouded under snow. Great sculptures of glass, wood and metal that served as spirit guides at the gateways to the cemeteries were light-gilded, like archangels. Haunted Hill, the mushrooming hovels, higgledy-piggledy tea shops and timbered guild houses were put to sleep underneath the ice, as if cursed by a snow queen, or anaesthetised.

Distracted by motion in the hospital grounds, she glanced down. Figures traversed a series of pebble-dash, snow-and-litter free paths; visitors, doctors, nurses, porters, paramedics, patients wheeling drip bag trolleys ahead of them, an armful of spaghetti-like tubes attached...She sucked her lips against her teeth. Harish's room might have overlooked a prison yard, the perimeter fence of which was invisible but still capable of shocking to death any inmate who tried for freedom. She cringed. City Hospital had always represented a band aid on the hallowed grime of Renegade. Now she felt as if she had been swallowed into the belly of some great, parasitic organism that was feasting on the city. Yes, that was it. Renegade was being emptied out, its corpse salted with snow then purified with so much reflected light it hurt her eyes. She stared at the sky, and tears bleed. Everything she knew smelt of blood and bandages.

A hand gripped her shoulder.

"You're not like other watchers."

She rubbed a hand down both cheeks then turned her head towards a tall, pale sliver of a man. Both insubstantial and striking, the doctor had abandoned his bedside ministrations to arrive noiselessly besides her. His face was cerebral with even, noble features. The thinning, silvery, cropped hairstyle accentuated the sharp profile and exaggerated the transparent quality of his skin, beneath which numerous veins were visible, like turquoise rivers under mist. While she might have imagined the statuesque figure in a doctor's coat and wire-rimmed glasses, she was startled by the crisp, white linen of his formal suit, the full moon of each eye.

"Other watchers?" Her tone was brittle. She didn't want to engage in conversation. She wanted to stay dissolved in what lay beyond the glass. At the same time, her natural defences were triggered. She despised being labelled.

The Darkled inclined his head towards Desdemona and Queenie, on guard either side of the hospital bed with its fevered occupant. "Those who keep the vigil," he whispered icily.

"And what makes *me* so different?" she threw back. "I'm still here. Throwing mental punches at myself for failing to save my brother from a life of rabid insanity. Sorry to disappoint, *Sir*, but there's nothing remarkable about this watcher."

The doctor released his grip on her shoulder. His skull-like face was strangely illuminated. "Mr. Denizel, if you please, and all I meant was that you look the type to see past the bruises to the suffering within. As I have just explained to Mrs Geronimo and Mrs Quirk, your brother has been through quite an ordeal." Cataracted eyes fixed on Harish's matted shape. "*He* can never be healed," he added so softly that Jezebel found herself wondering if the man had in fact said a word or if she had imagined it.

Her eyes flew about the room, alighting on Desdemona's delicate, harrowed features, then dancing off to Queenie's sterner face. "We'll fix him up alright," she said matter-of-factly, adding with a softness to match the DarkLed's own, "He's home now."

"But not home and dry." Mr. Denizel met the force of her gaze, then slipped away to retrieve the tablet PC from the foot of the bed. "Has the patient responded to your presence in any way yet, Mrs Geronimo?" He slid out the stylus and applied the nib to the screen, leafing through the charts.

"He's opened his eyes once or twice, but I don't think he's really aware we're here," Desdemona replied stiffly. Her radiant, black skin, a deeper hue than Queenie's or IQ's, was lacklustre. When she stroked her pregnant belly with a trembling hand, Jezebel felt a pang of anxiety, and guilt. It was cowardice to try to ignore what was going in that room. Desdemona deserved more from her, as did Harish. She turned her back on the window.

"Do you think so?" Mr. Denizel replaced the tablet. Indicating Queenie aside with his ghost eyes, he drifted over to the bedside. A veiny hand secured Harish's jaw, worked it side to side until the patient awoke with a jolt. Blooded knuckles arched, claws pawed at the thin blanket, and a whimpering noise bubbled up from Harish's trachea.

"Shhh there, Harish. Lie still." Desdemona unfastened the claws from the bedcovers and pressed them to the swell of her stomach.

"Who's the silly boy then?" The doctor raised his silver brows. He unclipped a pen torch from his breast pocket, leant in and manipulated the tiny spotlight, forcing each eyelid open in turn, then the mouth. "What a mess to get in, Harish, and what company to keep. What possible excuse can there be for jollying off when this lovely lady is expecting?"

"Circumstances were complicated." Desdemona glared at the man from under dark-kohled lids.

Jezebel nodded emphatically, adding, "It isn't always easy to say this is what makes you good and this is what makes you bad. Life isn't as regimented as that. Its borders are often muddled."

"How very true." Mr. Denizel met her gaze with unsolicited approval. Jezebel tucked her hands up under her armpits. The finer part of her wanted to ignore his elitist tactics. But she was also intrigued.

"And yet, if your brother *hadn't* decided to go off monkeying with a lawless crew of Skinwalkers, he would have remained one of the gracious and the good. In other words, he need never have shared his dirty secret." The doctor gestured to Harish's spine, and his thin, gelatinous lips crept up at a corner.

The sour smile set Jezebel on edge, and she saw that her distrust was shared by the other women present. Desdemona adjusted Harish's hand, fanning the grimy talons over her belly. Queenie plumped her breasts with the shelf of her crossed arms and grunted.

Concluding his examination in a series of swift, fluid movements, Mr. Denizel stepped back from the bed. He re-secured the pen clip on his breast pocket, paused as if sensing an air of resentment, and said in all graveness, "I know I am hardened, Mrs Geronimo, but trawling these corridors day in, day out, it's enough to crust the kindest heart. Sometimes we need to take account for our misfortunes, in the same way we take account for our Belief in this vaudevillian gala of a city." He laid a hand over Harish's brow, the fine skin at his wrist exposing the veins with the lucidity of a cold-water shrimp. His eyelids flickered. "So, another's paws chastised your husband for his lackadaisical attitude to family?"

"Crossin' the line, doc." Queenie puffed up like a squat toad on the defensive. "That boy believed 'imself a beast, one 'ose family was better off without 'im. And while I'm not saying I agree with what 'e did, it's not the work of a bleeding nun to understand or to forgive it."

Mr. Denizel kneaded the moist flesh under his fingers. "Well, this *beast* is running a fever, which is more the pity since he requires reconstructive surgery."

"Surgery, my aunt Fanny!" Queenie hooked her big, brown hands onto her hips. "All's needed is a good dose of the 'erbals, Plantain poultice, tinctures of Marigold, Cayenne, Comfrey..."

"Enough, madam!" Mr. Denizel glared at the witch, and Jezebel was reminded of a teacher chastising a wayward pupil in the assumed knowledge that that child is destined for a life of slop and strife. "I've every patience with Castclan hocus-pocus," he continued in a softer, more indulgent tone. "Lords only know your kind save me no end of bother with my more *imaginative* patients. Dole out a dab of this. Ingest a sup of that. But when a man is dying..."

Dying? Jezebel tumbled the word on her tongue like a piece of grit. It evolved into a secret, silent pain; fear of further suffering, fear of loosing Harish to a second afterlife. Draining her eyes of expression, she glanced at the others. Queenie's aged face was resin-like. Desdemona visibly sank into her chair, strength evaporated.

"I don't mean to alarm you." Mr. Denizel adjusted his cuff links at each wrist. "But something tells me not even Harish believes *I* am in charge of his destiny. Yes, I will do everything in my power to save him. However, the odds are not favourable. He's lost a lot of blood, the wound shows signs of infection, and most significantly of all, Harish demonstrates no *will* to pull through." The unfathomable eyes drifted towards Jezebel. "It's as if your brother has forgotten what it was that he believed in and resigned himself to a world without magic. A world of hurt, loss, and death."

This last word was uttered as a whisper, the patient having slipped back into sweat-drenched inertia, and it was all Jezebel could do to stare wildly at the broken man in the bed and think, *Wake up!* This *family needs you.* But Harish slept.

"So if you really want to do the best by my patient, I suggest giving him the space to heal. Let me work *my* magick in the operating theatre. If all goes well, he'll be free to leave here and be ministered to in whichever way you see fit." Mr.

Denizel produced a slim, silver PDA from a suit-trouser pocket, glanced at it then at Queenie. "I promise to be amazed at the speed of Harish's recovery once he's in your capable hands, but *only* once he has been treated by professional medical staff here," he added with a half-smile.

"Quack, quack," retorted Queenie. Her wise, brown eyes appeared to interrogate the doctor's opaque globes for some glimpse of deception. Then, gathering up her skirts, she crushed a kiss to the sleeping beast's brow, made her way around the bed to where Desdemona sat and gently secured her by the arm. "Come precious. Lets leave the doc to do his snip and sewing. Then we'll re-patch our best boy and get 'im safely 'ome again."

Desdemona bent to seal a kiss on Harish's lips. She allowed herself to be led away.

At the door, Queenie stretched out her hand to grasp the silver handle, paused, and glanced back across the room "You comin', Jez?" Her face, which was usually so solid, knowledge-etched and gladiatorial, was riven with emotion.

Jezebel felt life-weary. Harish was critically ill, a fact that weighed on her like a suit of iron. At the same time, she had committed herself to bringing him home safe. Tracing the scar at her neck with a fingertip, she said flatly, "No. I'm sorry Queenie. I can't."

Now it was *her* turn to be subjected to the witch's intensive gaze. Queenie nodded slowed. "Desdemona needs rest. As for me boy, IQ, I left 'im in charge of Belching Bertha and, Lords know, 'e's not a lad to trust with a stoked-up 'Aitch-U-V.'"

"And that's why you should go." Jezebel gave her attention back to the doctor. "Harish is to be prepared for surgery? Can I wait outside?"

Mr. Denizel scooped his pallid hands in the direction of the door.

"I'll take that as a yes." At her back, Jezebel heard a pneumatic swish of air as Queenie and Desdemona exited and the door drew to. Moving over to the bed, she curved her small, neat fingers over Harish's. There was no sentiment she could offer by way of comfort. Without word, she left the room.

Outside in the corridor, she seated herself on a bench of lucent, blue and silver polyester tiles, pressed her knees together and set her feet apart. She leant forward with her hands clasped in her lap, and glanced left then right. There were people seated outside rooms just like her, and others traversing the sterile floor tiles in either direction. Everyone was dressed ordinarily enough in frills, latex, vinyl, and lace, like the spirits of the insane haunting the clinical halls of a Victorian sanatorium. But in a city of lights, camera, action, and never growing old, their hushed footfall and unsure eyes were anything *but* ordinary. Jezebel studied a solitary man, a few quiet children, a pregnant woman carrying an overnight bag, and got no sense of the fantasia that was meant to underpin Renegade's noir-gothique paradise. Quite the contrary, what shone out from each pale face with poisoned brilliance was *disbelief.* In the acid-white of the hospital, all the theatrics were stripped away—no, that image was too gentle, she decided, twisting a little finger between her lips again, biting down and taking succour from the pain. Outside, the city was a whirlwind of sin-sparkle, blood-red exotica and thermals of mole-soft darkness. But in the ice field that was City Hospital, the dream was cancer-riddled. Inside those sterile walls, there was no such thing as Fae, Castclan, DarkLed, or Trawler, no such thing as Skinwalker, Grallator, drifter or even Drathcor, only flesh unconquerable, blood gone bad, and oh such suffering!

Her nostrils flared. What use were castles in the air when mankind was so very fragile? And yes, she had shelved the city's discrepancies for a time, in particular, its savage denial of those who did not make the grade of what counted as underworld beauty in its myriad, weird-glamorous forms, but pushed beyond the 'acceptable'. She had even dared to dream of a life outside of the hunt for Harish, thanks to D. Her breath tightened behind a hard wall of emotion. D was a freak of a jaded kind. He carried a heart's worth of secrets, tucked up beneath his flesh like a purse that held diamonds. But cut through the bitter words and guardedness, and D was strong as a lion. She felt *that* with every fibre of her being. Their paths interlinked, she had surprised herself by caring if *he* cared, a molten feeling that had culminated in her sense of invincibility amidst the cyber wasteland of the Blizzard Bash. And for a time, she had glimpsed what it was that made Renegade so goth damn special; the wonder and wilds of a life set to a nocturne. Hand in hand with D, she had downed the fierce, black, roiling waters of the madness, and she had started to get a taste for it. Then she got the answer that she had been searching for, and, just like that, their lives were no longer connected.

Because what she had wanted was to find Harish, wasn't it? Nothing else had come into play. Jezebel drew her coat about her knees despite the clement heat of the hospital. Her tongue pressed hard against her teeth, as if to gag her from disclosing a more selfish secret, and in confusion, she forced her mind back to Harish, curled up and fit to die in a white cell just a few short steps from where she was sat. Everyone was made a ghost in the hospital, bleached back to the shade of nothingness they were prior to a life in Renegade City. She was no exception.

Sighing, Jezebel pressed her lower spine to the back of the bench. Something hard dug into her hip and she twisted sideways, feeling about her coat pockets. With shame and curiosity, she remembered the book that she had stolen from D earlier. As she drew it out, an edge of the leather cover snagged on the silk lining of her pocket, a bitter reminder of her failure to produce the slingshot when it had been required a few hours before. Then she had witnessed D pay the price for her incompetence. Now she had the chance to learn more about the man, to pare back the flesh and expose his blooded clockwork...if she chose to do so.

Should she leaf through the pages of the book and discover whatever it was that D had recorded inside? On the one hand, it was a deceitful act. To forage into the man's subconscious, even if it was via the medium of words on paper, seemed tantamount to breaking open his skull and feasting on the contents. On the other hand, given that his lips had alchemised hers, was *that* a crime? Moreover, since D had demonstrated a propensity for keeping secrets when it came to any real details about his life and origins, did she have any alternative?

Her hand caressed the leather cover of the book as it rested on her lap, and the dilemma acted as a salve, distracting her from the bleak reality of Harish's being ill and her creeping sense of numbness. She ran a fingertip over the raised insignia: seal of the Drathcor, and a finer, more detailed version of the city key tattoo. Her forehead puckered, and she pulled at the collar of her coat, adjusting it to sit closer at her throat and protect the scar there. Wasn't it illegal to reproduce the seal? Its usage was restricted to the Drathcor and the strict applications they endorsed. And while she was sure that it was possible to counterfeit the design, what was the point? Desecration? Anarchism? Appropriation of some new divine right of kings? Her mind was a vortex, and every question threatened to pull her down.

One thing she *did* know was the power behind the seal. The foundation was a cross of sorts, spiked and angled as if to act as a barrier against outside invasion, which struck her as ironic given that she also recognised the style as a crusader's cross. The Drathcor had ordained themselves then as knights of a brave new order, leading their armies into darkness. Except the dream had failed, and Renegade lay in a deathlike state under a veil of silent white, she mused, lightly running her fingers over the central image of an eye. She pressed her hand to the spot, as if willing the eye to embed itself in her palm, let her carry it there, disguised behind her fingers until she chose to fold them out and see the world from a million different angles.

Forcing her hand back off the cover, she let her own eyes absorb the four symbols representing the Drathcor; the three ray glyph of the Awen, the black fist of a rose, the delicately unique luna-moth, and the ever-open petals of a lotus flower. She felt oddly protective of the icons, in a way she had never experienced before. Perhaps it had something to do with the world she knew seeming to break apart the more with each second, or the city being sterilised before her eyes as she had watched from the window in Harish's room. The seal of the Drathcor was so much more symbolic than the four, flawed human beings responsible for designing it. For all the loners, sinners, self-harmers, law breakers, rebels, freaks and outcasts, there had to be a *key* to unlock life in the dark. There had to be hope.

She took the book in her hands, stared at the proud insignia again, its blend of divinity and sorrow, turbulence and fluidity. Why was D carrying around that sacred tome? She moved her fingertips over the worked leather, tried to interpret any sign it might give her of what was held inside, and of the man who had written it; a man who carried a book emblazed with a holy emblem, who kept it tucked it into his inner coat pocket, next to his heart, who defended the city with every last fighting breath, but who seemed unusually exhausted by the whole black riot of a scene, who was known by the single letter D, who looked like a living god...a living god. *A living god.*

Jezebel felt turned to stone. She despised the Drathcor; they represented to her everything that was wrong, corrupt and cankered in their world. Was there a chance that the man she'd come to see as soul-broken, if mesmerising in all the splintered hues of dark and silver, was one of them? Did she want to know the truth in that case? Did she really want to rip open the book, knowing that once she saw what lay within those gilded pages, she could never go back?

She stared at the wall opposite, an expanse of inert, uninterrupted white, a void, and part of her wanted to stay dissolved, and absolved, in that nothingness. But part of her also wanted to tear apart the paint, steel and brickwork until her hands, skinned and bloody, plunged into the warm visceral of the city's vast, slow pumping, heart, and her Belief was restored. Her brilliant, black eyes flicked to the book of shadows in her grasp, flicked back to the wall.

No going back. She made her choice.

Aknowledgements

To Storm Constantine for her beauty, mentoring, gin sharing, and Belief in Tourniquet, to my editor, Donna Scott for her spooky-kooky intelligence and gentle nudging in the right direction, to Fiona McGavin for her light speed proofing, to my illustrator, Lucas Swann for his artistic like-mindedness and bringing Renegade to life, to Immanion Press for the fun, frolics and creative emancipation, to Catherine Hancox, Tamsin Lakin, Tim Miles, Kayte Redding and Zoe Ridley for their infallible support and patient editorial of countless first drafts, to my family for their tolerance, care and boundless love, to Scarlet for putting every frustration as a writer into perspective, to Del for faith and mapping the road to Renegade City with me every step of the way, and to my friends and all of the DarkLed for giving me a home among you, and for refusing to disappear into the void.

Thank you also to the following bands and artists for the music which inspired me to write Tourniquet:

Aerosmith	My Chemical Romance
Depeche Mode	The Cult
Marilyn Manson	Buckcherry
Sisters Of Mercy	HIM
Apocolyptica	Nine Inch Nails
Evanescence	Tori Amos
Metallica	Disturbed
Stabbing Westward	Lacuna Coil
Bat For Lashes	Rob Zombie
Godhead	Within Temptation

About the Author

After attaining a first class honours degree in English Lit and Creative Writing from the University of Glamorgan, Kim Lakin-Smith was awarded a Studentship to study for her MA in Writing at Nottingham Trent. There she was tutored by Graham Joyce, thrice winner of the British Fantasy award. She also became fascinated by the Internet; skills she later put to use in her work as a copywriter, advertising exec, and website designer. But it was her desire to write fantasy and science fiction novels which soon took precedence. Inspired by the time she spent living in Nottingham, a place she truly felt at home, Kim wrote *Tourniquet*, the first book in her 'Tales From the Renegade City' series and was delighted to find a home for it with Immanion Press.

Kim lives on the first floor of a Victorian gothic manor house with her mini demon of a daughter and dark lord of a husband. As a writer, she is inspired by artists who take pop culture, crack it open, and hatch something new; artist HR Giger, music video director Floria Sigismondi, god of fuck Marilyn Manson, alt.fashion designer Jeannie Nitro, and scriptwriter Joss Wheedon. She believes she is well placed to connect with her readers, having a lazy-hazy attitude to maturity, an eclectic dress sense, and a healthy dollop of vanity on the side.

Other Recent Titles From Immanion Press

Parallax View
Keith Brooke and Eric Brown
9781904853428
£13.99 First edition trade paperback, 2007

IP0073 Parallax View showcases the previously unpublished Novella 'In Transit', set in a future war-torn universe in which human expansion has come up against the implacable Kryte. Xeno-psychologist Abbott finds himself the guardian of a deadly Kryte on a mission to study it on his return to Earth. When the crash-land on the fortress planet of St Jerome, the Kryte prisoner turns the tables and takes Abbott into terrible custody. What follows is a terrifying journey across a hellish landscape towards a finale that might change the destiny of the Kryte and humanity, forever...

Plus six other stories that examine the interface between human and alien – a parallax view from two of Britain's top science fiction writers.

Mythanima
Storm Constantine
1904853323
£14.99 First edition trade paperback 2006

IP0013 An anthology of Storm's uncollected short stories, ranging from science fiction and fantasy to the truly bizarre. Some of the stories have not been published before or are available only in limited edition collections and magazines. Rare and sought after stories are available in one collection for the first time.

Storm leads her readers into far-distant worlds, as well as into ones that could be right around the corner. In her world, a town galaxies away can seem everyday, while the back room of the house next door could be a portal into another dimension, or a vortex of evil. Read *Mythanima* and find yourself wandering alongside characters as they discover that almost nothing in this world is straightforward or "normal" – and learn to cope. And enjoy it, like a box of chocolates.

Printed in the United Kingdom
by Lightning Source UK Ltd.
125091UK00001B/117/A